THE
BEST
AMERICAN SHORT STORIES
1974

THE
BEST
AMERICAN SHORT STORIES
1974

&

*the Yearbook of
the American Short Story*

EDITED BY
MARTHA FOLEY

Houghton Mifflin Company
Boston
1974

"The Deserter" by Agnes Boyer. First published in *Prism International* No. 12:3, Spring 1973. Copyright © 1973 by Agnes Boyer.

"Beginnings" by Jerry Bumpus. First published in *TriQuarterly* 26, Winter 1973. Copyright © 1973 by Northwestern University Press.

"A Summer In Puerto Rico" by Eleanor Clark. First published in *The Southern Review*. Copyright © 1973 by Eleanor Clark. This story will appear in a collection of short stories by Eleanor Clark, to be published by Pantheon Books in the Fall of 1974. Reprinted by permission of Pantheon Books, a Division of Random House, Inc.

"The Party" by Pat M. Esslinger-Carr. First published in *The Southern Review*. Copyright © 1973 by The Southern Review.

"Mansion, Magic, and Miracle" by Lewis B. Horne. First published in *The Colorado Quarterly*. Reprinted by permission of *The Colorado Quarterly* and Lewis B. Horne. Copyright © 1973 by the University of Colorado, Boulder, Colorado.

"Down the American River" by Rose Graubart Ignatow. First published in *Shenandoah*. Copyright © 1973 by *Shenandoah*, reprinted from *Shenandoah*: The Washington and Lee University Review with the permission of the Editor.

"Opening the Door on Sixty-Second Street" by Maxine Kumin. First published in *The Southern Review*. Copyright © 1973 by Maxine Kumin. From *The Designated Heir*, a novel by Maxine Kumin. Reprinted by permission of The Viking Press, Inc.

"Tom" by Mary Lavin. First published in *The New Yorker*. Copyright © 1973 The New Yorker Magazine, Inc.

"A Family Affair" by John L'Heureux. First published in *The Atlantic*. Copyright © 1973 by John L'Heureux.

"The Chamber Music Evening" by Phillip Lopate. First published in *Paris Review*. Copyright © 1973 by Phillip Lopate.

TO
WILLIAM SAROYAN

Acknowledgments

GRATEFUL ACKNOWLEDGMENT for permission to reprint the stories in this volume is made to the following:

The editors of *Antaeus, The Atlantic, The Colorado Quarterly, The Fiddlehead, Harper's, The Kansas Quarterly, Ms., The New Yorker, The Paris Review, Playboy, Prism International, Quarterly Review of Literature, Salmagundi, Shenandoah, The Southern Review, TriQuarterly;* and to Agnes Boyer, Jerry Bumpus, Eleanor Clark, Pat M. Esslinger-Carr, Lewis B. Horne, Rose Graubart Ignatow, Maxine Kumin, Mary Lavin, John L'Heureux, Phillip Lopate, Stephen Minot, Beverly Mitchell, Michael Rothschild, Peter L. Sandberg, William Saroyan, Philip Schneider, Barry Targan, John Updike, Arturo Vivante, Alice Walker.

Foreword

WHAT IS A SHORT STORY? The businesslike *Short Story Index* defines it as "a story of more than two average-sized pages and not more than one hundred and fifty average-sized pages." The more literary *American Heritage Dictionary* states it is "a short prose fiction aiming at unity of characterization, theme, and effect." Robert Penn Warren says, "It is a story that is not too long." Then a novel might be defined as a story that is not too short? Henry James said a story could be an anecdote or a picture and "I prefer the picture." Edward J. O'Brien thought the modern short story grew out of the essay. Others think its genesis was in tales told by prehistoric people around cave fires. A Supreme Court justice, struggling with a pornography case decision, exclaimed, "I can't define obscenity but I know it when I see it!" So it is, I believe, with a short story. You know a short story when you read it!

Years ago, however, during the Depression, a now famous author sent me another definition in a rather extraordinary way. When I was editing *Story* magazine, which was unique in those days because it was the only literary magazine devoted solely to the short story, I received a manuscript on densely typed yellow manila paper. The story was from a writer whose name I couldn't then pronounce — Saroyan — and was called "The Daring Young Man on the Flying Trapeze." It was like no short story I had ever read and it intrigued me. The other editors agreed that we should take it and I wrote the author that we were accepting his story. He answered that this was the first time a story of his had ever been accepted and he was so greatly encouraged that from now on he was going to write a story every day to send to me. I laughed and thought it won't last, that's the natural exuberance of any writer accepted for the first time. I went on to read other manuscripts of which we were receiving about a hundred a day. A couple of days later a story arrived from Saroyan, and the next day another, and the next day another, and then another and another and another. This was impossible. "Put them in the crank file," I told my secretary. By the end of the month the crank file overflowed. Something had to be done. So one weekend my co-editor, Whit Burnett, and I took them to the country to read. Every one was a good story. Conscience-stricken, I wired an apologetic telegram to the author explaining no magazine could use a story a day from an author but his stories were wonderful and I would try to interest other editors. Back from California came a telegram: "What do you mean sending me a telegram? I am not supposed to receive them. I deliver them." He had a job as a postal telegraph messenger.

In that stack of manuscripts was one which, although it was to be published as such in his first book, was not a short story. It was a letter explaining to me why he couldn't send me a story that day. He was too cold. The California temperature had sunk abnormally low, he was freezing and he had no money to buy fuel. There was an old tub and he thought of getting warm by burning in it some of his five hundred books, most of which he had bought for a nickel apiece. But as he turned over the pages and looked at the words, even German ones which he did not understand, he could not burn them. He simply could not burn any book. The important story he had hoped to write for me before being silenced by the cold which made him jump up from his chair and do bending exercises was lost forever.

"Well, I can tell you about it . . . I will tell you the things I was telling myself this morning while I was getting this story lined up in my mind." Then comes Saroyan's definition of how a short story should be written.

*Think of America, I told myself this morning. The whole thing.
The cities, all the houses, all the people, the coming and going, the
coming of children, the going of them, the coming and going of men
and death, the movement, the talk, the sound of machinery, the*

oratory, think of the pain in America and the fear and the deep inward longing of all things alive in America. Remember the great machines, wheels turning, smoke and fire, the mines and the men working them, the noise, the confusion. Remember the newspapers and the moving picture theatres and everything that is a part of this life. Let this be your purpose: to suggest this great country.

Then turn to the specific. Go out to some single person and dwell with him, within him, lovingly, seeking to understand the miracle of his being, and utter the truth of his existence and reveal the splendor of the mere fact of his being alive, and say it in great prose, simply, show that he is of the time, of the machines and the fire and smoke, the newspapers and the noise. Go with him to his secret and speak of it gently, showing that it is the secret of man. Do not deceive. Do not make up lies for the sake of pleasing anyone. No one need be killed in your story. Simply relate what is the great event of all history, of all time, the humble, artless truth of mere being. There is no greater theme: no one need be violent to help you with your art. There is violence. Mention it of course when it is time to mention it. Mention the War. Mention all ugliness, all waste. Do even this lovingly. But emphasize the glorious truth of mere being. It is the major theme. You do not have to create a triumphant climax. The man you write of need not perform some heroic or monstrous deed in order to make your prose great. Let him do what he has always done, day in and day out, continuing to live. Let him walk and talk and think and sleep and dream and awaken and walk again and talk again and move and be alive. It is enough. There is nothing else to write about. You have never seen a short story in life. The events of life have never fallen into the form of the short story or the form of the poem, or into any other form. Your own consciousness is the only form you need. Your own awareness is the only action you need. Speak of this man, recognize his existence. Speak of man.

There is a sequel. *Harper's Magazine* this past year published a short story by Saroyan. It is called "Isn't Today the Day?" and is all about why again he doesn't write a story. I shall not spoil it by telling you about it. It is included in this collection and you can read it for yourself.

Much more than usual, the short story has been a prime topic of discussion this past year. Lamenting the pressure put upon short story writers to produce novels which he considers a kind of publishing elephantiasis, L. E. Sissman, in an *Atlantic* article, emphasizes the fact that many excellent short story writers are unable to attain the same excellence in novels. Mr. Sissman does not say so but it is equally true that many fine novelists cannot write good short stories. I knew one, the Rumanian Peter Neagoe, who used to say "Give me a novel to write any time! If you get stuck in a novel you can always say, 'The next morning.'"

Mr. Sissman regrets that the publishing rating game with its continual emphasis on "bigness" in writing as in sports, architecture, production, and all American endeavors, has all but legislated a particularly apposite form of American writing out of existence.

I am talking, of course, about the short story. It could be argued that the short story, though not a domestic invention, has been perfected in America, and that, in an age of lightning disjunction and sleight-of-hand change, it is perfectly adapted to mirror and describe the way we live now. This is, after all, a time of short takes, of instant inputs, of kaleidoscopic sense experiences flashing and fading, dozens of times a day, before our eyes. Modern art has adapted itself to these changes by telescoping the space-time continuum: on a single canvas, we may see an object simultaneously in various elevations, in various stages of metamorphosis. Modern poetry has jettisoned the long forms — the epic and the narrative — in favor of short epiphanies, if I may use that wan New Criticism term just one more time. Modern film has invented the intercut, the jump cut, and the split screen to feed us different sequences of action and different levels of meaning almost simultaneously. But the prose narrative has, conversely, been moving from the short and timely to the long and irrelevant. . . . Why is this? Purely, I'd say, a matter of the rating game and the marketing structure that supports it.

Mr. Sissman goes on to cite two well-known authors as examples. "The granddaddy of manqué short story writers was Ernest Hemingway. The pouchful of glittering first-water half-carat diamonds he wrote in the twenties — of which 'In Our Time' is the archetypal example — was soon superseded by increasingly sprawling novels, none of which after *The Sun Also Rises* is really first-rate." Philip

Roth is another example he gives of a writer who had been cajoled by marketing considerations and perhaps a desire for wider recognition into abandoning the short story which he had mastered for an imperfect grasp of the novel.

There are ever so many more instances. One of the most heartbreaking I think, is Katherine Anne Porter, author of magical short stories. Many years before it was finally published, there was an announcement that she had contracted to write a novel. Every now and then all through those many years word was given out that the novel was progressing and would appear soon. When *Ship of Fools* did at last appear it was incredibly inferior to the short stories her readers love so much in *Pale Horse, Pale Rider* and her other collections. Only those who have been close to writers and know their struggles with the act of composition can guess at the agony Miss Porter must have endured trying to cope with a novel and waiting publishers. Worse yet, think of all the beautiful short stories she might have been writing!

Another writer whose early short stories I personally prefer to his later novels is Vladimir Nabokov. He, too, has been writing recently in praise of the short story, saying that he is confirmed "in the exhilarating belief that at the present time (say, for the last fifty years) the greatest short stories have been produced not in England, not in Russia, and certainly not in France but in this country." As his particular favorites he lists John Cheever's "The Country Husband," John Updike's "The Happiest I've Been," J. D. Salinger's "A Perfect Day for Bananafish," Herbert Gold's "Death in Miami Beach," John Barth's "Lost in the Funhouse," and Delmore Schwartz's "In Dreams Begin Responsibilities."

Critics, rather than publishers, bear the brunt of Vance Bourjaily's ire in his *New York Times Book Review* article, "Stories Should Not Be Their Own Reward." Since he has been associated with the Iowa School of Letters and a judge in the Iowa Short Fiction prize contest, he has become deeply aware of the importance of American short stories. He declares, "Two things must become clear to us: one is that the short story is not a satellite but as different from the novel as is poetry from drama. The other that, in terms of story talent, there are exciting people around, doing first-rate work . . . couldn't we encourage and support a separate criticism? Then we might hope to expand university activity in book publication, periodicals

and prize-giving — and how very welcome it would be to be joined
in this by the creation of a story-collection category in the National
Book Awards."

Fortunately for short story lovers there are a number of magazines
throughout the country publishing good stories. Three of the most
important are *The Hudson Review,* edited by Frederick Morgan,
which is celebrating its twenty-fifth anniversary, *The South Dakota
Review,* edited by John Milton, celebrating its tenth anniversary,
and *The Quarterly Review of Literature* with a thirtieth anniversary. This country is to be congratulated on possessing literary magazines of such high quality.

I am grateful to all the editors who have kept this anthology supplied with copies of their magazines and to their authors for gener-
ously granting reprint rights. The editor of any new magazine is
urged to send copies to me.

The editors and staff of Houghton Mifflin are entitled to gratitude
for their help. Finally, tribute is paid to the memory of Edward J.
O'Brien who founded this anthology.

                                                         Martha Foley

Contents

THE

BEST

AMERICAN SHORT STORIES

1974

AGNES BOYER

The Deserter

(FROM PRISM INTERNATIONAL)

THE DESERTER SITS at the kitchen table. He eats his cold beef sandwiches slowly and quietly.

"I only keep the fellows two days," I say.

The deserter looks at me and says nothing. His face is a blank page and the eyes that return every look I give him give back the same blank answer.

"I find it works out best that way," I say.

He still says nothing. His face is young-old; his wrists are very slim. The knuckles on his fingers show white through the thin skin. He continues eating in the same careful manner, but his eyes now move from mine to the open door and the green-wet shimmering beyond. He watches the little poplars flickering in the wind against the deep blue of the southern Ontario sky. It's very nice here, his look says.

He looks down at his plate.

"Most of them can't stand me much longer than that, anyway," I say, trying for a smile. "My husband is not — " I search for the word that will not wound too deeply, — "how shall we say? Sympathetic."

The eyes shift and move and come up to my face, then lower and rest upon my mouth.

"It's not been easy for him," I say. "Here. His life here, I mean. It wasn't easy for him before either, you know. When he was a young man, I mean."

His gaze moves just beyond me. His eyes reflect nothing at my words; it is impossible to know what he is thinking. His silence is beginning to nettle me. After all, I think, I could tell him what they instructed me downtown: "Promise one night only. See how it works out. Then you can extend your invitation if you like."

"And then, too," I say aloud, "it's my son's room, you know. And he may be trekking home anytime this weekend." I chuckle softly to myself. "One never knows about him, you know. He's that kind of fellow. A kind of a kook, you know."

His face has formed into a kind of rigid mask. "Would you like some more coffee?" I ask, jolting the table a little as I start up.

His arms lie inert on the table. I can see that it will not take a hard word to evict him, not even a frowning glance; he has already accepted his unacceptance. And yet, somehow, this one is different: I sense somewhere deep inside him, strong and hard, a person still; and him carefully maintaining that sure knowledge, even while the whole external world contrives to make something else of him.

"You got a lot more, then?" he asks, the sentence rising in the air just before the end, like a question that has changed its mind, and I hear the mountain highlands of central Pennsylvania in his deep voice.

, "I'm going out for a while," I say, pouring the coffee. "Do you think you might like to cut some grass in back?"

"Yeah, sure," he says, softly, drinking noiselessly.

I hover near the table; I am not through with him yet.

"Have you been to Rochdale at all? You should really try to find a place in Metro, you know. Where there are groups of people you could get in with; meet, I mean. Others like yourself, I mean."

The deep suntan on his face has already begun to fade. His eyes are grey, deep-set and penetrating.

"If you would just get one of those underground newspapers," I continue, trying not to show impatience, "you'd get to learn about these things — your way around and all."

How docile he is, I think. I sit down again, opposite. I want to tell him then about how it is with Sherman and how I usually give fellows like him a place to stay only when Sherm was gone to the States or the West Coast or someplace like that. I want to tell him that last winter Sherman made a trip to Japan and I had two fellows like him living in the downstairs room; but I am afraid he will

answer me with another blank look. I want to tell him he will have
to learn to be tough here, — tougher than ever, because there is a
stigma on him here, not from what he has done, but just from his
origin. I want to tell him how the hatred comes thick here now,
thick and virulent, a superficial amiability hiding an ill-concealed
contempt, a hatred spreading now and touching everything and
everyone, in its intensity making no distinctions among comers from
the south; — but he would not hear me now, at any rate, so very
wary has he become.

"Have you been to the Hall? They have a great meal down there
on Christmas and Thanksgiving, I've heard." He stares at me.
"You haven't been there? You should, you know. You should look
it up. You could make some good contacts there, you know."

"What's that?" His voice comes out loud, startling me a little.

"The Hall? It's just a place where the American exiles go." He
waits. "I've never been there myself, you understand," I add hurriedly, "I've only heard about it. It's right downtown someplace."
I wave my arm in that direction; as it drops, my fingers brush his
sleeve, and I pull my hand back to me quickly. A faint shadow
crosses his face then, like the shadow of a passing bird's wing, faint
and fleeting; I think I see disgust, or something very close to it, and
I suppress the little points of anger rising up in me. "The lawn
mower's in the garage," I say abruptly.

He smiles to himself then, a tiny smile, hiding his poor teeth. I
leave the room quickly to avoid his eyes. I go upstairs to get my
purse and keys and when I come down he has gone out into the
back and is standing next to the rose garden. Hands in his pockets,
his stance is detached, dreamy.

I am gone for half an hour before I remember another thing the
man downtown had said: "Never leave them alone in the house
when you're not there." I force myself not to hurry, to pace myself as if it were any other shopping trip, any other day. I visit the
supermarket, the bank, the liquor store. I buy every vegetable I can
ever imagine using, waiting patiently for each weighing. I look at
all the American magazines, glossy and blatant, stacked in the rack
near the check-out counter. I spend a lot of time reading the lists of
all the foreign wines at the LCBO outlet. I finally pick out a
Graves and a Portuguese rosé, declining the Puerto Rican rum be-

cause it is just too expensive here.' I write out the ticket. I add up
the figures twice, tear up the slip of paper, and start over again. I
don't know why I am so tense. I walk over to the library to return
a book that isn't even due yet. Coming back, I make myself stop
before a gallery window filled with bad portraits of somebody's
children, the kind of thing that usually turns me right off.

When I get back to the house, I leave the car in the driveway and
walk around the side and see that the grass in back has been cut. I
go in the house and start to put away the groceries. The young
man is nowhere about. Presently I am aware of him moving quietly
about in one of the little bedrooms in the back and I am overcome
with a compelling desire to get out of the house again. I wash my
hands at the kitchen sink, and taking scissors out of the drawer,
walk out into the front again. I will cut some flowers for the dinner
table, a regular early summer bouquet; Sherman will like that.

I am standing next to the gladioli bed when he comes out of the
house, carrying a large duffelbag. Scissors in hand, I stare at him.

"I'm shovin' off," he says. The slim face breaks out into a shy,
quick half-smile. "Well, thanks a lot for everything!"

He does not put out his hand and I do not offer mine; we remain
separate and inviolate. Only his long gaze holds us in our fixed positions, the space between us filled with unspoken words.

"But I said you could stay another night!"

"That's all right," he says. "I was going into Toronto anyway."
He shifts the weight of the duffelbag on his back. Standing away
from me, erect, he seems stronger, as if power has returned to him
with his newly regained ability to refuse. The small smile is pulling
down the corners of his face. "Well, thanks a lot!"

"Good luck." My voice catches and holds me back; he is already
walking away from me.

"Wait! Don't you want a lift to the Queen E?"

"No, that's all right," he says. He is already halfway down the
driveway; he seems to want to get away from me.

"Good luck," I call. I watch him walk away with the long blue
bag slung over one shoulder until he disappears behind the chestnut tree on the next property. Then I go back into the house.

I walk through all the rooms, up and down, and then out to the
terrace in back. I sit down and watch the sunlight playing on the

surface of the pool, the pale green moving shimmer reflecting through the heavy fluidity below.

After a while, guilt comes out and sits down in the folding chair beside me.

Beginnings

(FROM TRIQUARTERLY)

MUFFORD, SMALL AND QUICK, with white hair, a mask of wrinkles, and sharp green eyes, hurried through the French doors from the garden as the clock chimed and as Madeline poured the tea. They smiled at each other, and Mufford crossed the room to the easel. By it, Madeline's brushes and paints were neatly arranged on her shelf; the rest of the bookcase was filled with Mufford's books. "Aha," he said, "something new." Clasping his hands behind him, he studied the canvas. "I don't like it."

"I don't believe I do either, actually," she said.

"You're not ready for this sort of thing." He glanced over his shoulder for her reaction. In her brownish purple dress, high-collared and long-sleeved with lace at the cuffs, she sat staring at the floor. Her soft, pale face was especially vulnerable, pliable, in the yellow light of late afternoon . . . and Mufford saw she was, herself, a study: the portrait of a wistful young woman in a closed room.

"Stick to doing the garden," Mufford said. "After that, you may go ahead with — " he gestured vaguely toward the easel.

"You don't like it, so I'll throw it away," she said softly.

He came to the table and sat, head down, his eyes nearly closed. He looked up. "No. Complete it. I suppose I'll be fond of it when you're finished. But the fact of the matter is you're experiment-ing."

"I suppose I am." She nodded. "Yes. I hadn't realized."

"And you're going in the same direction as my own experi-ments," Mufford said, "which I find quite flattering."

"But I have no idea what I'm doing. The old way is much easier — and safer."

"I didn't see it at first, but you've gone beyond that."

"Not really."

"Oh yes. I should have expected it. This is what all the rest was leading to. So it's really what I wanted all along." Looking away, he said low, "Why don't you go ahead and finish it?"

"Right now?"

"Why not?"

She hopped up and went to the easel. Mufford lit a cigarette, sipped his tea, and listened to the whisper of her brush.

They heard the thump. Then the breathing.

Mufford went to the French doors. "Aha," he said. "He jumped right over the garden wall."

In white trousers, white shirt, and white shoes, the young man stood leaning forward, rather amazed, looking back and forth. Under bristling red hair, his head was narrow, his face compact and cunning. His yellow-green eyes fixed on Mufford's. He trotted up the garden path, padded across the terrace, and opened the glass door. "I want . . ." he whispered.

Mufford turned to Madeline, still at the easel, her eyes huge, her hands clenched.

"I want . . ."

"You want to stay," Mufford said, and the young man nodded. Mufford shut the door after him.

"I'm running."

"Yes," Mufford said. "And do you know from whom you're running?"

Madeline spoke, moving from the easel. "Let him catch his breath."

The young man nodded. "Thanks," he said.

"Sit down." Mufford offered his place at the table.

The young man sprawled in the chair, his knees wide apart, his arms hanging outside the armrests. He breathed deeply, staring straight ahead. Pinned to his shirt was a plastic name tag — *Teddy*.

He turned his head to Mufford: "I scared you when I walked right in like that." He laughed, his lips curling back from large teeth. "You should have seen your face. You sure were surprised."

He laughed loudly. But then he sat straight. He looked back and forth between them. "But I don't always do things like that."

Mufford nodded. "I'm sure you don't. You're just excited. I suppose you're in trouble of some sort."

His eyes narrowed and he looked away. Mufford leaned forward: "Tell us, Teddy," he said low.

"You'll turn me in."

"You must trust us, as we trust you."

"The hospital."

Madeline said, "You poor thing. Are you ill?"

"I'm an orderly."

"You've stolen something," Mufford said.

Teddy shook his head. "No."

Madeline said, "You fought another young man — about a girl." Teddy shook his head.

Mufford: "You failed to perform some duty, a doctor reprimanded you, and you struck him."

Teddy shook his head. "But you're getting warm."

The bell rang at the garden gate. Madeline and Teddy looked at Mufford who frowned and said, "That will be the police." Teddy slid from his chair and with a soft bump knelt before Mufford.

Again the bell rang.

Teddy ate three helpings of everything. At last he sat back from the table. "That was great," he said to Madeline.

Mufford offered him a cigarette. "Gee, thanks," he said, "but I don't smoke. It's not good for me."

"Tell us about yourself, Teddy," Mufford said.

"I live with my mother and father. Or I used to. Anyway," he smiled, "my mother was a really great cook, but she wasn't this good." He turned to Madeline. "You're really great," he said. "You know that?" He turned to Mufford and said loudly, "Does she know how great she is?"

"I suppose you will want to return," Mufford said, "when this is over."

"Oh no," he said and shook his head. "This won't *ever* be over. Not this. I'm really in trouble this time."

"Well then," Mufford said, "I believe it's time for you to tell what happened at the hospital. This afternoon the police were after a young man for questioning."

"But let's go into the parlor," Madeline said softly. "It's more comfortable."

In the parlor she served Mufford brandy, and put a box of chocolates on a table by Teddy's chair. As he talked, he ate the candy and licked his fingers.

The hospital authorities believed Teddy was murdering the patients. "But I love the patients," he said. "Those old men and women," he whispered, "their eyes stay with me. They lie there and watch me go down the hall. I stop and talk to them and see it in their eyes. They're waiting to die."

He lowered his head. Mufford glanced at Madeline. Her eyes were enormous. Mufford expected she would go to Teddy, put her arm around his shoulders, and Teddy would look up at her, his eyes shining, while she patted his bristly head . . .

Slowly Teddy straightened. Looking over Madeline's and Mufford's heads as if he were staring at a row of people standing behind them, he said: "I did it for five of them. The first a year ago. The last one this morning after breakfast." Then he leaned back, crossed his legs, and said, "That's it."

At last Mufford spoke: "They were locked in dying and you sent them on to life."

At once Madeline moved toward Mufford, whispering, "You don't understand. He *killed* them" — and Teddy sprang forward so that suddenly the three of them were so close their faces almost touched, and Teddy answered Mufford, "Yes. Life. Sent them on to life."

Mornings after breakfast Teddy walked barefooted in the garden, wearing the dark silk shirt and pants Madeline made for him. One day he took with him a book of Mufford's. But when Mufford looked out his study window he saw Teddy had laid it down somewhere and was simply walking along, his hands at his sides, his eyes wide.

Madeline and Mufford had just finished eating. "But I feel he *should* have lunch," Madeline said.

"He doesn't want to miss the sun."

"It will always be there," she said. "Perhaps if I made a sandwich you would take it to him."

"Don't worry about him. We're taking very good care of him." Then Mufford looked about the room. "Where's your easel? Aren't you working on something?"

"No," she said.

"Tired of it?"

"I am, yes. A little."

"A rest will do you good."

"Perhaps."

They were silent. She would not look at him.

"How do you do that?" Teddy asked, surprising Mufford who hadn't heard him enter the hot, dark shed. Teddy wore his pants but no shirt. His brown shoulders and arms glistened with sweat. "What keeps it turning?" Teddy said.

"Under here." Teddy leaned down and looked under the wheel at the kick. Mufford showed how he turned the wheel while he shaped the clay with his hands. "Here. Try."

"No. I can't do things like that."

"Certainly you can."

"I'd rather watch you."

"I could teach you," Mufford said. The steady whir of the wheel filled the shed. "I taught Madeline." He looked up at Teddy. The young man stared unblinking at Mufford's hands.

He moved closer. "Let me try."

Mufford stood at his side and guided his hands. Then he backed away. Mufford's eyes moved from Teddy's hands up his arms to his face. Teddy's eyes were large and his lips were parted. The windless shed was suddenly quite cool. Mufford closed his eyes.

Teddy lay in the afternoon sun, while Mufford knelt working in the flowers. Mufford glanced at Madeline's sun-glazed window; her shadow withdrew behind her easel.

Suddenly Teddy said, "What should I do?" He stood. "What should I do about . . . ?" He looked around the garden, at the sky, then toward the house, the window.

"What do you want to do?" Mufford said.

"I don't know. What am I supposed to do?"

Mufford laughed.

"Am I supposed to stay here? Would that be right?"

"It could be. There are worse places. Have you forgotten the hospital?"

Looking up at him, Mufford saw that Teddy had indeed forgotten it.

"If I stay here, then this is everything? The three of us?"

"Not quite," Mufford said, looking down at the flowers.

"He is young," Mufford said.

"And because he's young he's unhappy?"

"He wants more."

"More people?"

"Something like that."

"I still don't understand."

Mufford lit a cigarette and looked at her through the smoke. "He wonders why he's here."

"Oh." She hung her head. "You were right. I shouldn't have . . . experimented. You're always right."

Mufford chuckled. "Well anyhow, he's here and now he's ready."

"Ready," she said. A frown shaped an expression keener than any Mufford had ever seen on her face. "Ready?" Her mouth opened and her eyes grew large. "I'm sure I can't . . ." Her hand raised and touched her hair. Then her eyes clouded, the lucidity slipping from her expression, and her hand dropped to her lap, helpless.

Mufford turned away.

He and Teddy set up an easel in the parlor and worked mornings. Soon Teddy was on his own, though each time he finished he hurried after Mufford for his opinion. Occasionally Teddy showed Madeline a canvas.

Late one night Mufford heard a soft rapping at his study door — Madeline! She wore the blue peignoir he loved so much. Her eyes were red and swollen. He guided her to a chair. "He's leaving," she said. "I'm certain of it. He'll leave tonight unless . . . unless we do something."

"Well!"

"But what will we do . . ." her voice broke, "when he's gone? What will happen to us?"

Mufford stood. "I will talk to him."

"Thank goodness," she said and sighed.

Mufford knocked. "Come in." Before the fireplace Teddy sat in a black and red robe, but he wore his white hospital shoes.

"What's the matter?"

Teddy shrugged. "I keep waiting, but there's nothing."

"The garden? The painting?"

He shook his head.

"And Madeline?"

He looked up at Mufford. "I love her. I really do. She is wonderful." Then he spoke loudly: "But she loves you. I don't know why I'm here. It's unfair." He looked up at Mufford. "I mean . . . I can't do anything."

"You can paint." Teddy seemed not to hear.

A silence hung between them. Then the silence opened like clouds cleaved by cold air.

Teddy jerked forward. He stared big-eyed at Mufford. "What?" He stood and faced the old man. "I can't," Teddy said, his face tense, narrowed sharp as an ax blade.

"You are here," Mufford said.

"But *you* did . . ."

Mufford shook his head.

Teddy stared at him. "Madeline?"

Mufford nodded.

"Why didn't she tell me?"

"You were to find out for yourself."

"I'm stupid! Why am I so stupid!"

Mufford laughed. "Because you've just begun."

"Will I ever know more? Will I ever know . . . ?"

Mufford waited, then: "I'm certain we can teach you."

Teddy nodded slightly. He said low, "The two of you."

"Yes."

"Now I understand."

"Not quite," Mufford said. "There's more."

They worked every day. When it rained — and Madeline and
Teddy didn't paint, and when Mufford didn't work in the garden
— the three of them were together until Mufford retired to his
study. Now and then he heard them laughing in the parlor.

On one of these dark days Teddy went out to the shed and spent
the morning alone. Madeline and Mufford had sat down to lunch
when Teddy came running across the terrace and banged open the
French doors. "Stone," he shouted at Mufford. "I want stone.
And things to cut. Big hammers. And those things that cut . . ."

"Chisels," Madeline said.

"Yes," Teddy said, eagerly turning to her. "Yes." He grabbed
her hands. Then to Mufford, "You know. You both know." He
jumped up and down, shaking the table, the room, the entire
house.

He worked fast, devouring stone and crateloads of mallets and
chisels, and Mufford was at his side. But with the speed of urgency
Teddy learned to see into the stone.

One morning Mufford was working in his study. He stared out
the window, hearing from the shed the tapping of the mallet. Then
Teddy screamed.

Mufford sprang from his desk and ran through the house. He
met Madeline in the parlor — "Stay in," he yelled. "Go to my
study and lock the door."

"But you . . ." she called.

He was already outside and running through the garden.

The shed was dark. Then he saw the shaft of sun coming
through the skylight he and Teddy had cut in the roof: in the large
cube stood a figure half-emerged from stone. Mufford glanced at it,
and turned, looking for Teddy.

He was against the wall across the room, his mallet in one hand,
a chisel in the other.

Madeline waited at the window of her room. Then Mufford and
Teddy came from the shed. Mufford lit a cigarette and spoke.
Teddy laughed and Mufford smiled slyly. When Mufford came
inside, he smiled at Madeline and didn't say a word.

The next morning Mufford was in the shed with Teddy, but
Madeline didn't hear the tapping of the mallet. All afternoon

Mufford and Teddy sat in the garden. Mufford smoked and talked, while Teddy leaned toward him, listening.

On the second morning the men again sat in the garden, but while Madeline watched, they stood and started for the shed. They stopped at the door, Mufford spoke, gesturing with both hands; then he turned away, and Teddy went into the shed.

Mufford went down into the cellar and soon came up wearing his work clothes and carrying his garden tools. He walked down the path and disappeared into the garden.

Madeline turned to the shed and waited. She held her breath and as if from inside her came the steady chipping of stone.

At dinner Teddy said nothing. And Mufford, preoccupied and unusually nervous, left the table early. Madeline tried to make conversation with Teddy, but gave up. They sat in silence. Then Madeline blurted out, "Will she . . . ?" but stopped herself.

"What?" Teddy said.

Not trusting herself to speak, she shook her head and hurried from the room.

The next morning the chipping in the shed floated on the still air, and as Madeline waited the sound became the sun and the sky, the simultaneous wearing away and beginning. She leaned against the window and stared down into the garden.

The following day the three of them ate breakfast without speaking. Then Teddy asked Mufford for some cigarettes.

They stared at him. "Why, Teddy," Madeline said, "I didn't think you cared for cigarettes."

"Here," Mufford said hoarsely and pushed a pack across the table. Teddy put them in his shirt pocket. Then he took one out, asked Mufford for matches, and lit it. Mufford and Madeline watched him puff away. "It's not polite to stare," Teddy said.

"Indeed," Mufford said and rose from the table. Madeline also rose and went about her work.

But she found herself again at her window. Below, Mufford paced back and forth across the terrace. Then he turned and went off into the garden.

Madeline watched the shed, listening to the chipping.

It stopped. The air trembled with silence.

"No," she whispered, her heart racing. "Where is he . . . ?" She searched the garden for Mufford. He was nowhere in sight.

She leaned out the window. There was complete silence. "Where . . . ?" she whispered.

Teddy stepped from the shed and looked back inside.

Then from the shed came a young man — small and quick, with a face smooth as glass. He looked around the garden, and his quick green eyes turned to the house, the windows . . .

Teddy handed him the cigarettes. He lit one, spoke, and Teddy laughed. Then he put his hand on Teddy's shoulder and Teddy listened closely.

Madeline ran from her room, downstairs, through the parlor, and out the French doors.

On the terrace she stopped. Teddy stood alone. Cigarette smoke hung in the air.

Teddy turned to her, his face for a moment hard with certitude. Then he smiled and she went to him. In his yellow-green eyes she saw an amber valley without roads or paths.

ELEANOR CLARK

A Summer in Puerto Rico

(FROM THE SOUTHERN REVIEW)

June, 1938

ON THE BOAT the first morning almost everyone in Second Class, the second of two, was sick: mostly Puerto Ricans. Perhaps Latin American stomachs are more flighty than most, or it may have been the position of our quarters, in the lowest rear. Had visions of us all being shipped as slaves to P.R. from Africa. The food was appropriate too. Compote made of rotten apples, spoiled meat, and as a final gesture on the last morning they brought us three bad eggs. The crew probably gets the same rations, though if so I can't understand why they don't strike. Only a few yards of deck and none of it open.

I was struck by the resignation, or rather gaiety, of the Puerto Ricans. They would stagger to the rail, usually in little laughing groups, give each other all kinds of advice and even sing as long as possible before vomiting, and when it was over would smile cheerfully and go back to whatever they had been doing. It became a real distinction.

The first day there was a woman lying in a deckchair on the lower deck, a beautiful black-haired, black-eyed child in her arms. They were almost hidden by a blanket; beside the chair was the well-known paper-lined container, half full. The woman was so lost in keeping the child comfortable, she seemed wholly withdrawn, like a philosopher or a very old woman with her memories. And the child too was in a kind of trance. They hardly moved all day, except to pull the blanket up a little farther, or to be sick.

The next day she was well enough to sit in the saloon — they all seemed to have a superstition against the open air — and it turned out that she was very fat, with a great cushion of chin, stringy rat-colored hair, and that lovely pneumatic disposition that fat people so often have. She had made friends with all the women, at least all the "good" ones, and would chatter like a bluejay for a few minutes and then suddenly sink back and begin to listen, rocking her child and smiling partly at what she was listening to and more out of plain happiness. She was awfully distressed that I had no child and suggested that being in the tropics might help.

There were only two women on the boat obviously "bad." One had just been let out of an asylum where she had been for observation. F., the American would-be newspaperman who has been living in Indochina, said in his gay, saturated way, "By God if I were running an asylum I'd have let her out the minute she came in." She laughed, sang, and danced all day, especially sang. At the queerest moments she would erupt into song, in the same way that she was seasick. She wore slacks much too small — she was plump and wiggled a great deal, on purpose — and had a majestic black frizzle, like a French poodle's, on her head. She was very popular, particularly with a tall pockmarked man who danced well and had a vulgar smile and a lazy, seductive carriage. Sometimes there would be a whole gang around her, clapping, laughing, in what was partly the old primitive business of making sport of the insane. But the Bad Girl was not really crazy and sometimes the admiration seemed sincere, as if the others also had a craving to shriek in the dining room and wiggle up and down stairs.

An attractive young marine on board, going to be stationed at St. Thomas. He had joined because he couldn't find work — he was a mechanic — and was convinced that he was no good. His most usual phrases were "I don't know anything" and "If I could be dictator, just for a couple of months." He wanted awfully to find a girl but was too shy to dance. He sat next to a blasé Puerto Rican girl with a worn-out tubercular look, and when he tried to draw his forefinger along her shoulder she said, "Don't do that." It was all the English she knew. However, she gave in a little that evening, and we saw them standing together at the rail, he wiggling his long fingers and waving at the stars. "Venus!" he said, and she, very bored, "*Sì.*"

The F.'s, very companionable, are certainly taking an odd route from New York back to Indochina; just want to see a little more of the world, he said. He blond and paunchy, humorous, quick-moving and chronically restless, a good storyteller. She is the contrary, slow and over-resigned, somehow hangdog yet pleasant. She never initiates conversation; rarely speaks at all except to agree with him about something.

About the third day the clouds began to lower. They piled up into beautiful marble war-horses and palaces. I had never seen clouds so low and perfect. They hung very heavily; they seemed *built* only a few yards over the water, and hardly moved. The horizon was like a strip of yellow gauze.

San Juan harbor is magnificent, but it depressed me too; I kept looking for something else. A curious feeling of dissatisfaction, remoteness — and at the same time you feel a little like Columbus. They all do, everyone is making references to Columbus. After Ponce de Leon and Muñoz Rivera he is the national hero . . . We pass a kind of mystic line in the water, it is suddenly a brilliant turquoise green, and the Puerto Ricans begin to dance. They scream and shake imaginary castanets, and when El Morro is still only a little blot in the sun they are already waving frantically at the dock. Soon we distinguish, stranded on a tiny island, something like the ruin of a Roman temple. Splashes of scarlet blossom (the flamboyant), coconut palms, and the National City Bank. A half-caste official in a white uniform dashes out in a small red speedboat, cuts loops and figure eights in the water, whirls madly around the ship several times, at last lets the boat drift, and relaxes, his nose in the air, as though waiting for applause. A little Toonerville ferry is just setting out across the bay, piloted by an old, old man with a long beard and a dirty captain's cap; he sits and scowls in a little enclosure like a miniature chicken coop. The whole thing seems about six inches square, even from close to, but it actually has two

stories . . . The dock stinks of garlic and onions and maybe the
spoiled foodstuffs that are sent here because they can't be sold at
home. "Meester, meester, taxee! Taxee, okay queeck queeck *yes!*"
Even there at the dock, as on the voyage, we never have a glimpse
of the few First Class passengers.

On the edge of a precipice, overlooking La Perla and the sea, a
young goat is being taught to fight. His horns are very small and
tender but he does his best. The father lowers his head, looks
fierce, and slowly pushes him toward the cliff. The little one is
really frightened. He tries to look ferocious too but only succeeds
in wagging his tail and nodding rapidly like a young bird. He tries
to edge off to one side, he simply can't learn any more today, but
the old one shoves him back into position and he has to go through
it all again and again.

La Perla, slum of San Juan. Against the sea and the splendid old
Spanish palace of the military Governor who is trying to promote
the tourist business and the dripping crimson trees and the barracks
and the cemetery and the pseudo-modern Eleanor Roosevelt section, a residential quarter for the middle class. It is hard to believe
La Perla, looking from above, partly because it is early afternoon
and the sun casts a scintillating crust over everything.

There are several flights of steps down, all crumbling, some
hacked through the old Spanish fortifications. At the bottom are
heaps of garbage; there is garbage everywhere, green coconut rinds
that the goats munch at and try to tear apart. The children stare
like fish. They are almost all naked, even the big children, ten or
twelve years old. This is sometimes referred to as a Negro quarter
but very few of the children are black. Most are a sick coffee-and-
skimmed-milk color; a few look Irish; some have white Negroid
faces and yellow hair.

The section is squashed between the sea and the cliff; there is no
room for it. On one side the shacks push into the water, as if the
city were trying to get rid of them; on the other they cling to the
cliff like flies, held up by slim rotten timbers. Some are halfway
down and it seems as if they must be reached in a basket, but chil-

dren are born there — there is washing hung out on the projecting rocks.

At least half the women are pregnant.

We creep, we have almost to climb between the houses which are mostly pieced together out of grocery boxes and tin cans. Some of the labels are still clear: RICOMALT, BACARDI, CAMPBELL'S SOUP. Even without the animals and garbage there would hardly be room to walk in the alleys; the houses are all heaved together and press unbearably. Inside there is no light except from the door, often no other rooms, no beds. The women stare out from the stinking darkness, hating us, and we hurry and stumble against the walls. One house has a little more air around it and on the porch is a brand new Mickey Mouse, over two feet high.

Here and there a group of men squat in a doorway with a deck of cards, the naked children climbing over their shoulders, little pigs rooting under their knees for scraps of mango and coconut. Everywhere there is washing laid out to dry, usually on the ground in the wider alleys. Sometimes on boards held up by boxes, and the pigs and small goats run around luxuriously in the shade underneath.

Everyone looks sick; there is not a healthy face in all that stretch between the castle and the cemetery. Hookworm, malaria, tuberculosis, elephantiasis. A man shambles toward a sack of fruit and tries to lift it but he is too weak. Babies are crying, the special hopeless scream of disease, in every row. Little boys chase the pigs away from lumps of rotten food and the women lean with sagging stomachs in the doorways, their black eyes wretched and withdrawn. The sun throbs down on them, on the tin roofs and the washing and the blistering turquoise sea. Across the barbed wire fence are many splendid tombs, white with crosses on top. A lizard runs out from the rich grass at the bottom of an abandoned grave.

Went to Mayaguez in a "taxi," the railroad being a kind of euphemism here. Beside the driver were two tall, brown-skinned, Greek-nosed people, peasantlike, trying to get to the funeral of their *mamà*. But the funeral had been hurried so as to get the coffin out through the fields before the daily rain, and we were too late. The woman cried a little, stoically, and we left them trudging, tiny and philosophical, into the enormous mazes of the sugar cane.

Mayaguez a nightmare of heat, rain, and no place to stay. The hotels offer windowless, suffocating cribs at high prices; tried even missionaries, and ended up gasping in the house of a shrill, impecunious blueblood. And suddenly the next day found this village — Boqueròn — with a big stone Catholic church and a little tin Protestant one beside it, and a postcard dream of a tropical island bay. Introduced ourselves to the Postmaster, went through Spanish rituals with coconut cream and grapefruit juice, and by the end of the afternoon had a seven room house. It has no furniture whatever but magnificent spiders and a bathroom, the only one in town. We can eat on the floor but it would not be wise to sleep there, so bought what pass for beds, at two dollars apiece, at a store in Cabo Rojo.

There are two iceboxes in the village, one at Cretoff's where you buy chamber pots and rum and homemade cubes of water-ice called *linbergs.* The other is Don Jaime's, the ex-contractor; he talks about that and politics: "It is extraordinarily convenient. I put milk in it, for example, and it remains cold, absolutely cold, for an indefinite period of time." He sent us a rocking chair "from the time of Spain" and plums imported from Mayaguez. "Feel them. You observe? They are completely cold." The Postmaster and his wife send us rice, beans, and coconut cream every day by the orphan Juan who hurries along with his great black eyes down, hating to be seen. The Keeper-of-the-Woods sent boiled roots but the ones on the other side have nothing. Her name is Doña Claudia. The old man has had no work for years and lies on the stoop all day, waiting for food. She has nothing much to give him and nothing but bean juice for their little dog Niña who howls and howls. They are spiritualists, as are so many others; you wonder how the missionaries and their regular churches keep going. Sign after sign, on some dingy shack or other, announces spiritualist meeting-places, all the way from Mayaguez.

Doña Claudia makes handkerchiefs from five in the morning until after sunset, holding the cloth up as if to smell the stitches because she has lost most of her eyesight at the work. On a good day she earns ten cents: fourteen cents a dozen for men's handkerchiefs, eight for smaller ones. The agent takes them back to Mayaguez and eventually they are sold, twenty-five, fifty cents apiece, in New

York . . . But she managed to bring a present after all. I was trying to light the charcoal one evening and suddenly she was there below, in her yellow rayon negligee, with her plaintive smile, holding up to the window over her head a plate full of embers.

July 16

At the village end of the bay there are eight or ten curious palm-thatch bath houses at the water's edge, with a back door leading out into a circular enclosure that forms a pool about thirty feet across, fenced with high pickets and more palm-thatch. They are for protection, but the people are poor swimmers and generally timid about the sea, and we have been told there is no danger anywhere along the bay, so we go every day about a mile down the beach, where we are alone.

The other day when we were swimming there a group of children came by on their way to a picnic. Three were a long way ahead of the others. Suddenly one of them threw up her arms, did a little dance, and fell unconscious in the water. The two others, about six or seven years old, screamed hysterically and began running back down the beach. We ran to the child, who was writhing and already had a bubble of foam at the corner of her mouth, her head half under water. The others arrived, about twenty of them, including the Protestant minister who was conducting the picnic. He looked curious and resigned. No one would touch her. We carried her into the shade of a coconut palm where she went on twitching and rolling her dull brown eyes, while the children babbled, *"Un ataque, un ataque . . ."* Her older sister was one of the last to arrive and looked on with the others, bored and a little resentful. It seems the child has attacks frequently and the family is fed up with them; probably they are as poor as everyone else here and there is nothing they can do. In about ten minutes it was over. The girl dragged herself up, wavered and fell in my arms, pulled herself to her feet again and went off with the others. The sun was beating dreadfully.

Half an hour later a little girl came wandering back alone. She had left the group at the lagoon. She is terribly small and brittle, with wrists like twigs and strange translucent skin. Perhaps tubercular. She is nine years old but looks six at most, except for

the deep hazel eyes and a charming, too-precocious smile. We asked
her why she couldn't go to the picnic.

"*Yo soy catolica.*"

She walked back with us. She has seven brothers and sisters and
her father is a carpenter. Now and then she tried to pounce on a
big crab that was disappearing into its hole or scampered up into
the brush to pick bright yellow pods, like Japanese lanterns: her
mother uses the seeds for cooking. She is like glass, her voice too, a
tinkling upward cadence at the end of a phrase.

"Do you like to go swimming?"

"*Me gusta.*"

"And going to the movies?"

"*Me gusta.*" The phrase is so musical and lilting, it is as if she
were about to vanish into the air and were filled with a kind of
feathery amusement at the thought.

"And what do you do all day?"

"I work."

"Housework?"

Still the same smile and lightness: "Handkerchiefs."

I thought of Doña Claudia and the others.

"And do you like making handkerchiefs?"

"*Me gusta.*"

She was scared of being beaten when she went home, because of
trying to go to the picnic, so she left us at the bridge, putting it off
as long as possible, and went skipping over the sand as if the yellow
pods were carrying her away. Her name is Panchita.

I suppose if we had a car or even a bicycle we would have a different sense of distance, and of time. San Juan and our two nights
there are altogether remote. The F.'s gave us a rooming-house address and we spent the first evening with them in the manner of
shipboard buddies, knowing no one else and keeping up a few
hours longer an illusion of rapport, at the quite respectable little
apartment they had somehow arranged for. They did know someone else — a loud and commonplace American executive in one of
the big U.S. companies, who came in for a while with his dull wife.
It turned out the F.'s had brought with them a quantity of vast
packing-cases, which he proceeded to rip open in a state of half-

drunken euphoria to exhibit the stuff: a console radio about five feet square and other brand-new, big electrical things, kitchen equipment, etc., for their house in Indochina. Wild but quite witty and engaging even with that much scotch in him, she trying bravely to go along with his mood, though herself looking more spirit-crushed than ever. I suppose she was thinking of the trouble of re-boxing all those objects for the next leg of their journey.

The Trotskyite leader the next day — in his late twenties, all Spanish in looks, with fine intellectual features and great charm — was surprised and no doubt bitter that we were not there to work for the movement. Impossible to say you want private peace for a couple of months. He has the intensity and exhausted look of a man driving himself to early death, with no thought but for the movement, as though triumph were imminent. I have begun to learn not to feel guilty in such a presence, politics being so far from my native habitat, but L. can only bear this hiatus if he is putting it on grounds of his health, and in fact he is now covered with huge, infected insect bites.

A lovely jellyfish, flowing purple cylinder, dark and solid-looking at the top, with a loose-flowing skirt of very pale lavender. Beneath it long, branched tentacles like roots; it looked like a plant wrenched up and thrown in the water. It was breathing, swimming; the top rim of the cylinder rose and fell in a vague sensual motion that made the tentacles shiver and sometimes stream out behind.

There are so many strange noises around the house. A queer lit-tle subterranean thud that turns out to be the goats bumping their horns against the floor from under the house — their favorite nosing-ground. It is almost the same noise when they find the front door open and walk in, hesitating and staying close together like frightened young girls. Sometimes it's a tiny clatter of rain that drops out of a brilliant sky, lasts a minute or two, and for a few minutes longer trickles off the palm leaves. And the radios that go on and off in the same violent, tropical fashion as the rain — com-ing strangely from the packing-box or palm-thatch huts that make up most of the houses. And every day there comes from one house or another that ghastly sound of children being beaten. The blows dull and symmetrical, and over them the crazy rising-and-falling scream that goes with nothing else, as if everything in the world had become past endurance. Another sound, like an animal or a woman wailing, when a man wanders down the street announcing the new Argentinian movie through a little megaphone.

In back there is a family from Santo Domingo, ten children with fancy names, in pairs: Gardenio, Gardenia, etc. They have a one-room house; driftwood and boxes; but that is better than thatch. The kitchen is a shed of thatch and when it rains they throw sacks over their heads to run out and tend to the beans. They catch water in a rain barrel and in a big open pit in the yard, with a pail and string. Sometimes on sunny afternoons the eldest son cuts the family hair, sitting them on a pyramid of boxes in the yard. Their treasure is Johnny the Pig who runs like a dog after the little boy Gardenio and will roll over and play dead when they scratch his stomach. Gardenio walks toward the village calling, "*Toma*, Johnny! *Toma*, Johnny!" and the pig gallops after him. They feel fine about this and shake the baby to make him laugh too. The father works in the sugar cane when there is work: 25 to 50 cents a day for a few months and the rest of the year on credit. None of the children go to school because they have no shoes. The mother is brisk and sweet, with an acorn face and the walk of a headmistress. From 5 A.M. she washes, irons, cooks, cleans, never rests, slaps the children but doesn't beat them like the others around. The other day she sent Gardenio to borrow fifty cents, and since then there have been more presents — seashells from Mona Island, fruits that look like lemons, open to something like a pomegranate, and smell horribly. When we pump water or clean fish they offer to do it for us. But this is not really in payment for the fifty cents. It was the same before, and in the first days they sent us a plate of mangoes, "Because it seemed so lonesome," the mother said, "with just the two of you."

Lately there has been a great influx of handkerchiefs. Every house has work. Doña Claudia is doing scarlet ones; they hurt her eyes more than the white and when she sees us in the window she sighs and shakes her head mournfully. On the other side all the daughters of the Keeper-of-the-Woods are sewing, and walking down the street we see the old women and children bent over their handkerchiefs, their chairs pulled near the doors. They will not do it on the porches where the light is better; porches are for evening and visits, and probably it is not quite nice to earn one's living, as it were, in the street.

The upsurge comes now because the needle industry is threatening to close in October if the Wages and Hours Bill is passed and they want to fill advance orders. Also it helps to stimulate popular feeling against the bill. Doña Claudia says, "There used to be dresses and I earned 50 to 75 cents a day, that was splendid, then there were blouses, then embroidered handkerchiefs. Now there are only plain handkerchiefs and they'll go soon too. *Ave Maria!*"

Everyone is against the bill, they are frightened, they can't imagine what they would do without these pennies dribbling in.

This morning we watched a little white chicken gobbling up drops of water that dripped, about one a minute, from the top of a tar barrel. Mangy feathers and the usual hectic eyes of a chicken, as if they knew from birth that they would be decapitated. It stood very stiffly at attention, and when the drop came, let its head go like a released spring. Sometimes it had to wait longer than usual, and then would rub its beak forlornly back and forth across the damp stripe on the barrel.

This place makes for a most wonderful patience. The charcoal fire, for instance, simply cannot be hurried. I fan it desperately and for a few minutes it glows more brightly and then falls into ashes, so that I have to start all over. Water takes ages to heat and quite often doesn't boil at all, and to make coffee you have to stand quietly with the little cloth sieve in one hand and the pot in the other — no use trying to scratch or fidget or feel occupied — and wait. In the beginning, thinking of gas stoves, etc., it upset me, particularly in the morning, but I like it now. I watch the puppy below and the chickens and Doña Claudia trying to get all her handkerchiefs done before the agent comes. That is probably the main trouble with New York, that we are *able* to hurry so, and begin to think that every kind of human problem can also be rushed. Perhaps I had never quite accepted the thought that some problems, like the water that doesn't boil, are never solved. The best that can be hoped for them is that they will fizzle out.

July 25

Today is a Fiesta, commemorating the occupation of P.R. by American troops who landed at Ponce on July 25, 1898. Carloads of people have been coming all day for picnics, the young men and boys are decked out in beautifully pressed white trousers, and the old man next door, Doña Claudia's husband, is almost drunk. There are vendors of everything on the beach: water-ices, fried pork, mangoes, corn cookies, and candied grapefruit rind, all in little green and yellow carts with tassels. The coconut vendor, selling green coconuts at three cents per, is under a canopy of palm leaves. He carries a gleaming yard-long machete and glares like a pirate as he whacks the scalps off, but he is very skillful and always leaves a hole just big enough to drink from. All the palm-branch bathing enclosures are filled with screams and giggles and singing, and in between them the brown and white and coffee-colored children turn somersaults in the hot shallow water. A couple of rickety old miniature ferries have come from Mayaguez and are pulled up on a sandbar like a pair of patient horses. One of them tries to leave in a burst of music but gets stuck and has to be pushed by the children — the propeller kicking up an aggravated little spray in their faces — and a man with a long pole on deck. At last with a sort of grunt it tumbles into the deep water and everyone shouts and waves. Along the beach families, surrounded by mango pits, paper cups, etc., sit in the deep shade of the coconut palms under clusters of black umbrellas. And the fat woman scowls nearsightedly at the horizon across her half-kneaded, mountainous legs. It's a real sunshiny holiday; the children have ice cream on their noses and the Beach Club is papered with young girls too bashful to dance . . . But what is it all about?

Panchita, the little beach-girl comes every day. In the beginning she used to stand outside our windows and doors with the other children, all silently and portentously staring. They come right up on the balcony and gaze in the door, or lie on their stomachs on the steps, looking up. When we ask them to leave they smile bashfully, go away for a few minutes, then start all over again. Sometimes they stand on the cistern when I am working, so that their faces are level with the window and only a few feet away, and at night they crawl all around and under the house, calling our names over and over.

But Panchita has changed, and never did stare in quite the frontal fashion of the others. We gave her cookies, a piece of bread and jam. She was rather upset for a while at not being told to go away, didn't know how to behave, and used to eat the presents with her head down — almost tucked like a bird's under its wing — the little bright fluttery smile buried in her grubby hands. She would sit on the cistern for hours on days when there was no handkerchief work, playing with pebbles, waiting to be asked to do something, and went off skipping with delight when we asked her to buy ice. Whenever there is something to buy she comes and tells us about it; it was the only thing she could do for us, though she has found another now. One day I bought quinepas and gave her some. One kept dropping out of her fingers. Finally she let out her delicate tinkling laugh — an extraordinary sound here where the voices are so rasping, where there is no sense of music, only noise — and said, "It seems as if this quinepa wants to go off with the others," pointing to the ten-year-old vendor wheeling his funny little wheelbarrow around the corner of the house.

The night before last we gave her ten cents to go to the movies, and yesterday she arrived with a bag full of lemons that she had picked along the beach. She got one of her friends to come and ask if we wanted them first, and then came shyly, smiling, around the corner, holding the bag behind her. She wouldn't take money for them, though she never has a cent of her own; the seven or eight cents a day she can earn sewing handkerchiefs go to her mother. Later she came back and wanted my address in New York. "I'll send you lemons." I told her the postage would cost too much, but an hour later, swinging on the balcony railing in the dark all the time I was making dinner, she had another idea. "When you go away I'm going to bring you *muchos limones* so you can take them up there with you in your trunk." I offered her a piece of candied fruit, and when I put it into her mouth instead of handing it to her, the little laugh broke out, exquisite, running all through her tiny body like a shiver of cold.

She said, "If I'd been born in the United States I would have been an artist." I was horrified for a moment — because the people here are so often ruined by the fact of being colonials, so lacking in any *self*, it seemed as if it must have been said out of calculation, to please me. But it was not. She went on swinging on the railing, smiling a little to herself, smiling up at me beautifully when I came near. She likes drawing pictures and is going to show me some. She has not forgotten about the lemons, and is sad that we can't use more, though she has to go a long way down the beach to find them.

She showed the paper with my address to her friends and by evening they were all calling it outside our windows.

Government figure: 66 percent of the children of school age in P.R. are not in school. School attendance is less in the mountain districts, much poorer than the coast because of the ruin of the coffee industry. The children who do attend are not much better off since they have to be taught half in English. They learn geography, history, science and English literature entirely in English. The teachers themselves can hardly make a sentence in English and for the children it is so many hours spent in jibberish, they have no use for it outside the classroom and a year after school have forgotten everything. Panchita, who is about to be in sixth grade, doesn't know how many states there are in the U.S. — she thought it was 72 — nor when the Americans came to P.R., and can't pronounce United States. R.T., the American girl from Brooklyn teaching English at the high school in Cabo Rojo, teaches Shakespeare to students who can't understand her when she says good-evening to them at the dance.

The house beyond Doña Claudia's is large and painted. The family is fairly well off for Boqueròn: they own the movie house, the best store, and a café. There are twelve children. In back, next to the privy, is a wooden hut with a tin roof and no windows, used to lock the children in when they are bad. The one locked up most often is a wild-eyed girl, sixteen or seventeen years old. She is too

big for the mother to handle, so they send for the eldest son to beat
her and carry her screaming to the hut. They leave her there for
hours under a blazing sun, and we hear her screaming uncontrollably and sometimes for half an hour or more kicking and beating at
the door. The other day a friend climbed up and tried to give her
a glass of water through the slit between the roof and the wall, but
the opening was too small. The mother and other children lean
out of the house window, smiling, making remarks about it, and
laughing now and then when the one locked up — sometimes it is
one of the youngest — loses all sense and begins to thrash against
the walls of the hut. The heat there must be unbearable.

Sunday a young man in duck pants galloped in, stumbling on the
doorsill and again over the rocking chair, and introduced himself:
all smiles, all English. White skin and a juvenile kewpie-look. We
had sent a telegram that morning and his sister is the telegraphist
in Cabo Rojo, so he had heard . . . "Well, so I just thought I'll introduce myself, ha ha ha, I just love to meet fine American people,
get it? Well, well, well . . ." He had studied two years on the
Continent, so of course he liked to be with Continentals. He would
introduce us to the best people. "I'm a Porto Rican, but we're
Americans too, aren't we? Get it?" He said Porto, not Puerto,
and after every phrase laughed very loudly, switched from one hip
to the other, and said *get it.* "You see we have our four hundred
too, ha ha. They didn't come over on the Mayflower but they came
over on the Santa Maria, get it? Oh my yes, we have our Casa de
España and our Casinos, and I'm just going to show you . . ."
He is the librarian at the Agricultural College in Mayaguez; he
would get books for us, he would give us a party with real American
bacon. He leapt from theme to theme like a water-bug, switching
hips, rolling his eyes. And that book by Ellen Andrews! or is it
Helen? or Ruth? Well, naturally, Miss Andrews is a genius, he'd always said so, but that book! Imagine! The hero marries a Porto
Rican and the child turns out black. "Now you're fine American
people, you know yourself, we have Negroes here and white people
just like everywhere else, and my goodness you have poverty up
there on Broadway too, isn't that right? ha ha, get it? Say, and
have you been to the dances here? Oh no, not *here*" — he flitted

Boqueròn like a little piece of garbage off the railing — "I mean
the *real* dances where you meet the *real* Porto Ricans. Well now
I'm going to have a little party with some Continentals and a few
Porto Ricans, you know, the nice ones ha ha . . ." He stumbled
on the rocking chair again on the way out, ran on, ran back giggling to pick up the chair. "I'm just thrilled when some new Americans come here, we have a real colony now. Well, so long!
Cheerio!"

I am in love with the view from our dining room window; I
mean the room where we eat.   There is one palm tree very close —
the trunk is left out and you have only the large spiked branches
sweeping in from the left — and far away, along the sea, four other
palms make a lovely jigsaw symmetry.   The first palm is balanced
by a black-looking telegraph pole, very black after a rain, with its
wires slanting down across a little palm-thatch privy that is about to
fall down, a few scarlet splashes of flamboyant, and a beautiful
crooked line of red and yellow and blue washing hanging in the
sun. Today, on another clothesline, there is a bunch of yellow-
green bananas hung up to ripen.   The clouds form in shifting levels behind the four palms, sometimes two layers of rolling
marble-white and between them a mass of grey-blue, like dusk.
  The other night there was a vicious fight between a spider and a
kind of beetle. The beetle had been flying hectically around the
light, became dizzy perhaps, or worn out by the irresistible attrac-
tion of the hot bulb, and suddenly fell on its back in the corner,
where it lay waving its legs in a hopeless effort to turn right side up.
The spider, who has a den just above the floor in the corner,
emerged, spun a thread around the beetle and very slowly began
pulling him toward the wall. The beetle squirmed, twisted, flapped
his legs, all the time being drawn closer to the web that was hidden
in the wall. Once or twice he made a special effort to get free and
then the spider crawled out and put another thread around him.
Finally the spider disappeared into his hole and soon had lifted his
victim after him and out of sight. By that time the beetle had almost
given up. He went on gesticulating feebly with one of his legs but
the others were all wilted over his stomach.
  This scene, like the view from the window, is always new.

The inferiority complex of the island hangs over it like a cloud of soot. They love to tell about the tortures under Spain: men were tied by the heels to galloping horses, they had their tongues and fingernails torn out. They have never been a fighting people, there have been no revolutions — some of the Indians tried to defend themselves and soon there were no Indians left — but that horror, at least, belongs to Puerto Rico. It is about the only heirloom they have to show beside the splendid fighting history of Cuba.

There is nothing worse than the social apathy one feels almost everywhere. The island is by nature so rich, so lushly, saturatingly rich, that one becomes a little languorous thinking about it, but we have made it, or left it, a country of beggars. Sixty percent of the population, the lowest estimate, is unemployed, not counting men like our neighbor working at best half the year, for next to nothing, in the sugar cane. The streets of San Juan are lined with beggars, shambling old men and scab-headed children and little deformed creatures squatting on the sidewalks under the old eaves, holding their two palms up as if for rain. But in the schools the children learn to recite: "When the Americans landed, all our doors were open," and there is a grand holiday, with dances and fireworks, on the Fourth of July. As if that Independence had been theirs. Most of the middle class, at least those we have seen, who are also hopelessly poor but will not admit it — their one respectable possession is usually a radio and they can afford nothing better to eat than the same interminable rice and beans as the proletariat — dream only of sending their sons and daughters to be educated in New York. The Socialist Party has formed a coalition with the Union Republicana and is opposed to independence. And the Nationalists, for all their heroism, preach only an isolated, poetic struggle, as if the island were to live afterwards on its own mangoes and sugar and already ruined coffee industry.

They try to call him John instead of Juan — a minor result of the American occupation — but it turns out something like Jong, and like a little dog, he refuses to turn his head if I pronounce it differently. Not out of stubbornness; he is very obedient, a good boy everyone says. I think it is because he lives so much inside himself that he often doesn't hear. Only he is all attuned to the sound

"Jong," and when they call it he comes running, never answers, as if it were a bell. "Jong!" they call — and they all have the right to, even the little girl Carmen who is the same age as he — "Get some water," "Grate the coconut," "Take this soup up to Don Jaime's and don't spill it!" He never nods or smiles or changes his expression at all. He stands there with his hands hanging and his black eyes only half lifted while they tell him what to do, and then takes the soup or the pail or the coconut and edges out of sight. He seems to want to be out of sight, as if that were the only kind of home he had. When he has to carry things along the street he always stays as close to the houses as possible, and I think he hates pumping the water here, because he has to stand out in the middle of an open yard, in the sun. He is twelve years old.

He lives with our friends, Don Pedro Murillo the Postmaster and Doña Carmen. "He is our boy," Doña Carmen said when she sent him to us — it means our servant — but other times she says, "He lives here like one of the family, he calls me Mamà just like my own children." I have never heard him call her anything, nor speak at all except to deliver messages or ask if they have any more work for him to do. His older brother lives there too. Their mother was a cousin of Don Pedro's and when she died seven years ago and left them orphans, the Murillos took them in. One evening we spoke of the sadness of his face, and she seemed surprised for a moment, then remembered: "In school he writes themes about his mother, so sad . . ." She said it with a good deal of feeling, as she does all pathetic things, but it hardly seemed to strike her as a human problem.

I think it has never occurred to any of them that he is a child, and yet the Murillos are perhaps the most generous family I have ever met. They make, too, the least false distinctions. They are not aristocrats, are not even of pure Spanish blood, and they pretend nothing. How could they? — even if they wanted to. Don Pedro, to be sure, is white, also Selenia, the oldest daughter; Doña Carmen is plain Puerto Rican mestiza: thick features, dusky skin, and well-oiled, coarse black hair; the middle child has about the same skin as the mother; and Carmensita, though with very little that is Negroid in her face or build, is almost as dark as Jong — Doña Carmen refers to her lovingly as La Negrita. In the kitchen, cooking for them, on the same social level as Jong, is Tota, the only "Negro" in the district: coal-black, kinky-haired, with shapeless limbs and a total inability to refrain from singing.

Democracy becomes very delicate. The Murillos are friends with the financial aristocracy of Cabo Rojo: landowners, the manager of the Boqueròn Beach Club, *et al*. This is partly because of Doña Carmen's position as *Maestra*, schoolteacher. Pedro is something of an intellectual manqué, a dreamer, a knowledge-seeker without books, and was saved from failure only by the job of Postmaster, which carries a certain dignity. He still owns a tiny cobbler's shop in Cabo Rojo, where he goes every Sunday to empty the cash register.

In the evening the local rich young ladies, who say they will go to the U.S. to study medicine and at the age of twenty are still in an agony of *jeune-fille*-ness, rock and giggle in the bare Murillo parlor. Sometimes the washerwoman comes too, with some of her brood of eight, but not as far as the rocking chairs. She sits on the steps, ragged, barefooted, with only her broad athletic face inside the circle of light, and takes part in the conversation with smiles, which illuminate her wonderfully, and an occasional *"Sì"* or *"Verdad."* The darkness of her skin has all been beaten into it by the weather; she is tall, large-boned, and seems more Nórdic than any of them . . . The young ladies are mostly pasty-faced, with silken black hair and frail, pudgy bodies. They gossip, they titter about Pullman cars which they have seen in the movies, and ask if it is true that a big Negro comes through the train to see that everyone is in bed. When you ask about the bad fish here, sharks and *picua*, they point to the washerwoman smiling on the stone steps: "Ask her, she knows all about the sea." A little brown-skinned boy has already fallen asleep in the washerwoman's arms; a girl, in a transparent white dress, soiled and torn at the shoulders, leans across her lap and stares solemnly into the room.

Jong too sometimes stands in the doorway, watching, but more often he and Tota move into the dining room. Tota stitches herself ungainly garments on the sewing machine and Jong reads, keeping very quiet and tense, ready to jump up if they call.

This is the only time he can stay in the dining room. He eats in the kitchen, or rather, as that is a dark little hole without table or chairs and with a small tin box for a sink, standing in the doorway, or under the trinitaria tree in the yard, edging on the beach. He gets his bowl of rice and beans and hurries away with it . . . His room, their room, forms the passageway between the Post Office and the house. People run through all day, sometimes until late in the evening. Finally everyone else goes upstairs and Jong and his brother, who must be eighteen or nineteen, go to bed, together, in one flimsy little wooden bed.

This is a long, long tradition here; all the orphans live this way, and are as serious. But there is something special about Jong. There seems to be a deep sweetness and intelligence hidden away in him, and I keep feeling that if he would smile even a little it would be beautiful.

August 8

This morning word came over the radio that there was serious danger of a hurricane within twenty-four hours. Now, at 7:30 P.M., the danger is a little less. The hurricane started between St. Thomas and St. Martin, edged north of St. Thomas, and if it keeps to its course will avoid P.R. But it may shift; we will know by tomorrow noon . . . All day everyone has been talking hurricane but there will be no panic until the green flags are raised. The Mayor of Cabo Rojo put the green one up today by mistake instead of the yellow; the shopkeepers packed all their merchandise, barred their windows, etc.; the Mayor is obstinate and refuses to raise the correct flag. Here, people began lopping off leaves and dead branches of trees, and tying flimsy cords over their roofs; they tore down some of the palm-thatched bathing-huts and laid the stuff in neat piles on the beach. Everyone who could afford it has bought a lantern, and provisions. There was no one on the beach this afternoon and only one rowboat far out in the bay, struggling toward shore. The wind rattled in the palm grove — already you imagine the trees stripped, down, broken — and the village was full of the sound of hammering, people trying to hammer their roofs on a little tighter, putting planks across the seaward windows.

The young people are cheerful and excited, and the brightest of all is Pancha, ninety-six years old, though she knows that her house will not last ten minutes. Everybody loves Pancha. She dances and jokes and defends the Liberal Party, earns her own living ironing and picks the hookworms out of her own feet. Somebody will take her in afterwards, somebody will build her a new house and give her a new iron to earn a living with. But Doña Claudia next door can't bear it. What will she do when her house is blown down? This afternoon she crouched on the steps, her sticks of arms wrapped tight around her chest, a miserable shadow — she has been eaten away by hookworm — and said, *"Ai,* what will all the poor people do? I'm afraid . . ."

The hammering is still going on all around us.

August 16

The hurricane passed north, followed by a great wind that got people out of bed to tie their roofs on, if they hadn't already, at two in the morning. There was another possibility, but a small one and four hundred miles away.

The holiday of July 25 was not all so charming. In Ponce a group of Nationalists tried to assassinate Governor Winship, who was presiding at a grand celebration in honor of the fortieth anniversary of the American occupation. The chief of the National Guard and one Nationalist were killed, there were a good many wounded, and now there are nine Nationalists in prison, who will be tried for murder. One of them, Elifaz Escobar, had only recently finished a jail sentence for another shooting incident. The Governor said, "What bad shots they are!" and went on with his speech, saying that financial assistance to P.R. (and of course the island would need it for a long time before being ready for independence) would depend entirely on "how the Porto Ricans were thought to feel about the relationship to the U.S."

Don Pedro was frightfully upset. He is slow-moving, slow-thinking; he would like to be impartial. He crooks his forefinger over his nose and rubs it up and down a long time before making a definite statement. He is perfectly aware of all the Government violence of the last few years: murder of Nationalist students in Rio Piedras and protection of the police who murdered them, last year's "Ponce massacre" when a Nationalist parade was fired into, killing a great many, and so on. He told us all this, rubbing his long Spanish nose, looking harassed. He would like P.R. to be calm, to progress slowly toward a happier state — all this corresponding to his very admirable character: he is kindly, stern when necessary; he has worked all his life at very humble and unprofitable jobs without being ashamed of them (he started as a shoemaker; when Doña

Carmen was sent into the country as a schoolteacher he took up bee-culture, and had a taxi for several years here) and all the time he has been reading, plucking an extraordinary medley of information out of newspapers and bad magazines and perhaps a few books. He looks up as brightly as a child when there is something new to be learned . . . "We are all unanimously against this violence."

August 19

Went to the beach early yesterday, about eight o'clock. The light is extraordinary at that hour. The clouds hardly ever begin to mass on the edge of the sky before eleven or twelve. Usually by three or four they have all heaved up into the center, with brilliant blue gashes here and there; it rains violently, coming at the wooden windows like whips, then in a few minutes the gashes have spread out and torn all the grey away, and everything is hot and bright and still . . . At eight A.M. the sun is still low and almost as hot as at noon. It strikes the shadows of the palms, from deep back in the palm grove, like glistening black stencils on the sand. The colors are still clear and separate, not lost in the brightness as they become later. The flamboyant always seemed brighter even than the sun, it thrust back at it very impertinently, a sort of bullfight, but its month is over. The sea is pale turquoise, wonderfully clear like some kind of translucent stone, with a rim of candy green far out across the mouth of the bay where the fishermen's sailboats are. (They are really small rowboats with a mast stuck in, and the bay is so quiet, it seems brave of them to head out toward open water.) The lavender blossoms of the beach vines, scrawling from the brush toward the water, are still fresh. They look like morning glories but coarser, and they are not afraid of the high sun, but later in the day they seem tired, as if the vines were struggling to reach the water's edge, dying of thirst.

Don Antonio the crazy man, known as the *"Maestro,"* the sole inhabitant of this end of the bay, has not emerged. In a little while he will come out of his hut and cut grass with a machete, then haul a dead palm branch into the water and sit on it, the water up to his neck and his felt hat on, squinting through a pair of binoculars.

As we were swimming we heard a queer splash a few yards away, but were not frightened at first because there are always small fish jumping there. But this was a monster — and it was only by accident that we heard the little splash and saw the brown point sticking out for a second. We happened to be near shore and made it out, by the barest, with him after us from side to side in a slow, snakelike glide, until he was nearly scraping the sand. He was brown, seven or eight feet long and with a rather broad mouth. He swam a short way along the shore, weaving, as if waiting to strike, then turned out to the deep water. We saw the jagged point once again, quite far away. He must have been attracted by us, for that was the only time he came close to shore. We thought at first it was a shark, but I think it must have been a *picua* (barracuda), said to be more dangerous because they stay under the water, advance slowly and quietly, and then strike like a knife. We are told they can strike from a long distance. This one was very clever, not aiming in from the deep water, but circling around to the side and preparing to slice toward us straight along the shore. The bay closed over him so green and quiet it seems foolish to believe in these horrors gliding in it.

Every day now in the middle of the day I am overcome with *cafard*, past distinguishing between personal unhappiness and the great heat. For our siesta we lie infinitely apart in our separate miseries, like two trapped beetles, caught in our peculiar affection and companionship, which to our neighbors here evidently looks like the real thing, as it does sometimes even to us.

All the little boys have automobiles, very fast and frightening. They are made of a long stick with cross pieces at both ends, strings on both sides for stearing-gear, and excellent little wheels with tin tires. They are much better than store-bought cars. They can run around trees, turn upside down in the air, and in a pinch can be used as a weapon too. Some have streamlined Campbell's soup mudguards and the little boy next door even has a horn. It is a tin can with a wire passing through both ends, attached to the top cross piece, so that when the car makes a 180 degree turn the horn blows, i.e., the wire scrapes fiercely against the jagged tin. The only disadvantage is that the driver is behind instead of in the automobile, so that from a distance you might think it was meant to be a plough or babycarriage, but this never bothers the drivers. They go at every goat and corner as if it were a public enemy.

Crossed to the saltworks, the *Salinas*, yesterday in a rowboat. There is a little track jutting out into the bay on a long pier where the ships load, mostly four-masted sailing ships from Mayaguez. A pair of oxen had just hauled a small covered wagon filled with what looked like milk cans to the saltshed. They were very hot, and stood with their heads lowered almost to the ground, panting slowly and heavily. The back of one was ribboned with sores, perhaps from the whip, and the sores were black with little flies, not buzzing but settled, almost embedded in the open flesh.

The salt is piled in bright crystal hills; when you try to run to the top it cuts like paper. The sea water is let into a large pond, through a canal, then pumped by a windmill into the eight or ten flat beds. After evaporation, sometimes very rapid here, the salt is removed with picks and shovels. During the process the earth at the bottom of the beds turns a deep rose. The salt gathers first in fragile clusters like cobwebs against the wooden edges . . . There were thousands of crabs along the pond, most of them very young, about the size of a beetle; they look frantic, rushing from one hole to another with all their lopsided furniture. As we approached they would start up and run with a quick crackling sound over the dead palm branches. Carlos insisted on picking one up, a very little one, to point out its anatomy. He pulled its claw out and four of its legs fell off in his fingers. Farther on he wrenched a snail out of its shell. Along the beach are grape trees, about the size of a crab-apple tree, with a Japanese look, twisted and delicate, the grapes hanging in long tight clusters.

When the salt is being extracted and packed they have a good many men working, but yesterday there was only one old, old man in charge, the foreman. He is about as lumbering and asymmetrical as a crab — without the speed: it takes him ages to lift his arm to point toward the horizon. His face is all red and wrinkled and dry, and he wears two pairs of glasses. The inner pair is very thick; the other, enormous and pale blue, covers half his cheeks and has a cruel grip on his long red nose. His name is Don Juan. It seemed sad to leave him alone there with the oxen and the glittering little mountains of salt, but he likes it, it is as if that were his private estate.

It had begun to rain over Bouqueròn, the rain clouds were gal-

loping across the bay, and from the village to the lagoon — La
Boca — was a fine accurate rainbow, dyeing a small patch of palms
at either end.

Carlos, who took us there, a well-bred young landowner very high
in the local social scale, is married to the Jewish schoolteacher from
Brooklyn, R.T., who came down several years ago to a job at the
Cabo Rojo high school, intending to stay a year. They live in the
modest house he owns, new, comfortable, and very isolated, on the
promontory near the *Salinas*. She must have many lonely evenings
there. He seems to have no fixed occupation, looks generally bored,
with a roving Latin eye for sex and a strong suggestion of latent
bad temper. She is too intelligent and not nearly pretty enough to
satisfy him. A marriage about as ill-favored as ours, for different
reasons and though it has gone on much longer.

The moon is a milky mist over the mountains and the intricate
lush spread of the sugar cane; the palm leaves point down through
it to the black road like knives; beyond the railroad track suddenly
there is a smell of honeysuckle. The village howls with radios —
noche de ro-o-onda, que triste pa-a-a-sas — but in a few minutes you
lose them. The air folds around you like the sea, green milk-silver,
in the early afternoon. Here and there the softness is slashed
through with short plunging voodoo lights where stoves are still
burning in the kitchen shacks. The brown faces are bent over them
and on the wall the distended shadow of an arm thrusts stirring
into the glow; someone cries out. Someone sings, stops, people are
walking slowly down the road and back, waving ceremonial
branches to keep the mosquitoes away. *"Ave Maria, los zancu-
dos . . ."* From a one-room shack comes a collective murmur, on
and on, lilting like the sound of voyages: it is the death anniversary
of the father of the family; there is a spray of hibiscus at the door.
Another murmur farther on is from a gathering of spiritualists.
The frogs are chanting too in the damp places, and the crickets —
three careful pearl-notes, then a long listening — and beside the
fence a cow has folded its knees under, a green shadow; it com-
munes with itself in a sighing heavy breath that carries all its
bulk and all its introspection, and sinks away into an absolute of
rest. The banana leaves weigh like green rubber on the air over a
dried-up stream . . . Someone has put a nickel in the nickelodeon,

there is music at the Beach Club: hurry! hurry! All the boys run to the big bare dance hall but when they get there the record is finishing, it flaps itself over like a pancake and nobody has another nickel to put in. The boys shrug and wander back to the café. Cretoff has tipped his chair against the door and is reading the newspaper aloud, quick and excited, like a radio announcer. The boys spit, listen, watch the girls walking round and round the little plaza or sitting on the engraved stone benches that look like memorials and advertise the commercial houses of Mayaguez . . . A big crab runs across the plaza, everyone jumps up and chases it and someone picks it up gingerly by its claws. *"Ave Maria, qué grande!"* A little boy runs after his brother, laughing like a witch; he forgets to hold his pants up, they fall off and everyone laughs. The children are playing a love game, singing in a circle around the one who has to choose a husband . . . The moon is getting ready to go down behind the palm grove, the air is freshening; one by one the houses shut, their board windows tight as tombs. The children have gone suddenly. Cretoff sells his last pink *linberg*, drops the penny in the cash register and locks up — and the village closes like a flower into its tropical crowded sleep.

The big fish was a shark. It seems the *picua* has a long spear at the nose and doesn't glide before striking. It holds off, only moving a little from side to side, then plunges forward. After seeing the shark we began to hear all the danger stories about that part of the beach, where we have been swimming all summer. It was apparently a point of patriotism not to mention them before.

August 29

Doña Claudia paid us her first visit yesterday, and came again today. She put on a clean dress for the occasion, blue bedroom slippers and the remains of a pair of silk stockings, half of each leg in runs. She said she had become so used to seeing us at the window, it was as if her dearest friends, almost her own children were leaving. *"Ave Maria, Ave Maria . . ."* She twists her thin fingers and sighs, she sighs for everything poverty-stricken and hopeless in the world, and all her own lost health and youth, all the lost beautiful images. *"Ai! Virgen!"* Sighing, she looks down at her own weak shriveled body — the stomach dropped, her legs emaciated and

sprawling as if she had no more energy to keep her knees together
— and she seems to see there all the suffering she has ever dreamed
of. She could not do without it any more, she is uneasy speaking of
anything bright and strong. She told us how her husband had been
crippled falling from a palm tree and now he has dreadful pains in
his back; she has pains too, there is something the matter with her
ovaries. And her daughter who lives in San Juan: "*Ai!* she is a mar-
tyr . . ." It was clear that she came hoping we would leave them
some furniture or kitchen things when we go. She hinted at it, and
would look up around the room with a glimmer of shrewdness,
sourly, but that was gone in a moment and she gave way again to
her real hopelessness. She has no will left aside from that. "We'll
meet again," I said. "We'll come back." She gave me her first
honest look. "And what if I'm dead?"

The back-street hotel we stumbled on in San Juan, it soon became obvious, was a whorehouse, so no sleep; frequent banging at
our door in the night but nobody broke in . . . Had sent a card to
the F.'s, on the chance they might still be there, and hardly recognized him in front of the restaurant, a quite expensive one where
he insisted on taking us. He was in immaculate white suit, shoes,
and Panama hat, with an air of authority and a well-dressed orderly
or servitor of some kind walking a few steps behind. He has landed
a high-powered job at the PRA, has a car and chauffeur at his disposal and took us sightseeing, first to his elegant office, in the couple
of hours left before sailing time. It was out of tourist hours at El
Morro, but F. spoke a word to the guards and the gates were at
once opened for us.

The trial of the first of the Nationalists, Escobar, for the July 25
affair was in progress. It was front-page news and the sad half-caste,
half-starved looking face stared out from street, wall, bus, and gut-
ter all over the city. Had our first sight of the rich sections of San
Juan — country club, spacious houses, beautifully tended grounds
— where F. seemed much at home. On the bumpy ride from Mayaguez the tropical luxuriance of the island and its brilliance of color
were overpowering. On soil that can produce such enormities of
vegetation, you'd think people would be eight feet tall, strong,
healthy, and rich.

School started the morning we left Boqueròn. Doña Carmen,

charmingly proud of her *Maestra* role and wanting us to see her in it, asked us to stop by. She is also proud of the very pleasant new schoolhouse. The visit with its noise and distractions slurred over the sorrow of parting, especially from Panchita, whom we last saw waving and smiling among her friends in the school yard. She had come to be called *"la hija de la americana,"* and certainly in my love for her I have understood for the first time what being a mother is about. But how could I have taken her away with me, as she wanted, and as her family in their poverty would no doubt have welcomed too? If only they knew. The other most painful event of the summer was the news of my grandmother's death in July. The bathing enclosures on the beach, reassembled after the hurricane scare, had already begun to fall apart, to be rebuilt next June.

In our dark little quarters on the ship there was a magnificent basket of fruit sent by the F.'s.

In November, hurricane in New York: surely the first in my lifetime and presumably in much longer, since I have never even read or heard tell of one in this region. I always thought you went to the Caribbean for that. Some meteorological tomfoolery must be afoot. Perhaps they will start having blizzards in Puerto Rico, for Doña Claudia's despair and Panchita's delight. She was always asking about snow, and simply couldn't imagine it staying on the ground.

By a fine coincidence, later in November, the boss went off on one of his publisher's jaunts and I was told to work in his office that week, so I received the FBI man in grandeur. He seemed duly impressed, considering my age; and it was nothing about Trotsky at all. They merely had a note I had written to thank the F.'s for the fruit, and F. was somewhere on his way north from Miami, having suddenly lit out from San Juan with a lot of expensive government equipment, cameras, etc., from his office. It seemed he had been wanted on another charge, perhaps under another name, and mistook the reason of a government inspector's visit; the inspector had really been on his way there for some other purpose entirely. I was to understand that if he got in touch with me and I failed to report it immediately I would be party to the crime or whatever they call it. Loathsome predicament, even for such a chance acquaintance, with no ideological or other bond. I suppose this is just the point at which even the ideal government, if there could ever be one, has to be the enemy of human decency. In any case, I was spared. They got him through a trail of forged checks before he reached New York. His wife, who finally wrote me now that it is all over, has taken a room and found work as a waitress a mile or two from the penitentiary, to be near him.

My own brief marriage is finished. Elifaz Escobar, when we knew only through the newspapers, has been convicted of first degree murder and sentenced to life imprisonment.

PAT M. ESSLINGER-CARR

The Party

(FROM THE SOUTHERN REVIEW)

I STEADIED THE PRESENT on my lap and took a deep breath that stopped at my tight damp skirt band. The streetcar wheels clicked, clicked against the rails. I resisted the impulse to push back wet strands of hair at my temples and mash what little curl was left.

I didn't want to be on the hot trolley and I didn't want to go.

I pushed my glasses back up my greasy nose and wiped under the rims, carefully, not touching the glass with my knuckles. I had wanted so much more to stay in the porch swing with my book. John had just started telling his story; he was still with Beau and Digby, and we had all been together beneath sun spots of heat and sand, hearing the curses of the Legionnaires, smelling hot leather and camel fuzz. And then I had had to splash tepid water over my face, change from my shorts and wrap the hasty present my mother had bought at the dime store that morning. Matching fingernail polish and lipstick whose perfume made me slightly nauseated, but that Jan would probably like all right. I guessed she would, anyway, but I didn't much care. I begrudged the time I was having to lose. Over forty minutes each way on the trolley, and I would have to stay at least until 4:30 before I could break away politely. They usually played some kind of games until about 3:30 or so before they let you eat and escape.

I looked at the fat bland face of the watch hanging in its leather sheath beside the conductor: 2:20. I'd be a little late as it was and that would mean even more minutes lost at the end of the party; my mother said you should always stay at least two hours for polite-

ness' sake. And I had the other two Beau books waiting in their
faded blue covers when I finished this one. My whole Saturday afternoon wasted.

The click of the metal wheels chipped away at my world of sand
and dry hot fortresses until the desert sun fell into pieces and then
dissolved. I scooted the damp package higher up on my lap. I
could feel drops of sweat collecting under my bare knees.

We were passing the cemetery. The gawky stone angels dotted
the tombs and oozed green slime. They all had the same faces, the
same stone cataracts for eyes. Guardian angels, stiffened and blind.

I settled back against the wooden seat, feeling the wet patch of
blouse on my skin as we swayed along. It would be another ten
minutes on the trolley and then an eight block walk. My whole Saturday wasted.

When I climbed down from the awkward trolley steps, I realized
the afternoon was even hotter than when I had started from home.
The drops behind my knees gathered into rivulets that crawled
with itching slowness down to the tops of my anklets. Hot branches
hung like lank hair over the street, lifting and drooping with a
faint hot breeze almost as if they were panting.

Half a block away I saw the house with its tight cluster of balloons tacked to the front door and its pink ribbon trailing from the
brass knocker. Up close, I wasn't quite sure how to knock around
the pink satin ribbon, so I finally used my knuckles and left damp
imprints on the white door.

The door popped open immediately and a lady I guessed must be
Jan's mother stood there beaming greedily at me.

"Here's your first guest," she half turned back and called happily without taking her eyes off me. "Do come in," she added to
me and tried to open the door wider except that it was already open
about as far as it could go. She reached out to take my arm, but
when she saw me looking at her a little dumbfounded she didn't
touch me and just motioned me in with her hand. I saw Jan behind her.

"Hi," I said, blinking a little with the shadow of the room as the
door closed out the bright streak of balloons. I held out the little
package with its moist wrapping paper.

"Hi," she said and took the package.

"Aren't you going to introduce your little friend to me, Jan?" her mother said brightly, birdlike, from beside me.

I winced and glanced at her as Jan mumbled my name and held the present in her hands, not seeming to know what to do with it. Although not as fat as Jan, her mother had the same tight curly hair and the same plump cheeks. She said something else bright and pecking while I was looking at her that I didn't hear and then she put a hand on each of our shoulders and pushed us slightly ahead of her into the next room.

"We decided to stack all the presents on the buffet, and yours can be the first." I could hear her beam behind us.

The room was a dining room, but it was so covered with pink crepe paper I couldn't tell at first. Pink twisted streamers bulged low from the overhead light and swung to the molding of every wall. The tablecloth was scalloped with pink crepe paper held on by Scotch tape, and the buffet where Jan's mother put my present was skirted with more taped pink paper. A massive pink frosted cake with a circle of twelve pink candles in flower holders sat in the center of the table, and the whole rest of the table top was jammed with pink paper plates holding a pink snapper each and a pink nut cup stuffed with cashew nuts. Enough for the whole class I guessed.

"We thought we'd just stand up for the cake and ice cream," her mother's voice smiled around me. I knew we would have pink ice cream with the cake. "We just don't have thirty-three chairs in the house," she almost giggled.

I didn't know what to say and Jan didn't say anything, so her voice added, "Why don't you show your little friend your new room, Jan? I'll be down here to catch the door as the rest of your guests arrive."

Jan made a kind of shrugging nod and led the way out the other side of the room, up some stairs that smelled of newly rubbed polish to a converted attic room.

Everything in the room was yellow. Bedspread, curtains, walls, lampshade on the desk. It was a bit like having been swallowed by a butterfly, but it wasn't as bad as the pink downstairs.

"It's new," Jan said offhandedly. "Daddy finished the walls and my mother made the bedspread and curtains." She glanced around casually, but I caught the glint of pride before she covered it up.

"It's nice," I said. "I like yellow."

"It's so sunny." I could almost hear her mother saying it.

I nodded and grappled for something else to talk about. "What's that?" I pointed to a cloth-covered scrap book. The cover was a tiny red and white check, and I somehow knew Jan had chosen that herself.

"Just some sketches." But she couldn't cover up the pride this time.

"Can I see them?" I said too heartily, but she didn't notice as she put the book tenderly on the bed.

I started turning the pages, commenting on each one. Some of them were bad, the heart-lipped beauties in profile we all tried once in a while in math class, a few tired magnolias, some lop-sided buildings; but then I got to the animals. Round, furred kittens that you knew were going to grow into cats. Zoo monkeys, hanging on the bars, pretending to be people. Fat pigeons strutting among cigarette wrappers on their way to drop white splatters on Robert E. Lee.

I glanced up at her. She was watching me with the hungry expression I had seen on her mother at the door. "These are good." I couldn't keep the surprise out of my voice.

"Do you think so?" She waited to lap up my praise, her mouth parted and her plump cheeks blushing a little.

I nodded, turning to the animals again, telling her what I thought about each one. I don't know how long we were there when she said, "I guess we'd better go down." I hadn't heard anything, but she carefully closed the book and placed it on her desk.

Her mother was at the foot of the stairs waiting for us. There was a tight pulled look at the corners of her mouth. "What time is it, dear?" she said with that glittering, bird-sharp voice.

I saw the hall clock behind her in a brass star. The shiny brass hands had just slipped off each other and were pointing to 3:20.

"I can't imagine what has happened." Her voice slivered a little.

"You live pretty far out," I said, the excuse sounding pretty bad even to me.

She nodded abstractedly. "I suppose so." Then she added, "I'd better see about the ice cream."

She bustled off and Jan and I stood aimlessly at the foot of the stairs. I could see the pink crepe paper through the door of the dining room.

The silence lengthened uncomfortably and the hall clock pinged 3:30.

"You want to go in the back yard?" Jan said at last.

"Okay."

We trudged through the kitchen. Her mother was standing beside the refrigerator where I guessed she had just checked the cartons of ice cream. "You two go on outside. I'll be here to catch the door." Her voice was brittle, like overdone candy cracking on a plate.

I thought as we filed past that it would be better if she went up to take a nap and could have the excuse later of maybe having missed the knocker. It was getting awfully late.

We went out and took turns sitting on the swing in the oak tree they had out back and I told her about the book I was reading. I didn't much want to share it, but I had to talk about something. I told her she could have it after I finished even though I had intended to let my best friend Aileen read it next so we could make up joint Foreign Legion daydreams. We rocked back and forth a while, not really swinging, just sort of waiting and trying to limp along in a kind of conversation. I knew we were both listening, straining to hear a knock, a footstep on the sidewalk out front.

Her mother appeared at the back screen. "I thought you girls would like a preview lemonade. It's so hot this afternoon."

"It really is," I agreed hastily. She somehow made me feel awful. I guess it was the word "preview" that did it. As if there were really going to be something to follow, the birthday party when the other thirty-one guests arrived. "Pink lemonade sounds great." I hadn't meant to say "pink," and as soon as I said it I could have stuffed my sweaty fist in my mouth.

She gave a little stilted laugh and I couldn't tell if she noticed. "It's all made."

We waited and took turns in the swing until she brought the two glasses out on a little tray. I saw her coming from the corner of my eye and said, "I bet you can't guess what I got you for your birthday."

Jan shook her head, looking at me and sort of grinning.

"It's something to wear," I said prolonging it. Then as her

mother got there with the lemonade, I looked up, startled, as if I hadn't seen her. "That looks good," I said a little too loudly at the pink liquid. There wasn't any ice in it; the freezer part of their box was probably full of ice cream.

She strained out a smile. I thought I saw her lower lip quiver a little.

"I got so hot coming out here. I didn't know you lived so near the end of the trolley line." I tried to put over the idea of distance and maybe a confusion about their address. "This is great." I took a quick sip.

"Really great," Jan chorused.

But her mother was already on her way back to the kitchen, into the house where she'd be able to hear the door.

We stayed there in the hot shade, alternately leaning against the rough tree trunk and sitting in the swing until I guessed it must have been about four o'clock or so. We were still listening too hard to talk much.

"Want something to eat?"

I couldn't face that pink dining room with the crepe paper streamers and the thirty-three nut cups. I hesitated.

She must have understood. "We have some cupcakes, in case we ran out of . . ." Her voice trailed off.

"Fine. I love cupcakes," I said hurriedly.

As we came in her mother came from the front of the house.

"We thought we'd have a cupcake," Jan said.

"Oh, yes. That's a fine idea," she began. "And have a dip of the ice . . ." Then her face crumpled like a sheet of wadded paper. Her lips wavered over the word and a great sob hiccuped through her throat. She put her hand over her mouth as she turned and ran toward the hall, and I saw her back heaving as she disappeared beside the stairs.

We pretended we hadn't seen anything. Jan got the little pink cakes from a bin and dished out two great heaps of strawberry ice cream, and we stood beside the sink and ate them.

I had separate sensations of dry warmish crumbs and iced smoothness passing across my tongue, but I couldn't taste anything. But I ate the little cake and the bowl of ice cream and when she offered me another cupcake and more ice cream, I took them and ate them too.

I repeated some of my compliments about her sketches and added more as I thought of them and spooned up the chopped bits of strawberry in the bottom of the dish. We dragged out the ritual until shadows began to ease into the kitchen and I saw by the kitchen clock that it was after 5:30. I told her I had better leave to be able to get home before dark with such a long trolley ride back uptown. "Tell your mother," I began, but I couldn't think what she should tell her mother for me and I stopped.

As we went toward the front door I saw the pink paper of the dining room glowing in the afternoon sun.

"See you Monday. I'll bring the book," I said loudly at the front door.

She waved her hand and shut the door. The knot of balloons jogged, settled lightly against one another beneath the pink satin ribbon on the door knocker as I went down the sidewalk.

LEWIS B. HORNE

Mansion, Magic, and Miracle

(FROM THE COLORADO QUARTERLY)

THEY SAID OUR VALLEY had the softened light of England. That's why they were coming from Hollywood to make the film. Perhaps they were right if they caught us in the spring before the sun turned brazen and the desert dried to rattlesnake weather. For in the spring, when the desert was flowering and fragrant, the evenings sweater-cool, there was a gentleness in the blue sky, a serenity in the air that suggested some greener land that few of us ever thought of and none had ever seen. During World War II, distances challenged and evoked dream. We were isolated. We had, if not the shape, at least the *feel* of a hamlet or a dingle. To the south was the wide irrigated mesa where the town spread out, to the east the mountains, large and varicolored and hauntingly shaped, to the north the river bed, wide and sandy.

Near that river bed, even in spring, no one could have found the landscape of an England. In two places it served as the town dump. Beyond the dump that flashed sunlight into the eyes rolled the sand, throwing back like a reflection the sky's heat. For the sky was metal there, the mountains across the way sharp in upheaval. But the movie — it was about a conscientious objector in England — was not to be shot on the river but on the edge of the mesa. Near the Hill.

Any road coming off the mesa came downhill. But only the single paved road to town came down the Hill. There looking out over the alfalfa fields, the citrus groves, the farms and pasturing cows, advance crews built part of an English mansion. You drove toward it, looming large and dark, and looking at it hard enough imagined yourself in another place. But as you started up the Hill, it compressed, and you saw as you passed that the men had built a facade. It was beautifully done, that facade. Even if you drove up Lee Hiram's road and looked close it looked real. The windows worked. The big front door opened and shut with lock and hinges. The shrubs were real. Wide gravel walks crossed the front and a lawn was planted. But behind the front were braces and supports, the extra boards and materials.

We rode up there on our bikes one day — Ken and William Conner and I — hoping to get some scraps of wood. But there was a guard. He sat in the shade on a pile of boards behind the facade. He wore dress-slacks — not a uniform, not Levis — and a short-sleeved sport shirt. He smoked a cigarette fiercely and spoke so rapidly we could hardly understand him, so acidly he might have been angry.

"What?" Ken said.

"Boysmndre?" His mouth was wide, a thin and rubbery line with a twitch to it. He scarcely parted his lips.

"Yeah, we live around here," said William. "We came to see if we could get some of those scrap boards." The man uttered that they weren't his to give away. We asked when the movie stars were going to come. He didn't know and he didn't care that he didn't know. He was bored, had to stay up all night. What were they going to do with the mansion when it was all over? Blow it up. In the movie it was supposed to get bombed. Real airplanes? War so close to home? "I want to see that," said William as we rode away.

On the Hill we coasted down. Faster and faster across the little ridges of tar. Bumpbumpbump. The speed frightened towards the bottom. Suppose the machine failed and came apart? Suppose a tire blew? Fear increased exhilaration. "We'll have to find out when they're going to bomb," said William as we coasted together again at the bottom of the Hill. "I want to see that."

Looking back at the mansion, I said, "Yes, we sure will," for from this distance the mansion made you feel again you were in another place. Except for thinking of the guard. We wanted the scraps for a magician show we were readying, fixing a stage in our storeroom next to the chicken pen. No help on the Hill.

"Let's try the dump," William said. "There ought to be some stuff there."

Close to the river the ditches got shallower, the big cottonwoods gave way to mesquites, and we found ourselves panting the last half-mile through powdery dust the tire wheels tracked deeply. Oh, the heaps of papers, sofa cushions, car seats, radio shells — all the cast-offs from the town and valley. "There's nothing here," said Ken abruptly. "Let's go back. It's too hot."

"Just wait." We worked through piles, burning our fingers if we touched metal. In one spot were old toys we had thrown out during one of Mom's cleanings. Beyond the dump was the sand, bright enough to make you squint, and beyond that rocks and hills as red and raw as a sore. I said, "How long would it take to walk to those hills?"

"You'd dry up."

The danger intrigued. "Half day?"

"Don't expect me to go along," said William.

"Take a canteen — "

"Not me," said William.

Like a movie. I'd be a prospector struggling, a lone cavalryman crawling . . . The water hole at last — ah! I pulled up my shirt and wiped away the sweat. How ugly the dump was! "Let's go," I said. "Aren't you guys thirsty? What you going to find in this dump?"

William kicked over an old radio. Its insides glittered. "We'll have to figure out how to get some stuff from the Hill, I guess."

"With the guard?"

"I'll figure something out."

The storeroom that we were using barely kept out the rain and dust. It protected from no heat. We found mice in its corners, saw a garter snake once slide under its floor. One midnight my father even shot a skunk there after the chickens. The family trusted nothing of delicacy or value in it. But for the magician show no ordeal dissuaded. With old pull-down blinds we covered the walls of our stage area. We stitched together rips and nailed the long rolls across the bare boards. A quilt from William's mother, cotton spilling out, patchwork unpatching, got pinned to a line of baling wire for a stage curtain. We tacked black paper to a table, hiding it from top to floor, and sawed and hinged a small trapdoor in its top. William Conner was the magician, while Ken and I managed the mechanics of the performance. I crouched beneath the table to pull on the trapdoor and make a Buddha-like incense burner disappear. Ken from the other side of the stage pulled invisible threads and strings that gave life to a blue rope-snake, caused a flower to grow, handkerchief to float — such illusions we could create!

But what a greater illusion, I thought, had the people from Hollywood managed. When we came back from the dump, I could see from the western sunlight burning through the door behind me every nail on the blinds, every thumbtack on the black cardboard covering the table. Even the name spread across the back wall, shiny as it was, looked shabby. MISTOFO THE MAGICIAN. I remembered coming home from town in time for milking and Ken and William saying, "Hey, look what we did." With the same sun pouring on the wall, the letters had shown up as gold. Pure gold. Sabu might have discovered it in a sunken treasure cave. "Where'd you get it?" The dump, they said. Used Christmas wrapping paper. Up close you could see ragged edges from the dull scissors, paper so brittle it might tear, color flaking off in tiny chips. But back away and — MISTOFO, it glowed.

But what about now? Shabby. "Hell," I said to myself, turning to go put on my milking clothes. Still, if we could get some boards, William Conner insisted, we could raise the stage, paint it maybe. Something as good as the mansion on the Hill. What fantastic feats we could perform with an area open below! But the guard, what about the guard?

"Let's go up there again," said William one evening a few days later. "We'll scout." The guard was sitting on the front step of the mansion. He smoked his cigarette, peering out over the valley, eyes squinted against the sun, lowering to his left. When he stood as we approached, I saw that his trousers bagged because his legs were too thin to assert themselves, his arms were red-haired bones coming from his shirt sleeves, his neck a piece of food, pale and petrified, raising his head with a rubble of features. I hadn't remembered him being so small. He said something like, "Back, huh?"

William asked about the boards but he still didn't know. Didn't know who to ask, a man like him, all he did was put in his time, don't ask no more of him. "Can we scout around?"

"Stay out of them shrubs if you do. My ass if you break them shrubs. They start shooting soon." A spurt of words, face grimaced. Smoke hazed his face, flowing from his mouth and sifting double-plumed from his nose.

We followed William. I'd like to have walked through the doorway, but the watchman sat again, staring down at Lee Hiram's farm. William went from one spot to the next, up behind the facade, down to a mesquite along the road. He stood, musingly, peering through half-closed eyes.

"What d'you think?" asked Ken.

William nodded as a submarine captain might or a commando surveying his field of operation. "Yeah," he said. "We might make it." Back at the porch he said ostentatiously, "Too bad none of them boards is available."

"Up to me they'd be yours. But this country — Roosevelt and the rich they got everything sewed up. I don't give a shit if you take the boards." Bad talk. The three of us looked at each other. A spy? "Who lives in that place down there?" He nodded at Lee Hiram's farm. "A regular beaver, ain't he. Been going like crazy — whole yard full of kids. Everyday."

"He works hard," I said. "And all his nine kids, too." The Hiram kids were propped up as models for us too often to be praised lavishly. But defense of our valley's honor was another thing. They put their shoulders to the wheel, worked with a will like there was only today. Et cetera. "And Ronnie Hiram used to be scoutmaster." We praised him, though we weren't yet old enough to be scouts.

"One of them, huh?"

"He's in North Africa now," I said. "Fighting for the country. He's Lee Hiram's oldest boy."

"A brave soldier, I expect?"

"He's stopping Rommel," said William. That's the way the magazines and the newspapers described it. "Well, Dad," we had read in *Life*, "we stopped the best they had." Not as famous as Guadalcanal, El Guettar still flashed in our minds.

"He'll get his," said the guard. "Playing old Roosevelt's games for him."

Smarting with indignation, we coasted down the Hill, shadows long as a cloud's across Lee Hiram's field. He and Bob, the boy

LEWIS B. HORNE   57

next in age to Ronnie, were bringing the milk cans out for the
creamery truck. Lee Hiram was tall and cadaverous. But strong —
everyone knew that. Old as he looked. We waved as we winged by.
"What d'you think of that guy?" said William as we started
pedaling again.

"Probably a spy for the Germans," said Ken. "You see how he
watched Lee Hiram's place?"

As the home of the valley's one military hero, the Hiram farm
took on strategic import. We were proud of Ronnie. None of us
doubted he would come home like Barney Ross with medals
flashing. Besides his mail was getting censored.

By the churchhouse where William Conner turned to go home,
William outlined his strategy. We'd go up to the mansion about
sundown. One of us would talk with the guard while the other two
snuck off the boards we needed. Hide them in Lee Hiram's ditch
and come back with the car that Ken and I were learning to drive.
I was unsure. "That old fart has eyes in the back of his head."

"Okay. You do the talking then," said William, "and Ken and
me will get the boards. We aren't afraid."

Afraid! The suggestion rankled. I was brave as Ken or William
Conner.

But the next evening the cast arrived. Filming began at once —
an alfalfa field was turned into a haying countryside, an adobe
house transformed into an English cottage. It took a whole afternoon for Helmut Throne to hop a fence and greet a hayer. It took
another afternoon for him to approach a cottage, scattering carefully gathered white chickens. I would sit in the shade of a tree and
dream myself into some vision at one with the camera's, and then
our valley was England. The blue sky softened, the white clouds
blazed less fiercely, and the air to my skin was momentarily damp.

"Hell," said William a couple of weeks later. "People all over
the place."

But the weekend following was quiet. Saturday night we biked to
the mansion. William told me, "You just keep talking, keep his attention. Ken and I will do the rest." Talk about what?

"Where your buddies?" He sat like a scratchy-winged spirit,
brooding. Seeing him against the dark mansion with the pinprick
shade-and-glow of cigarette in the shadow, I felt disoriented, in
another place far from home. The lights of Lee Hiram's house —

kids bathing for Sunday School next morning — was a comforting
anchor, a grip for me in the dark drift I moved in. "Buddies not
with you?"

When the lie that blocked my throat broke loose, it came in as
swift a cataclysm as his own question. "Stayed at home." I listened
hard for Ken and William. The cigarette seethed. Frightened of
the silence, I engaged the enemy. "What do you do when they're
shooting?"

"Sleep," he said.

"You don't watch the movie stars?"

"Shit." I was about to say something else when the words shot
out like dozens of small rocks, as though designed — I thought — to
wound. "Look, boy, I have to work for my wages. Movie stars. I
seen plenty of them. And what are they? People — like you and
me. Only shit, they ain't as good. That Flake woman — beautiful,
you think? Well, let me tell you, boy, I seen her drunk as a skunk
many a time."

"Awww — "

"Drunk as a skunk, I tell you. Why didn't they finish up this afternoon? You want to know why? Because when she got out here,
she was too loaded to stand up. Fell down over there by them
flowers. Drunk, I tell you. If I got drunk on the job, you know
what would happen, don't you? Sure you do. I got to work for my
grub."

"Well, she is beautiful."

"You seen her when she gets out of bed in the morning, before
she gets that hair combed?" I was silent. I couldn't tell whether I
really heard skittering sounds or not. The guard asked, "What'd
you say that old man's name is down there?" He spoke as though
he referred to an antagonist. "The one with all them kids."

I told him and he wanted to know what Lee Hiram did for a
living.

"Farms."

"Bigger fool him. Much money in it?"

My dad worked in town, farmed on the side, so I couldn't say.
"He works hard," I said.

"You told me that already. Does he make any money?"

"He has nine kids."

"Eight," he said. "You told me one of them's off fighting Roosevelt's war."

"He's a good man," I said. "He pays his tithing. Nobody's ever heard him cuss. He's a good Mormon. And besides he's a Patriarch."

"What's that?" I told him about Patriarchs in the Church and about Patriarchal Blessings. He chuckled. "The things you people believe." He pitched his cigarette into the darkness.

"Don't you believe anything?"

"Sure," he said. He lit another cigarette. "Whatever I can see. These eyes right here — " he gestured at two gun muzzle cavities above the match light — "they see, then I believe. They don't — " The smoke he blew out touched my eyes and nostrils, its smell rubbing my lungs with brown fingers. "Look, somebody dies — he goes to heaven or someplace else, right? The ticker stops and he goes, one way or another. That what you say?"

"Something like that."

He shook his head. I could see that much. "No sir. Down there he goes, back into the old mother, that's where he goes. I seen. You ain't never seen a dead man, have you? Didn't think so. That's all he is. Dead. Bleed him out. Dead, dead, dead. Good for fertilizer, that's all. Cremation for me and let the old wind take me. I'll never know no better. Just what we see, buddy, what we see. That's it. The cemetery — it's a compost heap. The whole shitting earth's a cemetery."

"That's not what Lee Hiram says in church," I said, standing. Surely William and Ken had finished.

"Just what I see," he said. "What I hear." He called after me, "That's all you know, buddy."

William and Ken were waiting for me on the road. "Did you do it?" I asked.

"Sure," said William, full of braggadocio. "What'd you think we did?"

"I think he heard."

William was skeptical. "Why didn't he say something then?"

I didn't sleep well. I took my bath for Sunday but I felt smudged with the guard's cigarette, colored with the taint of his words. I didn't feel any better for lying to him, stirring up some of my own internal sediment, except I told myself he deserved it. What treasure did he with his smoking nostrils guard anyway? What business had he to make fun of the Hirams, of all of us in the valley?

All the same I wished we'd not taken the boards. I wished I hadn't stood on the Hill in arm's reach of the man. I could sense those eyes up there looking out across the valley, not with interest or liking or love, not with boredom or dislike or hate, but with indifference — looking out as though we and everything else in the valley were dross.

Next morning before Sunday School we drove up, the three of us, spruced in white shirts and slacks. Ken was at the wheel, barely able to see over the hood. No traffic on the roads then. There were not any boards in Lee Hiram's ditch either.

"Where the hell they gone?" asked William.

"He's got them back," I said. I replied quickly as though I already knew it.

They didn't believe. "He came down after we left. I know he got them," I said, itching all over with smoke. "He must of heard you like I said last night."

"Why didn't he stop us then?"

"He didn't want to," I said. "Don't you see? He wanted to let us go as far as we would. If we did that — ?" What, I wondered. If we did that then — ? It came on me. "We're as bad as he is."

I couldn't get him out of my mind. He squatted behind my eyes, bony, as though stripped of all superfluous beauty-making flesh. Body had no beauty, any more than the river bed or the out-used discards in the dump. He had only the essentials of energy and matter, being and bone. Nothing extra. I had said we were as bad as he. But what did that mean? Our stealing? It was wrong, yes, but we knew it. He didn't care, was no guard against moral decay. What then? If doing wrong meant nothing, neither then did doing right. That was it.

William and Ken were eager to get on with the magician show. Without more preparations. But what kind of entertainment would that be? "We got what we need," said William. "The disappearing Buddha, the snake, the floating handkerchief — "

"Hell," I said. "You won't fool anybody." I didn't ask the big question: Why do you want to fool anybody?

"We fooled your sisters." William was right. Melissa and Jane,

the two youngest in the family, had jumped with such curiosity that
we previewed a growing flower. They blinked at its miraculous rising on Ken's black string.

"Sure," said Ken. "Melissa and Jane were tricked."

"That was before," I said.

"Before what?"

"Before — " I felt afire, flaming inside as well as out. "Look,"
I said. "We were going to do things to the stage, right? Now we
can't because of — because of that old fart at the mansion. What
kind of show can we put on now? We can't play tricks — not good
ones — unless we have the right stuff. It's not worth it."

"You were ready before."

"That was before," I said. "Before we found out how to do it
better."

William cussed. "Tell you what. Let's go to the dump again.
See what we can find. If we don't find nothing — "

The dump seemed closer this time. The dust on the road pow-
dered our sweaty skin. At the river even William could see it was
hopeless. The sun drained away color so that the bare heaved-up
plain of garbage smote us. Our old toys. Discards. Paraphernalia
shucked off. Superfluous relics of a brighter time, living time —
now rubbish. We tried to salvage something. But we burned
fingers, cut knees, without reward. "Shit," said William finally,
"let's go."

Irritated that we'd come for nothing, wanting to say I told you, I
pedaled back silently, fiercely, hoping Ken or William would say
something, hoping they would give me an excuse to swear. But
they huffed up the dirt road as silently, as fiercely — perhaps as de-
spairingly — as I.

And then as news of the Tunisian campaign dropped away for the
question of where and when and how southern Europe would be at-
tacked, word came of Ronnie Hiram's death. My father brought
the news home from work. Probably an accident, I thought. After
he's been in battle, performed bravely, even heroically — probably
a jeep had overturned, a rifle misfired, something hideous that
would taunt the Hirams and the rest of us for all that Ronnie had
been and done.

In the midst of that news — all of us sitting at supper with no great desire to eat — William called. "Hey," he cried, "they're bombing tonight."

"Haven't you heard?" I told him above the murmur of voices at the table. He was silent. "You still going?" I asked finally.

"Probably not. You?"

"No."

Later while Ken and I were milking, Maud Connor called for the Relief Society. She wanted Mom to help with a meal for the Hirams.

Shy, Mom wanted someone to go with her. Because Dad was irrigating and I was the oldest, I was chosen. It was dark when we started off in the car, a kettle of soup beneath my feet, two loaves of bread warm between us. When we turned in to Lee Hiram's place, Mom asked, "What's that racket?" I remembered the bombing. Flares burst. Two large searchlights speared the sky. In brief flashes the mansion was lit up, smoke drifting across it. A voice squawked from a loudspeaker.

Mom muttered to herself and told me to take the bread while she carried the soup. Lee Hiram came in from the bedroom. Tall like Ronnie. For all the severity of bone and structure, his face had a gentleness to it. His mouth was wide with no tightness against the teeth. His eyes were large and pulled down slightly on the outer corners, tempering his weather-blown skin with sadness. His forehead was tall.

Mom handed over the food. They'd already eaten, he said. Two of the girls put the soup in the frig. Lee Hiram sniffed the bread. "It smells delicious."

"If we can help — "

"We're grateful. Very grateful."

He knew we were anxious to leave. At the door Mom said, "Give Jenny our love."

"Yes, yes." He looked up at the Hill. "They're very busy up there tonight."

"I don't know why," Mom said suddenly in a voice untypical of her, "I don't know why these things happen."

Lee Hiram pattted her hand as though she were the one who needed comforting. "It tests our faith, doesn't it? Severely," he said. He looked towards the Hill. The booms and yells beat against us. The spears of light leaned from one side of the sky to the other. We heard a scream. "Remember us in your prayers," he said as he turned back into the house.

That night in bed I wanted to pray. Help Lee Hiram, I wanted to ask. And Sister Hiram. Help all the Hirams in — I picked up words from Church — in their hour of distress, in their hour of need. But I was stopped by a vision of the guard. He stared out over the valley. I wasn't going to ask him. Not pray to him. Sitting there in the middle of all that racket, in the middle of bombs falling and houses crumbling, and bodies exploding. With his cigarette, not caring. Sitting there — as I tried, as we all tried, to sleep.

The bombing was the last big scene. The rest of the film would be shot in Hollywood. Monica Flake and Helmut Throne left. William wondered what would happen to the mansion, but I didn't care. I'd have been happy had it really been bombed. But that, too, was fake. The facade stood just as regally against the sky as ever.

I went up there by myself after the memorial service for Ronnie. The thought that the guard might know how Ronnie Hiram died — plainly, without glory, as I thought — humiliated me.

"What you back for?" This time he came around the end of the facade, buttoning the fly of his trousers, having urinated. "Don't know nothing about those boards. Tell your buddy that. How many times you gonna ask?"

"I just came to look around." Would he taunt me about the boards we'd taken? Had I thought a moment I'd have known. He didn't need to say anything: neither side would admit what it had done. To do so would make the incident a friendly jest. The guard had no friends. Of that I'm sure. I didn't want him for a friend.

"Been a lot doing down there lately." He nodded toward Lee Hiram's farm.

He wouldn't ask me what. So I said, "His boy got killed." He squatted on the steps without saying anything. So I went on: "He got killed in action — at El Guettar. That was the big battle. He was a hero, a real hero, like — like — You read about them. That was the kind of hero he was. Defeating Rommel's army."

"All by his self?" Like a single eyebrow raised.

"They did — all of them. They stopped the best they had. And Ronnie was one of the best."

"You know a lot about it."

"Sure," I said. "Didn't they call Lee Hiram from Washington?"

He didn't blink. "Roosevelt his self, huh?"

"Okay, don't believe me. You don't have to believe me if you don't want to. But I say somebody from the Secretary of the Army — not the Secretary himself — but somebody from his office — "

"Okay, okay." It sounded like *-kay, -kay,* ticks in the throat. "He's better off for it anyway. All them kids. Better off anyway." He continued speaking, looking out over the valley — across Lee Hiram's fields and orchard, over the cottonwoods lining the distant road, out to the low rim of mountains that looked so large and barren from the dump on the river. He muttered away. Something about kids, families, wives. He'd had wives, two of them — one an alcoholic, one a nympho. "D'you know what that means nympho? You'll find out. Have a daughter in Frisco, working in the shipyards or some damn thing, screwing around, making hay out of Roosevelt's war. Raised her by picking fruit with the Okies, doing God knows what, and look at it, piss on it, what d'you get for it? C'mon, what d'you get? Not one goddamn thing. Your soldier boy. What does he get? Tell me that. What does he get?"

"He'll get a medal," I cried. "You wait and see."

"I don't wait for nothing, buddy."

I looked at the mansion. They would be tearing it down soon. Already it looked morose. The stone covering was pulling off to show lathe underneath. Shrubs and grass were yellowing. Already — shabby. I thought of our magician's stage — shabby. Of Ronnie Hiram — not shabby. It couldn't be. But somehow rotten, wrong, that he should be killed, something miserable that took the prime out of what you looked at, drained the green, discolored the sky.

There was no joy to coasting down the Hill. No excitement. If only the bike would come apart, pitch me end over end into the Johnson grass, riding like a wave the big sob I could feel building up in my chest.

As I came to the bottom of the Hill, nearing Lee Hiram's fence, I saw his two youngest playing near the ditch. No water ran in it. But as I tore forward, the smallest ran into the road. I could see our paths colliding, my own trajectory leading to explosion. I yelled, twisting my wheel.

I thought for a moment I did fly. But I spilled into the irrigation ditch, bicycle on top of me. The sky pulsed a moment. The abrasions on my skin, hidden under clothes, burned. As I untangled myself I found a large rent in my Levis. My nose dripped blood.

A handkerchief appeared. Lee Hiram's. His face was above me. He helped pull off the bicycle. "You all right?" he said. "Elly should know better. I was just coming to get her. She really should know better."

Sister Hiram appeared. She was heavy, without shape, her hair pulled back into a low bun. "What's the matter, Lee?" she kept saying as the older of the two children cried again and again that Elly had run into the road. Lee Hiram explained; so they both helped me up. I was embarrassed by their concern.

More of the kids came out. Sister Hiram insisted I come in for a minute. One of the kids wheeled the bike which seemed not to have been hurt, and I sat at the kitchen table while Sister Hiram squeezed a lemon for lemonade. She even got the cubes from the frig. "Please," I said. "I'm all right."

"Any boy likes lemonade on a hot day." Lee Hiram and his wife sat at the table with me. Finally Sister Hiram said, "You were one of Ronnie's scouts, weren't you?"

"No, ma'am," I said. "I'm not twelve yet."

"That's too bad," she said. "I'm sorry you didn't get to know him."

"Yes," said Lee Hiram. "Mama and me — we know that there are more important things for him now." He went on to say that it had been hard, especially at first, but they knew the Lord had need of special souls.

"Yes," I said. I was anxious to speak a truth. "All us kids liked him. Whether we were scouts or not."

Lee Hiram smiled. A quiet smile. Resigned, pleasant — even happy. Register of his belief and faith. As though he knew something, had seen something face to face, for all that what was a part of the best was killed. With the trust he revealed, he looked as old, as ageless, as Abraham might. Hadn't angels visited that ancient Patriarch? Hadn't he triumphed over ordeal?

Coming out of Lee Hiram's driveway, I looked back at the Hill. There was the mansion. From here it looked real, two infant clouds riding above it. Real — the way it looked down across the valley. Like it was really someone's house. I could believe in it with pleasure because tomorrow the guard would be gone. I could smile even. Not the way Lee Hiram smiled. Lee Hiram had a special smile, so special, so miraculous, I could never match it. But I could smile and think of the magician's show, still ready to start. Sure. We could baffle the kids — William Conner, Ken, and I — we could create a mystery. Great, I thought. Great. To think of them, all of them, smiling wide-eyed with wonder.

ROSE GRAUBART IGNATOW

Down the American River

(FROM SHENANDOAH)

> *"It was a day of more pills
> and blood tests and visions,
> hallucinations, omens and
> ecstasies, which were not
> to go down the American
> River."*

my dear son
read over your letters of the years — including the piece of writing
titled I, JESUS — *I felt again the aches and love poured into the*
ground — where no seed comes up ever —

you in your madhouse — me in this life which sometimes has been
so frightful —

these years I've spent hoping — I even hoped again when you sent
those three pages —

people have a way of forgiving us and themselves — one can't in-
quire too sharply into their methods —

SHE FOUND THE ABOVE WORDS typed on a yellow sheet of paper. She
couldn't remember having written them. Her letters to him were
chatty; they were about the weather, trips to the orthodontist with
Janey and about the state of the garden.

In the summer she had told him about the robins who built nests
twice in the same fir tree. How the robin dived boldly into the tree

with food in its beak, even when she was nearby watering the lawn
and flowers. She could hear the babies; but the fir was so thick she
could not see them in their nest somewhere deep in the middle of
the tree.

She'd come across a letter of Gerald's from the summer. It was
one which still had its envelope so she could see its date: July 30.
She remembered it once she read it again:

Dear Folks,
I am held on ward. I am a prisoner. Can't move bowels for 3
weeks.
Come at own risk.
Contact Judge. Bug in ear for over 3 months.
You may not get out of ward for dangerous hallucinations.
Will peril your health.

> *& you may die*
> *Please,*
> *Gerald*

p.s. gassed to death by air, simple food & cigarettes.
" & you may die" was crossed out but still legible.

*

It was the first deep snow so she put out lots of seed, bacon and a
whole loaf of coffee-cake-bread for the birds. She was going to the
city to leave Jane with some summer friends — so she could go to
the hospital to visit Gerald and bring him a birthday, Christmas
and Chanukah gift of a small radio.

The hospital, at this time of the year, middle of December, always depressed her; with its Christmas and Chanukah decorations
and holiday expectations as in the outside world. But mostly it was
never knowing how he'd respond which troubled her.

He was now on massive doses of vitamin C he had told her on the
phone last week. He said he didn't want to see anybody until after
Monday when he would have finished another series of blood tests.
(He sounded phlegmatic about her proposed visit.) But he might
be surprised and glad when she did come. It was usually like that.

*

Gerald was ten when she got into Cooper Union Evening Art
School. They lived on St. Mark's Place, a block away.

The number of the school's office was poster-big beside his bed table. "All you'd have to do is phone and they'd come and get me right away . . ." she used to assure him.

"Mama, I'm a big boy. I'm not afraid to be alone," he told her. "You don't have to worry about me."

Even so she used to call him during recess break.

Sometimes he protested: "I was almost falling asleep."

But he was always awake when she came home from art school, panting, not even taking time to remove her smock. It would be a little before ten. She always started to clean up earlier than the other art students.

Whenever a drill siren sounded while she was in class she ran the block home. Once she found him outside their tenement, dressed. The identification tag, which the public school had given each pupil, was dutifully around his neck.

It was things like this she remembered after he got ill.

How normal he always had seemed growing up. He was a beautiful and friendly child. He shared his cookies with others, chipped in for milk for stray kittens — And how handsome he was in his cap and gown photograph taken right before high school graduation.

That photo of him, at seventeen, was always on her bureau in whatever new place they moved to. It was there the year in Lexington, Kentucky, where her one day a week maid dusted and exclaimed over it: "How goodlooking, mam . . ."

She let her think Gerald was back East in college. Especially, she had not wanted this woman saddened. Hattie had four children. Three of them illegitimate. Hattie had confided: "The only thing I was ever sorry for was that they were illegitimate. But I try to give them a good life, mam."

Hattie never told her she'd also had twin daughters whom she'd given away for adoption two months after their birth; because she had to go back to work to support the other children. She found this out about Hattie quite unintentionally from the lady who had recommended Hattie.

Hattie and she trying to spare each other sadness — how she had loved Hattie for this. She'd given Hattie an extra day. But not for cleaning. As a model — (how she had loved those Art Student days after Cooper Union . . . to work once again from the model). She did a portrait of Hattie. It was exhibited later in a Lexington Art

League Show. (How pleased Hattie had been to bring her family and friends to the exhibition. Those catalogues which she sent to people she knew in other cities —)

"Nothing like this will ever happen to me again," said Hattie to the framed portrait, in the living room.

"Now you talk to paintings like I do, Hattie," she told her.

"I don't mean the painting, mam . . . I mean you — "

She wept that night about Hattie — Because neither of them could speak of the time soon to come when they would leave Lexington, where her husband only had a one year position.

In May of this year — five years after Lexington — there had come a very sad letter from Hattie, containing a newspaper clipping about her eldest son, Ronald. His death by drowning in Tates Creek. He was in his high school graduation year. Ronald Williams had been the school's star athlete in basketball and baseball. She had photographed Hattie with one of the prizes Ronald had won, a mounted statue of a boy holding a bat. The photo of Hattie, smiling at Ronald's award, was pinned up on the cork board in her small studio here on the Island. How proud and happy Hattie had been that week, five years ago, in Lexington. Hattie was wearing the flowers they'd picked together and made into a corsage for the portrait.

*

How many times she had examined Gerald's graduation photo to see if there had not been some clue that he would be struck so tortuously in places of his being, in just another year.

For so many years that followed she had felt no fatal words describing his illness were beyond remanding. It only meant that what had been tried so far was at fault. They might still come upon something.

His patience and intractability. His humor and his despair. The casualness which disguised the intensities. They were in that piece of writing, *I, JESUS,* sent recently from the hospital. There were some of those qualities in his early letters.

He was twelve and they worried about his susceptibility to poison ivy. It was with some trepidation that they had sent him to camp . . .

Dear Mom & Dad,
No kidding, this is the life. You have to carry a 30-40 pound bag for four miles, up and down hills.

Sometimes you do it twice a day. In a tournament you have to carry doubles twice a day. You meet these rich guys! One man I had was Cornell Baxter, 83 and French, the oldest flyer in the world.

I'm starting to grow some hair so I need the shaver. Send all my popular songs along too. There's a piano here I can play on evenings in our mess room.

I've got some sunburn and P.I. So I went to the doctor and got a needle. Everything is alright because I am still living.
Your son,
Gerald

And the one of next week:

Dear Mom & Dad,
I feel fine today, only because I'm not working. A big tournament is going to be held this weekend and I have to carry doubles, 36 holes, three days in a row.

Caddying is a nice job when you have a good golfer, but when you have a duffer it's tough. They hit the ball into the water and they blame you for losing it.

However, sometimes you can put something over on them. I once had a fine golfer and I told her she was the best golfer I saw in two weeks. She gave me a quarter tip.

There's no point to calling. Costs too much money. The poison ivy went away after the injection.

I just received the candy. Looks good. I'm saving the sketch you sent. It's pinned near my bunk.

*Don't worry about me. I worry enough. And right now I'm not
worrying. Having a good time.*

Your son,
Gerald (get that ball caddie)

*

Now that he has his I.D. pass again, if he'd missed the early hospital breakfast, he could buy coffee and danish or a buttered roll at
nine or ten at The Exchange. Sometimes he phoned her collect afterwards, from the booth in the bus terminal across the way. He
mentions a companion waiting outside, whom he's treated to coffee
and cigs. He was always treating fellows who have *no folks on the
outside.*

His present drug, another brand new one — he's been in the ex-
perimental building for years — seems to have made him more easy-
going and sociable. He's phoned more frequently and written
more letters.

One letter contained that unexpected material, *I, JESUS.* It was
typed for him by an office girl in his wards. It came after a
particular phone call conversation.

It was good to hear his voice. Later, his calls always filled her
with fresh pain. Though by this time she should have been used to
them. Always the reminder: "Send your letter early." He liked to
receive her weekly letter with the two dollar bills by Tuesday. This
way he felt flush until Thursday when they handed out the *Store
Cards.* His was taken care of in advance by checks sent to the hospital. His card gave him credit for four dollars' worth of "eats, smokes
or goods," at the hospital's store building, The Exchange.

Invariably on his phone calls there was his appeal to her to give
him *hints on how to live.*

This made her smile sadly . . . She'd remember an earlier time
when she had tried to accede to just such an appeal. It was during
his first hospitalization at Brooklyn State. They visited him
Wednesdays, as well as Sundays at that time. And she wrote him on
each of the other days.

How he'd come right back at her:
"You write me advice as though I'm in a prep school away from

home," he told her on the next Wednesday. "I'm in a mental hospital, remember."

How foolish and guilty she felt. He'd been correct about her tone. At that time she could not always grasp how ill he was or what it might be like for him —

It was such a period of chains of explosions of guilt. Hers. His father's. Even his, the patient's. All of them were constantly struck with remorseful thoughts and remembrances of anything that had preceded and could be blamed for his illness.

In the long span of his illness, over eleven years now, newer theories had sprung up about schizophrenia and its causes. To the older, psychological, theories they'd added organic, or biological and chemical ones.

She and her husband were no longer full of self recrimination or blame toward each other. And Gerald himself, who kept up with articles about his illness, no longer had that righteous or accusatory attitude toward them, as in those first five years.

Those years had been hellishly difficult for her; but at least there had been some real feelings of hope for him then —

The head orderly at Brooklyn State, Irish Mr. Kimball, predicted Gerald would be home after six months and back at college. He was right.

They were so amazed and grateful that they easily forgot the first pessimistic prognosis by Dr. Blumberg, the Brooklyn doctor, who had immediately given Gerald shock treatments in his office. Thirteen weeks of them. Only to find he had to be hospitalized for a longer and more intensive series.

She used to take him by cab to Dr. Blumberg's office. She had to oversee him afterwards at home, under the effect of the insulin — He'd awake after a nap startled and sometimes frightening her too — She had to leave her job for this care; though they needed more than ever the money she had been earning —

It was a phenomenon of its own how they managed to get the money to pay for those treatments, and later on for his visits to psychiatrists. She phoned friends boldly and offered paintings for anything they could afford — And when this list gave out she shamelessly borrowed from relatives, giving paintings of their choice as securities — Many she never did get back —

She was so desperate to save him. He seemed to be slipping away from them. It was like watching the fierce waves eating the sand of a beach. You waited and prayed until the weather settled and the waves calmed; and you hoped the beach would be a restored surface again — It was like that for that series of office treatments. Ebb and flow. Flow and ebb.

Then came those six wracking months in which they visited him twice a week — his first hospitalization. During that time there were days when their missions were a dread more than a consolation for him and them. Then they learned about the eyes and ears of fear.

How flights of fear resembled what one knew about and had observed in animals or birds. (Once on the grounds of Rockland State where they were picnicking on a Sunday visit, a boy about fifteen was flying away from his visitors and actually landed in her lap where she sat under a tree —)

On one of their visits at Brooklyn State, Gerald had run from them and taken refuge on the floor of the coat room in the hall. They were on their hands and knees in the dark underneath the clothing, coaxing him out.

It seemed miraculous to them, after what had gone on during their visits at Brooklyn State, that he would be going home and would return to City College.

He had passed his first year, even as ill as he was at the end. And he continued at school for two and a half more years, always under drugs, and with weekly visits to Dr. Blumberg's office for observation and therapy.

"Be permissive. Don't be afraid to pamper him," kindly Dr. Blumberg advised. "Never mind reading text books on his illness. That's a mistake educated parents often make. Live by your mother's heart," he added to her personally. Dr. Blumberg was an old-fashioned German doctor. His American-born son had been in charge of Gerald's treatment at Brooklyn State. Then it didn't seem so much as if he'd been given up by one doctor for another; for Dr. Blumberg, the elder, also came to see Gerald at the hospital. It gave some continuity to their hopes.

When Gerald returned to familiar Dr. Blumberg's office he even felt free to complain about them to the sympathetic psychiatrist.

Gerald was oversensitive and his father overanxious about the care of a parakeet which they'd bought for him when he came home from the hospital.

Just as if Gerald couldn't figure out for himself — without reading the directions — how to slip the sandpaper lining on the floor shelf without opening the cage.

It turned out that Gerald had a way with small birds neither of them could match. They'd bought another bird right after, for company for the first one. The birds responded immediately. He trained them to fly around his room and return to the opened door of the cage. They kissed him and chirped at his endearments.

True, he occasionally lost a bird through an open window in some other room of the apartment. But they never made too much of the loss and replaced it. And one bird was even brought back from someone else's fire-escape.

"Oh, your father is too nervous at times. And your mother a little overgenerous," good Dr. Blumberg said, appealing to Gerald in front of them.

She was just trying to follow the doctor's own counseling. She didn't know for sure then nor for long afterwards — what comprised permissiveness and pampering. When did it stray its bounds? When did it ask or receive too much? Was it when life dammed up and became unlivable for the other, the one nearest the patient? But everything up to this point allowable? Needed, in fact.

Gerald preferred to practice piano all alone in the house. So she'd go out for hours, walking or shopping or ducking into a movie if it rained. If he was still at the music when she returned, she sometimes lingered outside in the hall, sitting on the steps in her coat. It was good to hear him play piano. Even if it was now just some of the easier classical pieces. And he began to add popular songs to his repertoire. He sang along with the piano. Not in an especially good voice. In fact, his tone was lugubrious. Yet, he seemed to enjoy this outlet.

They were grateful that he was doing all these things. He had even learned to drive their newly bought secondhand car. He passed the road test on his first try.

It made him so car-happy that he took a job delivering telephone directories. He asked her to come along; to sit in the car while he was double-parked. She did this for a few days until the car almost collapsed from the burden of those books. And cops came by to ask why she was in a non-parking area —

He enjoyed driving himself to the Marshall club where he'd won chess medals when he was younger. Or they'd have one of his friends or theirs who liked that game.

Their whole way of living centered around Gerald and his illness. It seemed worth the effort and the strain it cost all of them —

Then Gerald started to skip his medication.

"I want to see if I can function without it," he said.

And he baulked at visiting the doctor in Brooklyn.

"It's too far a train ride," he said.

They had moved to Manhattan to be nearer his college.

He used to wake her from sleep about one or two in the morning to prepare some food for him; because he liked company before he settled down to studying. He liked these quieter hours in the morning. She knew school was hard for him and she was glad enough to do this for him.

One day she prepared the tomato soup he'd asked for. He sloshed it around in the bowl with his spoon and said pettishly: "I'd rather have chicken noodle."

He spilled the contents of the bowl into the sink. He took a can of chicken noodle from the closet, opened it and heated it in a new pan, while she sat nearby on a stool in the tiny kitchenette.

He poured the chicken soup into a clean bowl and tasted it. He looked at her and said very casually: "I'll be glad if you died."

*

On that particular phone call Gerald had mentioned wearing a crucifix. He asked her what she did with hers when she took a shower.

"Honey, I'm your old Jewish mother, remember? I don't wear a cross," she answered. "I do have a cameo locket. My birthstone. My horoscope said it would make the wearer more tranquil. Even so I take it off when I go into the shower. I don't want the chain to leave a mark on my neck."

He was silent.

It was then she went on about those boyhood letters from camp. She'd come across them while straightening her desk drawers and file cabinets. His letters were scattered throughout her other correspondence and she had decided to put his letters together in a separate place.

She was surprised to see what a bulk had streamed from him during his years at the hospital. Someone reading them all together — all she'd found so far — might even have gotten a glimpse of their world as well as his. Their changes of residences, jobs, bits of their lives peppered his correspondence.

Dear Folks,
The weather has been rainy the last two months too. Hope the art shows and reading tours and Jane's dancing are coming along fine. I have lost my parole card for the time being and am doing ward work. So cannot call on Sunday.
Wrote a letter to Joe, waiting then patiently for a reply. One day it's possible that the last remaining credits for graduation will be completed.
Kani King won the Kentucky derby. Did you pick him? Next comes the Preakness and then comes the Belmont Stakes. The trots should be custom made for goodness sake.
More power for you and I guess things are complicated enough.
Dad sent a Pablo Picasso card. Gave it to a friend who's sleeping next to me.

Your son,
Gerald

Dear people,
I just can't wait until you reach Kansas. The whole building is being reorganized. They're putting in checkerboard floors and painting the walls.
Going to the lab and pharmacy.
Wunderbar??????

Your son,
Gerald

*

On her first visit to the hospital after their year in Kansas, she had observed that they had painted The Exchange a melba peach, instead of the old drab tan. And they had installed Formica counters, with revolving stools, instead of those huge wooden tables and heavy chairs she'd known for years of Sundays . . .

She was really pleased to come across Gerald's first communication, a two cent postcard when he was eight and away from home for two weeks at a camp. It made her smile.

DEAR MOM & DAD, SOMEONE THREW A ROCK AT MY HEAD. BUT DON'T WORRY. NO STITCHES. I FEEL FINE. I AM IN A PLAY WITH HIMEY. HE IS A TREE. I AM AN ARROW. YOUR SON,

GERALD

She had a job then and showed the card to some of her co-workers. "How's little hole-in-the-head?" they used to ask fondly about him afterwards.

These years of grueling factory jobs and painting at night; her husband's equally lousy jobs while he tried to write. He had jobs which gave him the day hours alone in the apartment: night shifts at the city garbage disposal plant where he weighed the truck loads of refuse; and during World War II he worked late shifts in a nearby hospital as admitting clerk. Those twelve unpublished years of fifth floor tenement walkups. Their serious and even grim lives at times; because it was only later that those years of writing saw print.

It wasn't until his fourth book that there was any break for him as far as jobs went. It was then he was invited for a year's teaching position in Kentucky and then in Kansas. After that positions in the East opened up for him. Their way of life became more integrated — Her husband no longer had to use a mask to hide his writer side for jobs.

There was also a change in their relations with Gerald. There had to be. Those years of continuous Sunday visits were over. Now they went whenever they could, separately — Only sometimes together. But her letters to Gerald continued — this uninterrupted and sometimes one-way correspondence.

To this day she sometimes had to redo an envelope. She'd address it to their home instead of the hospital.

"It wasn't called Jamestown but Camp Taber," he corrected her on that phone call.

"You're right! It was Camp Taber. The envelopes must have gotten misplaced. You have a better memory than I. And you have such a beautiful sense of humor in those letters . . ."

She coaxed: "Have you ever thought again about writing that book about the hospital? *Yeah, Yeah,* you said you'd call it."

"Yeah, yeah," he chuckled to himself over the phone.

It was not an easy laugh. It had his affectionate tone but it was so engrossingly self-mocking.

It was right after this phone call that Gerald sent her the chapter. She was more excited with tremors of hope than she'd been for years.

This feeling was partly nullified when she immediately came upon a newspaper article on the ill effects of shock treatment on the brain. They spoke of brain damage.

His world still came to her with griefs; but it did not pain as sharply as it would have years back when she lived so close to its edges herself; as if in this closeness she could reach him and persuade him back from the abyss. Once again his world made her ache and cry and still smile.

She typed a copy of his *chapter* and quickly mailed back the original because he told her on a phone call it was his only copy.

*

I, JESUS
by GERALD

It was a bleak, cold day, and as dusk unenvelops, daylight approaches. From the tops of the building the chateaulike spires come into being.

The changing of the guard was being formed, which meant simply that daily, day attendants were taking over in their jobs — their daily tasks at Rockland State Hospital in Orangeburg, New York.

At this particular ward (124), it seems that German was not on duty that day, so Lionel put on the lights and said: "Get up, boys!"

It was a day of more pills and blood tests and visions, hallucinations, omens and ecstasies, which were not to go down the American River.

The soap foam was spreading around the ward, and as you have probably guessed: Christ the Second was up and about.

You can tell by now that the author was this person, so if he had to be famous, he would have preferred it this way — in a book.

Philips was the day man, as long ago there was no special ward charge for this unit. Hall was on, and so was Donnie Steiner who had shrunk but was still one of the top pool men — for his size.

Cathy came (she was pregnant for three months), and the pretty Tom Boy E. J. Shirley, to give out the special and nonspecial amphetamines for patients on projects. Ursula came in, with Lisle not far behind. Betty was expected, with Liz already on the ward.

Breakfast was served for the blood donors, toothbrushing was worked out in a special place (a stretcher in the section, paste, brushes and combs), and coffeeshop hours were begun. All this time nobody paid any particular attention to Gerald (this author), who had busily started to write on his book.

Margaret's voice was coming out of the shop, so I decided to have a look-see.

Doctors were already coming on the ward. Dr. Deutsch, the German-Jewish one was on, and so was Spanish-speaking Dr. Areng. Dr. Simpson, who travels all over the U.S. and Scotland, was probably coming in later.

I would most likely have to explain some of my actions in front of a group of these men coming up soon as that would be after the dentist's, I suppose.

You, the reader, might want to know why the goings on in the different echelons were being performed as any other day — smoothly or not.

You see, today I decided to bare all the facts, as I am Jesus the Second, because it obviously started eight or ten years ago.

The only way sometimes in a State Hospital to save a person's life is to repeat the saying Jesus Christ in his ear by human voice ten times, until he wakes up out of his coma. This was done to me, so I am indebted to Rockland for saving my life. Since then I have had to pay them back, so to speak, by co-operating in the daily activities through my own skill and the rest with the Holy Ghost.

Please understand that that does not mean that I do not have any will; on the contrary, I am happy sometimes in doing this and working besides to regain my mental health completely.

Out on the grounds there is plenty of spiritual help, as the Church's doors are open every day. Please believe me when I say that I have received B's in Physics and A's in English in college, but, that, because the Church helped, I am partially in cahoots with them now, so to speak. It is Saint Dymphena, the Patron Saint of Mental Illness to whom I always go; partly due to Father Cox or Reverend Churchill, whom I think about. Let us not forget the Holy Baptismal Water or the candles or the figure of Christ on the Cross who winks and often hallucinates.

This is about what happens in the life of Jesus Christ the Second.

And then, of course, when I go to church, I'm sure to walk around the stations, where they put me on the 15th one, on top of Jesus Christ, and also of course, through the Holy Ghost I'm put into the ground at the feet of Jesus. So, you see, that is part of a busy day.

Might go to the library to read, dentist, doctor (psychiatrist), a visit, and then to gym at night. Though my head was burned by a Dr. Jarvis many years ago at some place and time, and then my father signed a project note for my benefit, authorizing the orderlies to take fifty blood tests, I feel in the pink. What a day! How's that?

*

It was mostly his having written that *chapter* that made her cling to some new feeling of hope. She asked if he would be allowed home for Thanksgiving. It would be his first home visit in five years. Two of those years they had spent in Kentucky and Kansas.

On his last Thanksgiving visit he's stuffed on candy bars on the trip home, ignored the dinner which she'd spent hours preparing and an hour or so later he asked for change to buy a piece of pizza from one of those stands in their old neighborhood.

"On this present drug," said his father, "I think he'll be able to take the long ride — " They now lived hours away on the Island.

"He doesn't hallucinate in front of you so much," said his father — "But even so, for Jane's sake, let's have him with other company around us."

Gerald's signs were mostly small ones, twists of the neck to avert the constant evil around him. Or he remarked the signs in others.

In one of his letters to her he wrote: "Glad there was no terrific wind when you flicked the ashes — "

He was on the phone a few times since their plan.

"Know who's standing next to me? My friend Jack. His people are taking him home for Thanksgiving too — And maybe for Christmas — "

Gerald was glad to hear some of their relatives were coming.

"Will I have to help with the dishes?" he asked. "I mop floors here. And sometimes help with the dishes."

"You can help stack them if you like. We have the dishwasher now — "

"Yeah, I remember . . . in one of your letters."

"Everybody is looking forward to seeing you, Gerald . . ."

Her family had always loved Gerald. He'd been the first of the children born and a favorite. When he first got ill they'd sent packages to the hospital.

Then they all had their own family problems. Right now her sister's boy, five years younger than Gerald, would be on his way soon to Vietnam as part of an advisory group. He had just finished his training program in Washington. They were glad he was in for the holidays and could come to the dinner. They had not seen him in years. He was a little shy with Gerald whom he'd not seen since he was a boy.

*

It was a fine, if expected, kind of Thanksgiving with concentration on food and the small talk of relatives who do not get together often. After the dinner they could hear the happy sounds of four girl cousins chatting and playing records in Jane's room.

Gerald held his own through it all, listening mainly and smoking cigarettes. Every once in a while he'd leave the room, go into her studio where a cot had been made up for him — And then appear again. His contribution to the talk was only about the eleven credits he needed for graduation.

It wasn't until the next morning that she could spend some time alone with Gerald. She took him for a ride to show him some of the neighborhood landmarks.

He repeated the names of the sights after she called them out. Then he complained that he couldn't remember them so she stopped naming places.

She turned into a marina and parked on the wharf. It was a pretty sight with the boats tied up and snow outlining the posts.

"I hope you go on with your book, Gerald. That was an interesting chapter. I showed it to a friend who's an editor. He was very enthusiastic. He'd like to see it if you make it into a book."

Gerald looked pleased at the praise. But he said: "I'm a physics student. I'm not a writer."

"Scientists write books too. People write about their experiences," she said casually. "I'll never forget how you made A's in English, as sick as you were."

"That was nothing," he said. "My father was a writer. I wanted to please him. I read digests of books. I didn't want to spend so much time on such courses. I was a physics major. I have only eleven more points to get. I'll take any courses — biology — music — philosophy —

"I get along with my father," he went on. "But he is a grouch sometimes . . . And you look fine. You didn't look so good when you came to see me last time. You were fatter and sunburned."

When they got home she went into her small studio for something. He followed her in and asked for a cigarette. Then he started looking at some of the magazines in which she had drawings. He seemed to be studying them.

"You have such a happy disdain for everything," he said.

At first she felt hurt and even a little guilty. She thought he was criticizing her. Then she heard him chuckling to himself and examining the drawings more closely.

"It's hard to follow some of your lines," he said. "They never break . . . But if you don't look at them too closely you can see it's just a simple drawing — "

Then his eyes seemed to dull and his shoulders looked a bit stooped as when he began to worry.

She went over to him and putting her hands on both his shoulders she kissed him gently on the forehead. A thin, widening smile spread over his face. It was a pleased smile but given not altogether to her. Other spirits were always present at their meetings.

Sometimes his acknowledgments to them were more obvious than
his to her.

                                      *

   Later, his father drove him back to the hospital. She remained in
her studio for hours, drawing and writing.
   He did not ask to come home for Christmas though they had
talked about it on the phone. The Thanksgiving visit might even
have been over-much for him, especially the long ride. And only
one letter came from him at this time. She read it over and over
again.

Howdy Folks,
Weather is fine. A little cold.
I read Franz Kafka's masterpiece, Amerika.
Okay, so he never came to America and it is fiction.
As Sir Francis Bacon put it: "Man, being the servant and inter-
preter of Nature, can do and understand so much and so much only
as he has observed in fact or in thought of the causes of nature;
beyond this he neither knows anything nor can do anything."
Think again; it is the speed of change.
Well, we missed the auto show and the circus but we can still see
Cinerama's Russian Adventure.
Hope dad enjoys teaching at Columbia where they probably have
also a new center for the arts and physics.
Trying again for confidence so I can take some refresher courses.
Much obliged and happy holidays.
Son,
Gerald

p.s. enclosed an American flag sticker for Jane. It can be used on a
*   car. Let's see what she will do with it.*

                                      *

   The visit to the hospital shook her up and haunted her for weeks
later. He'd lost weight again and his clothes hung on him carelessly. They were also spotted with food stains. A front tooth was
missing. He'd have to wait until after the holidays for a false
tooth. This gave him a slight lisp.

His new medication made him more assertive and bouncier than she'd seen him in years. He seemed years younger in tone and manner. He was talkative and fast moving — She hadn't seen him like this since he was ten. She remembered him like this when he was with friends up late on a summer porch in Rockaway Beach.

They took him for a ride to a shopping center where he could buy *supplies:* coffee, crackers, a carton of cigarettes, a comb, cards and some sucaryl. He was so boyishly pleased with all this *loot.* He'd just had a visit from his father a couple of days back and had been given five dollars for the holidays. So their coming on this extra visit was a surprise for him.

He asked to go to a restaurant though he'd just come from lunch at the hospital. He complained that someone else had gotten ten slices of bologna and he only two. So he ordered a western omelet and took a few hasty bites out of each half sandwich — He wasn't really hungry. He placed an opened napkin over the remains on his plate.

He kept talking away about how he took *plane* geometry instead of *solid* geometry. He repeated this several times with amusement. He remembered he'd made 96 in French. He said all this loudly again when the waitress brought their coffee.

Later they drove around the hospital grounds and he pointed out the buildings: the library, the church — It was closed so he couldn't play the organ for them — And they had to pass the building where he had his typing class. There were mostly girls and women in the class he explained.

"I might write something when I know how to type," he said offhandedly.

"Teach me to listen to T.V. Teach me things," he kept repeating. And he'd chuckle with amusement. Then he'd complain, "There are no good games on the wards."

In the car he stared at her, made senseless remarks with a chuckle, and the next second he'd pound on the back of the car seat until she thought he'd hurt himself. He repeated this ritual again and again, until they got to his building.

At the building he gathered all his supplies and opened the car door. They said *goodbye* but he didn't answer or look at them. She got out of the car and called *goodbye* up the steps. It was with much effort that he barely turned his head to them and said *good-bye* too.

"He was pleased with your visit," her husband said to make her feel good. "When we waited for you in the car while you were in the drug store getting the sucaryl, Gerald said: 'Let's not go without mother.'" And maybe to make himself feel better, he added strongly: "You know, I'd rather see him this way than like a vegetable."

"He was very bouncy," she agreed. Gerald had literally bounced up and down on the scat like a kid.

Back home, after a few days at a friend's apartment in the city with Janey, they found their mailbox full of Xmas cards. There was one envelope from Kentucky, from Hattie Williams. It did not feel as if it held a card. She nerved herself to open it. It was a two page letter on a folded, pretty flowered sheet:

I'm still full of grief, trying to fight the good life of faith and praying for strength. I still hope to see you all again. I'd like to tell you all about Ronald but it still makes me cry too much. I know having raised such a beautiful son yourself that you would understand my loss.

I tell all my friends that I am famous because you show my portrait in an exhibition, and to all your artist friends where you live now. Sometime I will come to see you, I invite myself (smile). I will help with the cleaning, I know how your back hurts. Please send me a picture of Janey so I could see how she has grown.
Love,
Hattie Wms.

MAXINE KUMIN

Opening the Door on Sixty-second Street

(FROM THE SOUTHERN REVIEW)

THE YEAR Jeffrey Rabinowitz was sixteen, his grandfather died at the Seder table. That is, he slumped over the ceremonial plate with its horseradish root and lamb bone and roasted egg, a sprig of parsley in his hand, and had to be helped into the living room to lie down on the horsehair sofa. An elderly doctor, summoned from his own Passover festivities in an apartment upstairs, had laid his ear to the old man's naked chest and pronounced the flutter of his heart to be only a little arrhythmia brought on by excitement. Nevertheless, Jeff's grandfather died on West End Avenue before the eight days of matzoh were over.

"Did you finish the service? I mean, after he slumped over like that?" Robin Parks wanted to know.

"I think we must have," Jeff said. "Because every year since I catch myself thinking, we opened the door for Elijah and the Angel of Death entered in. You know, it's the Angel of Death who's supposed to pass over the houses. Instead, he came for Grampa."

It was important to be on time; he was hustling her from the airport terminal, where he had gone to fetch her, to a cab.

"It was always such a joke, opening the door for Elijah. Dewey used to pull rank on me. Being the younger son meant I had to ask the four questions and he got to yank the door open with a flourish. Dewey always said we wouldn't know him if he came, Elijah. He'd never get past the doorman, he used to say."

"Well, he was right, I guess. Now everybody says it about Jesus. When I was little I used to wonder how Jesus could put a coat on."

"Why not?"

"Over his wings, I mean."

"I thought you meant he couldn't fold his arms back down."

"Well, that too. But Unitarians don't talk much about the crucifixion. Our Jesus didn't transfigure."

"Dewey had three apparitions of Elijah in his lifetime. Chariot and all."

"Was God driving?"

"I don't know. When he described it, though, I could see it too. It was a fiery buckboard, all right. Something like Pegasus pulling a hansom cab in Central Park."

The driver cheated a crosstown light and edged between two trucks. They were quiet a minute, considering.

"It must be awfully hard now," Robin said finally. "For your parents, I mean, having the holiday without Dewey."

"In a way, it's easier than his visions and things. They always hated surprises."

His parents were old, he told her. His mother was forty-five when he was born.

"But that's incredible! You're lucky you're not a mongoloid."

"Well, I missed it by a percentage point. My mother was married before. But they never had any children. I think we came as a great shock to her. And my father was one of those lingering bachelors who finally gave in. He can be very charming, but you always feel he was dragooned into the system. It's hard for him to cope with family life."

Before dinner there was schnapps in the living room — scotch in the palest violet glasses. Only the men partook. Robin inferred that women did not take their whiskey neat and shook her head when the tray went round.

Jeff's mother had blue hair and blue harlequin glasses. Her face was childish and well-kept with sweet small features, the skin finely wrinkled. Robin thought of a silk nightgown that wanted ironing. She wore four rings.

"It just lifts my spirits to have you young people around," she said, settling her plumpness with a little bounce. "I think a Seder is more *fun* when you can set a full table. Jeffrey and Dewey always brought their Christian friends home, we encouraged that, didn't we, Harris?"

"My wife prides herself on her Christian friends," Harris Rabinowitz pronounced equably. He too wore glasses and threw his head back so that the light glinted off them. What wonderful hair! Robin thought. All silvery and benign, that's where Jeff gets it.

"What Daddy means is that the holidays are hard when there's been a death," Mrs. Rabinowitz went on. "You know about Dewey, of course. He was the *best* baby. He went potty before he was a year old. Jeffrey here was impossible to train. You just never could catch him. He'd go in a corner behind the piano and grunt — I swear it was just to defy me. We used to say we'd have to send him off to college with Dydee service."

"Now Clara, does Macy's tell Gimbel's?" Harris Rabinowitz rumbled.

"Mother has a compulsion to tell all," Jeff said. His voice was even. Robin couldn't tell whether he despised or enjoyed her candor.

"Never mind, never mind," she said. "I'm sure Miss Parks wants to see us as we are."

Miss Parks has gone away, Robin's here, Robin thought fiercely, but touched thumbs in her lap.

"I suppose you're wondering where the hors d'oeuvres are," Jeff's mother said. "Usually we have hot and cold ones. But tonight there's so much ceremonial food. Jews don't know how to drink for pleasure, really. These little shot glasses belonged to my father, they're Bohemian glass, you know. It comes from being uprooted, this attachment to *things*."

And before they went to the table Robin had heard the history of three paintings, a bisque figurine and a pair of silver candelabra. It was a kind of promotional revelation that Robin's grandmother, who was, after all, of the same generation, would have shunned. "Good taste speaks for itself, Binnie," Gran would say. "Only an upstart waves a price tag."

"Ready, everyone?" Clara Rabinowitz trilled. "I'm lighting the candles! Sheila dear, will you say the blessing?"

Sheila Sheprow, Jeff's hugely pregnant cousin, stood at the head of the table like the figurehead of a Norse sailing ship and extended her hands, fingers paired, over the candle flames. "Any day now," Art Sheprow beamed. Her pleasantly freckled face shone as if buttered. Her parents, the Poppers, lined up opposite Robin. Downstream at attention stood the other aunt and uncle, the Szalds. Peter Kramer, who grew pot in the aluminum-foil lined closet of the apartment on West End Avenue he shared with Jeff, took a white silk yarmulka out of his back pocket, kissed it and put it on. Robin, who had not bowed her head with the others, caught Mrs. Rabinowitz's frown at this gesture.

"That's very sweet of you, Peter," she said just as Sheila cleared her throat, "but we're very informal here. You don't need a yarmulka on East Sixty-second Street."

The pot farmer took off his skullcap, folded and kissed it and stuffed it back in his pocket. Art coughed tentatively. And Sheila sang the Hebrew blessing in the clear, unselfconscious tones of a small child.

There was a general edging and tugging of chairs; the assemblage was seated. "Now dear," Clara Rabinowitz instructed Robin, "that was to symbolize the *joy* we feel when we can celebrate this festival in our own homes. Next, Daddy will bless the first glass of wine. It's called the kiddush. Oh Harris, wait! Not everyone is served yet."

Harris semaphored with his eyeglasses up and down the table. After he had spoken his portion everyone lifted his goblet. Robin sipped. Thick and sweet, the wine tasted like fermented grape juice.

"You have to drink all of it, you know," Jeff whispered.

"How many of these are there?"

"Four in all."

But his mother had overheard. Again the wide smile which ended in a little downturning of earnestness. "The four cups symbolize the four promises of redemption, Miss Parks. I forget what each one is, exactly. But on this night even the poorest of the poor were to be provided with enough wine to take part in the ceremony."

"It sounds like Thoreau," Robin said. "You know, the thing about 'none is so poor that he need sit on a pumpkin.' "

But no one knew except Jeff.

They had just gotten into the *Dayenus* when the phone rang.

" 'Dayenu' — how would you translate that, Harris?" Clara asked, while deliberate footsteps could be heard moving offstage to lift the receiver.

"Does Macy's tell Gimbel's?" he grumbled.

" 'It would have been enough,' Auntie," Sheila Sheprow supplied. " 'Sufficient unto the day thereof,' something like that."

It was the other Popper children — Sheila's two married sisters and their husbands — conjoined in San Francisco to wish the family *Good Yuntuf*. Everyone in turn, except for Peter Kramer and Robin, queued up at the living room extension. The senior Poppers hurried upstairs to monitor the flow of conversation from the bedroom.

Left to themselves, Robin peeked ahead in the *Haggadah*. Sixty pages to go, but a lot of it was music.

Peter furtively lifted a napkin, slid out a wheel of matzoh and stood in a corner by the china cabinet munching. "Starved," he explained. "Anyway, we're very informal here."

"That bothered you."

He shrugged. "She has her meaningful rituals, I have mine."

"Why did you kiss it?"

"You have your crucifix and I have my Grandpa's yarmulka."

"But Peter! I'm a Unitarian."

"So? A Unitarian's nothing but a homesick Christian."

"There will be a short wait for all seats," Jeff said coming back. "Sheila is reviewing her pregnancy long distance. She's up to the seventh month now. How's it going, Robinowitz?"

"Miss Parks to you."

"That's just Mother's way of indicating that you haven't been divinely elected," Jeff said. "Don't let it get you." But he looked unhappy; diminished somehow inside the frame of his curly hair and beard.

She relented. "No, it's very interesting, really. I *like* it. And I like having your mother explain things."

Between bouts of exegesis the service proceeded communally with each member reading a part. The Szalds shared one pair of bifocals which they passed back and forth between them like a dish of olives. Kramer, discountenanced by the English, chose each time to deliver his portion in Hebrew. Mrs. Rabinowitz promptly translated by way of reproof.

Symbols exalted her. She explained the parsley — gratitude to God for the fruits of the earth — the horseradish root, a warty phallus that made Robin think of John Donne's mandrake poem — the bitter lot of the Jews in Egypt — the haroses, unexpectedly delicious — mortar for the bricks the Jews made when they were the Pharaoh's slaves. And did Miss Parks know why the matzoh was scored in perforations? (Does Macy's tell Gimbel's?) To keep the dough from rising and swelling.

During the dinner itself, conversation found its urban level. The Szalds reported a mugging; they alternated details like a responsive reading. The Poppers brought up landlords. Art Sheprow defended rent strikes, bussing and peaceful acts of civil disobedience to disrupt the war machine.

"Have you ever done it?" Robin asked him. "Sat in, I mean?"

"I'd like to. But I can't risk arrest with Sheila in this condition."

Harris Rabinowitz sighed obtrusively. Conviviality sat heavily on him.

"The *schwartzehs,* the *schwartzehs,*" he said. "Between the *schwartzehs* and the dog-do the whole city is a slum. When I was a young man we went up to Harlem to hear jazz. Portaricka was a foreign country. A nice Jewish girl, if she had to work, went into teaching. Now she goes to CCNY and gets raped in the ladies' room."

Robin, prepared to despise him, was startled when he turned to her in supplication. "Don't get me wrong, young lady. You think I'm just a *kvetch,* a complaining old man. You think I'm some kind of a right-wing fanatic. But I want to tell you, I loved this city before it turned into a jungle. I was born here, I grew up in the Bronx in what they call a semi-detached. I had all kinds of neighbors, Italians, Polish people, even some coloreds. I went with all kinds, we had respect. The trouble with today is, there's no respect."

After dessert, they returned to the *Haggadah.* Art Sheprow, slightly flushed, read the grace and the company supplied the responses. When he came to "The door is opened for Elijah," there was a pause. Mrs. Rabinowitz unfolded a handkerchief and dabbed her eyes.

"We don't have to do this part," Jeff warned.

"No Jeffrey, I *want* to. I want *you* to do it." To Robin, she said, "It makes us all remember Dewey. Dewey *saw* Elijah, you know. Oh, no one ever believed him, I didn't at the time, but maybe he knew something we didn't. Dewey was such a bright child! Up until the eighth grade he always got all A's on his report card. Of course every night he read the same fairy tales over and over in his bed; we should have guessed that he was troubled, boys don't generally read fairy tales, but he loved them so! He *identified.* He was the frog who was going to turn into a prince. When all along he was the prince already."

Robin felt like a Strasbourg goose force-fed the unwanted grain.

Jeff stumbled from the table like a man fighting his way out of a hidden swamp. The front door was opened; the normal raw sounds of traffic swept in.

"O Praise the Lord all ye nations," Art Sheprow recited dubiously. After "Hallelujah!" there was the sucking sound of the door refilling its space. The latch clicked and Jeff returned to his seat with a marvelous show of self-possession.

This is what Robin read on his face: I shat in my pants to the age of four on purpose behind the piano. I played stoopball and kept porno magazines under the mattress and got C's in Latin. I have opened the door on Sixty-second Street and closed it again on the usual arrangement of furniture. It is not part of the divine plan that Elijah appear to Jeffrey Rabinowitz.

They went on into the psalms. "Out of distress I called upon the Lord. He answered me with great enlargement," Sheila recited. "Oh my God!" she said, pushing her chair back. Now she was standing, saying, "Oh my God, my God, I'm wetting my pants!"

In that suspended moment Mrs. Szald took off the bifocals and handed them to Mr. Szald who put them into his breast pocket. In her haste to get out of her chair Mrs. Popper knocked over a wine glass and Art Sheprow unaccountably buried his face in his hands.

It was all happening slow motion like a baseball replay; an awkward out-of-sequence pushing back of chairs against the heavy pile of the carpet, stick figures captured in various stages of arising, and a pool of wet unmistakably darkening the Aubusson.

Clara Rabinowitz found the first words. "It's all right, Sheila dear, your water just broke. Your water just broke and you're going to have your baby tonight."

"Let me take your shoes," Robin offered. Sheila stepped out of her navy pumps. Little puddles spilled from them.

Mrs. Popper, seeking equilibrium, exclaimed, "Isn't it lucky you're going to Doctor's Hospital? You're already on the East side, darling. Isn't that the luckiest thing?"

"Oh, get me a towel, somebody!" Sheila wailed.

"Come on, old man. You're not going to be sick or something," Jeff said, steering the father-to-be from the table.

Mr. Popper called a cab. Coats were located and handed around. Sheila tucked a hand towel into her pantics.

And the door on Sixty-second Street opened for the second time.

MARY LAVIN

Tom

(FROM THE NEW YORKER)

MY FATHER'S HAIR was as black as the Devil's, and he flew into black, black rages. When he spoke of death, as he often did, he spoke of when he'd be put down in the black hole. You could say that everything about him was black except his red blood, his fierce blue eyes, and the gold spikes of love with which he pierced me to the heart when I was a child.

He had made a late, romantic, but not happy marriage. All the same, he and my mother stayed together their whole lives through. They drew great satisfaction to the end of their days on this earth from having kept faith with each other.

They had met on shipboard — on the S.S. Franconia. My father had gone to America when he was young, and was going back to Ireland to buy horses for the man he worked for in East Walpole, Massachusetts. My mother was returning home from a visit to a grandaunt and granduncle in Waltham, where the granduncle was pastor of the Roman Catholic church.

My mother's family lived in County Galway. They were not very well off. They were small-town merchants who sold coal, seeds, and guano as well as tea, sugar, and spirits. My mother was the eldest of twelve. It used to puzzle me that the eldest of twelve should go visiting in a land to which most Irish men and women in those days went as emigrants. Such a visit suggested refinement, and this was affirmed by her classic beauty, her waist — which was thin as the stem of a flower — her unfailing good taste, and her general manner. My father had set his eye on her the minute he went up the gangplank — she was already settled into her deck chair, reading a book.

They did not marry till three years later, when, after a correspondence conducted more ardently by him than by her, he sent her a diamond ring and money for her passage out again — this time to marry him. They were married from the parochial house in Waltham.

My mother hated living in America, and on three occasions when my father let her go see her people he had to follow and fetch her home. When she spoke of her ocean crossings, whichever way she was going, my mother referred to them all as visits, until the last one, when, eastward bound and taking me with her, she knew she'd never have to go back. My father had drawn out some of his savings and given her money to buy a house in Ireland. She bought it in Dublin. Then he gave up his job, took the rest of his money out of the bank, and went to Ireland himself — for good.

My father never seemed to feel resentment against my mother for forcing him to return to the land of his birth. He may not have felt any; his savings, although modest, enabled him to cut a great dash in his native land. He had brought home with him a car that looked so large on the narrow Irish roads that when we went for a drive of a Sunday it seemed at every minute as if the sides would be taken off it by the thorny briars in the hedges — hedges so high they made other cars look like cockroaches. Sitting up at the wheel of that car in a big coat with an astrakhan collar was a far cry from running barefoot across country in County Roscommon, where he had been born.

"Why didn't we go back to Roscommon to live?" I asked him one day.

His blue eyes blazed with contempt for my foolishness. "I have to educate you, don't I?" he said. And I suppose he imagined, like all poor emigrants, that in the place of his birth time would have stood still — the children going barefoot to school, doing their sums on a slate, and mitching every other day, until at last, like him, most of them would run off to England and thence to America with scarcely enough schooling to write their names.

Although my father had a deep and a strong mind and was the subtlest human being I ever knew, he had had small schooling. He could read and write, but with difficulty. He came, indeed, from stock that had in the penal days produced a famous hedge school-master, and of this he was very proud. It may well have been his pride in this scholarly kinsman that led to his own premature de-parture from a one-room schoolhouse in Frenchpark. For one day the schoolmaster, in a poetic discourse on spring, invoked the cuckoo, and he made reference to the cuckoo's nest. My father's hand flew up, and, without waiting for permission to speak, he gave voice to his shock and indignation. "The cuckoo doesn't build a nest! She lays her eggs in another bird's nest!"

"Is that so?" The master must have been sorely nettled by this public correction. "Well, boy, if you think you can teach this class better than me, come up to the blackboard and take my place." Abandoning sarcasm, he roared and caught up his cane. "I'll teach you not to interrupt me!" he cried.

"You're wrong there, too," my father said. "You'll teach me nothing more as long as you live!" And with that he picked up his slate and fired it at the master's head. Fortunately, for once his aim was bad and he missed. Instead, he put a gash an inch deep in the blackboard, and in the hullabaloo he lit out the door and down the road for Dublin. He was in such a rage he forgot to say goodbye to his mother, whom he never saw again in this life. He spoke of her to me three or four times, and I'm sure it was of her he was think-ing on occasion leaning over a gate staring into the deeps of a field in a mood of utter blackness.

From Dublin my father went to Liverpool, from there to the po-tato fields in Scotland and the hop fields in Yorkshire, and finally, one Palm Sunday morning, he arrived in Boston, then a leading port. All he took with him to America was the memories of the boy he had been, running barefoot over the bogs and the unfenced fields of Roscommon with a homemade fishing rod in his hand, or maybe a catapult. That boy used to think nothing of running across country from Castlerea to Boyle, and even into Sligo. Towns that lay twenty miles apart were no distance to him — leaping stone walls like a young goat, bounding over streams like a hound, and taking the corner off a lake if there was wind would dry out his clothes. Whenever I think of what it is to be young, I find my mind invaded by images of a boy — a boy running over unpeopled land under a sky filled with birds. My father had made his memories mine.

My mother had her memories, too, but she had so many of them they seemed to take up all the room in her head. She never discarded duplicates. She had a hundred memories of summer evenings when she and her sisters and cousins strolled around the rampart walls that enclosed the small town where she was born. There was the same tinkle of laughter in every one, and the same innocent pretense of surprise when the girls met their beaux taking the air in the same place at the same time. Winter evenings could have been reduced to the tale of one evening in one parlor, my mother at the piano, with her sisters in a half circle around her singing high and the beaux in an outer ring singing strong and low. I was an only child, and when I was small I liked to think about those gay young people swaying back and forth, their mouths like swinging censers spilling song to right and to left. But I got tired of hearing about them, and in the arrogance of my own youth I thought those memories of my mother's had used up all passion in her. Long before I knew what passion was, I knew there was no passion between my parents. Not that my mother wasn't always telling me proudly about all the American women — that is to say, Irish American — whose expectations had been dashed to the ground when my father arrived back from Waltham with her as his bride. And she displayed with amusement his bachelor trophies — a topaz tiepin, a set of silver-backed brushes, and a half-dozen or so pairs of gold cufflinks. He had been the most eligible bachelor in East Walpole, she many times assured me. He was nearly fifty and had never been caught. It was my mother's code that nice girls never tried to catch a man but had themselves to be snared. She herself was thirty before she was snared. Everyone thought she was much younger, she said, until the midwife took the opportunity of asking her age in a cloudy moment just as I was about to emerge into the world.

"Your father's admirers were all a lot older than that, though," she told me. "They must have been out in America for years to be able to buy those expensive presents, because you may be sure they left Ireland empty-handed."

My mother's own trunk could not have been very heavily laden, but she based her estimate of what the others brought with them on the fact that they had traveled steerage. She had traveled cabin. My maternal grandfather, as well as wholesaling grain and guano, was a shipping agent for the Cunard and White Star Steamship

Lines, and my mother knew all about poor Irish emigrants, no matter what grandeur they later assumed.

My mother had a stateroom to herself, and the courtesy of a reduced fare arranged by the Queenstown agents of the line. It was her firm conviction that no one — no woman, that is — could ever live down the stigma of steerage. Her stateroom in cabin class was a symbol to her of how my father had lifted himself up by his marriage, he, of course, having gone steerage on his first crossing. By the time they met on the Franconia he had elevated himself to cabin, else they would never have met.

"He would never have been happy with any of those women," my mother explained to me in East Walpole. I knew them all by sight. They were plump and jolly and usually to be seen in the company of their husbands — at a ballgame, or watching a parade, or just sitting side by side with them in matching rocking chairs on their front porches. My mother never rocked on her porch. She never went to a ballgame. She watched only one parade, and that was when the United States entered the First World War. Then she stood at the gate of our house on Washington Street to see the American boys marching to camp. She cried all the time, thinking of her brothers back home in Ireland. Mostly she stayed at home, doing embroidery or reading. She didn't believe in tagging after a man everywhere he went.

I had my doubts about the wisdom of this, and once made a sly reference to my father about his former admirers.

He looked at me with astonishment. "They'd never have given me a daughter like you," he said. "You have not got your mother's looks, but you have her ways." I understood then that my mother's ways were an abiding source of his pride.

Sometimes I wondered if it was my father's lack of education that had kept my mother from marrying him in the three years that followed the voyage on the Franconia. He'd asked her as they parted on the quay-side at Queenstown, she told me.

"But I took a dislike to him at first sight," she said. "I'd noticed him coming on board and I objected to the way he was staring at everyone, especially at me. I wasn't surprised when he came up to us and broke into our conversation." She had become acquainted in the departure shed with two elderly English gentlemen, who had helped her find a porter to carry her steamer trunk and arranged with the steward to have her chair placed between theirs. They also urged her to choose first sitting, which was the sitting they favored. Their company was most enjoyable, she maintained; it was they who made the voyage so pleasant. They were both married and spoke very nicely of their wives, who hadn't accompanied them because this was a business trip. They showed her photographs of their wives, and said that their wives, too, had read and greatly enjoyed *The Weaver,* by Parker, which was the book my mother was reading when my father caught sight of her from the gang-plank.

It was in this book she'd left on her deck chair while she went down to the dining saloon on the second day out that my father wrote his name. He scribbled it in the margin of the page at which she'd left it open. And after that, every time she vacated her chair he wrote his name on whatever page was open.

"It was a very cheeky thing to do," my mother said. "My sisters would have been horrified."

Then one day, when she was playing quoits with the nice elderly gentlemen and the one who was partnering her put down the quoit for a minute to rest, my father picked it up and finished the game. Naturally, they won, my father and herself. And after that he partnered her into the finals, and victory. They were presented with a silver rose bowl, which he immediately gave her but which I never saw. It vanished into thin air during the three years that passed between playing quoits on shipboard and playing at marriage on dry land.

The two gentlemen between whose deck chairs my mother's had remained stubbornly placed used to tease her about Tom. "He'll propose to you before we dock in Queenstown," one of them prophesied, and the other agreed. They urged her to accept him. "He's a good man, Nora," they said.

"But I refused him!" my mother would insist, with a laugh that still rings in my ears. It was a pretty laugh; her face was only a small part of her charm. "He had a cheek, scribbling in my book." I think she had suspected from his handwriting his lack of schooling, and it would not be long until his letters proved her right.

I have often wondered what became of his love letters to my mother. What did she do with them? Surely bad spelling and grammar would not be cause for a woman to destroy her love letters? His letters to me, written the times she took me away from him to Ireland, told so much love it lies on the pages still, although the ink has faded and the paper frayed. I have them all treasured away. Among them there is one on pink paper that he wrote me after he'd come back to Ireland to join us. It was written on the eve of the Grand National, and he was going to Liverpool for the night. He had just had time to come to a hockey match in which I was playing left wing, but he hadn't been able to stay for the finish. I should explain that in his day he had been a great athlete — a champion hurley player, but at a time when everyone on the team was expected to score from any place on the field at any time and however he could. He wrote:

DEAR LITTLE DAUGHTER,
   This is a Pound For Pin Money and I hope ye will win. I was very Much Disopinted how you Plead you Seem to wait till the Ball Came to you that is Rong you should Keep Moving and Not to stay in the One Place. God Luck,
                                                    DADEY.

   "Dadey" is nothing unusual — just "Daddy" spelled his way. I wish he hadn't written "ye" for "you" — it looks like stage Irish. But it also shows that my father never felt obliged to spell a word in the same way in the same sentence, much less the same page. It was as if he felt that he could give new meaning to a word with each new spelling — or, at least, a different inflection of meaning. It was as if for him a letter had a visual quality and could impart a message beyond its mere words. How often I saw him, after he had laboriously composed a letter, lean back from it the way a painter might stand back from his easel and, grabbing up his pen, jab at the page again, dotting an "i" or crossing a "t" and adding "t"s and "s"s or doubling an "l" or "n" at a furious rate, until he felt he had given the composition a more powerful effect.
   His letters to me must have roused at least as much love as was put into them. I keep them in the velvet-lidded box where my mother kept the trinkets he received from other women. In this box I also keep a few souvenirs that my mother herself seemed to treasure beyond their value: a silver Child of Mary medal, a gold-

plated Communion cross, and a buttonhook of real but hollow silver. That buttonhook baffled me — it seemed to emphasize what I thought was the shallowness of her feelings. Why had she kept a thing like that throughout her life? It had been a casual gift, and an odd one, from a customer in her father's shop — a customer whom in her lifetime she always "Mistered." Mr. Barrett — that was how she referred to him. It seemed a distant way to refer to any man.

"But he always called me 'Miss Nora'!" she said when I questioned it.

Mr. Barrett was a land agent on a large estate called Multyfarnham, a few miles outside the town ramparts. My mother met him one afternoon when she and her sisters were picking the daffodils that grew in rings under the trees in such numbers they never regarded it as stealing to pick them.

"When he caught us, Mr. Barrett said we were only thinning them out," she explained. And she said it was to make sure she was happy in her conscience that he called that evening to buy a drink in her father's shop. "Only a glass of port wine," she hastened to add. "He never drank anything else." It was clearly a token drink to make his call acceptable to her family — as if anything could, it seemed from the tone of her voice. Why they disapproved I did not at first understand. "I used to stay out in the shop talking to him for hours," my mother went on. "My sisters would be furious. We all played the piano, but I was the best. What made them mad with me was that I stayed out in the shop until closing time."

"Couldn't you bring him into the parlor?" I asked.

"I thought I told you!" my mother cried. "Mr. Barrett was a Protestant!"

"Oh?" That was all I managed to say, but I looked with my first real interest at the crescent-shaped scar on her index finger. It was more than a crescent; it ran almost the whole way around her finger, like a ring. It was hard to believe it was not a real ring made of ivory or whalebone that had somehow sunk into her flesh and over which, like grass on a grave, the skin had grown. I don't think it would have been visible at all if her skin had not been the deep olive of a Galway woman's, which tradition credits to the wrecking of the Armada off the coast of Ireland. Even when my mother was an old woman, the texture of her skin was soft and smooth. And then, too, that scar shone bright as the sickle moon.

"I was polishing a glass for his port wine," she said, "and when the glass broke in my hand he pulled out his handkerchief and tore it into ribbons to bind up the cut. It was a silk handkerchief with his monogram on it."

"Do you ever hear from him? Where is he now?"

"He's dead," she said. "He was found dead one morning in a little ditch that ran between the road and the woods. He used to take a shortcut over it when he was going home at night. He must have slipped on the plank across it. He fell face downward into the water." She paused. "There was only half a foot of water, but he drowned."

"Was he drunk?" It seemed a natural question, and I didn't think I deserved the look she gave me.

"I told you he only drank port wine," she said, "and never more than one glass."

"How frightful!" I cried. "Did you feel awful?"

"I didn't hear a word about it for two years. I didn't hear until the time I came back with you — an infant in my arms — to show you off to my family. It happened only a few days after I left for America to marry your father. I inquired about him the minute I came in the door — I was wondering if he ever called when I had gone." She looked down at the scar on her finger. "That's when they told me." She paused again. "But no matter what they said I knew he never drank to excess — only the one glass of port wine."

I never asked my mother about Mr Barrett again, even when my father was dead and she might have been prepared to talk more about him.

My mother lived for twenty years after my father — her due, considering that was the difference in age between them. It was not a fair bargain, however, because he had had her beauty when he could proudly display it but she did not have his support when she needed it most. "Poor Tom," she'd say. "If he only knew that I'd be left so long after him, to fend for myself," or "If only Tom could see me now, crippled like this, it would break his heart." And while he had always spoken of death as being put into the black hole, she always spoke of it as "joining Tom." And the implication was that now wherever he was would be home to her. And a place of happiness, too.

She used to speak of him during those twenty years she survived him in much the same way that her sisters and brothers used to speak of him in his lifetime.

"Poor Tom," she would say. "He was so good to me."

"Poor Tom," *they'd* say. "He is so good to Nora."

One day when my mother had been dead for two years, I was paying a duty call on an unmarried aunt who kept house for one of her bachelor brothers. We were sitting in the little parlor that had been the scene in my mother's stories of so much brightness and laughter and song, but the day was dull, and our talk was sad, and we often fell silent. In one of those silences, my aunt picked up the newspaper and was glancing at it idly when she gave an exclamation.

"Listen to this!" she said. "Yesterday some poor young man was found drowned in a small drain with only a foot of water in it. He was lying face downward. They thought he had drink taken, but from the evidence given at the inquest the coroner decided it was suicide."

"Where did it happen?" my uncle asked listlessly, and when my aunt said it had happened in another part of the country his interest evaporated. But my aunt was devouring the print. She caught my uncle's arm and shook it violently.

"Suicide!" she repeated. "Just like Nora's Mr. Barrett."

A hundred questions leaped to my mind, but I was silenced by the look on my uncle's face. "What are you talking about?" he cried. " 'Nora's Mr. Barrett' — as you call him — was accidentally drowned. You know that as well as I do. What would Muggie think if she could hear you saying such a thing?" Muggie was the name by which my maternal grandmother had always been called by her grown-up family; it was meant to be an endearing diminutive, but to me it had always seemed more appropriate than they knew. In one way or another, she had smothered most of her children.

Had my mother known the truth about Mr. Barrett, I wondered. Had my father? Had that knowledge had anything to do with his rare but terrible drinking bouts, and the less frequent but more terrible depressions that came down over him like a snuffer? I had seen that snuffer quench joy in him at times when he should have been happiest, looking over a gate at his purebred horses thudding across pastures flowing rich as rivers. Yet his face would darken, and I'd be sure he was thinking that, even before him, they would be put down in the black hole. Tiepins and silver brushes, he knew too well, could outlast a million men and a million horses.

I was twenty. I had just finished my first university examination, and while I was waiting for the result my father decided to take me to Roscommon, to the place where he was born. He had taken me to Killarney, with its lakes, and Connemara, too. We had gone together to the Glens of Antrim and the Burren in full flower. But I knew these places were nothing compared to a bogland bathed in the light of his memory, a light he thought had no night and over which he thought no cloud could ever settle.

It was midafternoon when we reached the town of Boyle and took the road to Frenchpark. What would he feel, I wondered, when he'd see the changes inevitable in the time since he'd last been there?

To my astonishment it did not bother him at all that where there had been golden thatch there were gray slates, where there had been plowshares there were tractors. He hardly seemed to notice that the boys wore boots and not one girl had a waterfall of hair. His eager eyes fell short of these changes and fastened on unchanged mounds of earth, on unchangeable stone walls, and on streams that still ran over the same mossy stones. "Look at that!" he would cry, stopping the car one place after another and pointing out with delight something familiar. "Look at that five-bar gate! Many's the time I vaulted it. Look! Look! By God, that's the same old bank I put Dockery's ass over, digging my toes into its sides like it was into butter I was digging them!"

Then his eyes fell on something so exciting he could hardly speak. "I didn't believe it'd be still standing. By all that's holy! It's the old schoolhouse!" he cried. "God be with the master! I wonder if he's still alive."

The little schoolhouse was no longer used as a school, of course. We had passed a large new school a mile or so back the road. But Tom got out and stood staring at it. At last, he went over and tried the door. It was locked. He looked up, then, at the windows, which were very high up so the scholars of those days couldn't be distracted by looking out.

"I bet the mark of that slate is still on that blackboard," he said, and suddenly he lifted me up as he used to when I was. a child in Boston lifted up to see a parade. "Can you see anything?" he cried.

"Only cardboard boxes piled up everywhere." The classroom was evidently used as a storage place for the jotters and copybooks, erasers and pencils that had replaced the old slates and slate pencils of his day.

He set me down. "But I'd guarantee the mark is still on that blackboard!" he said. He gave a laugh. "If I thought the master was hereabout, I'd call and let him see you." His eyes traveled over the countryside again. "There were eighty-four scholars in that little schoolhouse," he said. "And I could name every one of them." As if I didn't know! I myself could sing out that litany of names: Micky Dockery, Tom Forde, James Neary, Ethel Scally, Mary Morrisroe, Paddy Shannon . . .

"Most of them went to America," my father said, "and I met many a one of them out there. I'd be in a bar and it crowded, and suddenly I'd see a face, and I'd know it at once for a Roscommon face. You wouldn't have to give me a minute till I'd put a name to the face as well. I'd leave my drink and I'd go over and I'd slap the fellow on the back and I'd call him by his name. But if he saw me coming he'd beat me to it. 'By the hokey — it's not you, Tom?' And after that it would be round for round as long as either of us had a dollar in our pocket. And it wasn't only the fellows but the girls. I was with your mother and you one day in Boston sitting in Childs Restaurant, and I caught sight of one waitress that was shapelier than the rest, with red hair that could make you think the evening sun was on it. 'Stop staring, Tom!' your mother said. She was easy embarrassed. But although the girl had her back turned to us I could have laid a five-dollar bill she was from the County Roscommon. 'Wait till she turns around,' I said, 'and I'll give you her name into the bargain.' But when she turned round she beat me at my own game. 'Tom!' she screamed, and she left down the tray she was carrying and ran over to us and began shaking hands with your mother and taking you in her arms and throw-

ing you up in the air. And everybody in the place gaping. With all
the commotion, it wasn't long till the manageress arrived on the
scene, but seeing it was Molly Murray she turned away and let on to
notice nothing. Molly wasn't the kind of girl any boss would attempt to put down. She'd have pulled off her apron and lit out of
the place if anyone ventured to say a word to her! A real Roscommon woman! Do you know what happened when we'd finished
eating and I asked for the check? She went over to the cash register
and ran up a zero. 'On the house,' she said. That'll show you
what she was like!" My father laughed.

He looked around him again over the flat land, where, among
the new cement houses, there were still a few mud-wall cabins. But
there was more grass growing out of their thatch than could be seen
in the little fields around them. They, too, would soon turn back
into the clay from which they were made. "She lived over there,"
he said, pointing to a cabin behind one of the new cottages. It
seemed now to be a cow byre. He sighed. "But that was a long
time ago. I don't know if she's alive at all. There can't be many
of the old folk left. There must be a lot of them laid to rest in — "
He paused, and I waited for the familiar phrase about the black
hole, but the memories of boyhood were too strong. "In Drumshanbo cemetery," he said quietly, pointing to where in the distance I could see a small, walled cemetery, dotted with marking
stones not much different from the rough field stones that
surrounded the little plot.

"Is that where your parents are buried?" I asked, thinking of his
mother, to whom he had never said goodbye. I thought he'd want
to visit their grave.

But he shrugged. "They're put down somewhere there," he
said, with what I took at first to be a strange indifference. "I sent
money back to the priest one time and asked him to put a tomb-
stone over them, but he returned it and said no one could find the
exact spot." A dark shadow fell over us both for a minute.

"It's a wonder he didn't keep the money to say Masses for their
souls," I said, and at that the shadow lifted and a smile broke like
sunlight over my father's face.

"I never thought of that," he said. "Ah, but the priests that
were going in those days weren't like the priests today. He was a
gentleman even if he was a priest."

We were walking back to the car when we saw an old man coming toward us on the road.

"Let's have a word with this old-timer," he said, "and see if there's anyone left around here that I knew in my young days." The old man was so bent and was walking so slow that we got back into the car and moved forward to meet him. As we got nearer, my father took his hand off the wheel and nudged me. "He's making his way to Drumshanbo to save people the trouble of carting him there," he said.

Yet when we drew level with him the old fellow looked spry enough for his age. His face was weathered by wind and rain, but he seemed as hardy as a wild duck. It wasn't poverty that had him bent double, either; he had a suit of good frieze cloth on his back and a pair of good strong shoes on his feet. As the car stopped, he came over to us with a courtesy not common today.

"Good day, sir."

"Good day to you, sir," my father replied, but I saw that he was staring at the old fellow with a puzzled look on his face.

"It's a nice fine day, sir, isn't it, thanks be to God," said the old man. And, as my father had said nothing, he looked appraisingly at the car. "That's a fine car you've got there, sir," he said. "I suppose it's visitors to this country you are? Is it wanting to know the way to Dublin you are, sir."

At that my father gave a laugh. "No," he said. "I know this part of the country well enough. I wish I had a dollar for every time I walked this road!" he cried with a reckless note in his voice.

"Ah, I knew you were from America, sir," the old man said. "Sure, Americans have plenty of money for traveling the world and going anywhere they like." Then he frowned, as if he, too, were puzzled by something.

My father hesitated for a second, and to my astonishment he turned the key in the ignition and put the car into gear. But just before we drove away he leaned out. "Did you ever hear tell of a young fellow called Danny Kelly?" he asked.

"Is it Danny Kelly? Usen't us two sit on the one form beyond in the old schoolhouse!"

"Is he still in these parts?" my father asked slowly.

The old man gave a dry chuckle. "He is!" he said. "He went to Scotland for a while, but his family brought him back here a while ago. And he'll never be leaving again." With a jerk of his thumb, he pointed toward the Drumshanbo cemetery. "The Lord have mercy on him."

"The Lord have mercy on him," my father repeated, and both of them took off their hats. "There was another young fellow by the name of Egan," my father said then. "Did you know him?"

"It would be a queer thing if I didn't! I'm called Pat Egan," said the old man, but now his blue eyes filled with mild inquiry. "If it's not an impertinence to ask, sir, where did you hear my name?"

Now, I thought. This is the moment. But my father was letting in the clutch.

"There was a fellow I knew in Boston that came from here," he said. "He told me if ever I passed this way to inquire about a few of the scholars that were in that schoolhouse there with him." He nodded at the little school.

"And what was that man's name, sir, if you'll pardon my asking?"

My father seemed to expect the question, he was so ready for it. "I declare to God I knew him as well as I know myself," he said, "but at this moment I can't recall his name."

Pat Egan was satisfied. He laughed. "Wait till you are my age, sir," he said, "and you'll be forgetting your own!"

We drove away.

"What do you make of that?" my father asked. "Pat Egan and me are the same age to within a day. I didn't know him from Adam when we drew up beside him. But when we were a minute or two talking I knew him by a bit of a blood mark that you maybe didn't see at all, because it was under his left ear. But I remembered it, because the female teacher, when she'd be expecting a baby — which was every year — used to make him keep his cap on in class, pulled down well over his ears so she wouldn't see it and it maybe bring bad luck on the child in her womb. I knew him by that blood mark. But he didn't know me from Adam!"

"Why didn't you tell him who you were?" I asked, looking back at the figure of the old man getting smaller and smaller behind us.

"I don't know," my father said quietly, and then, to my surprise, he abruptly swung the car into a narrow laneway on our left. "There used to be a cottage up this lane," he said, "and many's the time I was in it. I near wore the seat off my pants sitting on an old settle that stood by the hearth. Rose Magarry was her name," he said. "She was my first sweetheart." And now with every word he was giving little light laughs like a stream frolicking over stones. He was so lighthearted I thought I could tease him.

"Oh, you must have been a right boyo in those days," I said.

He turned angrily. "What makes you say that?"

"I was thinking about those tiepins and cufflinks you got from admirers. That's all."

"Is it them things?" he scoffed. "A few dollars is all that kind of thing cost in those days. Gold was cheap in America then. The girls could earn as much as us men then. And some were earning more! They gave presents like that to every fellow they met."

He had slowed down the car and was looking from side to side of the lane. "We ought to have come on the cottage before now," he complained.

We were passing a mound of dung that looked like rotted thatch, and among the nettles and elderberry bushes there were foxgloves and hollyhocks, twined together with honeysuckle, and a white rose-bush gone wild. Hundreds of bees were buzzing over it, and white butterflies dancing. "Do you think there might have been a cottage there at one time?" I said cautiously, because I was thinking that if it is true, as legend tells us, that nettles grow out of the bones of monks and men of combat, perhaps honeysuckle and roses grow from the bones of young maidens.

My father was looking where I'd pointed. "You're right. That would be the spot. I knew I couldn't be so far out in my calculations. The old people would be dead, and she'd be married and gone. Come to think of it," he said, "I heard she was married and a widow into the bargain." He looked ahead, to where there were four or five new cottages, the ground around them as bare as a hen run. "We'll stop at one of those cottages and ask if anyone can tell us where Rose lives now," he said. He winked at me. "Just for fun."

We stopped in front of the first of the cottages, at the back of which a young woman was hanging out wet clothes. She turned and stared at us, more aggressive than curious. But an old woman, who had been sitting inside the window, got up and came hobbling out.

As she came down the cement path, my father called to her, "I'm sorry to bother you, Ma'am, but I wonder could you tell me anything about a girl by the name of Rose Magarry used to live in that cottage back there." He nodded back at the mound of rotted thatch and flowers.

The old woman had a touching simplicity. "Magarry was my own name, sir," she said. "Would you be meaning me? I am called Rose. I married Ned Malone, but he's dead these twenty years."

I looked anxiously at my father. He was gripping the steering wheel and staring straight in front of him. "I was only wanting to ask because of a young lad that used to know her long ago," he said stiffly. "A fellow I met in America. He asked me to call."

"And what would his name be, sir?" the old woman asked, and it broke my heart to hear the deferential note in her voice. But next minute she threw up her hands. "Ah!" she said softly. "Don't I know who that was! Tom! It's his son you are, sir, isn't it?" She darted close and peered into my father's face. "Tom's son. Sure, you're the dead spit of him!" Then, stretching out her hands, she caught at his and went as if to drag him out of the car. "How is he? Tell me, is he still alive? But wait, what am I thinking about, you'll come inside and be telling me over a cup of tea? And you too, Miss?" she said, recalling my presence. But next minute she glanced back uneasily at the young woman who was all the time standing by the clothesline staring.

"You'll have to excuse us, Ma'am!" said my father. "We've a long journey ahead of us yet."

There was a strange little silence.

"Ah well, in that case, sir!" the old woman said then, and she seemed relieved. "But wait a minute, sir," she cried. "I'll open the two sides of the gate, so you can turn your car in comfort."

I waited till we'd turned and driven down the narrow laneway and were back onto the road. "Why didn't you tell her?"

He said nothing for a long time. "Why do you think?" he said, and the black mood that came down on him didn't lift till we'd crossed the Shannon.

JOHN L'HEUREUX

A Family Affair

(FROM THE ATLANTIC)

I

IN THAT COUNTRY there was never a wind. Sun beat down from April to October, and the fields that surrounded the town grew pale yellow and then dark yellow and then brown. There was no green anywhere.

Dust hung in the air, flung by the wheels of jeeps as the soldiers tore down Finial Street to the Blue Spider Cafe. Cozy Oaks was also located on Finial Street; in fact, it was separated from the Blue Spider only by Adam's Bakery and Johnson's Wood and Hardware, but the soldiers never went to Cozy Oaks. The men from the farms went there, and the men from the foundry, but the soldiers went to the Blue Spider.

All during February and March they sang around the jukebox, and the sound drifted slowly past Adam's and Johnson's until the regulars at Cozy Oaks would shake their heads and shrug their shoulders, but nobody ever complained because, one way or another, everyone was a little better off since the soldiers had come. In April, with all the windows open, the singing and the short high whoops that meant they were having a good time could be heard far out in the fields and sometimes even beyond that, in the pocked desert where the base was located and where the lucky soldiers with cars brought the girls from the Spider who would go all the way.

It had been like this every spring of the past four years, even when the base was new and nobody had yet sorted out how they really felt about the soldiers. Beryl Gerriter gave birth that first

spring to her son Jason, her deep moans and howls punctuated with
the drunken singing from the Blue Spider. Luke Gerriter waited in
the sitting room with his daughter Elissa. They said nothing,
though from time to time he would send her to the kitchen to get
him another beer.

"Why can't I go in?" she asked him.

"Shut your mouth. You're not old enough."

"Twelve is old enough."

He held his beer can to his mouth for a long slug and then he
looked at her. Nothing. A face like an ax, everything pulled out
to a point, with her mouth pinched already like Beryl's, a worried
face. And skinny. How in hell would he ever marry her off?

"Twelve isn't old enough for much," he said.

She knew his voice when he spoke like that, she was afraid of it,
she didn't know why. She leaned over Pal and hugged him, rubbing the fur along his back.

"We should get rid of that mutt. It stinks. That's what the
hell's the matter around here. That mutt. One of these days I'm
going to take him out and shoot him."

She said nothing. He was just drinking; his threats didn't mean
anything.

Voices drifted in from the Blue Spider. They were singing "Poor
Lil." In the other room Beryl smiled sourly at the idea of poor
Lil. Poor Berla, she thought, and she pushed again. By Christ,
she'd never have another baby. She could feel her skin tear, she
was being ripped apart. Someone mopped her forehead, someone
pressed at her thighs. And that bastard in the other room, getting
drunk, it was his fault. Oh God! She pushed again. There was a
huge surge between her legs, and for a moment she went unconscious. She woke screaming.

Outside the room Luke waited out the scream and then slammed
his beer can to the floor in fury. "If she don't hurry up in there!
Hurry up, you!" he shouted at the bedroom door. "I said, hurry
up!"

The bedroom door opened and Dr. Pharon stuck his head out.
"We've got problems," he said, "serious ones. It's gonna be a
while, and I can't promise anything. But I suggest, if you got a
brain left in that addled head of yours, that you stop drinking and

start praying and, whatever else you do, you shut up." And he closed the door.

"I'll be at the Oaks," Luke said to his daughter. "You can come and get me when the mule is born."

Elissa nodded, her eyes glazed with fear, and she hugged Pal again. "It's going to be all right, Pal," she said, rocking back and forth, the dog's muzzle in her lap. "Everything's going to be all right. Everything."

She was awakened later by Dr. Pharon, who told her to go find her father; he had something important to tell him.

Outside she paused for a minute to think what she was doing. She did so many things automatically that sometimes she had to stop and tell herself what came next. She had trouble catching her breath; the sun had gone down, but there was no breeze. In the distance she could hear loud shouts and singing. She tried again to catch her breath, and in the still air she could taste the dust. She crossed the lawn to the evergreen tree and held a spiky branch to her face, breathing its sharp smell of oil and gum, a bitter smell, but special to her. The tree was yellow, almost green, and with her face buried in its branches she could forget the damp heat and the taste of dust.

Pal whimpered at her feet.

"It's all right," she said, and ran down the dirt road to where it met Finial Street. A small stone caught in the sole of her sneaker, and she stooped under the streetlight to poke it out. It had wedged between the rubber sole and the canvas lining, and the more she pried at the hole the deeper she pushed the stone.

A jeep roared by, throwing dust in her eyes and hair.

"Damn," she said, "damn it."

And then the jeep screeched to a halt and backed up, crookedly, weaving from side to side.

"Hi there, sweetheart."

"She's too young, Ron."

"They're never too young."

Elissa stared at them, not frightened. They were soldiers from the base. Nobody minded the soldiers. The men had jobs now that the soldiers had come. Even her father had a job.

"What do you say, sweetheart? You want a ride?"

He was blond, with a wide funny smile. He was the most beautiful man she had ever seen.

"I've got to go to the Oaks to get my father."

"Well, you jump right in here between me and my friend and we'll take you straight to the Oaks." He leaped out and held the low door open. She hesitated.

"Come on. You'll be all right."

"For Christ sake, Ron," the driver said.

"What about my dog?"

"Bring your dog too. Come on."

She climbed into the jeep and held out her arms for Pal, who wriggled from the soldier's hands into her lap. Ron climbed in beside her, slamming the small door. "And away we go," he shouted as the jeep took off. His arm, thrown over the seat at her back, drifted gradually to her shoulder. She could feel his hand lightly touching her bare arm.

"What's your name, sweetheart?"

"Elissa," she said, throwing her head back to feel the air blowing in her face.

"Elissa. Well, that's some name. I never heard of a name like Elissa. I think I'd call you Cookie, 'cause you're so sweet." He put his hand on her knee and ran it slowly up toward her thigh.

"Ron, if you want to get your ass in jail, you're going in just the right direction," the driver said.

"What's the mattter, for Christ sake? I'm only petting the dog." The two men in back laughed. Ron rubbed Pal's ears and his back. "Isn't that right, Cookie? No harm in petting the nice little doggie."

Elissa thought she had never been so happy.

"My mother just had a baby," she said. "I've got to tell my father."

"That right?" Ron said, his hand going back to her thigh. "You gonna have a baby? Hmmm? Would you like a baby?"

His hand was hot on her thin dress and she could feel sweat break out on her thigh and up higher. She wished he would move his hand there. She wanted him to touch her all over. But most of all she wanted to put her two arms around his neck and lay her head on his chest and just stay like that for a long, long time.

"Cozy Oaks," the driver said, slamming on the brakes.

And then she was out of the jeep and it was roaring off, the men in back laughing and Ron shouting, "See you around, Cookie." She stood for a long while watching the trail of dust the jeep left behind. She could still feel each of his fingers on her thigh and his thumb moving back and forth.

All the way home she repeated their conversation in her mind. I think I'd call you Cookie, 'cause you're so sweet, he had said. And he had asked if she would like a baby. She put her hand on her thigh where he had put his. For once she did not care that her father was stumbling along in the dark, cursing every goddamn stone in his path, the goddamn wife who called him away from his buddies, the goddamn baby that would put them all in the poorhouse. She had not even minded going into Cozy Oaks to get him. She had only half heard the sarcastic comments of the men at the bar, the double-meaning jokes, the laughter. While he bought a round of beer for everyone, she had stood at the screen door looking down toward the Blue Spider, where Ron was probably dancing or drinking with some pretty girl he was calling Cookie because she was so sweet, but it didn't matter. He had been nice, and whether he meant it or not, he had said it.

"You said it's a boy."

"What?" She stopped and tried to wiggle the stone into another part of her shoe.

"The baby. You said it's a boy."

"Yes."

"Did you see it?"

"No. Dr. Pharon said to go right away."

"Then how do you know it's a boy?" His voice was angry.

"I don't know. I just think it is. I don't know."

She put her arm up to ward off the blow, but he had only meant to caress her. They stood looking at one another.

"I thought you were going to hit me."

"I never hit you. You're like your mother, you try to put me in the wrong. You try to make me look bad."

"No. I don't. I . . ." She lowered her eyes.

He put his arm around her shoulder now, stiffly, feeling the small tense muscles beneath his fingers. They walked this way, fa-

ther and child in a book of photographs, until they reached the
little house where all the lights were on.

Dr. Pharon explained patiently that Beryl had had a breech birth
and, though there was not necessarily a connection, the child was a
mongoloid and would probably not live long. The mother had required many stitches, she was seriously ill. She should be in a hospital, but there was no hospital, and so he would have to pay Mrs.
Botts to stay with her.

Luke Gerriter listened with his head in his hands, and when the
doctor left, he saw him to the door. Then he went into the bedroom, where he looked in the crib for a long moment, for the last
time. He stared at the gray figure in the bed.

"So you had to do this to me, too," he said. "One lay in three
years, and you had to produce this. You bitch." He turned at the
door to look at her again. "You miserable bitch," he said, and
lumbered up the stairs to Elissa's attic room.

Elissa stretched out on the sitting room couch where she stroked
Pal and whispered over and over again, "It's all right; it's going to
be all right."

II

The next morning Luke bought a bed frame that folded in half
and a mattress to go with it, and he set them up in the tiny bedroom. He said nothing to Beryl — everything between them
seemed to have been said already — and she remained with her face
turned resolutely to the wall. She had not asked to see the baby.

With the double bed taking up most of the room and then with
the dresser and the baby's crib, Mrs. Botts found she had no place
for the chair she had brought in from the kitchen. So she perched
on the edge of Luke's folding bed, knitting, talking to herself, and
at regular intervals feeding the baby. This sort of thing had happened before; the answer was to wait. The little thing would die
eventually or, if he lived and grew up, they'd adjust. People always
did. She moved closer to the window hoping to catch a breath of
air, though she knew there was never a breeze here. Elissa would
be along soon to relieve her.

Almost at once they had settled into a regular routine. At three o'clock Elissa returned from school and Mrs. Botts went home. Elissa prepared her father's dinner and then he disappeared until midnight or later, when he came stumbling home from the Oaks. Meanwhile Elissa sat with her mother, saying nothing.

Elissa had instructions from Mrs. Botts about caring for the baby, and she went about the work methodically, automatically; it was the way she made dinner, the way she did schoolwork; it was as if there were some more important part of her that simply stepped out and walked away, leaving the methodical, automatic Elissa behind to do the work.

School was the worst part of the day. The others teased her about her idiot brother, and once one of the teachers had called her aside in the schoolyard and asked about her mother and her father and finally about her brother. She wanted to know if he had a big head and if his eyes were pink; she asked her to describe him. Elissa said she didn't know and tried to pull away, but the teacher had hold of her arm.

"You tell me, you hear. I've got to know these things. I'm only doing my duty." She tightened her grasp on the girl's arm.

Elissa tried to run, but could not get away. And then something inside her took over, and it was as if she were talking with her father when he was drunk and impossible. She said in her dreamy way, "He's just a baby, just a little ordinary baby. His eyes are blue, a pretty light blue they are, and his head is only as big as a baby's head. He cries when he's hungry and then my mother feeds him, but most of the time he just laughs and plays with his toys and sleeps. Just like any baby."

"Are you telling me the truth?"

"Yes, ma'am."

"That isn't what everybody says. What do you say to that?"

"Maybe they haven't seen him," Elissa said. "He's a real nice baby."

More and more she found herself alone; she played with the dog and sat with the baby in her mother's room, waiting.

Luke found himself more and more in the center of things. Somebody was always standing him a beer at the Oaks, and the men went out of their way not to mention births or babies. Work was going well, too, with a good raise following the birth of the child and the foreman keeping out of his way at the foundry. It was only at home that life was impossible. He had to be very drunk before he could get courage to come back to that small bedroom smelling of sour sheets and milk and lie there knowing Beryl was not asleep and that thing lay in the darkness between them.

He thought sometimes he would get up and place a pillow over the baby's face and put it out of its misery. He thought of shooting it. Some nights as he turned off Finial Street into the dirt road that led to his house, he saw himself approach the door and walk through the house and down the cellar stairs and get a gun — the small pistol maybe, with its shiny blue barrel, or one of the rifles — and go back up the stairs, through the sitting room and into the bedroom, and there . . . He could not imagine the rest in detail, but there was one small shot into the crib and then a scream from Beryl, followed by two shots and then a silence. He held the gun at his own head. On those dark nights staggering home from Finial Street, he would weep at how rotten life was, how wrong everything had turned out. He would go home and fall into bed, and it did not matter any more that Beryl was lying there awake, staring straight ahead.

Beryl seemed to be awake all the time. She lay in bed motionless, turning from side to side only when she had to be washed or when Mrs. Botts changed the sheets. She ate whatever they brought her, and when they asked if she wanted more, she shook her head no.

After the first day Mrs. Botts gave up trying to talk to Beryl but she could never be sure whether Beryl was asleep or awake. Sometimes it was as if she were staring even when her eyes were shut. She'd be plumb glad, she told herself, when this whole thing was over.

Only Elissa was indifferent to Beryl's silent stare. Often, coming home from school, she would stand at the bedroom door and look at her mother, thinking, she'll never come back, she's gotten away to some place where there are trees and air and no more shouting and she'll never come back. She envied her.

And Beryl lay there, with her gray face on the pillow, staring. It was almost a month before she asked to see the baby. There had been no warning, no signs of a return to life; suddenly one afternoon she simply turned in the bed, lifted herself on one elbow, and spoke to Mrs. Botts. Her voice was clear and strong.

"Let me see it," she said.

Mrs. Botts looked up from her knitting. "How's that?"

"Let me see it. The baby."

"Well, now, Berla. Are you real sure you want to do that? Might be as how well enough should be let alone till you're feeling better."

"I'm real sure."

Mrs. Botts picked up the baby and laid him in the bed next to Beryl, who twisted beneath the sheet so that she could get a better look at him. She took a long deep breath, and her chest heaved twice, as if she were going to sob. And then she whispered "No," a breathy sound that turned into a deep moan. She picked up the baby and crushed it to her breast, bending from the waist and swaying her body from side to side as she clutched the white, unresisting thing.

Mrs. Botts stroked Beryl's hair and said over and over, "That's all right, Berla, you go ahead and cry. That's all right, Berla," and she went on stroking, waiting for the release of tears. But the tears did not come. Beryl stopped moaning and released the baby. She placed it on her lap and forced herself into a sitting position.

After a long while she said, "Look at it. Just look at it."

The baby had smooth, almost puffy skin, moist in the airless room. His ears were small and round, and his nose only a blob of flesh, not like a nose at all. His lips were thick, the color of raw meat. Beryl bent closer and looked at his tongue. It had two deep grooves and protruded from his tiny mouth. But it was his head that astonished her most. It was small and hard and completely round. She had expected something huge, a monstrosity, an enormous watermelon head. Looking at him at first, she had been relieved, she had almost begun to hope. And then she recalled the doctor's warning. "He's a mongoloid, he will never be normal, he will probably not live very many years," and she saw the huge lips and the tiny slits for eyes. With her thumb she gently pushed up one eyelid. The eye was milky blue and empty.

She had not wanted him, she had not wanted sex in the first place, and now this had happened. She crooked her finger under his tiny palm and looked at his hand. Even his hands were wrong. There was a space between his first finger and the rest. His feet had that same strange cleft, as if they were paws, as if he were Pal.

"Put him back," she said, and then a long while later, "I'm

going to call him Jason." Her mouth bent in a thin, bitter smile.

She was herself again for a few months, and then in the fall she had a hysterectomy, and after that she left the baby's care entirely to Elissa. She never wanted to see him again, she said.

Jason died just before his second birthday.

III

Elissa missed him. He was not a mongoloid to her, some strange monster her father would not look at, or a mockery her mother hated. He was that ordinary little baby she had told her teacher about, a baby who cried when he was hungry, but who most of the time played with his toys and slept. She would have a baby of her own someday, in a place different from this one; and she would be loved someday too.

Elissa was fourteen now and plain. Her hair was long and thin, falling straight on either side of her wedge-shaped face. She looked nearsighted, though she was not. The glassy look in her eyes came from daydreaming, her teacher said, but Elissa knew it was something different from daydreaming. She was escaping, she was going away.

With Jason dead, no one teased her at school any more. Among the other girls there was even some grudging admiration of her breasts, which were rounder and fuller than their own. They could tell she didn't use cotton either, as most of them did. But she was plain, she was no threat to them. They merely laughed indifferently when she was called on in class and admitted she hadn't heard the question. The boys ignored her altogether, except to joke about her breasts as they passed in the corridor. "Maybe with a bag over her head," they would say, cupping their hands in front of their chests. Elissa was oblivious. School would be over if you waited long enough.

Soon after Jason died, she had begun taking Pal for walks each evening. After supper, when her father left for the Oaks and her mother settled into her chair by the radio, Elissa took the dog and walked slowly down the dirt road to Finial Street. She pulled a stick of straw grass from a clump by the road and chewed on it, kicking stones ahead for Pal to chase. She walked slower as she came into sight of Finial Street, and under the streetlight she stopped and waited. When she heard one of the jeeps approach she bent over as if she were taking a stone from her shoe. She liked the feeling of the blood racing to her temple, the hammering in her chest. This was how she had met Ron. It could happen again.

And then one night a jeep did stop and come roaring back.

"Hi," a girl said, giggling. She was in the front seat beside a soldier, and there were two other soldiers in the back. Her dark red hair tumbled around her shoulders in big curls and her mouth glistened with lipstick. It took Elissa a full minute to recognize her as Florence Kath. Florence was also a freshman at the high school.

"Hi," Elissa said, her eyes darting from face to face. Ron was not there. "Oh, it's you. I didn't recognize you, you're so . . ."

"We're going to the Spider," Florence said. "Want to come?"

"Yeah, why don't you come?" a soldier in back said. "Here, you can sit right between us. We'll take care of you." The other just grinned.

"I'd like to," she said. "I really would, but my dog . . . I've got to get back home." She could not take her eyes off the soldier in front who had his arm around Florence and was pushing the shoulder of her peasant blouse lower and lower.

"Fresh bastard," Florence said, pleased, and she pushed his hand away. "Come on, Lissa, you'll really love it."

"I can't," she said, "I just can't. My father . . ." She stood there speechless as the jeep took off, scattering dust everywhere.

Elissa and Florence became friends. Each morning during third period they met in the girls' room and smoked a cigarette. And they ate lunch together. Though they ate in the cafeteria with everyone else, there were always empty chairs at their table. Florence was cheap, everyone said; Florence did it with the soldiers.

"You ought to come to the Spider, Lissa, it's really terrific. I go only on Saturdays now, but next year I'm gonna go on Fridays and Saturdays too, once I convince my old lady. You ought to come."

"My mother would never let me."

"Well, you ought to come anyway. Last Saturday there was this guy. Oh my God, he was so cute. He bought me a beer by buying it for himself, you know, and letting me drink it. He had real curly hair, black, and we necked like crazy right in the booth. I didn't care. And when he took me home, woo, woo."

"What happened when he took you home?"

Florence sang, "But I ain't gonna tell you what he did to me."
She sang loudly so the kids at the next table would hear her. "I
don't care about them bastards," she said. "I don't care about any
of them. They all ought to go get laid."

"What happened when he took you home? Tell me."

"Nosey bitch, aren't you. I'll tell you on Saturday when we put
up our hair."

Every Saturday morning at Elissa's house they put up their hair
in huge pink rollers, whispering and giggling at the kitchen sink,
splashing water everywhere. Then they sat outside on the back
steps letting the sun dry their hair.

Beryl would sometimes come out, not actually joining them, just
leaning against the doorframe smoking a cigarette. She had put on
weight since her operation, and the faded housecoat she invariably
wore bulged now with two small rolls around her waist. She kept
her hair tied back with a blue and white bandana.

"Boy-crazy," she would say, and the girls would giggle. "I
know," she said, nodding in agreement with herself, "don't think
for a minute I don't know."

And sometimes she would study the two girls. Elissa was devel-
oping a good bust. Funny about that, because she was so skinny,
especially in the face. She'd get a man someday, all right. Beryl
smiled bitterly to herself. Florence was pasty white, with a plump
face and a red mouth that was always pouting. She's looking for
trouble, Beryl thought, and she'll find it.

"You keep going to that Spider," she would say, "and you'll get
what you're looking for."

And once she said, "You kids, you think you know. I was like
that once. Everything looks rosy. You think getting married is
going to be the greatest thing in the world. Hah!" She lit another
cigarette, her face pinched in concentration. "I remember when I
was a kid, about your age, maybe younger, I thought getting married was the best thing that could happen to anybody, just getting
away, not having to answer to nobody for nothing. I thought men
were . . ." She was looking out over their heads, squinting
against the sun, and then suddenly she threw down her cigarette
and ground it out. "Men," she said. "They only want one
thing." She went inside and slammed the door.

Florence waited a minute until she was sure Beryl was gone and then she said, "Jesus, your mother, is she ever some kind of nut! She's worse than mine. My old lady just keeps nagging and nagging, but at least she's not crazy." She touched the rollers on top of her head. "You know something? I think she's really crazy. I really do."

"It's since the baby died," Elissa said. "And then her operation."

"Maybe it's the change. They get crazy during the change, that's what Tussie told me. Tussie's my aunt, and is she ever gorgeous. She's the one that showed me how to put on makeup and everything. She told me all about sex and everything. Woo woo. As if I didn't know already." She shrieked with laughter, and Elissa laughed with her.

Florence rummaged through the large embroidered bag she carried everywhere with her. She pulled out her makeup box, flat plastic containers of base and powder and rouge, and she gazed into a small round mirror as she drew the crimson lipstick across her mouth. She was making it larger, she explained. Men liked lips that way, it was sexy. She held the lipstick lovingly, caressing her lips with it, gently expanding her lip line above and below its natural ridges. Her lips looked wet. She pursed them at the mirror, lazily stuck her tongue out and curled it to one side of her mouth, tossed her head back, and gazed into the mirror with half-closed eyes. She was thinking of tonight, of what might happen.

Elissa looked at her and ached. The pancake makeup, the hair in rollers, the glistening red mouth. Some day she would go to the Blue Spider. Some day all that excitement would be hers.

IV

On the night before her fifteenth birthday, Elissa woke to angry shouting. It was a sweltering night and she had kicked the sheet off, but now she pulled it over her and pressed the pillow against her ears. Sweat was running from her forehead into her eyes. Her head ached. She took the pillow away from her ears. They were still shouting.

She could hear her mother's voice screaming "bastard" over and over against her father's drunken laughter, a choked, hollow laugh with no joy in it. Pal was whimpering at the foot of the bed. Her mother's voice grew louder and she heard her father's voice too, thick and angry, though she could not make out what he was saying. And then there was a crash. A table must have been tipped over or something heavy thrown. The voices stopped. The house was completely silent. A floorboard creaked and Pal whimpered once again, but the house remained silent the rest of the night.

The next day Beryl and Luke did not speak to one another, nor would she sit with him while he ate. When Luke returned from work the table was set for him and Elissa, and the dinner was ready on the counter next to the stove. Beryl sat in the bedroom looking out the window. Elissa and her father ate in silence, Elissa only toying with her food. She was not hungry.

On the third day Luke said to her, "Where's your mother?"

"In the bedroom."

"Doesn't she eat at all? When does she eat?"

"She eats before you come home." Elissa pushed the beans around her plate with her fork. "Can't this stop?" she said. "Can't this all stop?"

She held her breath, fearing what he might say or do. But he only went on eating, mopping his plate finally with a piece of bread. He leaned over the table, his head in his hands. Elissa listened to the kitchen clock ticking, saw her father shake his head from side to side. It will always be like this, she thought, nothing will ever change. She will sit in the other room looking out the window and he will sit here with his head in his hands and I will be between them listening to the clock tick and tick and tick. She wanted to run, she wanted to scream, it was better to be dead.

Luke stopped shaking his head from side to side. He looked up from his plate, his eyes strange and wild, his face bruised-looking.

"Oh, Christ," he said. "What's the use? What's the goddamn use?"

The next day he went back to his guns. He had three of them; two were heavy-gauge shotguns and the other was a twenty-two, revolver size, with a snub barrel. He had not touched them since the soldiers came and he had gotten a regular job. But before that, in that endless time when there had been no work and he had a wife and daughter to support, he had spent the days hacking at the sand and stone that stretched for miles behind the tiny house, trying to coax the sterile land into producing vegetables. And at the end of the day, when they had eaten dinner, he would get out the guns. With Beryl and Elissa by his side he would trudge to the end of the garden, where he placed tin cans on a large rock to use for target practice. He was quiet and methodical, setting up the cans and walking back to the shooting box drawn in the sand, lifting the gun to his shoulder, clicking back the safety catch, firing. Elissa would watch as his face tightened in concentration, his jaw went hard as he focused on the target, and his chest expanded in a sort of sigh as the bullet struck the can and sent it spinning into the air. He would do this over and over until it grew dusky, and then they went into the house. None of them enjoyed the shooting; it seemed, somehow, a necessity. He had taught Beryl to shoot the twenty-two and insisted that Elissa learn also. But all this has stopped once the soldiers came and there were jobs and money. He had not bothered since then to oil and polish the guns; weeds grew here and there in the patch that had once been the garden. They should have been happy, Elissa thought, but it had not worked out that way. And now he was back with his guns.

"What's he do that for, anyhow? What's he want to shoot tin cans for?" Florence narrowed her eyes and stared into the distance where Elissa's father was shooting. It was Saturday and they were doing their hair. "That makes me really jumpy, boy, that gunshot."

"It's just a hobby. He just does target practice."

"Jeez, your family. I'd be afraid to live here. Honest to God. With your mother in the change and everything and your old man shooting out back, I'd be afraid he'd go off his nut and shoot me. How do you know he's not gonna miss some day and hit somebody by accident? Or your dog, maybe. Where is he, anyhow? Maybe your old man shot him. Maybe he's using him for target practice."

"No, he's up in my room. He's afraid of guns. He's always been afraid of guns. The noise."

"He smells, that dog. He really does. If there's one thing I can't stand in a house, it's a smelly dog. I like everything really clean. That's why I wash all my own stuff. I like it really clean."

"Wait a minute. Shhh." Elissa stared out across the ruined garden at her father. "I think he called me," she said. He was waving his arm at her. "He must have," she said, and began walking toward him.

"Watch out he don't use you for target practice," Florence said, adding softly, "what a bunch of nuts."

Luke was standing in a litter of tin cans holding a small bunch of purple flowers, weeds that had somehow grown through the barren soil and bloomed now in the shade of the rock Luke set the tin cans on. The stems were thick with brownish green leaves, and the blossoms were small but numerous. "Here," he said, handing the flowers to Elissa. "Wait a minute," and he stooped to pick two more and then a third stalk. "Here, take these."

"What should I do with them?"

"Take them in to her."

"What should I say?"

Luke had turned from her and was bent over picking up cans. "Don't say anything. Just give them to her."

"Should I say they're from you?"

"I don't care what you say. Say whatever you want. Just give them to her. Say, yes, you can say they're from me." He was lining up cans on the rock. He was sweating.

"I'll tell her," Elissa said.

"Oh, and kid, Elissa." He scratched his head and stared at the ground. He spoke so softly she could hardly hear him. "Tell me, uh, tell me what she says."

Elissa ran to the house, her heart pounding. It would end now, the fights and the anger and the silence. She showed Florence the flowers and then ran up the porch stairs.

"Flowers," Florence said. "Big deal. Big fat hairy deal," and she giggled to herself. Elissa had already disappeared into the house.

Suddenly she was shy. She did not know how to give her mother the flowers, how to say they were from her father. She went slowly into the bedroom and stood there. Beryl was sitting with her face to the window. Her blue and white bandana had come loose and the hair at the back of her head stuck out in little clumps; it was matted and damp at the temples. She turned and blew a stream of smoke from the corner of her mouth. Her eyes were swollen and there were dark smudges beneath them. She looked at Elissa questioningly and then she saw the flowers.

"What are those? What the hell have you got there?"

"Look." Elissa held out the bouquet to her.

Beryl began to tremble, her mouth working furiously and her eyes darting from Elissa to the door behind her and then back to the flowers.

"Where did you get those?" she said, breathless. "Are they from him? Did he tell you to bring me those?" Her voice rose; she was almost screaming. "Get those out of this house! Get them out of here! Out! Get out!" She stood up, one hand at her hair.

Elissa backed to the door. "They're only flowers. He just wanted to give you some flowers."

"Look at them. They're death flowers. Death! You put those on coffins. Don't you see? Don't you see what he wants? He wants to get rid of me. He wants me dead." She dropped her voice to a whisper. She was clutching Elissa's arm, her thumb and fingernails deep in the soft flesh. "He can get rid of me, you know. He has grounds. You can get rid of a woman like me. Once you can't have children any more, once you're like a chicken with its guts ripped out, they can get rid of you. He'd like to too, that's what he wants."

"He just wanted to make up. He just wanted to give you the flowers."

Elissa pulled away from her but Beryl continued on, talking rapidly, in a whisper, her words piling furiously on one another.

"You're with him too. You're like him. The both of you, you want to drive me crazy. You want me to go crazy and then you can get rid of me. Bringing me those flowers. Death flowers." She began to scream again. "Get them out of here. Get out."

Elissa ran out of the house and stood on the back porch, white and gasping for breath. Inside she could hear her mother sobbing wildly. Florence was staring at her, motionless, one hand gently touching the pink rollers on her head, the other suspended halfway to her mouth. Somewhere in the distance her father was waiting. And all she could feel was the sun, beating heavily on her head and shoulders, numbing her entire body. There was a terrible crashing sound in her head, rhythmic and painfully loud, like a gunshot; but is was not a gunshot, it was something inside her head and it would not stop. Florence was saying something, but she could not hear it.

"Wait. Wait," she said, "it'll stop."

Florence watched her come stiffly down the stairs, walking as if she were in a trance. Her arms hung limply by her sides and the flowers in her left hand trailed along the ground as she step by step approached her father. He was standing with one foot on the rock, staring off into the space that stretched out forever behind the house. As she approached him, he turned and saw the flowers. He made a sound that was half laughter and half groan.

"She didn't want them?"

"No."

"What did she say? Did you say they were from me?"

"She said to get them out of the house."

"But did she say why?"

"She said they were death flowers. She said you wanted her dead, because . . . She said you wanted to drive her crazy, that we both did."

Luke's face went gray and he put the gun down carefully against the rock. He began walking toward the house. Elissa ran after him.

"No, oh please no," she said. "Don't say anything to her. Don't do anything. Please. Please no."

She was snatching at his sleeve but he pushed her away and kept on, a furious determined walk. She turned and went back to the rock where he had left the rifle. She picked it up and held it in position, the butt against her shoulder, her eye at the sight. She turned the barrel toward the house, toward Florence, but Florence had gone home. Without thinking, she sighted the kitchen window and waited and waited, and then pressed the trigger. Nothing happened. She had forgotten to release the safety catch.

Voices came to her now, she could hear them shouting. The word "crazy" drifted toward her on the windless air and then "bastard." She shook her head; she would not listen.

And then — she did not know why — she turned the rifle so that the barrel pointed to her chest. She reached for the trigger, but her arms were not long enough. She crouched. She placed the gunstock on the ground. Nothing worked.

Yes, she thought, you'd have to use your toe. You put the stock on the ground, the barrel at your chest, and you push the trigger back, away from you, with a toe. It would work perfectly.

She smiled at the thought and then looked around, suddenly self-conscious. She put the rifle back, leaning it against the rock just as it had been, and she walked slowly to the house.

V

"Look, kid, you can go if you want to, but if your father finds out, don't come crying to me."

Beryl had said this to her late at night on that same Saturday Elissa had brought her the death flowers, and now it was Saturday again, and she had been going to the Blue Spider for almost a year.

Elissa stood in front of the bathroom mirror touching her hair. She wore it in immense curls that tumbled about her head, some of them only half combed out, still springy from the rollers. Florence wore her hair this way; it was the fashion, she said. Florence helped her with everything. She taught Elissa how to spread the thick layer of pancake makeup evenly over her face and how to blend in the little dot of rouge so that her cheekbones stood out flushed against all that pink. She had helped her pick the peasant blouse, elasticized at the shoulders, and the plaid skirt, yards and yards of material that swirled around her when she danced and that concealed her thin legs and hips. And she had taught her how to act at the Blue Spider. She called Elissa Cookie, and Elissa called her Candy. The soldiers liked their names.

She smiled at her reflection in the mirror, tipping her head from one side to the other to catch a glimpse of herself in profile. She pursed her lips the way Florence did. Minutes went by and Elissa continued to pose before the mirror, distracted from her own image by the thought of Len.

She had met him on her first Saturday at the Blue Spider. They danced once or twice that night, but she did not remember him a week later; she had been too excited, too confused. Everyone seemed to like her. They laughed and drank and danced. How could she have remembered one soldier out of so many? But when he reminded her that they had danced together only a week earlier, she was embarrassed and grateful. She fell in love with him at once. And now, every Saturday night, they drifted together early in the evening, kissing and touching in the booths and on the way home.

"He loves me," she said aloud to the mirror. She touched her hair one last time and then put on the soft pink lipstick her mother liked; she would put on the deep red just before she reached Finial Street.

"Don't get in trouble, you," her mother said.

"Oh, Ma."

"And you better get home before he does. If he finds out, he'll kill you."

"I'm always home before he is. Don't worry."

Elissa let the screen door slam behind her, but Pal had wriggled out before it closed and was wagging his stubby tail excitedly.

"No, Pal. Go back," she said. "Go back!" She stamped her foot and pointed toward the door. The dog only lowered his head and put back his ears. "Goddamn," she said. Pal began to whimper. "Ma," she shouted, "call the dog, will you? He's gonna follow me." The dog slunk into the house.

Beryl watched her daughter walk down the dirt road, her hips swaying, her curls tossing with the movements of her head. "You look nice, Elissa," she said to herself, and then turned away, back to her empty house. Pal was in her way, sniffing at the screen door. "Get out of here, damn you," she said. "Damn dog." She kicked him lightly and he yelped and ran. Suddenly she found she was angry. "Damn you!" she shouted at the dog, and then she turned and leaned against the door, watching her daughter disappear down the road to Finial Street.

At Finial Street they were waiting for her in the jeep, but Len was not with them. The two soldiers in back made room for her, and even before she sat down the jeep roared away. One soldier had his arm around her shoulders, the other put his hand on her knee; she settled in comfortably between them.

"Isn't Len coming tonight?" She tried to sound casual.

"Hey, is Len coming tonight?" The soldier repeated her question, laughter in his voice. He tightened his grip on her shoulder.

"I don't know. Is Len coming tonight?" The other picked up the question, nudging her leg with his.

"What's the joke?" she said. "What the hell's so funny?" She leaned forward. "Hey, Candy, what the hell's so funny?"

"Wouldn't you like to know?" Florence said, rolling her eyes.

"Come on, tell me."

Florence leaned back and whispered in her ear. "Len's gonna get a car. And you know what *that* means." She laughed wildly, rocking from side to side, wriggling against the driver. "Woo woo."

"Woo woo," Elissa said, laughing, but her heart lurched, and she could feel the blood rushing in her arms and legs.

She loved Len. She loved the feel of him as he pressed up against her in the booths or when they kissed in the jeep on the way home. She would twist around in the seat so that her whole body would be touching his, and then she would move gently back and forth so she could feel him thrusting against her. She wanted to be naked under him.

She looked down at her lap and then at the lap of the soldier next to her. She could see that soft bulge. She could reach over and put her hand right on it. What would he do? She didn't even know his name, and yet she could reach out and do something like that. She would, too, someday. She would tonight, maybe, with Len.

"See anything you like?" the soldier said, shifting a little on the seat. "If you were a squirrel I'd be worried."

"Bastard," she said, and hit him in the ribs with her elbow. She tossed back her head and began to sing the "Pocaluma Polka." It was going to be a perfect night. Nothing could spoil it. She was still singing when they reached the Blue Spider and went in.

Elissa was thrilled by the air of excitement in the place. Everyone was in motion, talking and laughing. There were some girls in the booths already, but most of them were dancing, and there were soldiers lounging against the jukebox waiting for their turn. Someone called to her from one of the back booths. She waved to him and laughed. She was dancing, gliding backward to the heavy beat of the music, humming. She could feel the soldier's hands moving on her shoulder and at the small of her back. She didn't care. Let him. She was dancing with someone else now, she could feel his thighs against hers. She was floating, and always there was the music blaring and bodies touching hers. She was safe here. She was alive. Someone handed her a can of beer and she was surprised at the sharp bitter taste. She took a long slug from the can and everyone applauded.

"Jesus, are you ever the one!" Florence said to her, and then she whispered something to one of the soldiers. They laughed together and then he whispered to her. "You pig," she said, and pushed against his chest with her fist, laughing. They sat down in a booth.

Len had come in and was standing by the jukebox waiting for

the music to stop. They were dancing to the "Chicken Bop," and every few steps the girl would pull away from the boy and do a little hop. It was a popular dance because it gave the girls a chance to show what they were made of, Len had once told her. Elissa moved away from her partner, hopped, and returned. He grinned and said, "What've you got down there?" He pulled at the elastic on her blouse.

"Pig," she said. She was flirting more than she would have if she had seen Len come in.

She swung out from her partner once again, did her little hop, and returned, and this time he said, "You've really got something. Let's take a look." And he pulled again at the elastic. The blouse slipped from her left shoulder, and she pushed it back easily with a flick of her thumb. But she was annoyed.

"Come on," she said. "Cut it."

The dance was about to end. "I'll be good," he said. He held her tight against him, but when she swung out and returned for the last time, like a small boy he said, "Just one little peek," and he pulled at the elastic.

She stopped dancing and stood there. "Now look what you done," she said. The elastic has broken and her blouse dropped low on the left shoulder.

"Let's see, let's see," he said, being funny. The music had stopped and everyone was beginning to stare.

"Come on, let's get out of here," Len said. He came between her and her partner.

"Hey, hold on there, soldier," he said. "You stealing my little girl friend here?" And he pushed Len to the side.

"Look at this. Look what he done," Elissa was saying. "How can I go home with my blouse like this?"

"Quit shoving," Len said to the soldier, and took Elissa by the arm.

The soldier spun him around. "You didn't answer my question, friend. You stealing my little girl friend here?" He waited for an answer. "Huh?" He pushed Len in the chest with the flat of his hand. "Huh?" Another push. "What do you say, soldier boy?"

The crowd around them had fallen silent, the faces hungry for a fight. Len glanced at them, and knew what was expected of him. But he didn't want a fight. Not now.

"Don't try that again," he said, and spat on the floor.

"Try what? Try this?" He pushed Len harder. "Why, this is the easiest thing in the world, no trying involved." He pushed him harder still.

And then before anyone knew what happened, before anyone could holler "fight," Len lashed out with his right fist and caught the soldier on the side of the head. He lurched back, but as he fell, he struck the other side of his head on one of the upright beams. It made only a dull thudding sound. He slid down the beam to a sitting position, a look of surprise on his face, blood beginning to drip from the side of his head. Len took Elissa's arm and pushed her to the door.

"Hey, no rough stuff," the bartender was shouting. Everyone was talking loudly. "Who got hit?" "Who did it?"

They stood for a moment outside the door, Elissa holding the blouse together with her hand. They were breathless, flushed with excitement.

"I got a car," Len said.

"I know it."

He paused, and she stood there fiddling with the material of her blouse.

"Do you want to?"

"Yes. Do you?"

Laughing, they ran to the car.

"Yellow bastard," they heard the soldier shout as they drove off. "Come on back and fight, you bastard."

They drove out of town, out beyond the houses and the fields and the base, deep into the pocked and sweltering desert. They were silent the whole way, an odd formality between them. Finally Len stopped the car and they got out.

"This looks all right," he said. "What do you think?"

"Yes, this is fine," she said. What had happened? He was a stranger, she thought, he was just someone else she did not know. But I love him and he loves me. We're going to make love, she told herself, trying to recapture the excitement of the Blue Spider. He was naked now, standing on the blanket he had spread over the sand. He was caressing his fat stomach.

"Come on," he said. "Get those clothes off, for Christ sake. We haven't got all night."

They made love and afterward she said, "Is that all?" It had happened so quickly, just a brief hard pain that spread upward into her chest, taking her breath away, and then nothing more.

"What do you mean, is that all?"

"I mean, should we go home now?"

"Oh, yeah," he said. And as he picked up the blanket and walked to the car, he added, "Hey, uh, thanks a lot."

"That's all right," she said.

They were silent as he drove her home.

*

Luke had been home for more than an hour. He had gone upstairs and sat, waiting, on Elissa's bed and then he had come down.

"Where is she?" he asked Beryl.

"She's out for a walk. She was too hot up there."

"Yeah, I hear she's hot up there. I hear she's hot down at the Blue Spider too."

"Who says?" He was drunk, she knew, but canny drunk. It was best not to antagonize him. "Men gossip," she said, "they just make things up."

"My own daughter, a friggin whore. I have to hear about it at the Oaks. My wife don't tell me. Oh no, she's helping her do it."

"Who said . . ."

"It's been going on for a year, they tell me. 'Hey, Gerriter,' he says to me, 'I hear your daughter's getting it plenty.' I call him a dirty liar and he says, 'No, it's true.' So I'm gonna punch him in the face and they tell me, 'No, Gerriter, it's true. She's down there every Saturday.' And there I was listening to them laugh about my own daughter. I'll teach her. I'll beat her to an inch of her life."

"I let her go. I'm the one. I said she could go as long as she got home before you did. So if you're gonna blame anybody, it's me."

"Yeah, I should beat you too. I should have years ago."

"You're not going to beat anybody, Luke Gerriter. Get that straight."

"I'm not gonna be made a fool of by my own daughter. I'm gonna teach her a lesson." He stormed into the kitchen and took a beer from the refrigerator. Beryl followed him. " 'She's getting it plenty,' he says to me."

"Don't you touch that girl."

"I'll touch anybody I goddamn please."

They stared at each other in silence for a moment, and then Luke took a long slug from the beer can.

Beryl spoke very slowly. "If you put a hand on her, I warn you, I'll kill you." She continued to stare at him for a moment, and then she went to the bedroom.

She sat by the window trembling. They had not fought for almost a year now, not since the day he had sent Elissa to her with the flowers. She had changed since then, she knew it. Something strange had happened inside her and she found herself, despite the stored anger between them, wanting him, wanting him with her in bed. She could not tell him this, but there were times when she ached, when she lay in bed listening to him snore and had to keep herself from going to his cot and saying, "Come to bed with me, I want you." And now it was all going to change again, within an hour, as soon as Elissa got home. She could foresee it, the accusations, the heavy hands, the screaming. She shook her head to clear it.

In the kitchen Luke had finished his beer and took down from the pantry shelf the bottle of whisky he kept there. He sat at the kitchen table and watched the whisky rise in the tumbler; he filled it only half full. He put his head on the table to rest, to wait for her. As the time passed and the whisky sank in the bottle he wept for himself as a betrayed father, for his daughter being used by filthy soldiers, for everything. He would grow angry and violent, pace around the kitchen, cursing and threatening to beat her half to death. And after a while he would sit down again. He dozed fitfully. By the time the small gray car turned off Finial Street onto the dirt road, Luke had finished most of the bottle and was thoroughly, violently, drunk.

*

The car stopped in front of the house and the two people inside sat there in silence. They had not spoken once since leaving the desert. Finally Len cleared his throat.

"Um, there's something I should tell you. I'm being shipped out soon."

"Oh." As if she had expected it.

"Yeah, this week. They're sending me overseas."

"Oh."

"Yeah. Maybe I should have told you before. Maybe you wouldn't have wanted to do it."

"No, that's all right," she said.

"Well, anyway, it was, um, great."

"Yes," she said.

She got out of the car and closed the door softly.

"See you around," he said and drove off, fast.

"That's all right," she said, and drifted toward the door, her hand at the shoulder of her torn blouse. Vaguely she noticed that the light was on behind the screen door. She couldn't breathe very well. She stopped by the evergreen tree, bending into its spiky branches to inhale the bitter smell. The screen door creaked, but she did not turn around.

Her head jerked sharply back and there was a tearing pain in her shoulder as Luke grabbed her arm from behind and pulled her into the light.

"Look at you, you whore, you pig," he said softly, staring at the curls and the makeup and the crimson slash at her mouth. He slapped her hard on the face. In the silence, the crack of his hand against her skin was like a gunshot, and involuntarily he drew away from her, hesitating for a moment. And then he saw the blouse. "Look, look!" he said. "Is that what happens in the cars, huh, they can't wait to get at you so they have to rip your clothes off."

Elissa backed away from him. He was crazy drunk. He might do anything.

"Or do you like it that way? Damned whore," he said, "some like it that way. Do you? Huh? Do you like it?" And with one hand he reached out and tore her blouse down the front. His anger grew as he looked at her. "Look at you," he screamed. "Look at you." He tore at her brassiere, and as she struggled it came loose in his hand. She stood stripped to the waist in the light shining through the screen door. "Whore," he said, "pig," and slapped at her breasts, pulling her closer and closer to him as they struggled. She was screaming, pushing him away, and he was calling her whore, whore, while his neck and chest heaved with the violence of what he was doing. He felt fists on his back and heard someone calling his name and them something struck his head.

"Luke, Luke," Beryl was saying. "Luke."

He took his hands from Elissa and turned, with the face of a stranger, to Beryl. He looked at her, confused.

"Get in the house," she said, her voice firm and low.

"She . . ." Luke said, pointing to his daughter.

"I know. Get in the house."

Luke went up the stairs slowly, bent like an old man, never having noticed the pistol in her hand.

Elissa and Beryl looked at one another, uncertain, questioning.

"Nothing happened, did it," Beryl said. Elissa continued to look at her. "Nothing happened," she insisted.

"No. Nothing happened."

"I know," Beryl said, "I know," and she threw her arms around the girl, sobbing uncontrollably. "Nothing happened. Nothing. Nothing happened."

VI

It was almost October and still the heat was unbearable. Luke wiped the sweat from his forehead with the back of his hand and then mopped his plate with a piece of bread, swooping on it to catch the drippings.

"How come she's sick again?" he asked. "What's the matter with her?"

Beryl pushed back her plate. "You want another beer?" She rose to get it.

"What's the matter with the kid?"

She placed the beer can at his side and sat down at the table facing him. "She's pregnant."

"Oh no," he said, and groaned.

"She told me this afternoon. She's over three months."

Luke sat staring at his empty plate, his hands at his head. After a minute Beryl saw his shoulders shake. He was crying.

"How do you think I felt?" she said. "I told her she's gonna be punished and good. I feel like she tore something right out of me, like she killed something I had, the only thing I had."

His shoulders shook again. He said nothing.

The clock ticked above the table. They could hear Pal upstairs, as his nails clicked against the wooden floor. Beryl glanced at the ceiling and waited for him to say something. Finally she couldn't stand the silence any longer.

"It's not yours," she said.

He looked up at her, shocked.

"It's not your baby. I asked her."

He shook his head and looked back down at his plate. In the three months that had passed since he beat Elissa, none of them ever mentioned what had happened.

"Well, I had to know, didn't I? After that . . ."

"Yes," he said. She could barely hear it.

"Do you want to know something? Do you?" There was fright in her voice, and he looked up at her finally.

"What?"

"Do you know what I felt first of all? I was jealous."

He stared at her.

"You don't know what it's been like," she said. "Oh Jesus, sometimes I want to just die."

"It's not mine," he said. "I was drunk that time. I didn't know what I was doing."

"I know," she said. "Nothing happened anyway. Nothing happened."

There was a long silence between them and, tentatively, she moved her arm forward on the table until her fingers touched his. He did not move away.

"Can I tell you something?" she said.

He moved one of his fingers against hers.

"Sometimes I want it now. With you."

After a long moment he took her hand in his. "Oh Christ," he said, "what a mess." And for the first time in years, they went to the bedroom to make love.

*

Upstairs Elissa lay in her bed, one arm across her stomach. She studied the boards in the slanted roof above her head, and whenever Pal put his muzzle against her, she scratched behind his ears. But she noticed nothing, was aware of nothing.

At first, after that night with Len, she had tried to understand what had happened. He didn't love her, she knew that, but that hadn't mattered. Not that he was going away either. It was something different. Everything seemed to have come to an end — the excitement of going to the Spider, men brushing against her, touching her, knowing that something was going to happen, that it was all going to be different. But nothing was going to be different now. By the time she discovered she was pregnant, not even that mattered very much. That seemed only to prove what she already knew. She was trapped forever in the sweltering heat, fighting for a breath of air.

*

Around midnight they awoke and made love once again. Luke collapsed against her, breathing hard, and then rolled away, half asleep already.

"She's got to be punished," Beryl said. "She's got to be taught a lesson."

"I'll shoot her dog," Luke said. "She loves the dog."

"No. No, that's not enough."

There was a moment of silence.

"I'll make her shoot it," he said.

"Tomorrow."

Before dawn Luke walked to town and borrowed the Garners' car. He was back before the sun was fully up. Beryl had prepared a large breakfast for them and they ate it, as they always did, in silence.

Afterward Beryl said, "I told your father."

"You got to be punished," he said. "You know that."

Elissa pushed her hair back from her face but said nothing.

"We're gonna shoot that dog of yours. You're gonna shoot it, that is."

Elissa nodded.

"Now you're gonna take us out to where he did it and you're gonna show us the exact spot, and then you're gonna shoot that dog."

"You killed something I had," Beryl said, "and now you're gonna do the same."

Elissa nodded. It was all crazy. Nothing mattered.

The sun was high when they passed the last of the farms and took the road to the airbase.

"Left here," Elissa said, numb. She stroked the dog and looked out the window. Miles and miles of sand, with the sun beating down. Nothing could live here.

"Where is it?" Luke said. "It must be around here somewhere."

How could you tell, she thought, everything was the same. In a few minutes she said, "Here. Here's the place."

They got out of the car and stood by it awkwardly, looking around them. No one would ever hear a gunshot out here. They walked a long distance from the car until Luke said, "Where are you going? I thought you said it was here."

"Yes, it is here. It's right here."

Luke drove a stake deep into the sand and tied the dog's leash to it. He walked five paces distant, readying the gun. He cocked it, examined the shells, snapped it shut. Only twenty-twos, but at such close range enough to kill a dog. He released the safety catch and handed Elissa the pistol.

"Do it," he said. "Do it or we just drive off and leave you. It's your punishment."

Luke and Beryl moved off and stood at a distance, watching.

Elissa looked at the pistol, turned it over in her hand, and then looked at Pal, who wagged his tail and tried to come to her. She looked up at the sky into the blinding sun and thought she saw a cloud coming, perhaps it meant rain, but it was just the sun against her eyes, and when she looked back at Pal she saw only a blazing dog shape against the sand. Slowly, evenly, she raised the small gun, placing the barrel firmly beneath her right ear.

The only sound in the desert was the dog whimpering in the terrible heat.

PHILLIP LOPATE

The Chamber Music Evening

(FROM THE PARIS REVIEW)

I

THE LIGHT THAT DRIPPED through the Venetian blinds was so inviting that the doctor, waking up, wanted to lick it like caramel syrup.

He slid away from the sheets, lowered his naked feet onto the rug and put on a flannel bathrobe with the idea of following this light out the door. Marlene was still asleep, face downward. Her broad shoulders had slipped past the lime-colored sheets.

He overcame the urge to study her asleep, knowing from past experience this would lead him to melancholy thoughts.

In the front hall, by the umbrella stand, the sunlight had made a sailboat out of a triangle and three parallel lines on the brown cork tiles.

Werner Hartmann stepped outside and heard the birds, the buds, a truck laboring uphill, gnashing its gears. All was blissful across the United States. Good day. Then he remembered the chamber music gathering that night, and felt a contraction, a pinch at the heart.

It was all because Geary, their violinist, had phoned the day before to say he couldn't make it. He had to pick up his wife's brother at the airport. Werner was upset; he had been looking forward to playing the Brahms piece and thought Geary was taking the group too casually. Either they would have to postpone the evening or else play trios. Then Annette, his oldest daughter, volunteered. Werner didn't know if she could handle it. She was only thirteen, a willing but not noticeably gifted musician. Furthermore, she had the habit of sticking her tongue out when she played. Her violin teacher had warned her he would not allow her to be in the music school recital unless she cured herself of this ridiculous habit.

Well, this would be a good experience for Annette. He phoned the others for their opinion and they thought it was a wonderful solution.

So today Annette was going to have her debut.

II

"Pick me up!"

Terry scooted over to her father as soon as she saw him in the garden. Annette, who had been playing a game of tether ball with her younger sister, followed chastely behind, her chinked eyes frowning from sunshine as she waited beneath the rope-swing and the dogwood tree.

"Pick me up!" demanded Terry.

"There goes my gardening," said Hartmann. He was more amused than put out. His chest hairs tickled Terry as he lifted her with his bony arms. She got right up close to his face to see it as if for the first time: the crusty brown pores, flabby lips and crag of a nose with its nostril hairs at the entrance of the cave, and the omniscient eyes, alien, watery blue, that looked into hers from a distance that could never be crossed. "Hee-hee," she laughed apprehensively.

Higher she rose, and now it was perfect. She giggled and her cheeks bloomed. "Once . . . twice . . . thrice!" he pretended to drop her, and let her gently down.

"Again. This time a piggyback ride."

From her kitchen window Marlene Hartmann laughed to herself at Terry's directness. Pick me up! She knew just what she wanted, that girl. Heaven for her would be to swing in Daddy's arms forever. But see how Annette hung back, already with that adult's look of missing out. Maybe she thought she was getting too old for Daddy's pickmeups.

Werner had a tightening sensation and immediately straightened his shoulders for Terry to slide down.

"That's enough," he grumbled.

Terry pulled a long face.

"No more now, no more."

"Why don't you give Annette a turn?" Marlene called from the back door. "I think she wants a piggy ride too!"

The girls were stunned that their mother had been "spying" on them. Hearing her tensely gay accent Annette made a sarcastic face. In fact she was glad someone had noticed her hovering and hovering, with her arms folded across her chest like a crushed bird.

"Well come here Annie! Soon you'll be too heavy for me. One two three four Alley Oop!"

Annette closed her eyes and went limp. She thought she smelled the white dogwood blossoms growing on the higher branches.

"Come on, let's finish the tether ball game, Terry. I'm winning 18–7."

"Okay, but one more pickmeup." Terry ran to her father's knees and hugged them.

"Kids, let your father have some peace. I'm sure he doesn't want you in his hair all Sunday."

"We were *going*, mother," Annette said.

"Well I should say so. Gosh, what a tone of voice!" Mrs. Hartmann said.

Her husband waved to her. He looked so charming in his new goatee. She fancied him as a German courtier: distinguished, cultured, handsome to the ladies, a shade of melancholy. She remembered his face when it had been suffering but now that vulnerability was losing ground to the warm fatherly fuzz of his beard, and a good thing too; perhaps she could relax and stop worrying about his discontent — begin to think of her own satisfaction more.

"Breakfast is in five minutes, okay?" Marlene called out.

"Très bien."

III

At breakfast Hartmann had it on the tip of his tongue to suggest that Annette practice. But Terry was keeping everyone in stitches with her babble and he decided not to darken the mood. He would suggest it later on, but casually.

Werner scanned his subscriber brochure of radio listings. Grieg, Prokofiev, Schubert . . . Sunday fare. There would be an interesting discussion at 4:30. By that time they would probably have left for a walk.

He switched on the program: it was his habit to leave this station on all day Sunday, good or bad. Then he sat in his favorite chair and reached by instinct for the new periodicals. There were the scholarly journals that he told himself he should catch up with, but instead he opened a magazine that had nothing to do with his field. It was a journal of political thought which he noticed seemed every year to get fatter and more infrequent.

The double issue at hand was a collection of essays on the blue-collar worker. Turning pages, sensing the tone, Hartmann felt an older brother's protective indulgence for the Left. There was something so touching about these writers with their *gymnasium* faith in correct analysis; their lyrical trills when they came to expose the true enemy; their controlled anger, hissing underneath the dialectics like a delayed fuse under a rock.

He remembered now his Communist days, the general meetings at Köln, standing up in back to hear, the perennial stray dogs moving among the crowd. The first classes he gave as an instructor, all that came back, and suddenly the memory of the Gestapo ringing his house, and his walking calmly through the troops with an ear-flapped cap over his head. Was it his blue eyes that deceived them? Or the worker's cap? To walk past Death as casually as going through a turnstile, when so many, so many he knew were unlucky . . .

They had hidden him in the cellar of a rectory for a year. In Holland. A low-ceilinged room lit by naphtha lamp, with nothing to read but sermons. It was not a bad year. His mind reached a sort of stillness. He would have accepted whatever happened to him. Gestapo or liberation. He thought that if he ever survived he would like to give up university life and earn his bread with his hands, as a bookbinder or gardener.

And now look! He had turned up like a rabbit in a strange country and was making good money for an intellectual. This country respected European brains. They paid you well to spin out theories. He enjoyed the American comfort of life, the natural grandeur of the forests and the continental sunsets. But deep in his heart he longed for some strong conversation. The people who surrounded him seemed like white bread, inexcusably bland.

IV

Hartmann had had a puzzling research career. He had always been interested in unexplained phenomena, those stepchildren considered beneath the attention of medical science. Faith healing and the laying of hands engaged him for a time. Then ritual fasting. Then he moved on to the ability to discern color through touch. Now he was investigating placebos.

It was not that he believed any of these approaches should necessarily be adopted. No, what excited him was just the delusional, the imaginative underside of the idea. When this had faded he let the research slide, not without leaving behind a slim article arguing that the evidence was "inconclusive" while chiding the medical establishment for its dogmatic neglect of the subject.

His more powerful emigrant friends were perplexed but continued to help him get grants. They still believed he would make a contribution. Certain other colleagues welcomed his conversation at lunch and appreciated his skepticism, but now there was the tiniest condescension accorded someone whose obsession with integrity begins to seem part of a pattern of self-defeatism. Poor Hartmann! He lacked the blind spot, the childishness necessary for deep enthusiasm. Whenever people urged him to publish more in the scientific journals, or better yet, write a book, Hartmann always answered:

"Why should I add to the rubbish in print? The world has seen enough half-baked nonsense already."

He was fifty. He still had fifteen years to come up with a good idea.

V

"Oh no Regina you peed all over the floor. Stop that — bad dog. Look at this flood! And I just mopped up half an hour ago."

"I'll mop up, mother."

"You bet you will. I would appreciate it. I must go to Shopwell for tonight. — Come, out of the kitchen, Regina. Such bad manners to pee on the floor. Are you so old and senile you can't hold it in?" Marlene dragged the dog through the kitchen door and then stopped back in the living room.

"What do you think would be nice to serve them? I was planning some ice cream and fruit. How does that sound?"

"Fine."

"What kind of fruit, do you think?"

"Mhm . . ." he pointed to the fireplace.

"Maybe a salad would be better. A nice garden salad on a summer night?"

"A salad would be excellent too."

"What kind of salad? Fish or ham?"

A bird was warbling nearby, the same repeated call: two long ascending notes and eight short pips.

"Fish," said Hartmann.

"Then I'll have to go buy some. I have ham in the house but no fish."

"Use ham instead, Leni, it makes no difference. It's silly for you to go out of your way."

"Not at all! I was planning to go to Shopwell anyway. Did you see how Regina leaked all over this morning?"

"I heard . . ." Werner began warmly. But he realized he had nothing to add.

"Disgusting, hmm?" said Marlene with a flirtatious laugh that puzzled him and reminded him of something. What was it? he wondered.

Probably she just wanted to make contact.

A moment later his wife was back.

"Black bread! That's what Klausner likes. I could pick up some fresh warm pumpernickel at the bakery in Georgetown. Warm black bread and sweet butter. Mmmm . . . That's lovely. That will be a treat for all of us."

"Ya. Sit down and rest for a minute."

"I don't have time to rest," Marlene laughed ironically. "Who's going to make lunch? And someone has to see that Terry gets her room clean."

Werner's brows were furrowed, as if trying hard to understand.

"And then I must do a wash so you can have shirts tomorrow."

"Terry!" he called out.

"Wait a second."

"No waiting, you come here when Daddy calls," said Marlene.

Terry wobbled in on high heels and an old-fashioned floppy hat.

"Excuse, gutt afternoon, I am just goink for a valk. Could you tell me von der vich vay to the zooo?"

"Sprechen Sie Deutsch?" asked Werner, bending down to her level.

"Natürlich," Terry rolled her eyes.

"Gosh! She's such a scream when she puts on that German," said Marlene. "Where did you get those *earrings?*"

"Excuse, ein moment," Annette ran in, "this lady has stolen my purse!"

"No, I want to be Grandma," Terry whined.

"You can be Grandma in a minute, I promise," said Annette.

"No, I'm the only Grandma, look!" Terry said, and struck two throw pillows under her shirt.

"What a riot! — Hey kids, your room must be upside down with those costumes. Go and tidy up."

"My room is perfectly neat."

"Terry, go and clean right now," her father commanded.

"Awl right."

Terry sloshed off in her high heels.

"And you too, Annette."

"Aber der *my* room is zo clean you could lick off der floor."

"Stop it now. The joke is wearing thin."

"Boy," Annette muttered. It was a curious thing, this business of jokes wearing thin. Sometimes they could go on with the joking for a long, long while, and both parents would be laughing; and then suddenly they would say it had gone too far.

Presently Mrs. Hartmann left the living room. Annette sat down on the fireplace stones, looking into the grating. Then she reached for her novel and opened it into her lap. She wore a brown wrap-around skirt and a heather sweater. Her bosom was already well-developed.

"What are you reading?" Annette asked her father.

"An article on American factories."

"Is it good?"

"Mm, fair . . . What are you reading?" he asked politely.

"*Wuthering Heights.*"

"Didn't you finish that yet?"

"I've read it twice. I like it."

Werner returned to his article.

"I'm reading it again for a book report," explained Annette.

"When you finish maybe you can try something different. Have you tried *Arrowsmith?*"

"Who's that by?"

"Sinclair Lewis," Werner said with subdued irritation.

"Oh, right. Didn't you bring that to me once from the library?"

"I did, and you let it sit around for three weeks."

"I had to read another book for school. *Microbe Hunters.* If you bring it again I promise I'll read it."

"No, I'm not getting it out for you. This time you get it out yourself," Werner said coldly.

Annette shrugged. She returned to her book, and he to his magazine. She read another chapter, though it was difficult to concentrate.

"There are books in the house already that you could read. Have you looked at those short story collections in the bookcase?"

"Uh huh. I couldn't get into them," said Annette.

"De Maupassant you couldn't get into?!"

"Which one was he?"

Werner almost lost his temper. Was she purposely being obtuse with that flippant tone of hers? Maybe he was wasting his time trying to educate her. He looked at the article — to return to it would be the most inviting course. "Bring me the volume of short stories from the bookcase."

Annette obeyed immediately. "The de Maupassant or the *250 Great Short Stories?*"

Werner reflected. "The *250 Great Short Stories.*"

The book was hardbound and very heavy. Hugging it against her chest like a leaded anchor, Annette felt she was going underwater. She meekly placed it on the end table by his arm. Hartmann opened it to the contents page. His eye ran down the listing, and the sight of some old friends gave him comfort and professional pleasure.

"Get me a pencil, please. I'll check off the ones I think are good."

She fetched a pen for him from the dining room address book.

"Conrad . . . de Maupassant . . . Poe . . . Kipling . . .

Mérimée . . . Faulkner . . . Flaubert . . . And here's an excellent little-known writer, Heinrich von Kleist. Have you heard of him?"

Annette nodded. He could not tell if she were telling the truth or not.

"I'm surprised they put him in here. A double check for Kleist. Who else? . . . Gorki . . . Jack London? He is more of a journalist. I remember enjoying his stories as a boy. I'm not sure how I'd feel about them now. I'll check London, too."

He handed the book back to her. Suddenly she wanted to get rid of it as fast as she could. She looked wishfully at the bookcase; if she put it back she knew her father would be annoyed. But she didn't like to have it next to her. "I'll just keep this in my room," said Annette.

"Mhm." A silence fell, like a sip of red wine. Instead of going out Annette waited, hung on for something more.

"By the way," Werner said, "you might practice a little the Brahms for tonight."

"I practiced it, Daddy!"

"You did? I must not have heard it."

"I practiced when you were gone yesterday. I've been practicing it all week. Remember?"

"I don't remember . . ." He wanted to tell her to practice it this time in his hearing. But he controlled himself. The best performance would come if she felt relaxed. He might tend to be a perfectionist in music; there was no point forcing her to overrehearse. Nevertheless, the worry showed on his jowled face. "Did you find it manageable or difficult?"

"A little difficult. — Daddy, do you think I could ever be a violinist?"

"That depends." Werner filled his pipe bowl slowly with tobacco.

"Depends on *what*?" Annette said exasperatedly.

"If you were to take it more seriously you might. Most professional violinists practice five or six hours a day."

"What I meant is, do you think I have the talent to become one — even if I practiced six hours a day?"

Werner thought it over. "Music is a very hard life."

Annette squinched up her nose.

"Well you asked me my opinion. If you want me to say just what you would like to hear — "

"I don't care what you say."

"Lucky for you. That makes you very independent."

"Pffffffft — !"

I'm always offending her, he thought. The younger one is brazen but you have to laugh. There's something jolly, healthy about Terry. This one gets her back up so easily. She's poisoned with my melancholy.

"I'm going out to the garden," Werner announced.

VI

The sun had recently come out. A cloud had just passed over the land and was sweeping in dips toward the Potomac. Through a V of cleared foliage the hill could be seen with its alternations of light and shadow, each farm patiently waiting its turn.

Werner stationed his garden chair in front of the clearing, his back to the house, in order to get the most distant view. As a result of clever landscaping one could imagine their land stretched for miles over rolling plains, though actually this plot held no more than half an acre.

The tiger lilies had come out marvelously this year.

Ah! . . . Let them say what they want, let them do what they want. As long as they leave me this beautiful garden to look at, this warm sky, this *earth*.

A noise shook the grass behind him. He was afraid it might be a human but it was only Regina waddling up for affection. Werner dug his fingernails into the dog's shaggy mat. The animal sighed and Werner widened his massage, letting his fingertips soak up the heat, losing his train of thought, guided only by the whirlpool of muscles, indulging himself on flesh.

Werner hoped no one could see him. Then he began to wish that someone would take notice of his popularity with the dog, he who had always felt estranged from the natural.

"How much easier life is when there are all these living things around us — children, flowers, animals. How much lighter, how much heavier the burden! Look how grateful Regina is. I am such a success with her. She asks to be petted, I do, and she is happy. Terry asks to be picked up. I do, and she is happy. Incredible!"

Just then an extraordinary sweep of light and shade came over the garden. He rose automatically. In that gust of wind the twigs seemed to stand out against the trees with iron clarity. Accents of sunspots were strewn over the grounds like drops of rain after an electrical storm. Each blade of grass and each pine cone seemed to have shivered into its final outline. This must be how Adam saw, Werner thought.

He had known such bountiful moments in Nature before, when attentiveness came as easily as breathing and everything smelled very grand and he knew they didn't last longer than a half-hour . . . even so, even so, he thought stubbornly, this was all happening and it was marvelous, marvelous.

Marvelous, marvelous, he kept repeating, hoping to prolong it. Already he felt the blood was draining from the scene, the crispness was retreating. He listened to his heavy breathing, the sharp bird noises . . . If heaven were to speak to him now he would not miss the signal.

Maybe an angel passing overhead would be lured by his antennae.

No?

He thought of Rilke, and of the passage in *Duino Elegies* about going through life with the attitude of always lingering, forever taking leave. "So leben wir und nehmen immer Abschied."

Well, I've had my moment of happiness for the day.

His neighbor on the right side, Purdy, came out with a hose to give his garden a sprinkle. Mr. Purdy was a lanky businessman with white hair that rose in a dependable cowlick. He had shrewd common sense, Werner had decided once, but he liked to play dumber than he was.

Werner was in the mood to talk now and strolled over.

"Afternoon . . ." Mr. Purdy said. "I see you been puttering around in your garden here."

"Yes I was trying to, but I puttered so much that my engine went kaputt."

"Oh ho, yes."

"And now I must put away my putter," Werner nodded sagely.

A silence arose. Purdy seemed to have forgotten he was talking to anyone. His eyes took in the tricycle, bicycle and other hardware of his neighbor's yard.

"You have a sun tan. You have been away for a while?" Werner brought him back politely.

"Yes . . . on a business trip, to Austin, Texas. Had myself a ball. Say have you got a number five spade I can borra?" Purdy asked in his Maryland drawl.

"A number five spade, a spade," Werner tapped his forehead. "Hmm . . ." He was eager to oblige in some way. Rarely did any of his neighbors ask him for a favor and he took it as a sign of growing community acceptance. But he knew he had no such article, so his mind began to work the answer into a joke, possibly: No I haven't — to call a spade a spade. His clouded face had already given Purdy the answer.

"Thanks anyhow. I'll just drive down to Sears and pick up a new one."

"And what are you planning to plant?" Werner asked.

"Well there's a good question!" Purdy said with a hint of fun in his eye. "It depends on if we get the cabbage in soon so's we can utilize the patch by the side of the house, because Mrs. Purdy wants tomaters and I'm thinking we can diversify over by that fence. That is if there aren't so many rabbits as we had last year. But even if they're back I got a little surprise for them. You see that metal thingamajob over there?" Purdy went into an explanation of catching rabbits and the varieties of fertilizers that passed over Werner's head.

Werner gave himself over to staring shamelessly at his neighbor's Adam's apple. It had a loose flap of gooseflesh that slid up and down every time Purdy took a swallow. This man is priceless, thought Werner.

Finally Purdy's mouth went dry and he turned to hook up his rubber snake.

Werner hurried inside to tell his wife. "I have just been talking with Mr. Purdy — " he announced. Marlene was not immediately visible. Soon she came up the basement stairs carrying the wash basket. She brushed past him and into the kitchen.

Werner pursued her with his juicy anecdote. "I have had a most interesting tête-à-tête with our neighbor Purdy," he said suspensefully.

"Yes? What did he have to say?"

"He was giving me a course of instruction on the uses of fertilizer. You can't believe how he went on. I know he is a salesman for a living but I never knew what he sold. Perhaps it's fertilizer."

"I should think so, with that smelly garden. — Lunch is now. Can you call the girls?"

"Terry! Annette!"

"What?" Annette stuck her head in mistrustfully.

"Your mother informs me that we are to eat lunch. Please kindly join us ladies . . ."

VII

The children took chairs on one side of the maple table, which was large even without the center leaf, and barren except for four straw Mexican place mats. The girls were banging their forks on the place mats. Werner sat at the head of the table, absently watching them.

"You weren't supposed to tell Mommy we were saving for her present," Annette said.

"Oh yeah? Well you're the one who made me tell her!"

Marlene called from the kitchen: "Who will give me a hand to bring in the food?"

Annette looked at Terry. "Your turn."

"What??"

"You remember I had to dry dishes this morning."

"Okay, okay," Terry said and went inside.

Werner tapped the table to get his daughter's attention. She would appreciate the story about Purdy.

"Do you know Purdy our next door neighbor? Well he is starting to speak freely with me. For the first time we had a decent chat . . ."

"Thank you for being so polite!" cried Marlene as she struggled in with a large dish. Werner cleared his throat and helped her set it down. "Help yourself. There is some leftover macaroni salad also if anybody wants it. You can start on the jam and peanut butter and cheese."

"Peepee butter," Terry said brightly.

"Pass down the cheese, please?"

"I don't want no peepee peanut butter mommy."

"That's enough. What kind of nonsense is that to talk at the table."

"Me no talkee nonsense," Terry said solemnly like a movie Indian.

Her mother laughed in spite of herself. "Who would like some milk?"

"Mommy, you should hear the way Susan Edmonds does it. She was teaching us at Brownies. 'I no is crazy. No I me.'"

"I'm not surprised she teaches you it. Such trash, that Brownies!" said Marlene Hartmann, leaping up to fetch something.

"Why do you call it trash, Mother?" Annette challenged her.

"It's rubbish, that's why. Trashy is common, low, worthless. Darling, would you like some wine?"

Hartmann shook his head. He had fallen into a bad mood. It was childish he realized, just because they interrupted his story!

"What's the matter?" asked Marlene.

"Sit down. I've been waiting for you to eat with us."

"Oh I? I eat when everyone is finished!" Nevertheless she sat down. "Who would like some more bread?"

"I would!" said Annette.

"Of course you would! Here, help yourself, but go easy on the slices. You watch your figure, girl. You don't want to get like Mommy do you? Gosh I am on a diet and I can't eat a thing! Now who would like the rest of the macaroni salad?"

"No thanks," said Terry.

"It's a pity then," said Marlene. "I'll have to give it to Regina. And she gets so fat she won't be able to waddle from the kitchen to the bathroom. Poor Regina, under the table — maybe she would like to join us for a meal! What do you say, Regina? Look how she always goes to Daddy. Clever dog, she knows who is the master. Mhm, what a gorgeous day outside. It's a shame we didn't eat on the patio. So much more fun to take meals in Nature! Who wants to be stuck inside on a day like this. We should go for an excursion.

I have an idea, kids, listen. Please stop that for one second. Who
would like to take a ride this afternoon?"

"I would," said Annette.

"Me two. Me three," said Terry. "Me four."

"Wonderful! Maybe you can ask Daddy if he takes you."

"Yes if you like," Werner said. "I could take them to the mu-
seum of the woods."

"Mu-seum!" Terry wiggled up her nose. "Every time we go anywhere it's the museum."

"You could go to the old canal," said Marlene.

"*That's* no fun, the canal."

"No we can have a nice time," Annette poked her sister. "Come
on Terry, say the canal."

Terry refused to budge.

"Is there anything for dessert?" asked Hartmann.

"There's fruit and cheese."

"We had cheese for lunch. That's not dessert," exclaimed Annette.

"You don't have to take it if you don't want it! In Europe it's
considered a very elegant dessert."

Annette shrugged off this statement. "So what happened with
Purdy?" she turned to her father.

"Yes, you never told us that story," Marlene said.

"He is going to lay traps in the backyard to kill the rabbits."

"Barbarian!" exclaimed Marlene.

"Why is he a barbarian?" Annette asked.

"Will you let me continue? . . . He thinks the rabbits are coming from a farm coop on Muehlenhill Drive. And that the owner
opens the cages at night because he doesn't like the small home-
owners. Purdy suggests that everyone in our row buy rabbit traps
and leave them at the fence."

"I wouldn't dream of it!" Marlene said. "Think if Regina gets
hurt."

"Yet I enjoyed talking to him. You get an idea what America
must have been like. He is unique, Purdy, a vanishing type of
Americana."

"What do they do with the rabbits when they kill them?" asked
Terry.

"They cook them in a stew. Hasenpfeffer. Very tasty."

"Yuck! I wouldn't eat that if you paid me *ten dollars*."

"You might change your mind someday," said Werner, taking a peach from the fruit basket.

The discussion seemed to have reached its end, when Terry muttered: "He'd kill a rabbit just for some old lettuce!"

"Lettuce means cash, no?" Marlene remarked. "In this country they worship cash, it's only natural they kill for their God."

"I don't think Germany's any better," Annette injected.

"No, Germany is worse! There's no comparison. Germans are very greedy, certainly. But at least in Germany they don't destroy the natural beauty for a few extra dollars."

"That's ridiculous," said Annette scornfully.

"You may not agree, that doesn't make me ridiculous! . . . Besides, when were you in Germany, miss?"

"I read an article that said Germany was one of the greatest polluters in the world. And that some of their big lakes are already dead."

"Where was this article?"

"In the *Christian Science Monitor*."

"I never heard of such a magazine."

"Oh mother, you don't know what you're talking about! Right, the students are protesting because the German rivers are being polluted and the forests are getting cut down?" Annette asked her father.

"That is unfortunately correct," said Hartmann, who had been keeping out of it.

"I thought it was true for the cities," Marlene said doggedly, her voice catching, "but that they had a plan for protecting the countryside."

"What plan? You think everything is trashy over here and it's all perfect in Germany, Germany! You don't know."

"I know you don't talk to your parent that way. Go to your room," Marlene blurted out. She fled the table instead. They could hear her sniffling in the kitchen.

Annette looked ashamed of herself. "I'm sorry. I'm really sorry." Then she went into her room to begin her exile.

Werner and Terry were left alone at the table. Neither particularly wanted to look at the other.

"Golly!" said Terry. "I didn't even expect that."

Her father gave his assent, as if to say: I know, you didn't have any part in it.

VIII

Marlene was loudly weeping in the kitchen. For about twenty seconds he considered not going in to her. Then he picked himself up. She was not just crying but efficiently cutting a tomato at the same time, the blade pressing through the tomato and stopping just short of her thumb. Werner found her very lovable in this mode. He came up behind her and wrapped his arms around her waist. He could feel her thighs through the apron.

She turned around and her face was dripping with tears. She's like a mango, he thought, when you squeeze her the juice runs out. How amazing that mysterious wetness, like her vagina which is always sopping every time I go to touch it.

"Marlene, Marlene," he rocked her.

"Did you see what she said to me? Oh, you wouldn't let it upset you! To be talked to so cruelly by your own daughter."

"I understand. But listen, you shouldn't allow yourself to be dragged down to the level of a thirteen year old. — I agree, she shouldn't have said that to you. I'm only saying she's an immature child and if you consider that you won't get as hurt by her."

"She has such a cutting tongue, you don't know!" said Marlene, wiping her eyes with her apron string. "It's easy for you to ignore it. She's always polite with you. Mother is fair game though."

He sensed her crying spring was about to run down. He put his arms around her; but just this tenderness set her off again.

"What hurts, what hurts the most is that they learn it from *you.* You are always being so clever and I'm the idiot. Mother is a fool, that's what *you* think of me. You stick up for her. What do I know? I'm a common housewife. Is it my fault my education was stopped by the war, that I married so young and to someone who was smarter than me?"

He had no easy words to answer her. I could agree, thought Werner; I could poke holes in her statement, I could find exceptions, historical reasons. *In the end I am powerless to take away certain kinds of inequalities.*

Werner stayed with her a long while near the sink. It was getting cloudier outside. Soon they would drive out to buy ice cream, and maybe take a walk along the canal, and get home just in time to start receiving company, and something else would happen, and something else, and they would forget what had made them cry two hours earlier. That was the real sorrow. One activity was always following the next, taking them further along a path that was never explained, further away from some point back there that never got cleared up. One's spirits lifted and collapsed a dozen times a day with no fidelity to up or down. From upstairs came the sound of a violin being practiced.

Marlene blew her nose. Then the family drove out to the Potomac Canal.

IX

"Geary could not make it, eh?"

"No Geary had to pick up his wife's brother at the airport."

"So this young lady will be our violin master. *Enchanté de vous avoir dans notre ensemble.* You understand French? Geary should be careful," Klausner winked at Werner. "He may come back next week and find he has lost his seat."

"If you heard me play you wouldn't say that."

"We shall see tonight. Your father says you are the new Heifetz."

"She will do well. Come, have some food," said Werner. "Marlene has gone out and gotten *Schwartzbrod* especially for you. I think you have made a conquest."

"At my age I have my doubts." Klausner followed his friend into the dining room. He was a great-shouldered, bullish man, with a plodding walk, a psychoanalyst. At the cello he was a pillar of strength.

"Mar-lay-na!" he pronounced it, kissing her hand. "You are looking so lovely tonight if I were ten years younger I would not let you stay with this rotten man."

"And your eyes are getting weaker!" Marlene laughed. The doorbell rang again.

"Stanley, I'll bet," said Hartmann.

Stanley and Joy Morrison came into the dining room. He was

tall as a basketball player, with black-rimmed glasses and a slow grin. His shirt pulled tensely against his bony shoulders when he put his big hand forward to shake hands. He and his wife worked at the Department of Health, Education and Welfare. They were in group therapy together and had recently joined a nudist colony. Stanley, at thirty-five, was the youngest member of the quartet, capable of beautiful playing, but insecure, and hence the weakest link.

"Your front door is open," he observed.

"We leave it open for wandering gypsy violists," said Werner. "Have a chair. Have some Camembert."

"Joy, what happiness it is to see you," Klausner exclaimed, "particularly for an old Freudian like me."

"Why do you keep saying that?" asked Joy.

"Because Freude means *joy* in German, get it?" said Stanley.

"White wine anyone? — to wash away the taste of Klausner's bad puns." Werner filled the glasses with great zest.

"Aren't you going to offer any to our violinist?" Morrison nudged him. "What are you, an adult chauvinist?"

"No, but I am cautious just the same. — Here Annette, have a little."

"Oh, more than that!" Annette exclaimed. Everyone laughed.

"Refills?" Werner asked after a silence of some moments.

"Any more for me and I'll make Brahms sound like — "

"Boogie Woogie!" Klausner finished Stanley's sentence.

"That would be nice for a change," said Marlene.

"How's the research business, Werner?" asked Stanley.

"So-so. And you, are you doing anything for my welfare? What about my health and education? I keep expecting you to pull some strings with the President."

"No . . . It's only old Hans here who's saving any souls."

"Not so!" said Klausner. "Just last week I let two of my patients go crazy."

Everyone laughed, Klausner heartiest of all. Marlene Hartmann smiled to herself; she loved the sound of laughter in her house, and had a special affection for Klausner.

"Well, shall we start?" said Werner. They moved into the living room, where four wooden folding chairs had been set up facing the orange couch.

"I was looking over the Brahms score this morning and I noticed," said Stanley, "that Brahms has the habit of making the tempi difficult for amateurs — "

"Brahms has no longer any habits," Klausner interjected. "Except decomposition."

"Which is rather peculiar for a composer," added Werner.

"On that note . . ." Stanley said gamely, sitting down and taking his viola out of the case.

They began to tune up. It was the moment when each man had to go into himself, leaving the social comfort behind. Stanley frowned and listened to his tone; Klausner, bowing, stared into space; at the piano Werner's profile had turned into the outline of severe nobility.

"We will start off with the Mozart trio," he said calmly to Annette, "and then the Brahms. You can tune up now or later."

"I'd rather later."

"Fine. Would you like to be my page turner for the Mozart?"

"All right. That will give me something to do. — I'm so nervous!" she whispered to him.

"That goes away," he whispered back. "Remember, keep your tongue in."

"I will!" she said, and laughed ruefully.

"What's the order?" asked Stanley.

"I thought first the Mozart piano trio, to warm up, then Brahms' third quartet, then solos if anyone wants, then if we have time, another trio, the Haydn we did before. How does that sound?"

Klausner nodded. It was assumed that Hartmann would make those decisions. Though not necessarily the best musician, he was the guiding spirit of the group, its backbone.

Werner gave the signal with his chin to begin. Stanley was there from the first note. Klausner liked to hold back, to let the other players set the scene, and move cautiously in and around their energy. Then when he felt rooted in the piece, he would charge like a buffalo and everyone would go flying to the end. That Klausner loves to steal the show, thought Marlene.

"Soon you should go to bed, you have school tomorrow," Marlene remarked to her younger daughter.

"I want to see Annette play."

"Of course you'll see Annette play." Her mother was touched

by this loyalty. They were learning to be friends, those two. Such
flowing music! Lovely. Like mountain springs when the snow
melts . . . Interesting how Stanley and Klausner always look down
at their instruments, while Werner keeps nodding to them and giving quick glances in their direction. That funny giving-approval
with his chin. He was not always so attentive to the people around
him. And look at Annette — leaning like a swan over the piano to
turn the pages. That girl has such a beautiful neck! Where did she
get it from? Not Werner or herself, it must be Grandma Hartmann. What a pity she wears her hair wild and keeps it hidden.
Tonight she looked very neat with the brown tortoise-shell barrette.
Barrettes are such funny things. Father and daughter in a space of
their own. How she bends down to turn the pages, practically
putting her breasts in Werner's mouth! Does he notice it I wonder?
Of course he notices it. The way she parades around him in her
slip, sitting in front of him with her legs open and panties showing.
I'm jealous of my daughter! Silly! Of course, she's younger and
prettier than me. Werner is surrounded by women. Poor man, it
must be a strain on him. Sometimes I think we give him too much
love. He feels stifled. But I can't help myself — how can I hold
back my feelings? When I see him I feel so grateful. Every day I
can have him in the same house with me I want to say it's a miracle. Ridiculous! You'd think by now I would take him for granted.
But he's so impressive-looking. You see how the other women are
drawn to him. Joy as well. Ich! I love him so much more than he
loves me, it's pathetic. If I were to hold back more but I can't.
He's getting tired of me. Certainly, I can't stimulate him enough.
I'm no intellectual. He talks to Annette before he talks to me. I
am like a visitor in my own house. Gosh, my eyes are getting wet.
This music makes me so sad. It's like that other one, who proposed
to me on the lake. I didn't understand what he wanted! Crazy girl
— just seventeen. I asked Mother what it was all about and she
said I was much too young. He had such strange unhappy eyes:
that's what sticks with me. And later on he went off and committed
suicide. But certainly not because of me! I wonder what both men,
so sensitive and educated, saw in me. Was it something they made
up? Was it that they needed a hausfrau who was practical and
down to earth? To balance their soaring? Maybe I did look "mysterious" at one time, the way my lip hung down in the old photo-

graphs. Now I don't think I'm specially attractive at forty. It's Werner who draws people to the house. All these brilliant people, our social circle, the group tonight — of course they made small talk with me at the table but they don't care anything about me. If Werner were to die before me they would see me a few times out of courtesy, and then I will be thrown back on myself. Gosh, how lonely that will be! And why do I keep thinking he will die before me? Now I must hold back the tears. It's over. Everyone will be looking round. How did the piece go so fast? Good music is such a treat for me, but I always think about something else! Next time I must really listen to every note.

"Anyone for some coffee?" She jumped up. "You must be thirsty, you musicians. That was marvelous!"

"Bravo," Joy Morrison called out. She followed Marlene into the kitchen. "Can I help you with the dishes?"

"No, everything's taken care of."

Joy lingered all the same. Then she moved to help Marlene lift the tray — which was quite light to begin with. Not because I can't manage, thought Marlene, but for her own conscience. I should really invent some task for her to do. If I were nice. But I'm not feeling so nice toward her.

As she passed the kitchen doorway Joy stopped her to confide. "I feel foolish sitting there and clapping at the end, don't you?"

"Foolish, why?"

"Because it's making believe that we're the audience — an audience all of three — when really they're playing for each other. We're just eavesdroppers. I don't know, it makes me mad."

"That's interesting. I'm not sure I see what you mean," said Marlene.

"Well skip it," Joy murmured. "Probably making a mountain out of a molehill."

Coffee mugs were passed around and again the players tuned their instruments. This time Annette joined them. Annette went over the score: it was the C minor piano quartet. The first movement was allegro non troppo, the second a scherzo, the third andante — which was good because by that time she would need a rest — and the fourth allegro again. How convenient that the slow part came in the middle! She wished the whole thing was andante. Stanley gave her a wink, as if to say: Just stick with me!

"I'm all ready," she said.

Her father nodded and hit the first note with such incredible firmness his finger almost went through the keyboard. The beginning was fairly somber: she wasn't going to try any fancy phrasing, if she kept up that was enough. Daddy was giving her approving nods, so far, so good. She looked across for one second at her father's hands: they were like knotted roots growing from a tree. She knew their feel when he took hold of her hand on a walk, their special temperature. How I hate him sometimes, but I always love his hands. Elbow's up! She hadn't made one mistake yet. I'm going to have to make a mistake soon. This next part is where I always make the mistake. I feel like I'm on the merry-go-round and can't get off. I have to make a mistake soon. It's coming up, it's coming up, one bar away, train going around the curve. I got it! Now let's see if I make this next one. This part is too hard for me. They can't expect me to do this, this is getting too fast for me. This is a nightmare . . . Why am I putting myself through this? Oh, first mistake! (Hartmann winced at the sour note but nobody else seemed bothered.)

He doesn't like it when I mess up. But I like it. I'm going to mess up some more before this is over. I'm only thirteen years old! Funny that time we played the duet and I goofed on the last note. Boy, was he upset. Why do I always do that? I know why.

Terry waved at her and she lowered her eyes. Her fingers were swelling from the tension of the bow. Her forehead was hot; her nostrils itched. She tried to scratch her nose and bring the bow back in time but lost the rhythm. Don't think about that mistake, just let it go by. If you get stuck you'll never be able to find your place again. But that mistake was so interesting! It was like watching a glass roll off the table and knowing and knowing and not being able to stop it. Those are my favorite kinds of mistakes.

Why was Stanley smiling at her so weirdly? Through those goggly glasses. He was a friendly one.

Annette rolled her eyes in mock exhaustion: Difficult, whew! Stanley returned the expression: Impossible! Klausner noticed their clowning and made a wry jab at them with the bow. You two are having fun, his bushy eyebrows said: What about me? Klausner played the next phrase in such a way that Annette imagined it was for her benefit. She could not say what made it stand out, but it

was somehow droll, as if placed in quotes. She looked sideways at
Klausner and tried to play the same way in response. He returned
with an extraordinarily robust sawing motion. Annette smiled to
herself, then tittered.

Werner looked sternly at her. He had the feeling he was whipping them along like a steward. He would do justice by the owner,
Brahms. Maybe there was no justice in the world but they would
have justice in music. For instance this passage: he would show
them how it was done. Tenderly, but with no relinquishing of
strength. Each note asked of him to be played with sympathy, to be
stroked on the face, while the other notes were crying in the corner.
How hurtful art was to all the things it left out. No you can't come
in, only C minor, he gets work today! That was what Nietzsche
meant by: "Genius always has a streak of cruelty." Even Fra An-
gelico was cruel to the vulgar subjects he refused to paint. Let's see
what Stanley will do with this solo. Not bad . . . Ow, little crude.
There is that crudeness in his character. He takes pains to disguise
it. Annette is playing astonishingly. Maybe she took to heart what
I said before about her laziness. She is being forced to play beyond
her capacity by the stronger players. Here everything is laid out
and we have only to follow. Time knows how to behave for once.
We do God's bidding. Music is God's inexorable thought.

What are these flowers on the piano? I don't want flowers. I am
only interested in one thing, music! Like four horsemen we are
plunging off the cliff.

At the end of the cadenza Terry pulled her mother's face down
to her and whispered: "Mom, Daddy looks really mad."

"Not mad at all, dear. He's concentrating hard. It only looks
like frowning."

"Oh."

They were in the andante. Werner felt a globe of anger in his
stomach. He watched it grow vertically into a glass rod across his
lower chest. Then the glass cut deeper into him. It was like a deep
gash, a valley between two sharp ridges. He knew the gash had always been there, covered up, the only companion in his loneliness.
Now it was coming out, like blood under white scar tissue. It was
very satisfying to feel it. But also so painful that it swelled him like
a sausage that soon must burst.

The others, as if sensing his anger, moderated their playing.

They surrounded him sorrowfully, like three graces. They were picking him up and rocking him. He did not like their protectiveness. He was grateful when the adagio began and he could again be an avenging angel. It was hard to imagine a music as anguished, as sickly as this piece. They had reached a pitch that was as keen as a dentist's drill piercing an open nerve. How much longer was this agony going to build? Was this what he was supposed to give himself up to, this yearning and infinite ache?

Suddenly the melody lifted right up and they were on a plateau overlooking broad plains . . . a field of waving wheat . . . it seemed an unimaginable solace was offered shortly ahead. Don't let this stop, don't let anything spoil the harmony that is meant to be. Just once let my soul overflow its banks. My heart is flooded with good strong feelings. It's going to be all right, my life will be redeemed . . . let no one dare to spoil it. If only they can let me have it this once. Oh coolness, sorrow, earth everything together . . .

Annette bit her lips. I just know I'm going to make a mistake, I can't help myself, she whimpered inside. I know I'm going to miss it. They came to the finale, her elbow dragged and she played the penultimate note. It screeched horribly.

"WRONG NOTE! WRONG NOTE!" he screamed.

She let the violin drop from her hands. Hartmann saw blood and slapped her face.

A force had carried him out of himself. Something magnetic, something loving, and she must have sensed this love because even as the others tried to separate them she wept in his arms.

"Oh, yes," he said, wiping the tears away. How easily tenderness came now. Then Marlene moved in to protect her, and Stanley and Joy Morrison. They're convincing her that she should be frightened of me, he thought bitterly.

Klausner took his friend Hartmann aside, into the hallway, away from the other's hearing.

"Werner," Klausner shook his head in private. "You just don't do things like that!"

STEPHEN MINOT

The Tide and Isaac Bates

(FROM QUARTERLY REVIEW OF LITERATURE)

HE'D WRECKED HER. No doubt about that. He'd been careless and his luck had run out, finally, and what was a man to do then?

He was standing high on the bluff they had just climbed. Below him his *Diana* lay broadside to the wind and to the fist of the sea. Each breaker drove her hard against the black raw edge of the ledge. Her cockpit was flooded, her decks awash. There was no saving her now. It was enough to make an old man sick.

"Rest here," he said to Cory, his daughter. "Catch your breath."

He started to reach out, to reassure her. But, hell, she was all of twenty-five and still a tomboy — she could take whatever came along. Besides, how can you offer an encouraging hand to someone done up in lobstermen's rubber pants and hooded jacket? Almost his height, she could have been some fisherman's adolescent boy, tall, lean, and undernourished. Her thin lips were tight and a little blue with cold, but her expression was blank. She wasn't complaining. Hell, she could shrug off anything.

A wave of exhaustion swept over him without warning and he sat down in the coarse brown grass, his muscles trembling. Carefully he reached under his torn yellow slicker, under his leather jacket, down to the wool shirt where he kept his cigarettes and matches. They were in a plastic case. He took out one cigarette and the box of wooden matches and tried to strike a light, his hands cupped against the November wind. The head of the first match came off like putty. The second merely smeared the striking edge of the box.

It hardly seemed fair. Silent, drained of profanity, he put the case back into his inner pocket and chewed on the end of the cigarette.

All this time his eyes never left his boat. Four, five, six breakers had come and washed back. Turning his head, he spat tobacco juice downwind. Then a leviathan wave lifted his *Diana* up on her side, cracked her on the solid face of the ledge, sucked back and let the hull jounce after it. This time the shock shattered everything above deck, canopy, cabin and all scattering into bits of flotsam, the glass of the windshield exploding noiselessly into an instant of glittering spray. Isaac Bates heard himself utter a startled "Aaa!"

And then, embarrassed, he said to Cory, "Well, it's just a matter of time now."

He tried to make it sound off-hand. The two of them never talked much about their inner feelings. They got along best just sharing chores — repairs around the house, chopping wood, or sometimes going over the books down at the cannery. The rest of the time she helped her mother. If anything bothered her, she didn't feel obliged to tell him, and in return he didn't burden her with his own worries. Of the eight children, she was the only one who would stay home, and he wasn't about to drive her away.

So there were times — like on early-morning crow hunts or off fishing somewhere — when her eyes would fill with tears for no reason and he wouldn't ask why. And right now he had cried out and she had said nothing.

Because it *was* nothing, really. The *Diana* wasn't his livelihood, nothing fundamental had been shattered, there was insurance and he wasn't poor anyway; they had not been injured, and they were lucky to have ended up on the mainland rather than on some tide-scoured ledge. She knew all that. She had a level head, she did.

Again the dark November water slithered back and this time he saw that her hull had been stove in. There was no longer any hope of salvage. Isaac squeezed his eyes shut, wincing from the sting of salt. He would not look at her in that November way. He would see her as she had been twenty-two years ago, newly built and still unpainted, red oak planking pink as a baby's rump, the admiration even of strangers.

Maine craftsmen had built her, some of them using the hand tools their fathers had given them. The oak itself came from

Isaac's own woodland, a section so rough that only oxen could get the logs out to the truck on the highway.

"What's a man like you messin' around with a *lobster* boat for?" That's what Elias Skolfield had asked when the *Diana* first took shape on his ways. He wasn't being critical; he wasn't even asking a question. He was simply approving the design, nodding because she was to be the solid, high and dry design of the Maine coast lobster boat. He was also noting the fact that Isaac Bates was no simple fisherman, that the slogan "You can't beat Bates for frozen fishcakes" had done more than pay off the mortgage. A man in Isaac's position — at his crest then at only thirty-six — might easily have invested in one of those factory-built speedsters. But he hadn't.

"Well, it's got honest lines," Isaac said, his trumpet muted as it had been for the birth of all eight children.

"*Proud* lines," Skolfield said. There was just a bit more sheer to her than the average lobsterman, but only a builder would have noticed it. "And power enough for three boats."

"Good to be on the safe side," he said, but he was thinking about the feel of the throttle and the lurch forward at his command.

As they talked there in the yard, the shifting May breezes brought to Isaac odors of cedar planking, mahogany shavings, tar and pine pitch. The sun was warm in his face and anticipation radiated in him like a good rum.

"Let's go," someone was saying.

He watched a shipbuilder on *Diana*'s deck take wood plugs from a keg and hammer them into drilled holes, setting each with the first blow and driving it home with two more. With his left hand he caressed the surface before setting the next, checking the level of each plug, a regular motion, rhythmical . . .

"Let's go now."

Rhythmical as waves, breakers pounding . . .

"Come on now," Cory was saying. "We'd better get moving."

The November gale suddenly tore at his face again. His cheeks felt raw. He looked down at the ledge below them and then quickly up at Cory. She had taken off her bulky foul-weather pants and stood there in wet, clinging Levis. The hood of her jacket was thrown back now. Her hair, sand-colored and stringy, was soaked.

He felt a rush of concern for her. She was a strong girl, but still . . .

Pulling his sleeve up, he tried to read his watch. The crystal was clouded with droplets on the inside.

"Your watch working?" he asked her.

She reached up under her jacket and pulled out her wrist watch from some dry pocket. She looked at it and put it to her ear.

"It's working," she said.

"What time is it?"

"Five fifteen."

"Well, it's turned now. It's on the ebb. Might as well go."

He had planned to wait until the tide had passed its peak at five. There had been a slim chance that some boat might have passed and with the tide still on the flood they might have tried to get her off. The odds of that were hard against him, of course. The tourists were all gone by Labor Day and half the lobstermen quit for the winter by the first of November. What few remained wouldn't tour the traps on an afternoon like this. Still, a man had to be an optimist if he was going to get a thing out of life.

Like coming through the gut in the first place. He and Cory had navigated that channel between Black Island and the mainland a number of times. It was risky, of course, but there was always enough water so long as they were twenty minutes before or after the peak of the tide — always until today. Still, for all this, he didn't regret the other times. Summer folks used to shake their heads, seeing them run through a channel that was naked ledge at half-tide. A man had to take chances just for the sake of living.

Like having women-friends. It was no mean trick for a married man in a small town like that to have his pleasures on the side. His old Mercury sedan was familiar all over that part of Maine. Even school children knew that he was the one that owned the cannery. And the risk of hurting his wife was a real one since his love for her was honest and full. Ella was a good woman. But any man worth his salt had to run risks just to keep himself alive.

"There was still a chance to save her," he said, "until her side was stove in . . . if only someone had come along before the tide changed."

"It won't change for another hour," she said flatly. "It won't be high until six."

He looked up at her sharply, squinting. It wasn't like her to contradict. "Not that it makes any difference now," she added.

"It was high at five," he said. "Just fifteen minutes ago."

That settled, he heaved himself up and with a grunt set the duffle bag on his shoulder. It held all they were able to salvage from the *Diana* — her personal effects, so to speak.

"Got to get to the highway before dark," he said. Then he set off with his back to the sea, assuming that Cory would follow close behind.

The grass bluff gave way to a tangle of spruce and hemlock with clumps of briar between, which waved like whips in the wind. As they moved inland, the sound of the surf died behind them, but always there was the moan from the tree tops. It was growing dark much more suddenly than he had expected. He wanted to stop and try looking at his watch again — perhaps the condensation had cleared. It was an uneasy feeling to have the crystal clouded like that. He hated having to depend on Cory's. Still, what time *was* it? And when was sunset?

They walked for what must have been an hour — or was it only half that long? — all the time expecting to come out on the highway. Somehow it retreated darkly before them. His luck was still bad.

Suddenly he heard his wife Ella cry out from her hospital bed. He stopped dead. Time hung motionless in the twilight.

"An owl," Cory said flatly. "Did you hear it?"

So they continued without a word. An owl. Yes. Of course. He had taught her to identify the cry of birds and she had been a good student. So much for that.

But the picture of Ella lingered there in the gloom. Poor Ella in a strange city in that miserable hospital bed, alone and wondering what would become of her next month. She was strong — she was strength itself — but she'd never had to face anything like this.

"First trip to a hospital in eighteen years," she had said with that taut smile of hers. That was only three days ago. Eighteen years previous she had given birth to the last of their eight children. It was, he remembered, quickly done, neat and on time. Just like her. And in those days the nurses and friends always commented on how strong she was, how healthy. But this time the swelling in her uterus was not a new life. It was a lump which at best was bad.

The doctors in Portland had consulted, tested, and talked more. So Isaac made some long distance calls, told Cory to pack, and drove the three of them down to Phillips House, the expensive wing of the Massachusetts General Hospital in Boston.

The first thing he did there was to tell the doctor in charge that in any event he was to "talk straight." Then sitting awkwardly on the edge of the easy chair in Ella's private room, he made plans for the family:

"This may take time," he told them. "And I don't intend to do much commuting. So as soon as we get the place closed up and the *Diana* over to the yard for the winter, Cory and me will find a hotel room nearby."

"Don't go to all that trouble," Ella said. "I'll be all right."

"No trouble. Never did think much of a Maine winter anyway," he said, echoing his own annual refrain.

"Been suffering in silence?" she said with a hint of a smile.

A wave of affection caught him off balance.

"Only thing that makes me suffer," he said, "is having you in this goddamned nunnery instead of where you should be."

"Never you mind about that," she said. Then she began with a long list of things which would have to be done at the house: kitchen cleaned, refrigerator emptied, linen packed away.

"I sure hate leaving all this to you two," she said, shaking her head. "But I guess I've got no choice."

That struck him hard. She was right, he supposed. But it was a terrible thing to hear someone utter the words "no choice." Worse than dying. Perhaps the same.

And now, in this miserable, darkening forest, did he have any choice? He was heading for the highway with his head down, driving one foot before the other, mindless.

When they finally broke through onto the tar road they almost fell, stumbling giddily. The rhythm of effort had been interrupted. Legs tingling, they turned this way and that in the middle of the road, surprised and without plan. What had been a gray, fast-moving overcast was now a dark, blood-tinted haze. Looking up he saw three gulls flying hard and into the wind. It was a bad sign — only during the worst of gales did they risk crossing straight through the center rather than riding it out.

"Rest yourself," he said. "Someone's bound to come by."

They waited, sitting silently in the winter-killed grass next to the road, leaning against the duffle. He tried to take a look at his watch again, but even when he turned it so as to catch the last dull glow from the sky, he could not see the hands.

After a time — more or less — a pickup truck came by and stopped without Isaac having to make a gesture. He slung the duffle in back and got in the cab. Cory climbed in after him.

"Mr. Bates?" the driver asked. His voice was adolescent. He sounded like one of the Skolfield grandsons, but Isaac could never tell them apart.

"Right," Isaac said. "You're one of the Skolfields?"

"Pete."

They drove in silence. As they passed a cluster of three houses by the general store, Isaac noticed a kerosene lamp in the window of one. The electric line was down again. But there was no need to comment.

Finally the boy gave in to his curiosity. "Been hunting?" he asked.

"Lost my boat," Isaac said. "Had to beach her."

That wasn't really honest, of course. He had driven her hard on the ledge. An incredible miscalculation. Baffling. No, he hadn't beached her; he'd wrecked her. But how could you say that aloud?

"It's a bad night," the boy said.

When they came to Isaac's mail box the boy turned in without a word. It was a five-minute drive in over that rutted dirt road and another five out, but the boy was offering his time as condolences.

When they came out on the hillside where Isaac's house and barn were, they were hit with the gale again. The truck shuddered with a gust before they drew into the lee of the house itself.

"Can we get her off at dawn?" the boy asked as they got out. "Tide's high again at six-thirty."

"*Five*-thirty," Isaac said sharply. "Besides, it's too late. She's broke up."

A wave of despair broke over him. He opened his mouth to say thanks, but he couldn't utter a word to the boy. What did *he* know about such things?

"You're lucky to be alive," the boy said.

"You think so?"

But Isaac's answer never reached the boy; it was lost in the wind and in the decades that lay between them. The headlights swung sharply and soon were only a winking flicker through the forest on the other side of the pasture, streaking back to town, leaving the night blacker than ever.

They entered the kitchen like two blind strangers. It hardly seemed possible: for more than twenty years the house had been filled with children — eight of them in the peak years. They had gone, one by one. Scattered. And was there, finally, only this blackness? Was that all?

The power must have been off for hours, for without the oil furnace going the place had picked up the dank, tomb-like chill of a house long deserted. Isaac flipped the light switch from habit and the blackness became more intense. He shivered, groping for matches.

When in doubt, Isaac gave orders. "Find a flashlight," he said to Cory. "And get the kitchen matches." It didn't pay to speak softly if you wanted action. "We need about four lamps going. Start with the ones in the pantry." They hadn't had electricity in the place until 1935 and a part of him had always resented all that too-easy glare. "Then get some spills for the range."

He groped about for a flashlight, but before he could locate one there was a flicker of orange behind him. She was lighting the lamp. The room appeared and the storm outside was forced back hissing.

"Now some kindling," he said. She lit a second lamp for her own use and then tossed to him the matches and a fresh pack of cigarettes. When she was safely out in the woodshed, he began to study the tide chart which was hanging on the wall. His hands ripped carelessly at the cigarette package as he squinted to make out the blur of fine print. "November . . . November . . . November 10, High . . ." He lit a cigarette and inhaled deeply. "November . . . 10 . . . High 5:05."

"Ha!" He whooped and called to Cory.

But the black wave which had sucked back for an instant thundered down on him once again: November 10th they had driven Ella to Boston. And the 11th they were still there. This was the *12th*. He put his hands to his temples. Gears had slipped.

"Was that you?" Cory asked. She was standing there at the door with a coal hod half-filled with the spills — wood chips and bark.

"Me? No," he muttered, taking the hod from her. "Just the wind." He started laying the fire.

She didn't question it. He could hear her behind him, bustling about like a young Ella, lighting lamps, stuffing wads of paper in the windows that rattled, mopping the front hall where the rain had driven under the door, filling jugs of water from the last remaining trickle from the faucet. When his fire was roaring with pine slabs he converted to oak and she put the kettle on the hottest section of the stove.

"You'll be needing a hot whiskey, I suppose," she said in an offhand, affectionate way. The echo of Ella was startling.

"We both will tonight."

"Now don't get me all giddy," she said, setting the kitchen table for two with quick motions. "I've a lot to do tonight."

He didn't press it, seeing her set out two white mugs. That was something his wife would never have done — not once over the course of decades. And there had been times — like this one — when it would have been good to have shared a drink.

She brought him the bottle of *Kings* whiskey and he measured by eye a double shot for them both, the slosh in each mug as quick and accurate as a bartender's. Then she filled each with steaming water from the kettle.

"Sugar and lemon for yours," he said. "Nothing for mine."

He watched her as she went to the pantry and sliced lemons. It seemed senseless to him to have pants cut like that. All the young folks were wearing them. He sniffed the steam from his drink and felt sweat come to his forehead.

"You should get out of those wet things," he said abruptly.

"They're drying out."

"Women shouldn't wear pants anyhow."

"First I've heard you complain," she said lightly. She was holding her mug in both hands, warming them, and taking quick sips.

"Just change them."

The smile went from her face. He thought he saw a flicker of fear there and cursed himself for speaking roughly to her. Still, why not? She hadn't been raised to be just another fair-weather girl. Not like the other two — fooling around with men too old for them and stumbling into marriage and moving away. No, Cory had her feet squarely on the ground.

And as if to prove it she obeyed him by heading up the stairs to her room. She was back down only half a mug later with sweater and skirt over her arm.

"It's winter up there," she said. "Turn around so I can change without freezing."

He faced the stove, his mug in hand, and listened as her wet Levis hit the floor with a "splot" and her dressing filled the room with a charged silence. The heat from the range prickled his face.

"Stove heat makes sense," he said, speaking only to hear his own voice. "You know just where it comes from. Keeps people together. As soon as you put in a furnace, the family scatters all over the house, each to his own damn room. Good feeling to have the heat at your face and cold at your back."

"So who put the furnace in?" she asked, hanging her wet clothes up on the pegs behind the range.

"Ella did," he said. It was meant as a kind of easy joke, but strangely the name of Ella cast a pall on the place. Cory paused, hand on peg, and took in a deep breath. Isaac took a scalding slug of his drink. He wished he hadn't brought her name into that kitchen. She was gone. He and Cory had the place to themselves.

"Will she live?" Cory asked very quietly.

"Live?" It was a rotten question to ask about a dying woman. "Of course she'll live. Good God, don't you know that *all* wives outlive their men? What's the matter with you, d'you want to wish her right into her grave?"

She was looking at him now, her mouth open, her eyes squinting, and her face pale.

"Oh, come on, now," he said, jovial again, "don't take everything so serious."

"Sorry."

"Nothing to be *sorry* about. You sound like your Uncle Will." She grinned. His older brother, William, was a perpetual victim. The very mention of his name brought smiles in Isaac's home. "Like when he was trying to teach your cousin Tina how to drive . . ."

"And was standing in the garage?"

"So as to direct her in backing out . . ."

"But she wasn't in reverse?"

"In first. That's right." They were both laughing now. "So Uncle Will gets pinned to the wall . . ."

"Between the studs?"

"That's all that saved him. And she gets flustered and shouts at him . . ."

" 'Why do you have to stand right in front of me?' "

"And he says," Isaac could hardly finish. " 'Sorry.' "

Isaac wiped the tears from his eyes and poured more whiskey in each mug. It was the first time he had told the story without Ella shaking her head and saying "Poor Will." Cory added the hot water to his drink from the kettle. She hesitated over her own mug, then shrugged, and added the water.

"You won't tell on me?" she said with a grin.

"I wouldn't tell on my Cory," he said.

"You may just have to do without supper."

"There's more in this world than a goddamned series of home-cooked suppers."

"Let's drink to that," she said. They clinked mugs. "No more meals, no more brooms."

" '. . . No more teacher's dirty looks,' " he chanted.

"Doesn't rhyme."

"Say, did I ever tell you about your Uncle Will and the mop salesman?"

"Never," she said. He knew she was lying, but neither of them cared. He loved the telling and she loved the listening so he started right in. The pieces of the story fitted together, link by link, building. Then, finally, at precisely the right moment they exploded into laughter.

After a lull he said, "You know, we're goddamned lucky to be alive."

"Sure are," she said. "You've got a genius for picking the right ledge to land on."

He snorted a laugh right in the middle of a gulp. Whiskey sprayed the air. They broke into laughter again. The sound sent him back years to a rooming house in town and some Latvian woman named . . . what *was* her name? But by heaven she could laugh. From the gut. Free and open. God she loved life. And everyone else. Danced until you were out of your pants and then brought you down with a whoop.

"No one really loves a cook," he said to Cory, sloshing a careless round into their mugs. "A man who hauls himself off a black ledge doesn't cry out for a meal. No sir!"

"And what *does* he cry for?" She was heading for the kettle.

"Celebration. Thanksgiving."

"So you shall have it," she said, kettle in hand. "Today is a holiday."

"Celebration for being alive."

"We'll have one every day. This place *needs* a celebration every day. Forever."

She was pouring the water with a flourish, kettle a foot above the mugs. It splashed over the table, steaming. Some ran from the table onto his pants and he jumped up, laughing.

"God but you're sloppy," he said, delighted with her. The room turned on its mooring; the deck rose and fell under him. The kettle went somewhere and she was laughing, her head back, and he was holding her, dancing about the room singing "O sole O mio" and feeling her close against him and laughing and his hand drove itself down beneath the fabric of her skirt onto the round of a buttock firm as youth itself and the other hand wrenched at the cloth, ripping it.

Her fingers were suddenly at his face, ripping like winter spray. He threw her back from him and with a crack of timbers she went down hard.

He staggered back, sober. She was lying there on the floor, broadside to the black cookstove, rocking. Her hands were over her face; she began sobbing like the winds, lost.

Later that night, the electric lights glared back on. That was when she stood again, solemn, dry-eyed, white, and unreal. Ghostlike.

"We'd better eat something," she said.

She heated some tasteless spaghetti. Silently they ate, knowing that it would be the first of many like that — just the two of them there like figures in a waiting room, afraid to touch each other even with words.

BEVERLY MITCHELL

Letter from Sakaye

(FROM THE FIDDLEHEAD)

I FOUND THE LETTER FROM SAKAYE today when I was looking
through a box of old books in the basement. It was stuck between
the pages of my Sunday School Bible, and at first I didn't recognize
it. After nearly thirty years, the cheap wartime newsprint is worn
and creased, and the writing just barely legible — but I can still
make out most of it, even if it is in pencil. Besides, I don't think
I've ever forgotten it — and I know I've never forgotten Sakaye.
She wrote the letter just after she'd been sent away, and I can remember how excited I was to find it waiting for me when I came
home from school — and how disappointed I was because she
didn't really say anything. Just that she was living on a farm on
the prairies now and she missed Mission, and she wondered if Billy
Hunter was sitting in her old desk behind me, and had Mrs.
Grimsby come for rehearsals yet, and who was to be the new May
Queen. Nothing really important in that. At least, that's what I
thought nearly thirty years ago — and I can't remember if I ever
answered it. I didn't think then that Mrs. Grimsby or Billy Hunter
was important enough to bother about. And I didn't realize when
I was eleven how important I was to Sakaye — and I didn't know
how important she was to me. That's one of the hardest things
about growing older — remembering all the opportunities you
missed because you didn't have the understanding to appreciate
them when they were offered — and then realizing when you do
have the understanding, that it's too late.

I suppose our relationship started on the first day of school in

Grade One. That was the same year the C.P.R. Empress liner nearing Hong Kong at the end of her voyage was turned back to Honolulu without even going into the Hong Kong harbour — and the people on the ship could see smoke rising from the buildings as the Japanese planes dropped their bombs. Some of the passengers were businessmen returning to their families, and some were the wives and children of businessmen whose offices were not far from the harbour . . .

In Mission City the desks in the Grade One classroom were shining with new varnish that smelled sickly-sweet, and the floor was slippery from the fresh oil the janitor had coated it with during the summer holidays. I sat in my desk, hugging the wonder that I was finally a school-girl with a desk of my own, with a fresh bottle of white paste stuck in the inkwell and a board to rest my feet on if they got tired on the floor. There were pictures all around the room and charts and blackboards with real chalk and new erasers and a sandtable with real sand in the corner and a small table at the back of the room with little red chairs — and books open on the table and on the shelves. And piled on the ledge beside the teacher's desk were boxes of plasticine — coloured plasticine. And the smell! The delicious grown-up smell of chalk dust and oil and the teacher's perfume and rubber erasers and soap and my new school bag. The teacher was busy writing the names of pupils who hadn't registered, questioning the mothers who were in a straggly, whispering group beside her desk. We sat in awed silence, overwhelmed by the strangeness and importance of being in school. I could see my mother standing at the back of the room with the rest of the parents who had finished registering, and when she caught my eye she smiled.

Margaret Barry sat a few desks up in the next row, swinging her foot very carefully in the aisle so everyone would notice her new school shoes, and Billy Hunter was scrunched in front of me, furiously uncomfortable in a starched white shirt and bow tie. I didn't know all the kids, but most of them looked as excited as I felt. I poked Billy on the shoulder to show him my new school bag, and we were just undoing the buckle when I noticed the little girl beside me. There were no sleeves in her cotton dress and her arms were covered with goose pimples — and she was sitting perfectly still, wrapped in an envelope of private misery and crying without making any sound. Billy and I stared at her, astonished that anyone would cry on the first day of school, and in front of all the kids. She wasn't very big — the tips of her canvas shoes just reached the floor. I could see the splotch marks on her desk from tears, and while we watched, more tears splashed off her cheeks. Suddenly my mother came down the aisle. She squeezed herself into the little desk beside the girl and put her arm around her. Billy and I could hear her whispering that when she had been a teacher and Sakaye's brother was a little boy, she had taught him in this very room. So that was her name — Sakaye. Billy and I looked at each other — we'd never known anyone with a name like that. And when my mother pointed to me and told Sakaye that I was her little girl and Billy Hunter was my friend, Sakaye glanced at us shyly and then looked down at her desk lid again. She sat there huddled against my mother, not crying any more, but not looking around, either.

I guess my mother made Billy and me feel protective towards Sakaye from the beginning, because when Margaret Barry and some of the other kids started to giggle at Sakaye for being a baby and at my mother squeezed into a Grade One desk, Billy and I just glared them into silence. And we didn't laugh when Sakaye refused to tell the teacher her name, and my mother answered for her and pointed out Sakaye's brother, standing at the back of the room with the parents. I hadn't realized that my mother had taught in my Grade One classroom and I hadn't realized she had taught someone as interesting as Sakaye's brother. I'm afraid it made me feel quite important to know all that.

It made me important in Sakaye's eyes, too. I think she always liked me because of my mother — and sometimes when we were playing in the yard at recess she would come and stand beside me without saying anything. She never said anything in Grade One — not even when it was her turn to read out loud. I knew she understood English, but she wouldn't ever say anything in English at school. She was smart, though — she always got a gold star on her paper for number work, and her printing was so good the teacher would put it on the board for everyone to see. That pleased me. Somehow I felt that it was because my mother had taught Sakaye's brother that she was so smart. And I didn't mind it when I had to take Sakaye to the girls' bathroom in the basement and show her how to use the toilet. That was after she had wet her pants one afternoon during printing.

We must have been going to school for at least a month then, because most of the novelty had worn off and I was sitting uncomfortably correct for printing: back straight, feet together on the floor, in the exact centre of my seat, scribbler making a diagonal with the top left of the page and arm resting loosely on the desk — loosely, Miss MacDonald insisted — and the right hand holding the pencil loosely so it rested on the joint of the first finger. Rested loosely. Miss MacDonald crept around the room, up and down the aisles, swooping down on you suddenly from behind and flicking your pencil or jogging your left arm. If the pencil flew out of your hand you had been holding it correctly; and if your left arm slithered across your desk, knocking your scribbler to the floor, *that* had been the correct printing position. My neck and shoulders ached from the dreadful effort of keeping my left arm and right hand loose, and the circles I was making were woefully inconsistent — some above and below the blue lines, some not even touching the lines. The classroom was unusually quiet, save for the whisper of pencils on paper and the tiptoe tread of Miss MacDonald.

When I first heard it, it was like the slow sibilant hiss of an old steam pipe which increased in volume and persistence to the first splash and steady drumming on the floor. It was coming from Sakaye's desk — and when I looked over I saw that the last of the perfectly formed, loose, round circles on her page was wandering uncertainly above and below the blue lines, as the puddle kept growing and growing under her desk, and little yellow rivulets spread in all directions on her seat, dripping down the back and running down the cast-iron scrollwork at the side. It seemed to last forever, and all the time Sakaye kept making her pencil go round and round the last circle, which wasn't a circle at all. The kids began to snicker — I almost laughed myself. Not because Sakaye had wet her pants — that was horrible — but because Margaret Barry was making frantic and futile efforts to keep her new school shoes out of the puddle which had spread all the way to her desk.

Miss MacDonald came down the aisle to see what the commotion was all about. I guess when she saw the size of the puddle she realized that Sakaye hadn't been to the bathroom for a long, long time.

She wasn't mad or anything. "Sakaye, why didn't you put up your hand if you had to leave the room?"

We had this elaborate system of hand signals in Grade One. If your hand was up, that meant you wanted to ask a question. Your hand up with one finger showing meant you had to leave the room, but it would only take a few minutes. Hand up with TWO fingers involved a longer absence. Sakaye didn't answer Miss MacDonald.

"Sakaye, do you know where the girls' toilet is?" This in a whisper from Miss MacDonald. Still no answer from Sakaye, but she stopped making the desperate circle and shook her head. "Jennifer will show you."

So that's how I came to take Sakaye down to the girls' bathroom in the basement for the rest of Grade One, and I suppose that's when we really became friends. She never did put up her hand to leave the room, but when she had to go, she'd reach over and tap my arm gently and I'd understand and put up my hand with its important one finger in plain view.

I was scared of the girls' basement — especially in the afternoon after the janitor had swept the floor and sunlight streaming through the little high windows swam dizzily through the swirling dust particles. The cement on the floor wasn't quite even and the shadows and dusty light chutes gave me the feeling that I was half floating. And noises from the classrooms above us echoed with terrifying intensity — the clatter of rulers dropping, the heavy measured tread of a teacher's feet, and the distorted voices coming from a great distance. But I couldn't let Sakaye see how scared I was. She had taken my hand when we left the Grade One classroom, and we crept down the old wooden stairs that creaked with each step. She didn't seem to mind having wet her pants once we got out of the classroom, and I had the impression that she was rather pleased to be away from it all.

The worst thing about the girls' basement was the fact that the toilets flushed automatically — and, to me, unpredictably — with a thunderous swoosh of water. That and the smell: Lysol so strong it grabbed my throat and gagged me — and the horrible green soap in the dispenser, and wet paper towels and orange peels and apple cores in the waste basket.

When we reached the little room with the toilets behind their

swinging wooden doors, I pushed one open to show Sakaye where it
was. They were all innocently quiet. When I realized that Sakaye
didn't even know how to sit on one, there was nothing for me to do
but demonstrate. Sure enough, while I was sitting there explaining,
all the toilets flushed together. It really wasn't so bad as I had imagined — just a little cold and windy on my bottom — but it still
frightened me half to death. I couldn't let Sakaye see THAT. But
after the first expression of amazement had widened her eyes, she
began to laugh. Politely, of course, and she put both hands over
her mouth so she wouldn't offend me. But I knew she thought that
I had made all that thunderous swoosh. I guess I started to giggle,
too, and after I had finished what the fright made me do, I made
her sit on the little wooden seat. And I made her stay there until
the toilets flushed again, and when the cold wind reached her bottom we both started to giggle helplessly all over again. It was really
kind of fun — naughty fun, perhaps — but fun, nevertheless. After
that first time, she would never close the swinging door behind her
when we made our daily visits, but had me stand where she could
see me. We always giggled — but Sakaye still wouldn't say anything, not even to me . . .

I can't remember anything about Sakaye in Grade Two. Perhaps
she wasn't in my class that year, or perhaps the Grade Two teacher
took a dim view of two little girls leaving the room at once. I just
can't remember now. But it's strange that Sakaye should ask about
Mrs. Grimsby and Billy Hunter and the May Queen in her letter,
because what I remember of her in Grade Three is inextricably
linked with them . . .

Mrs. Grimsby was the official accompanist. Come the end of
April, she appeared with inexorable regularity at the old grey
annex which served as the elementary school gym. The janitor
would have nailed the scarred and battered May pole to the centre
of the gym floor and screwed the wooden circle with its old coloured
streamers into the top. In many ways, Mrs. Grimsby was very like
the old May pole: she was grey with a certain battered dignity; she
was much smaller at the top than at the bottom; and the emblem
on her Legion tam had the same faded droop as the May pole
streamers. She always wore her Legion Auxiliary uniform for rehearsals.

A few days before Mrs. Grimsby came for rehearsals, we would

have a series of "dry runs" in the gym. First we would be paired
off with the boys according to height. Then we would line up in
the corner, holding hands, and walk to the May pole. I always got
paired off with Billy Hunter. By Grade Three, my relationship
with Billy had undergone a subtle change. Deep down we were
still good friends, but certain things about Billy bothered me in
Grade Three. For one thing, he had not taken to school with the
same gusto I had, and was afraid of the teachers. Of all the teachers, not just Miss Buckley, who terrified everyone. For another, he
had very sweaty hands. I suppose it was the sweaty hands that
bothered me most. If Miss Buckley glared at Billy, the perspiration
oozed from his palms in direct proportion to the height of her impatience. A little glare, a little sweat; a big glare, a big sweat; a
glare and a shout, a veritable flood. In the middle of the walk from
the corner of the gym to the May pole I would slip and slither in
the frantic clutch of Billy's sweating hand until he would finally
snatch it away and wipe it on his pants. Miss Buckley would bark
at him and he'd grab me and leak horribly all over my hand for
the rest of the rehearsal.

The dry runs were never much fun. Miss Buckley would bang
time with a ruler and we'd walk around the May pole, in and out
singly, then in and out in pairs, until she would be satisfied that the
majority of us had at least a dim idea of what we were doing. Then
would come the skipping — dust would fly up from the floor, the
old gym would shake, and we'd all be red from exertion. And
Billy's hands would sweat. If we were really smart, we'd get to use
the streamers the first day. Usually it was the second. Or the third.
If we had dared, we would have tangled the ribbons on purpose,
just to watch Miss Buckley get mad. But we didn't dare — and the
knots and tangles that sometimes needed the janitor to get them
undone were the result of sheer ignorance.

By the time Mrs. Grimsby came to the rehearsals, we were fairly
good. She'd be sitting at the piano waiting for us when we came in
ranks from our classroom, the shiny seat of her Legion Auxiliary
skirt firmly settled on the piano bench and the emblem on her Legion Auxiliary tam quivering expectantly until she got the nod
from Miss Buckley to begin "Come Lasses and Lads." With the
first bar, Mrs. Grimsby would undergo some kind of mystical trans-
formation — the greying figure in the old blue uniform would swell

visibly until she became Boadicea leading the British Empire in the paths of glory. "Come Lasses and THUMP, take leave of your THUMP, and away to the May pole THUMP". And away we'd go magnificently until the dust from our banging feet swirled in giddy, ecstatic clouds.

But this is where Sakaye comes in again. Half the pupils in my Grade Three class were Japanese and they hated the May pole dancing. If one of the Japanese boys had to have a white girl for a partner, he'd squeeze her fingers until they were white and then stick his fingernails in the soft flesh. We didn't dare tell on them because we were almost as frightened of them as we were of Miss Buckley. So the boys were never punished. But the girls were. Miss Buckley would be driven to near maniacal frenzy by the fact that Japanese etiquette demanded the girls never walk with the boys but follow them from a humble distance. She would shrill at them, making a rainbow of saliva that half-delighted, half-terrified us — but it didn't have much effect on the Japanese girls. They would skip obediently — but still just a trifle behind their partners. And Miss Buckley would spank them, turning them over her knee in front of everyone and smacking them with the ruler until her arm was tired. She never hit one of us, so we could only guess how much it hurt.

By Grade Three we were used to the heavy orange and green socks the Japanese girls wore with their cheap canvas shoes, and we took the cotton dresses they wore on even the coldest days as a matter of course. But when they were turned over Miss Buckley's knee and we saw the heavy flour sack petticoats and panties — still with PURITY stamped on them — and stitched together with coloured yarn, we were shocked. We could tell that Mrs. Grimsby didn't like it either, because she'd sit rigid at the piano — and when she played after someone had been spanked the music sounded different — "COME lasses and thump". The day that Sakaye was spanked, Billy and I stood there holding hands, and I didn't even mind that his was sweaty and trembling. But we were only in Grade Three then, and there was nothing we could do except look away and pretend that we hadn't noticed anything. I think that Sakaye understood — but even in Grade Three she wouldn't say anything in English — and I just couldn't find anything to say to her. My mother didn't say anything, either, when I told her — but I can still remember the expression on her face. I saw the same expression on Mrs. Grimsby's face three years later one Sunday in the United Church — and recalling all this now, I have suddenly realized that Miss Buckley's ruler was somehow responsible for my leaving the church when I was eleven.

The Japanese had their own United Church up on the hill behind the fair grounds. Their minister was a white woman who had spent most of her life as a missionary in Japan, so that even her walk resembled the obsequious shuffle of the Japanese women. I found her fascinating — not that she made any effort to become friendly with the ladies of the white congregation — but fascinating from the fact that when she did stop to talk to my mother, her English had a peculiar sing-song intonation. And when she met her Japanese parishioners on Main Street, she would make three jerky Oriental bows to the men — not to the women — before speaking to them. And the quality of the respect she got from the Japanese youngsters in my class impressed me. She taught them in their own language for two hours after school in the plain grey building that was also their church, and whenever they met her down town on Saturdays I would see them bowing very politely from the waist — three times, just like their fathers. They would stand in shy groups talking to her, before whirling off like autumn leaves, just as gay in their bright colours, and just as elusive. Apart from Sakaye, who would half-wave if she saw us, I never really got to know any of them — nobody did. They came from a world that was different from any we white children knew, and they endured ours for the five hours they had to be in school — then they were off. I used to wonder what they did — but they would never say. Sometimes I think that by the time we had all reached Grade Five, the girls might have talked with us — but if one of the boys noticed a girl talking to us, he would snap at her in Japanese and that would be the end of it.

Their minister tried to explain their culture to the Ladies Auxiliary, and came to one of their meetings with lantern slides. But I guess no one was really interested, because she tried only once. She offered to show them to my Sunday School class, too, but Mrs. Hancock was our teacher that year, and she was interested in the mission in India. I don't think Sakaye ever knew about Mrs. Hancock, and I'm sure Mrs. Hancock didn't know Sakaye — and Mrs. Hancock made it plain to everyone that she barely tolerated the Japanese minister. But the minister came to a few of the suppers the women put on in the basement of the church, and she always looked rather out of place among the potato salads and pumpkin pies and cold ham and pickles — and the women in aprons, red with exertion and Christian fellowship, and the men with cigars, and the kids running around and squabbling.

There were always squabbles at the church suppers, and too much food, and too much smoke and too much noise. And we always had to clap for Mrs. Hancock, because she had worked so hard and washed so many dishes and done so many wonderful Christian things. And Mrs. Hancock would accept all this homage as if it really were her due, smoothing down the pink ruffled apron she had made and then bought back at the bazaar, her powerful hands red and wrinkled from the dish water. Beside Mrs. Hancock, the Japanese minister was dwarfed almost to the point of oblivion. Mrs. Hancock was a big woman — but she contained herself admirably with a corset which must have been in constant struggle with her rebellious flesh. Even when she sat down we could hear the battle going on with mysterious creakings underneath her dress, on which the ridges of whale bone stood out in full relief. Although I still can't really forgive Mrs. Hancock, I suppose I must give her her due — she must have suffered like the early martyrs in that corset. Her corset didn't always triumph over her flesh, either. Frequently the interior turmoil was made audible in explosions of sound that even today I have a grudging admiration for.

Like a boiler taxed to the point of explosion, it would start with deep intestinal rumblings — heavy at first, then a series of staccato thumps — a high whining soprano as it reached her great bosom — then brawpp. Oh, a magnificent brawpp! Followed by "My Jesus, mercy." Why she called on the merciful Jesus, we never quite understood, but she must have astonished even Him. Over the clatter of knives and forks as the women set the bare plank tables, and the crash of lids on the old stove, and the thundering of us youngsters as we ran back and forth unsupervised on the stage, it would echo magnificently. "Brawpp. My Jesus, mercy." There would be a few seconds of awed silence — even the grown-ups were impressed — or startled — and then the women would clatter just a little louder, and the men's voices would rise politely in an effort to appear as if they had noticed nothing. It was useless, of course, because the lovely thing about Mrs. Hancock's gas attacks was that once they started they kept right on. And we knew it. The scuffling on the stage would stop abruptly — even the kids who were fighting about chopsticks on the piano would abandon their position — and we would all melt quietly to the kitchen door. Mrs. Hancock's performance made the church suppers worth coming to as far as we were concerned. We would squeeze ourselves against the wall and wait fascinated for the next eruption, not even daring to laugh for fear we'd miss something.

The highlight of Mrs. Hancock's religious experiences, as she told her Sunday School classes with unfailing and relentless regularity, had been a minister's sermon on the holy women in the gospel. Why it had impressed her I never knew, for a more boring and stupid existence than theirs I couldn't imagine. But watching Mrs. Hancock washing dishes in the church basement I could see that she really fancied herself as THE holy woman of the gospels, trudging after Jesus and His disciples, and washing their dirty socks and cooking their meals. Somewhere down the years Mrs. Hancock had forgotten they were originally WOMEN, and she seemed determined to do her Christian ministrations all by herself. At least, that's what it looked like to us watching from the door. There were always crowds of flustered women in the kitchen, basting turkeys and spooning pickles out of jars, and slicing homemade bread. But Mrs. Hancock was the Queen Bee, and made the others insignificant as drones. It would be one of the drones — usually my mother or Mrs. Grimsby — who would notice us at the door, and make us move reluctantly to the other end of the hall, "out of the way."

The Japanese minister had been invited to the last church supper I attended, and had spent most of her time at the small sink in the corner, scrubbing cocoa out of the blue enamel pots that had to be used for coffee. She seemed unmoved by either the fluster of the women or the importance of Mrs. Hancock — and her face was as tranquilly impassive then as it was later when she clapped politely. I saw her shuffle out quietly in the grey cloth coat she wore to church functions, and I don't think the others even knew she had gone. That must have been the last time I saw her, because a few weeks after that was the attack on Pearl Harbor . . .

Pearl Harbor was the event that really shattered our illusion on the West Coast that the war was "over there." The *Eine Kleine Nachtmusik,* pale flames in December sunlight, Sunday afternoon security — all are linked irrevocably in my memories of Pearl Harbor. I was eleven then. The sun was streaming through the windows in the living room while I sat half-asleep in an armchair watching the flames in the fireplace and waiting for my grandparents to wake up from their Sunday afternoon nap. My father was dozing on the chesterfield and my mother was reading peacefully — no one was really listening to the symphony on the radio. The sudden interruption of the music startled us — and I could tell from the expression on my father's face that there was something frightening in the announcer's terse message. It was over almost as soon as it began — the sun was still shining, the fire purring quietly, and again, after the announcer's voice, the Mozart. But something was irretrievably lost — perhaps it was security, perhaps it was the illusion that our lives were contained in the small world that was the family — perhaps it was something too elusive to define. It changed the pattern of that Sunday afternoon. My grandfather woke up with a snort and came into the living room with his hair still tousled from sleep, followed by my grandmother, crease marks from the pillow zigzagging across her cheek. Where was Pearl Harbor? And we looked it up in the atlas, frightened to discover that only the Pacific Ocean separated us from the war now.

At first I didn't associate the attack on Pearl Harbor with the Japanese people I had known all my life — and I never associated it with Sakaye. We were in Grade Six that year, and she sat in the desk behind me. That was the year she started to speak English and she was the one who started whispering to me during school. I can't remember now what we used to whisper about — but that isn't important. What was important was the fact that we had discovered that communication went deeper than words, and it wasn't so much what one said that mattered, as it was that you knew you liked each other, and this was being communicated — and we had known that since Grade One. But of all the Japanese girls, Sakaye was still the shyest. Perhaps that is why the teacher pretended he didn't notice us whispering, because he never got after me when I was talking to Sakaye.

But the rumours that followed December seventh made it clear that for many in Mission City the association of the attack with the

Japanese living in the Fraser Valley was only too real. Where did all the money go that the Japanese had been making on their farms? Not to the trades people of Mission, that was sure. And what about the Hyakawas' son who had gone to Japan last year? What business could he have over there? And then reports about the fishing boats on the West Coast began to drift into Mission — the fishermen had been charting the coastal waters in preparation for the invasion of B.C. Someone even discovered that the fresh straw carefully laid down between the rows of young strawberry plants pointed directly to the Mission bridge — and because we boasted one of the three bridges that crossed the Fraser River, we suddenly saw ourselves as a strategic location, infiltrated by the enemy, and a prime target for attack.

All this never made any difference between Sakaye and me, but the other Japanese youngsters in my class must have realized what was being said, because there was a change in their attitude. For one thing, they stopped huddling together in little groups and talking in Japanese. After Pearl Harbor, I can't remember hearing Japanese spoken again, except for the occasional swear word — and that was just as likely to have come from the white youngsters. For another, they were much friendlier than they had been. Roy Hoshira started bringing enough jawbreakers from his brother's grocery store for all those who sat around him — not just for his Japanese friends. The girls were different, too. I think we had always liked the Japanese girls — Miss Buckley's ruler and the May pole dancing had achieved that in Grade Three — but until Pearl Harbor, they had remained quiet and inscrutable. Pearl Harbor never made any difference in my friendship with Sakaye, though, not even when people started saying that her uncle was the admiral of the Pacific Fleet . . .

It must have been only a few weeks after Pearl Harbor that the Japanese woman came to our United Church for the morning service. The minister had already begun the short sermon he preached for the children before they went downstairs for Sunday School, and I was sitting in front of the church with the junior choir, facing the congregation. So we saw it all. The door opened quietly and Sakaye's mother walked in. In all the years I had been going to St. David's, I had never seen any Japanese at our service. Furthermore, no one ever came to church that late. She shuffled noiselessly

down the aisle with a polite, half-apologetic smile, and slipped into
the empty space beside Mrs. Hancock near the back of the church. I
don't suppose many in the congregation even knew she was there.
But the junior choir did — we saw it all — we saw Mrs. Hancock
turn to look at her, and we heard Mrs. Hancock sniff. And we saw
Mrs. Hancock rise self-righteously and walk out of the pew, leading
her daughters to a place nearer the front of the church. Only Mrs.
Grimsby kept her seat in the pew as one by one the others followed
Mrs. Hancock's example. Mrs. Grimsby was strangely lost without
her Legion Auxiliary uniform, and although we recognized her expression as the one which followed Miss Buckley's ruler episodes, it
was useless without a piano on which to thump "COME lasses and
lads," and she couldn't rally us as she might have. So she sat erect,
trying to people the empty spaces in the pew between her and
Sakaye's mother at the other end with her will alone. The minister
ended his sermon abruptly, and in a tired voice announced the
hymn. When everyone else was singing "The Church's One Foundation," Sakaye's mother got up and walked out as quietly as she
had come in — and I was suddenly reminded of flour sack petticoats
and panties stitched with yarn. I guess the other kids were, too, because nobody in the junior choir sang that morning. Just nobody.

And nobody said anything when the junior choir filed out into
the vestry and we hung up our surplices in the cupboard. The
younger children who had been sitting in front of the church with
their Sunday School teachers came bursting through the door and
clattered to their places in the different sections of the big room.
Mrs. Hancock's class were all members of the choir, and we sat
silent on our benches as she eased herself carefully into her chair
and opened her lesson book. Nobody answered when she said good
morning to us. And nobody said anything when she asked who
could say the Bible verse for the day from memory. We wouldn't
even look at her. And when she began reading the lesson, we all
just sat there, staring at the floor or looking out the window. It was
Billy Hunter who started it, and I suppose it was the bravest thing
he had ever done. I was sitting beside him, and I knew how scared
he was, because there were splotches of sweat all over the cover of
his Bible. Mrs. Hancock was still reading from the lesson when
Billy swallowed a great mouthful of air and belched. "My Jesus,
mercy," he said firmly, and looked at me. I caught on. And as

Mrs. Hancock went on reading, I swallowed air and belched and said, "My Jesus, mercy." Then everyone caught on. Sometimes it was a solo; sometimes as many as three of us at a time belched and said, "My Jesus, mercy." Some of the girls weren't too impressive, but the boys produced some beauties. We knew the other classes were looking at us, and we could hear their shocked giggles. But not one of us laughed. We just sat there, and every time Mrs. Hancock opened her mouth to speak, somebody belched, and we all said, "My Jesus, mercy."

That was a long time ago. I don't know what became of Billy Hunter or Mrs. Grimsby, and I don't know if Mrs. Hancock kept on teaching Sunday School, because I never went back. I never said anything about it to Sakaye — and then one morning when we got to school we found that all the Japanese youngsters were gone. My mother had been dead for two months when Sakaye's letter arrived, so there was no one to tell me that Sakaye had had to get permission from the Canadian authorities to write to me, and that her letter had been censored — and it was only a few years ago when I read about the Japanese internment that I realized how Sakaye must have waited for my reply.

I wish I could answer Sakaye's letter and tell her all this, because now I know that it was important after all. She must be nearly forty, and she may still be living someplace on the prairies.

But I can't read the address on her letter any more.

MICHAEL ROTHSCHILD

Dog in the Manger

(FROM ANTAEUS)

I

ALL NINE GREYHOUNDS whimpered as their trainer approached the runs. They danced on their hind legs and clawed at the chain-link fence. Long necks craned to the ground, haunches thrust up, they lashed their tails and stretched away the afternoon nap.

The trainer raised a pin from the door of one compartment. A sleek black greyhound hurtled out of the pen, his coat purple in the November sun. The dog bounded ten yards, swerved, and twirled around his master. The trainer clapped his hands; the dog depressed his wedge-shaped head and crouched through the grass, entire body waggling, up to the man's high boots. Indignant at being so quickly curtailed, the dog flicked his hot tongue on the hand fastening a slip leash to his collar and snarled at the pickerel-like brindle bitch who lunged past her opened door. The trainer clicked his tongue, leashed the bitch quickly, and jogged down the dirt road that wound to a stop at his farm.

The seven hounds left behind chorused their frustration.

The trainer jumped the shriveled ferns in the roadside gully and headed on toward the orchard and high meadow. Both greyhounds paused by the rows of bleached cornstalks scraping in the residue of the garden.

A succession of frosts had withered the landscape. From a ledge above the orchard the surrounding maroon and blue hills appeared close, sullenly compact.

Both leashes jerked taut in his fists and the trainer was lurched forward.

Halfway up the meadow a fat woodchuck began to burr. The woodchuck sat on its haunches unperturbed, its black forepaws lax. The greyhounds snorted from the pressure of the collars against their throats. Their front legs pedaled the air.

The trainer slipped the leashes and away the greyhounds sprinted over the meadow.

The woodchuck hesitated and rolled nonchalantly toward the mouth of its burrow. It was too sluggish, dazed with fat for hibernation, and the trainer felt a nausea mingle with his excitement. He began to run after his hounds.

The bitch was upon the woodchuck first, clamping its tail as it dove into the burrow and flinging it into the air. The dog seized the neck, the bitch its spine, and they began to shake it. Yoked by the screeching woodchuck, they cantered in circles on the meadow.

The trainer ordered the greyhounds to stop. He cupped his ears to muffle the woodchuck's long shriek. Greedily, the hounds paraded their catch. The woodchuck's chestnut belly had come unseamed and a loop of intestine popped through the masses of stored fat.

The greyhounds did not eat the carcass, but neither would they abandon it. They sprinted after one another, taking turns dragging and tossing it, and playing tug o' war.

The woodchuck had lost its shape and the sky was darkening before the dogs' blood cooled. They dropped the pulp in the grass and frisked happily around the trainer in reunion.

The trainer absently slicked back the whiskers on their greased hot muzzles. It was a shock to see how a chase transformed them and to share something of it, if only a rapt electric distemper. A raccoon, a rabbit, a nerve-frozen doe triggered the blood of a greyhound's eye and discharged tension that unstrung with the crack of the rabbit's neck, the collapse of the doe, her lungs exploded in a cedar swamp. Afterward, smeared and spent, they would slouch back to him, feral creatures reduced to dogs, comprehensible. He knelt to the level of the two slender heads. Ears tucked back, eyes protuberant, their dry tongues scraped his nose and mouth.

The two hounds led him through the dim meadow to the ledge.

Mist rolled off their shoulders: there would be another frost that evening. The light turned on below over the farmhouse porch. Shafts of light from the kitchen, dining room, and upstairs bedrooms sloped to the ground. Despite his distance from the farm, he saw the yellow windows of the kitchen and dining room glint, blotted by his wife setting the table, and the glint stirred his appetite.

He wrapped a leash around each fist and trotted down into the orchard. Abruptly, both greyhounds stiffened. An apple thumped in the dry grass and the branch above it wavered. The trainer stumbled ahead and yanked them to go on, but they balked and gazed across the orchard, ears cocked in the direction opposite the farmhouse. He slapped the leashes on their flanks but they did not move. They howled a prolonged, piercing alarm.

The trainer squinted through the black apple branches. He could see nothing but the long row of stakes on which the snowfences were to be hung. The hair finned along his hounds' spines. They wrenched angrily to the ends of their leashes. He worked to restrain them. Baying and coughing, the two hounds tugged toward the far corner of the orchard. He wrestled them up toward the house. Hauling and hauled, the three staggered directly between the two points, to the road.

A bulky form, an outline darker than the air, hunched one hundred yards down the dirt road.

The trainer whipped the hounds to quiet them. "Hello?" he shouted. His eyes engraved a bear into the outline. The bear was injured, he thought, perhaps drunk from bushels of apples fermented in its gut.

The hounds shrank lower to the ground. From the farm in the distance behind he heard his wife call. The bear slouched forward.

At fifty yards, a man stooped in its place.

"Are you okay?" shouted the trainer. There was no reply.

People seldom walked the dead-end road to his farm and never at night. His hounds lagged shoulder to shoulder as he approached the stranger, halting ten feet from the lowered head.

"Hey, you all right? I didn't know what you were. In fact, I thought . . ." The stranger sidled a step closer, raised his head, comically waved his palm beside his ear, and said, "Hi, Jack."

As if fingers cinched the trainer's larynx, his voice was stifled.

The trainer stared into the face before him, a caricature of the face he had known. No skull seemed to frame the head or anchor the features. Indolent eyes appeared to float like buoys no longer moored in the brain. Nothing looked symmetrical, nothing solid to the touch. The hounds' jaws clacked as they absorbed the tension which flowed through the leashes and they moodily encircled the trainer's boots.

Again he heard his wife, her voice become strained and insistent above the belligerent cacophony of the kenneled hounds. "I'm speechless," he said, shifting leashes to his left hand and extending his right hand in greeting.

The hunched man lowered his head, glanced at the dogs, and limped around them to the other side of the road. "What's wrong with them?"

"They are very high-strung. Jesus, I thought you were a bear," said the trainer to fill the space between them. Dumbly, as if motion required all his concentration, the stooped man swayed ahead.

"We have a son. He's almost three now."

The man turned into the driveway. His tortoise indifference, his laborious rocking motion, ate away the trainer's disbelief.

"You know, we actually heard last spring that you went out a window."

"Really?" The man dragged his fingers the length of the jeep.

"Yes, last spring we heard you had committed suicide."

He stopped and twisted back his head. After a moment he murmured, "I didn't come to see *you*." The trainer rapidly walked ahead.

A woman stormed onto the porch and seeing the green glow of the hounds' eyes, stopped short. "Didn't you hear me?" Television voices followed her outside through the ajar door.

"I'll lock up the dogs, I'll be right in." The trainer pulled the hounds around the corner of the house.

The crippled man entered the globe cast by the light and stood on the lowest step. He smiled up at the woman, porch light whitening the part in her coarse black hair. "Who are you?" she said.

The man made a pained noise, scowled, and looked away. His jaw hung and he turned back to her and gawked at her dark wide-set eyes.

"Mark, remember me, I'm Mark Craeger," and his mouth stretched into a long grin. Craeger crouched up the steps and moved around her as if she were not alive but a marvelous inanimate thing he had happened upon and wished to inspect. He touched her hand. He rubbed the fabric of her loose khaki trousers between his fingers.

"These are not your pants," he said.

"We both wear them."

Craeger grimaced theatrically as the trainer opened the door behind her. His stoop intensified. His shoulder brushed the woman's hip as he lumbered past her husband and into the house.

Straightaway Craeger scrutinized the face of the child. He stroked a twine of black hair from the boy's fleshy bright cheek and it sprang back. Transfixed in the highchair by a giraffe dunking its neck between splayed forelegs to reach water, the boy chewed a porkchop bone and continued to ogle the television. The woman watched Craeger hover near her son and quickly brought another plate and silverware to the table. Craeger sat next to the child. His acrid smell saturated the room.

"Joel," said the trainer, "this is Mark."

A herd of wildebeeste smoked across the savanna, an elephant fanned its ears, a parrot squealed, and from nowhere a lion straddled the gouged remains of a zebra.

"Zebra horse," burst Joel, pointing with his chop. Joel's upper lip protruded and he rested his wet chin on the brass buttons of his overalls. Sideways, he regarded Craeger, who was bent close to the plate, noisily swallowing the porkchops, beets, and salad placed before him.

"Mark eat porkchops," Joel observed aloud. "Mark eat cucumbers." Craeger contorted his face, stuck out his beet-mauve tongue and wiggled it at Joel. Joel banged his head against the back of the highchair and let out a long ticklish laugh. The vein in his temple distended and his small mouth showed sharp, spaced teeth. "Mark funny man," he announced.

Craeger took the last chop and stuffed it into the side pocket of his navy suit jacket. "Do you like him?" he mumbled. Joel climbed down from his highchair, toddled to the latched door leading to the playroom, and twisted the knob with both hands. Unsuccessful, he slapped his palm against the door.

"Does who like who?" the woman said to the bristled peak of Craeger's head.

"No, Joel," his father said. Joel flushed, fell on his rump, and gaveled on the door.

"*You* the *boy*," said Craeger.

She snorted smilingly and did not reply.

"This is some place, Fran, you must love it here," said Craeger.

"We do," said the trainer.

"Must put a lot of pressure on one another, so far from people. Not to get bored, I mean."

"There's a lot to do," said the trainer.

"Gee, those are some animals you have," said Craeger. "How many do you have anyway?"

"Ten."

"Ten dogs! That must cost a pretty penny. Why so many?"

"I raise them for the track."

"Gives you something to do, I suppose." Craeger bent forward with a warm smile. "Why do you answer all the questions, Jack; is Fran forbidden to talk?" The trainer laughed and as his laughter died, Craeger added, "Is something *wrong* here?"

The trainer slumped back and benignly enlarged his eyes. "What can I say? Fran, have I cut your tongue out?"

Joel's rhythmic hammering ceased the moment his father rose to unhook the door. Joel pulled himself up by his father's leg and turned the knob. Listening behind the door, a greyhound scuttled to its feet, its claws clattering on the bare hardwood as Joel darted into the playroom.

"This is inane," said Frances. She snapped off the television and began to clear the table. Joel returned from his toybox with a miniature dump truck and fire engine and placed them on the table beside Craeger's elbow. Craeger ignored them.

A white bitch stared from the open door. "This is Milka. We're about to breed her. See what happens, Mark, when they're in heat," said the trainer. He pressed his knuckles along her sinuous back. When he reached the base of her spine, the tail switched mechanically to the side.

"This pump truck," said Joel, steering the red fire engine on the edge of the table. "Hydraulic dumper." Craeger pursed his lips, his eye fastened on the bitch.

Twice the white greyhound warily stalked around the table, stirred by Craeger's new scent. Her serpentine body crouched at

last, sphinxlike, behind Joel. "Wow, she's something," said Craeger and started to growl louder than the hose noises that Joel
whooshed to accompany his fire engine.

"Don't make that sound."

Craeger persisted. Suddenly Craeger batted the fire engine and
dump truck at the hound. Milka started before they hit the floor.
Her black lips twitched back to unsheath her fangs. Craeger hissed
and taunted. The trainer clutched Milka's collar, dragged her to
the playroom, and held the door closed.

Joel gathered his vehicles and rushed to clasp his mother's legs.
She hoisted him to her breast. Belatedly his face puckered and he
wept. Craeger remained seated. He withdrew the porkchop from
his pocket and in a droll, passive manner commenced to chew at it.

The trainer felt his hands and feet go cold. "Take Joel upstairs.
Latch this door behind you."

Craeger deposited the cleaned bone on the table and, as if he
would nap, sank into himself.

"There are rules, Mark, human decencies. I don't know what
has happened to you and I don't hold myself or Frances responsible
for it. Do you understand that? This is our house and if you stay
here you'll act like a human being. You won't provoke the dogs,
you will not . . . do you understand?"

He saw that Craeger's compliant posture had deflected all his
words. For emphasis, that some contact be made, he seized Craeger's wrist. Craeger's parted lips dropped to kiss the back of his
hand. His hand retracted. Craeger raised his varnished sulphur-
colored eyes and scrolled his upper lip beneath his nosetip.

"What do you want here?" said the trainer. He fixed upon
Craeger's white skin, hairs separate on the boneless cheek. He had
no more words. Craeger's exorbitant expressions failed to signify
any state of being which he recognized. 'Human decencies, human
decencies' — uncanny, drained of sense — resounded like a heck-
ler's voice and heat compressed around his eyes.

"He's a great little boy," said Craeger. He wrinkled his nose
and averted his head.

The trainer turned wearily and paced through the kitchen to the
dark corridor of the shed. The cold burned his wet face. In the
kennel below, the ears of the nine hounds crooked to follow his

footsteps. The hounds scurried from their stalls down ramps to the runs outside. They fidgeted hungrily, barking, anxious to be let out.

He switched on the floodlights and descended to the kennel. Hardened by the wind, the ground was already crisp beneath his boots. He let out two males. The larger sauntered over the moonlit field and waited for the smaller fawn greyhound to challenge. Nose to the ground, the fawn dog carefully meandered, urinated on the smoking grass, sniffed, all the while closing the space between them.

Swiftly the challenger bolted and left the other champing in pursuit at his flanks. Their sharp-knuckled paws drummed across the field. They shrank in the distance, merged and vanished. A faint drumming continued, grew loud, and neck and neck they pelted toward the trainer, humped, lashed out, humped like giant ferrets. The fawn greyhound rippled past him, a muzzle ahead. His tongue slapped on his lathered cheek, his lemur eyes limpid, emerald in the moonlight. The fawn greyhound, the trainer decided, would sire Milka's litter.

Craeger stood back from the kitchen window, sucked at the milk carton spout, and once more reeled forward to peer into the yard. He hooted contentedly. Under floodlights outside, the greyhounds wriggled like snakes around the trainer.

Craeger jeered and tilted back the milk carton.

Frances' voice cautioned Milka. Girded by an air of preoccupation, she slipped into the dining room, hooked the playroom door, and directly strolled to the kitchen. Craeger set the milk carton on the window sill and crossed to the sink. Silently he hunched beside her. He watched her strong fingers scour fork tines and spoons. He confronted her quietly with his close huddled presence until she acknowledged him. "Joel takes to me," he said.

"He doesn't see many people," said Frances.

"I think this is a bit extra special, don't you?" Craeger nudged her and with a grunt, stood straight.

"Why do you walk all doubled over if you can stand up?"

Craeger whistled admiration. "Fifty-four bones I broke. I am a cripple. Fifty-four," he blustered. To stress the point, he clownishly resumed a deepened slouch.

"How are you doing? You're not as pretty as you used to be, you know that, Fran?"

"No?"

"And I know why."

"Well, then, tell me," she said archly.

"Because Jack is a *bad* person," he declared.

"Think that," snapped Frances.

Craeger pressed against her hip. His lower lip drooped and he stretched to kiss her blunt jawbone. Frances lightly shoved him and he collapsed at her feet. He smirked, reached up, and patted the buckle of her belt. "You're going all rotten in there. All rotten." Craeger knit his limbs and folded up at her feet like a great-headed fetus spilled from a jar of formaldehyde.

Frances petulantly filled the sink with dishes, made a bed of the playroom couch, and led restive Milka to the isolation pen at the side of the house. "You can sleep in the playroom," she informed Craeger stiffly. He lounged at the table like a drunkard, swished the carton and swallowed, milk drooling down his neck into his collar. "There will be towels on the bed. The bathroom is on the left," Frances concluded and headed upstairs.

"I wouldn't shit in your toilet," he exclaimed.

Craeger rolled the empty milk carton from one corner of the table to the other and waited. When he heard the heavy footsteps on the porch he listed forward on the table and closed his eyes. The trainer softly locked the front door, turned off the porch light, and stepped to the playroom door. His fingers were checked on the doorknob: "It was this time of the year five years ago we first saw Fran," said Craeger. Craeger had not shifted position. His gray lids remained shut.

"I remember," said the trainer, uncertain whether he should go on, stand, or join Craeger at the table.

"On a red horse. She looked so fine." Craeger's words seemed to roll out by themselves. "What a beauty. I loved her, you know that?" Craeger shivered and sat up. He chewed as if his mouth had gone dry. "What's happened to her anyway?"

"What do you mean?"

"Frances is a *bad* person," he pronounced.

The trainer stood arrested. "And why do you say that?"

"You know full well." Craeger's smile assumed a complicity.

His lids flagged. "Good night, Jack," he said with a nod of dismissal.

"Good night," the trainer repeated. That he had not refuted the charge in Craeger's smile annoyed him the instant he left the room. He climbed upstairs and paused. He listened to Joel's breathing, crossed the landing, and sat on the foot of the bed to tug off his boots.

"Well?" The shade-blackened room amplified her voice.

He undressed and lay beside her. He reached out and touched the flannel over her hip. "Nightgown?"

"Craeger," replied Frances. "You shouldn't have let him come. My God, he was supposed to be dead, I thought."

"I didn't invite him."

"Make him go," she demanded, "tomorrow. I don't want him around Joel. He stinks."

"How generous."

"Isn't it true? And he's crazy, Jack."

"You have an awful short memory." She did not answer. "Besides, where can he go?"

"That's not our problem," she said. "You can't help him."

"I care about him."

"Why? He hates your guts."

"Oh?"

"He said as much. He said you were a bad person."

In the next room Joel thrashed a bar of the crib and squealed in his sleep. Frances tiptoed to the crib and patted his back until, calmed, Joel hummed briefly and resumed an even sleep.

"He didn't come to see me, you know," the trainer said decisively on her return.

She was silent, thinking for a long while before she said, "Sometimes I wish I didn't even exist until we got married."

"That's nonsense."

She was still awake when her husband twitched and his breathing deepened into sleep. She heard the dogs stir in the kennel and moan dismally for access to Milka's swollen heat.

Past midnight the high-pitched moans changed to a fearful and aggressive summons. She shivered from a doze. She leaned over her husband and wrinkled back the shade. She shook him. "He's leaving, he's leaving," she cried.

In the white moonlight below, Craeger trundled toward the orchard. He rummaged in the frost-stiff grass at the edge of the garden. Then he lowered his trousers and for some minutes crouched
on his white hams. Then, he shambled back to the farmhouse.

II

Impatient that his day begin, Joel clutched the crib bars and rocked
the crib.

"Fine thing, to dread going down your own stairs," said Frances.
She tucked her trouser leg into the woolen sock and laced her boot.

"I said I'd talk to him. It doesn't have to be brutal," he said.

"It is already. Why did Joel toss all night? And the dogs? Get
him out, Jack. That's more important than your sentimental
manners."

"Sentimental? He was a close friend, you were in love with him.
Is that sentimental?"

"Get him out," she repeated, her voice styptic.

"All right, I said I'll tell him."

She left the room and with Joel slung on her hip reappeared at
the door. "Morning, Joel," crowed the trainer. Joel happily
whipped his body.

"We'll be outside today," she said and went down.

Untouched, the two towels hung on the back of the couch. The
bed had not been slept in. She kneed open the door and saw Craeger's back curved over the table. Eggshells circled a stack of Joel's
books, the milk carton, and the pork bone. "Look! Look here,
Joel. A panda is snoozing in the bamboos," said Craeger. He
flagged the picture at Joel. Joel squirmed and reached to Craeger.
"Get down, get down," he insisted.

"Help Mommy make the oatmeal," countered Frances. She hu-
mored him into the kitchen and while she prepared breakfast, held
him on her side.

When she perched Joel on the counter, however, his lips refused
to unseal for the spoon. At last she yielded and sat at the table.
Craeger flattened his ear to the table and frowned like a physician
discerning an irregular pulse. He proceeded meticulously to cleave
the eggshells with his thumbnail. Each time a shell cracked, Joel's
mouth gaped with hilarity and Frances deposited a spoonful of oat-

meal. She felt blood rise suddenly to the surface of her face; Craeger's decoy was not for Joel — he had tricked her into sharing a domestic travesty, and each time an eggshell was splintered on the table, it was as if he snapped a beetle's shard.

The trainer heard Joel's laughter before he entered the dining room. This day he had not expected to hear laughter and find everyone seated together. "Good morning, Jack," said Craeger, lifting his head. "Are you as hungry as I am?" He smirked askance at Frances, who had offered him nothing. She worked Joel's feet into the gum-rubber boots and snapped up his coat. She failed to catch her husband's eye as he ambled to the refrigerator. "There's enough oatmeal for both of you on the stove," she said, grabbed her jacket, and led Joel tripping outdoors.

He put up coffee and dished the thickened oatmeal into two bowls. He placed a bowl at Craeger's littered end of the table. "Been eating an egg?"

"Eggs," said Craeger.

The trainer ate his oatmeal. He watched Craeger's forefingers swab viscous cereal from the bowl.

"Well, what do you have planned, Mark?"

Extravagantly perplexed, Craeger tilted back his head and narrowed his eyes.

"What do you want to do, I mean?"

"Visit."

The trainer noticed the red light glowing on the percolator. "How do you have your coffee?"

"Cream and two teaspoons of honey."

"Honey?" He smiled, shrugged, filled the order, and served the coffee. He swished hot coffee through his teeth and said in a tight pleased voice, "So, you really think I'm a bad person?"

Craeger concentrated on the trainer's soft eyes.

"I know you said it. How could Fran have known you used the exact same words about her?" The logic braced him and he sat.

"She does know, then?" asked Craeger.

The trainer paused a moment too long, nodded, and Craeger drank coffee and spoke nothing.

"It would be better if you left."

"But I just arrived."

"We both think it would be better."

"Better?"

"We have to breed dogs today. You antagonize the dogs. And last night Joel . . ."

"Joel likes me," interrupted Craeger, "a lot."

"Yes, but last . . ."

"I wanted to be with you and Fran. There are a lot of people I want to see again. I've spent too much time alone in hospital rooms, so much that I forget how to talk. I wanted to visit you first . . ."

"It's not possible right now."

"And then maybe afterward I'll travel around, maybe go to Peru with somebody, or British Columbia."

"I'll drive you to town this afternoon."

Craeger drew in his neck and settled sulking, contracted in his chair.

"You'll be able to catch a bus." Resolve drove each word out his mouth. His eyes avoided Craeger and he walked outside to the porch. If he remained in the room, discomfort would prime more words and in the end, he would relent.

He ignored the hounds' hallooing and strolled down to the garden. Cusps of frost lingered in the shadows of the house. In the open the day was brilliant and warm. He pulled cornstalks and flung them onto the pile of frost-lurid tomatoes, purple squash, and wizened black peppers. With a stick he chiseled the hard ground and crawled down rows where turnips, beets, and carrots had grown, his fingers rooting the cold broken dirt to harvest whatever Frances had overlooked.

He stopped working and knelt back on his heels. All at once the fact that he had left Craeger alone in the house surged through his body strewing images of a room on fire, a rifle aimed at a greyhound's brisket. Anxiously he scanned the side of the house. His eyes fastened to a darkness shifting upstairs behind his bedroom window.

He sprang up and ran to the house. He charged through the empty dining room, the playroom, and up the stairs.

Gazing into the rectangular mirror which rose behind the opened drawers of the commode, Craeger gritted his teeth as he raked a brush over his stiff cropped hair.

"What are you doing here?" gasped the trainer, pounding into the room.

Craeger replaced the hairbrush on the marble top of the commode and said, "You never showed me your house."

Only after he had noticed Craeger's navy suit jacket pouched on the sheets of his unmade bed did he realize that his own tweed sportcoat was draped around Craeger's body. "Get out of here," he screamed. He bunched Craeger's suit jacket in his fist and halted. Beneath the jacket was an album of photographs taken from a shelf in Joel's bedroom. The album was turned to a page on which Frances crouched in a meadow to forage for blueberries, opposite Frances in her gold swimsuit counting periwinkles with naked Joel on a pink granite shore by the ocean.

"Do you need this jacket?" Craeger asked, holding out the wide tweed lapels.

"Get out of here," the trainer said. "Here." He tossed the blue suit jacket to Craeger. The jacket hit his shoulder and fell to the floor. Craeger disregarded it and lurched slowly downstairs. The trainer picked up the jacket and followed. Craeger returned to his end of the table and sat.

"Let's go, Mark, you can catch the bus."

"I don't have any money."

The trainer walked to the kitchen counter and wrote a check for one hundred dollars. He slapped it on the stack of Joel's picture books beside Craeger. Craeger officiously read the check and folded it in half. He slanted on one buttock to slide the check into his trouser pocket.

"Now let's go. I'll drive you to the station." Craeger refused to move. "Don't make me force you."

Craeger chose a book about steam shovels and leafed through its pages. The trainer wrenched him from the seat by his elbow. Craeger slackened and was dragged out to the porch. "Now get in the jeep."

Craeger squirmed loose and simpered, "No."

"Walk, then," and he threw shut the front door. He spied the suit jacket dumped in a chair seat, rushed it to the door, and slung it onto the porch. Craeger stood where he had left him, the suit jacket coiled about his shoes. Once again the trainer closed the door. He listened a moment, locked the door, and with his open palm began to sweep the bone and eggshells over the edge of the table into the empty milk carton.

Outside, Craeger scuffled to the end of the porch and as if he had reached the prow of a dinghy, stopped short to survey the long hazardous swell of field, orchard, and tapering road. Around the corner of the house he glimpsed Milka prowling the margin of her isolation pen. Craeger stretched and, crooning, squatted against the clapboard wall, his knees drawn under his chin. He took the check from his trouser pocket and from inside his tweed sportcoat retrieved a small photograph: Frances' head was lowered and her cheeks facetiously bulged as she perused her pregnant belly; her fingers interlocked to measure, to substantiate its impossible girth. Expressionless, Craeger examined the photograph carefully before he inserted it in the creased check and replaced both inside his new sportscoat. He felt the tremor of pacing through the downstairs. The tremor diminished, dogs began to bark, and Craeger watched the road. A truck had stopped far down the road and he saw two tiny figures begin to unroll slat fences and fasten them to the row of stakes.

Joel took him by surprise, roaming from behind the shed. He climbed the porch steps and approached, coyly drawing cider from a brown apple. "Where's Mommy?" Craeger asked.

"What Mark doing?" Joel asked and quickly answered, "Mark sit on porch." Craeger giggled and pointed out the men putting up the band of snowfencing. Delighted, Joel tittered and sucked on the thawing apple. Presently Frances tramped around the shed, fronds of asparagus and milkweed pods bunched in her fist.

"That's a pretty bouquet," remarked Craeger.

"Isn't it lovely?" said Frances. "Is that Jack's coat?"

"No," said Craeger, "he gave it to me. Know what those guys are doing? Quarantine."

Frances smiled, pushed on the locked door, turned the knob, and rapped. "Is he home?"

"I think so," said Craeger.

Frances knocked again. "What?" answered the trainer fiercely.

"We're back."

Craeger chortled as the door opened and Joel heaved his apple

off the porch. Frances took Joel's arm and pulled him into the dining room. The trainer slammed and locked the door.

"I forgot the watchword," bantered Frances.

He shoved her against the door. Joel scooted to the kitchen
chewing his fingers. "It's no joke, he's warped."

Frances sidestepped meekly and placed the palms of asparagus
and milkweed pods in an amethyst-colored jar. She centered the arrangement on the table. "What's happened?" She restrained Joel
as he streaked toward the playroom and removed his coat.

"I wanted to give him every chance. Malignant is the only word,
malignant."

"Did you ask him to go?"

"He made me kick him out." She saw the edge was gone from
his anger.

"Aren't you going a bit overboard?" She opened the cupboard
and pushed cans.

"I caught him ransacking our bedroom."

"Are you serious? What was he doing?"

"He'd been into the drawers. The photo album was out. He was
using my hairbrush."

"And so you gave him your tweed jacket?"

"He already had it on. I don't want a thing he's touched. I
threw the brush in the trash."

Frances locked a soup can in the can opener and ground off its
lid. "Then call the county sheriff," she suggested calmly.

"Just keep the door locked. Ignore him. He'll get hungry. How
long can he stay? Pretend he isn't there."

"What should I tell Joel?"

"Nothing. It would confuse him. Keep Joel away from him."

"He's gone out of his way to be friendly to Joel."

"It's a trick. Just pretend everything is the same. During Joel's
nap we'll breed Milka. We'll use the shed door, that's all. Stay
away from the porch."

"It's not reasonable, Jack. If he's out there we can't ignore
him."

"You heard what I said."

He selected two short leashes from a peg in the shed. In pairs he
exercised six of the greyhounds. The dogs tried to maneuver to-

ward the isolation pen. The brindle bitch, who slashed jealously at
the dogs, and a large surly red dog, he ran separately. When he at-
tempted to coax the red hound back to the kennel, the dog bucked
and pinwheeled but failed to slip his collar. The trainer whipped
the leash twice. The red dog glared and cringed into the run.

The fawn greyhound seemed to understand he had been selected
for stud. Leashed, he trotted obediently at the trainer's thigh. He
brushed the hound's fine yellow coat in the shed and they entered
the house.

"I'm not sure Joel's asleep yet. He was all keyed up," said
Frances, turning from the sink. She walked to the landing, listened,
and returned. "Don't you want something to eat first?"

"No. Get a roll of gauze, I don't know how Milka will take to
this."

Frances trailed them to the isolation pen. Milka greeted the fawn
dog at the gate with a histrionic assault and darted into a corner.
The trainer shut himself and Frances inside the pen, released the
dog, and waited.

The hounds stamped formally and frolicked. Frequently they
halted and the dog nuzzled the bitch's ear or butted her shoulder
and throat. She stood rigidly, switched aside her tail, and he
dabbed his tongue over her unfurling heat. The dog mounted.
The white bitch yelped, twisting back to gash his tensed neck. He
dodged and paraded about her. His eyes bulged from his narrow
head. Upright, his tail stirred the air like a sickle.

The trainer took the gauze roll from his wife. "She's too flighty.
Hold him." He straddled Milka and wound the gauze around her
closed snout. "Now bring him here to me; you steady Milka." He
tugged the dog away and his wife held Milka's collar. His wife
knelt on one knee and with the other braced the bitch's concave
belly. She blinkered Milka's eyes with her elbow while her husband directed the fawn greyhound from behind.

The dog's glistening red nozzle emerged as he reared to clasp
Milka's haunches. The trainer bent to guide it into the breach.
Muted by the gauze muzzle, the bitch's screams persisted until the
sperm jet was lodged, fully dilated, inside her.

"A tie," he said happily. He was sweating. The clonic lunges of
the dog's body softened and the bitch relaxed.

Tousled black hair stuck to the bridge of Frances' wet nose. He looked at Frances and began to laugh.

"What modesty," said Frances. "Poor Milka." Frances scratched Milka's ear. "Christ, my legs and arms are all cramped."

"Why don't you go back in?" he said. "It could take another half-hour."

"You can manage by yourself?"

"I think so." He switched positions with Frances. He supported drowsy Milka and held the dog's tawny withers to prevent him from rolling off. Frances kissed his brow and groaned to her feet.

"Bravo, bravo," shouted Craeger before she had unpinned the gate to leave the isolation pen. "Do it again. What a show," Craeger racketed from the edge of the porch. His neck was lewdly crooked around the house corner, "Encore, encore, encore."

Frances indicated her disgust and trudged stonily to the shed entrance.

III

Saddled on the arm of the playroom couch, Joel peeped noiselessly out the window. Like the white wing of a moth, the back of Craeger's left ear was suspended outside the lower corner of the window. Joel pressed nearer to the glass. The navy suit jacket turbaned the rest of Craeger's head and his body was clenched against the chill.

"Dessert, Joel," Frances called into the playroom.

Milka looped back her neck and haltingly licked her loins. She gobbled the bit of chicken breast the trainer pitched by her snout and resumed the methodical bath. "We'll breed them again tomorrow."

Frances placed three dishes of pudding on the table. "Tapioca," she hollered.

The trainer considered the white bitch sprawled by the front door. "This litter should be something special." Frances nodded and marched into the playroom. Joel hovered by the window and watched her shadow stretch over Craeger's head and fill the cube of light cast from the playroom to the dark porch. She cupped her hand on Joel's shoulder. "Come on, honey, tapioca pudding." He jumped to the blankets covering the couch. "Mark sleeps on the porch," he said.

Frances carried Joel to the dining room and inserted him in the highchair. He dug his teeth into the center of the dish and wiped tapioca on his chin and throat.

"Are you tired?" his father asked him. Joel scooped more pudding and greased the deck of his highchair. The dish was confiscated. "He's overtired, Frances."

"Mark sleeps on the porch," said Joel.

The trainer glared at Frances. "What did I say about that?"

"About what?"

"Mark sleeps on the porch, Mark sleeps on porch," Joel agitated. His incantation worked.

"Not to say a thing to . . ." He completed his meaning with a nod at Joel.

Frances reached over Milka and snapped on the porch light. "What do you think Joel is, a moron?"

"Turn off that light."

"No."

He rose and slapped down the light switch. Milka moved skittishly to the kitchen. "Because you wanted him out *today*, I put myself through living hell this morning. I did what you wanted. Don't go back on it."

Frances lifted Joel between them. "And? Is he gone?" she said pointedly. "No, but we slink in and out of the back of the fort. You think that's what I wanted? To play this asinine game?" Joel gabbled loudly. "And don't say I'm upsetting Joel," she added. "He sees him camped on the porch. He feels how unnatural all this is."

The back of his hand flashed up, faltered, and his fingers lightly stung her temple. Redness stippled her throat and ringed her eyes. Joel went silent, vague. "You had better get hold of yourself, Jack," she said blandly. "Go outside. Feed your dogs."

He followed her into the playroom. She picked out the farm puzzle and the circus puzzle and said, "We'll be upstairs." He loitered, resting on the blanketed couch. A wrecker truck, cement mixer, ferris wheel, two wagons, a sprung Jack-in-the-box, Noah's ark, and dozens of plastic barnyard and exotic animals had overflowed the plentitude of Joel's toybox and were stranded on the braided rug. Unnatural? Her adamant hostility toward Craeger, Craeger's uncanny, insolent, obsequious and idiotically sinister behavior — that was unnatural. And now, after she had prodded him to turn Craeger out, she called it asinine. He glanced out the window behind him and discerned cowled Craeger huddled serenely in the half-light, asleep.

Listlessly, he walked through the downstairs and into the shed. He clustered nine dishes and filled them with dry meal. He left the floodlights off. He watched the woolly blue clouds mass along the hills and conceal the moon.

Blocking the entrance to each run with his body, he slid the feed dishes past the doors. The greyhounds tried to squeeze outside. Milka's season dwindled their appetites.

A thin cap of ice had formed on the water pans. The trainer cracked the ice and refilled the pans. Tonight the hounds were all the same to him and it was a chore to feed them. Bitter wind seared the matted field and forced him to the shed. He decided to renew his offer to drive Craeger to town. Perhaps the chill wind had changed Craeger's mind.

Milka accompanied him to the front door. As if she were readying to break from a trap, the white bitch crouched below the doorknob. He dragged her to the playroom and hooked the door. Then he flicked on the porch light and went out.

Craeger dropped a drumstick into the tiny heap of picked chicken bones on the porch deck and snuggled the patchwork quilt about his neck. He revolved his head, raised his eyes and said pompously, "Yes?"

The trainer noted Craeger's new supplies. He stooped, and one by one gathered the moist bones. "These can injure dogs," he said remotely. He turned and walked to the door.

"Very well," said Craeger, "dispose of them."

The trainer softly closed and locked the door. He switched off the porch light, threw the chicken bones in the waste can, and cleaned his hands at the kitchen sink. His body moved heavily. A nerve mass in the base of his neck had begun to sting, and with each step he made through the house and up the stairs, the smart quickened.

He watched from the door of Joel's bedroom. Frances hushed

him and resumed the lullaby. Her legs were tucked beneath her and one arm rubbed Joel's back through the bars of the crib.

He leaned on the doorjamb and isolated a puzzle piece by her heel, a ballerina in a handstand on a speckled draft horse. Humming the song, Frances got carefully to her feet. She checked Joel and whispered, "I thought he would never fall to sleep. We made those puzzles fifty times." She moved close to the trainer at the head of the stairs. Her broad angular features appeared to him unusually distinct, yet much farther away than he knew she was.

"Are you okay, Jack?" She did not wait for his answer. She passed him quickly and walked downstairs to wash.

"Why did you feed him?" he asked, but she did not hear or did not wish to reply.

He was leaning on the doorjamb, his back to her, when Frances returned and she was frightened. "I'm bushed. Aren't you coming to bed?" she asked, retreating to the bedroom. He held the banister and as if plated with mail, descended.

He sat on the couch. Hanging from brass chains of the playroom chandelier, the blue coronas of four bulbs nettled him. The rhythmic clack of Milka's tread deadened on the braided rug. When he put his face against hers, the ceiling light, her long skull, and his head were momentarily aligned, just so, and he looked through her eye. He saw only a dark-red web of vessels squirm in amber liquid. It was there, in that web, a sight hound lived.

He turned off the four lights and in the dark massaged the base of his skull and let his neck loll over the back of the couch. Silently, Milka bounded onto the couch and nestled into a ring beside him, her sharp muzzle across his lap. Again and again his fingertips traced a line from her damp nostrils to the bone ridge between her warm velvet ears. When he quit, she whined and nuzzled his stomach. He drooped his head forward and pushed Milka off the couch. His foot bumped the Jack-in-the-box and it whistled like a bellows as he moved along the wall.

He fed Milka in the shed and whisked her by the mob of hounds to the isolation pen. On his way back through the downstairs, he put out the remaining lights. He pulled back the blanket and sheet on the couch and, fully dressed, stretched into the makeshift bed his wife had fixed for Craeger.

Like a blizzard, the baying of the confined greyhounds filtered into the house and he straggled in and out of sleep. Before the night had elapsed, Joel's murmurings, the dogs' rutting din, the rumble of the furnace in the cellar all blended together and the air seemed to jangle and scream as it circulated through the playroom. He started up in the blackness, uncertain whether his eyes were open or shut, if he imagined the chaos blaring from the kennel. He turned to the window to see if Craeger had left the porch to defecate but could not determine even the outline of the window.

He kicked aside the sibilant Jack-in-the-box, jarred three carnival notes from the ferris wheel and stumbled his way toward the shed. The tumult of the greyhounds had grown frenzied. He groped about the mortised timbers in the shed to locate the floodlight switch.

The abrupt effulgence of the floodlights dazed him. From the shed steps he squinted, white-blind, to comprehend the pandemonium below.

Two enormous many-colored wings flapped spookily back and forth along the block of runs. Fanning the patchwork quilt like plumage of a mating display, Craeger strutted past the fawn and black greyhounds, stamped outside the red hound's door, and gesticulated his quilt. Purple and white jaws clapping the air, spines bristled, the greyhounds lunged at the fence. The red dog thrashed and crazily rammed the chain-link wall.

The trainer seized Craeger's back and hurled him to the ground.

Craeger drew in his head, doubled up, and sheltered himself beneath the quilt. The trainer stabbed his foot into the mute cushion and waited.

Motionless as a garish fungus under the floodlights, Craeger did not respond. "Bait the dogs," screeched the trainer, and his heel once more came down on the quilted mound.

Timorously the quilt began to creep, over the frozen ground. Craeger draped a quilt-corner on his shoulders so he could see, and lumbered out of the spotlit ring on all fours.

The trainer kept pace, exactly beside him. Craeger turned the edge of the house and crawled before Milka to reach the raised porch. Breathing quickly, he clambered onto the porch and wound himself in the quilt.

The trainer scanned the flat black sky. Little as yet suggested the coming day. He addressed the murky shape on the porch: "It will

be light in less than an hour. If you are on my property then, I'm
going to call the police and have you arrested."

An amused gasp erupted from Craeger's throat. "Arrest this
man, Sheriff," he gruffly imitated. "The charge?" he inquired.
"Well, sir, he's Joel's rightful father." His dialogue completed,
Craeger forced a yawn, cocked the side of his head to his kneetops
and watched the trainer's silhouette fade by the corner as if it had
melted into the clapboard wall.

Milka jostled the fence of the isolation pen. He drifted by her
and the row of pent hounds pranced as though the pebble floor
seared their footpads. He made no attempt to pacify them.

From the shed cabinet he selected a box of cartridges and took
down his rifle. He pulled the cord of the single bulb above the
workbench and wiped a rag along the cold barrel.

He carried the rifle and ammunition into the house. He vaguely
distinguished Joel's toys on the playroom floor. He sidestepped
them and sat on the couch. He removed the lens caps, drew back
the bolt of the rifle, and loaded five cartridges. He worked with
precision.

He lay the rifle on the disheveled couch and, one level at a time,
moved up the flight of stairs. He crossed his bedroom and furrowed
back the shade next to the bed. All he could make out were ribbons on the prim collar of her nightgown. Her deep, distanced
breaths did not convince him she was sleeping, but it made no difference, so far had she and the bed receded from his eyes. He let the
shade fall and slid into Joel's room. He did not stop to look into
the crib. He parted the curtains of the window opening on the
road, raised the shade, and began his vigil.

More than an hour he watched the dark enclosure of sky. Joel
chirped and smacked his lips. The first light appeared, to seep up
through the bone-colored road and the hoarfrost between rows of
apple trees. Still, he lingered at the window and listened for a
signal.

A silver-red sunspot filled a niche in the one-dimensional hill
line. Like a snake issuing from a black fissure the spot stretched
silver-red along the undulating rim of hills until its limbless train
encircled the horizon.

Momentarily, the alert sounded, remote, inexorable, from the
kennel and he spied Craeger slouching from the porch and down

the driveway. He watched the pallid form veer suddenly toward the garden. It was not the form of any person he had known. It was not a person at all. It was the distorted shape of his life that he saw, wile without spine, the lies and deception on which the center of his life had rested.

Craeger made a dozen laggard and undecided steps and halted. He stood absolutely stiff. He turned slowly, all the way around, and he looked up at the single shining pane of glass behind which the trainer kept watch.

The trainer hastened down the stairs. He clutched the rifle and stalked through the house to the kennel where greyhounds ricocheted off the chain-links.

He swung open the red greyhound's door.

The red dog vaulted from the run and vanished before the trainer was able to discharge the black dog, the fawn dog, and the brindle bitch, one after the other.

He replaced the pin in each door and walked around the corner of the shed.

Beneath an apple tree, halfway between the garden and the snowfence, the hounds swarmed over the bulge of Craeger's body.

The trainer sat on the frigid turf.

The greyhounds' pointed heads converged, bobbed, and wagged savagely. They flipped the body on its back and the four snouts plunged to carve. The swarm became clear, stylized, the revolving figures of a merry-go-round. He steadied the circular reticle of the scope behind a dog's shoulder blade. He was deaf to the report of the rifle as the fawn greyhound twisted into the grass.

Bewildered, the brindle bitch arched her head at gaze and somersaulted when the bullet tore into her chest.

The black hound bolted fearfully toward his trainer. Steaming muzzle, throat, and forelegs were dark silver with blood. Shot, he sagged and flattened on the driveway.

Frances burst screaming out the front door.

The large red greyhound cowered in confusion over Craeger's body and the trainer fired. The dog yelped and hobbled toward the woods. Frances shoved his shoulder and his last shot hit nothing. Her face was deranged. She saw the figure heaped at the edge of the orchard.

"Set, set," called the man after the red greyhound.

"Good God, no please . . ."

"Three dogs."

"My God . . . no, no, you didn't, no."

"They jumped the run to get at him." A red slash, the grey-hound disappeared into the leafless trees. "The dogs, I killed them."

A squeal broke from the upstairs bedroom. Frances crumpled on the ground. He put down the rifle. He clamped Frances' elbow and jerked her to her feet. "Call the sheriff . . . hurry . . . do you hear, quick, he may still be alive," and he glided over the streaked frost.

PETER L. SANDBERG

Calloway's Climb

(FROM PLAYBOY)

THE NORTH FACE of the mountain was still in shadow at midmorning and the lead boy's yellow parka showed brightly against it as a small and now immobile sun. He stood in web stirrups suspended from *pitons* he had finally managed to drive into the granite roof of an overhang that jutted 15 feet out from a point almost at the perfect center of the steep 2000-foot wall, so that he stood suspended over 1000 feet of space. For two hours, Nils Johnson, a half mile distant at timber line, had watched through his binoculars the agonizing progress of the climb and he knew now, had known for many minutes, that this lead boy was going to fall.

The second boy seemed to know it, too. Less conspicuous in a dark-blue parka, he sat face out, legs dangling from a small ledge 60 feet below and 30 feet west of the center of the overhang, holding tightly in his gloved hands and across the small of his back the rope that linked him with his companion. Through Johnson's binoculars the rope was a taut golden cable that ran on a bold diagonal up from the second boy's gloved left hand through four equally spaced *pitons,* then through a fifth *piton* driven into a crack in the angle formed by the wall and the overhang. From this final protective *piton,* the rope went out to the waist of the lead boy, around which it had been passed three times and secured with a bowline knot.

The boy continued to stand immobile in his stirrups. His head was close under the roof of the overhang, bent slightly, and he held on to the upper quarter of one of the stirrups with his left hand and kept his balled right fist jammed into a crack that began several

feet from the lip of the overhang itself. Occasionally, his companion on the ledge below would crane his neck to follow the diagonal
of the golden rope, but he would not look, Johnson observed, in
that direction for long. It was as if he did not wish to witness the
accident that seemed imminent, as if he were not sure of the sound-
ness of the *pitons* the lead boy had placed (and upon which the
lead boy's life would depend in the event of a fall) nor of his own
ability to handle the rope skillfully.

Johnson had two sons, at home in Denver now. His older son,
Tommy, was 12: only a few years younger, he guessed, than these
two boys who for two days had been inching their way up the steep
north face. His wife, Elizabeth, had been the first to notice them
from the camp Johnson had established beside the clear stream
below the first gentle rise of the mountain. It had been his idea,
which he had carried out against her will, to move their camp to
the bleak terrain at timber line from which he might better observe
the attempt the boys were making.

The guidebook evaluated the climb as moderately difficult, ranging on the Sierra Club scale from 5.6 to 5.8, with several pitches, including the central overhang, requiring the direct aid of stirrups
and ranging in difficulty from A1 to A4. Johnson remembered it as
a long, sometimes arduous climb, steep and very exposed. When he
had done it a decade earlier, it had been customary to allow two
days for the ascent, bivouacking on the area above the overhang;
but in the years since then, numerous ropes of two had completed
the wall in a single day.

The two boys who were attempting the climb now had not managed to reach the overhang in their first day, had spent what Johnson knew must have been a miserably uncomfortable night on the
small ledge from which the boy in blue now payed out the rope.
He had guessed from the poor time they were making, their long
delays and awkward movements on the wall, that they were too
inexperienced, too wary to succeed; and he had been surprised this
morning when, instead of roping down the face, they had prepared
to climb the overhang, which, once passed, would cut off their retreat. The first 1000 feet of the wall were the least complex, the
central overhang was a reasonably straightforward technical problem, and it was only in the final 100 feet that the climb became
rigorous in its demands.

Johnson put the binoculars in his lap for a moment, closed his eyes, realigned his back against a rough concavity of sun-warmed stone behind him. He thought he knew what that lead boy was feeling: how he had reached or nearly reached the limits of skill and, perhaps, of nerve; how his ability to act, to go on or go back, was suspended now as he was suspended over 1000 feet of space; how a seven-sixteenths-inch-diameter rope, passing as it did through a handful of *pitons,* was his umbilical link with his companion, upon whose courage and skill as belayer his life would depend, should he fall in what would have to be his attempt, finally, to advance or retreat.

I should have gotten my butt over there, Johnson thought. *I might have been able to call them down.*

But she, whose bitterness, like a stream that had run deep underground for years and had begun to rise and threaten the surface of their life together, would, he knew, have used his concern for the boys against him, would have managed to manipulate it toward something sentimental with which she then would gently mock him as one more coupon torn from her book of payment for what had been his recent and disappointing infidelities.

He'll make a move out of his stirrups. He'll try to clear the overhang, but he's much too far back. If he does fall, and that last piton pulls, or his friend panics, or the belay is rigged poorly . . .

*

Then he knew she was coming to join him, heard her deliberately clumsy-footed approach as she came up across the rock-strewn slope from the last line of stunted firs beside which he had stubbornly carried out last night his erecting of their tent. Aware he admired grace, she kicked stones from her path with the toes of her climbing shoes, stood over him finally, looking down, her face even more attractive in its maturity, he thought, than it had been when, years ago now, he had been a young, cocksure instructor of English, and she, with an impassivity that had captured him, had led half a stadium in cheers for the Colorado football team. She wore her high-cut faded Levi shorts and scarlet long-sleeved jersey well, for she had scrupulously maintained her figure and even through her pregnancies had gained so little weight that Johnson had wondered since if this might account for the slightness of his sons. Her brown hair was long: She had arranged it this morning into a ponytail that spilled across her left shoulder, down the front of her jersey almost to her waist. She had, in recent months, left off wearing a bra, an emblem, he knew, of her liberation not from men in general — she had not yet pursued her instincts that far — but from him in particular. Her breasts were well shaped, but her nipples were large and it embarrassed him to see where they jutted against the fabric of her shirt.

"I thought we had a date this morning," she said. Her voice was pleasant and only one long familiar with it would have detected the slight vehicle of contempt upon which it rode.

"I was worried about those boys," he replied. He made an effort to stand.

"Don't get up," she told him. "I'd like to sit in the sun for a while. It hasn't managed to reach the tent."

"Did you warm up the eggs?"

"I ate them cold. Your fire was out." In recent months, she had become deft with the apparently innocuous phrase, and this both amused and troubled him, for until now, the ironies of their relationship had been his to define.

"Look," he said. He handed her the binoculars. With a studied lack of interest, she took them, making the adjustments necessary to adapt the lenses to her perfect sight.

"So?"

"So he's been there too long. Almost half an hour."

"Maybe he's resting."

"I don't think so."

"Well," she said, laughing as she returned the glasses. "What do you want to do — go up and bring him down in your weight-trained arms?"

"It won't be funny if he falls."

"I wasn't implying that it would."

"I don't think the other boy is very well experienced: He handles the rope awkwardly."

"Really."

"Look, if all you can do is be bitchy," he bristled, "why don't you go back to the tent?"

"Because, Nils, I've been in the tent all morning." Then, as if sensing that he could become angry and end by his silence her pleasure in tormenting him, she added: "Somebody's taken the place we had by the stream."

"Oh?" he said. "Who?"

"I haven't the slightest idea. I saw the smoke from his fire this morning. He has a small blue tent, an orange parka and moves nicely. I think he's alone."

"Is he a climber?"

"I don't know."

"Are you sure he's alone?"

"Yes. Quite."

This range of mountains was remote and the season was still early, but the area was popular with climbers and Johnson, who had come here in what had proved so far a futile effort to mend his relationship with her and — though he had not told her this — to revisit scenes of his earlier and more successful climbing days, was not surprised that others had come here, too. He wore new steel-rimmed spectacles, a stylish departure from his customary horn-rims. When he raised the binoculars now, he found they had lost clarity from her adjustments and he had to make adjustments of his own.

The lead boy, he observed finally, had driven yet another *piton* into the roof of the overhang, close to its outer edge, had clipped a stirrup into it and was testing the integrity of this stirrup now with his right hand, yanking its webbing back and forth. Then, slowly and awkwardly, he transferred his weight from the first and second of the web stirrups to the second and third.

"Good." Johnson breathed hard. "Good. Now you've got it. Now get up and over before you lose your nerve."

"Is that what happened to you this morning?" she asked lightly.

"Betts, I told you; I was worried about them."

"Wouldn't it be better to assume they know what they're doing?"

"I don't think they do know."

"We were going to make love, I think," she said. "Then have breakfast."

She pulled the jersey over her head, folded it and put it on the rough ground beside her.

"Do you think that's smart if other people are around?" he remarked.

"Don't tell me you care."

"Don't you?"

"Not really. No."

He glanced instinctively in the direction from which the stranger she had mentioned might appear.

"You used to be modest," he said. "I remember that from the start. When we had our first apartment, that depressing place downtown, I'd tell you to take things off during the day, remember that? And you wouldn't do it. You used to get angry as hell."

"I've changed. I'd do it now, but you don't ask."

"I still like the way you look. You know that. It's just been so bloody long — "

"I know what you're going to say," she said. "All of your clever arguments about the value of fucking around, and I really don't want to hear them again, all right?"

He sighed. "I thought we were going to try to do better, by getting away . . ."

"So did I. But it's been a big nothing so far."

"Were you willing to let it be anything else?"

"I don't know. Maybe not. But I think I was willing to try last night, and again this morning, if you had stayed around, if you'd been half as keen about me as you were about those damn boys."

He started to defend himself, but his position seemed hopeless and he lay back against the concavity of stone. She knelt before him, aware, he knew, that the sight of her familiar breasts unconcealed in this new environment could still arouse him.

"I'm not one of your pretty coeds," she said. "But I do feel like screwing — according to Plan A of our reconciliation — and as far as I know, except for whoever that is by the stream, you're the only man around."

"Well, go ahead, then," he said. "Help yourself."

"Thank you, Nils. I'll do that. Just try to be up to it, all right?"

"I usually am, aren't I?"

"Oh, yes. You're very big in the erection department."

He could not help laughing, but she was not amused and prepared him with a masculine detachment that, along with her coarseness, was not characteristic of her.

"Whatever you think, I still love you," he tried to say, touched by this sentiment as she arranged herself over him.

"That's not a very big deal for me right now."

"I've said I was sorry. I've told you it was an empty, meaningless thing; that it didn't work out."

"I've heard that before."

"Well, why don't you pay me back, then? So we can forget it and be civil again? Why don't you have an affair of your own?"

"Maybe I will, Nils."

"I think it would make a lot of sense. I really do." He had argued endlessly with her that they should accept what had become the new morality: relieve themselves of some of the burdens of a confining and fixed relationship, with its absurd prerogatives of jealousy. He had buttressed his persuasions with his customary and careful logic, but she had surrendered nothing to him, and his own attempts to enter a more exciting life that seemed increasingly to be passing them by had failed so far partly, he knew, because of her stubborn refusal to join him, at least in spirit. In this way, it had come to pass that he lived in a state of perpetual agitation that he had with wretched poor luck been born, as he saw it, a decade too soon.

"My students tell me that marriage is quaint," he said.

"Keep still, will you," she told him.

Halfheartedly, he took her breasts in his hands. He felt too exposed here on this open upslope of rock and was distracted by the possibility that the man who was camped by the stream might wander up this way and find them copulating. The concern surprised him, for he had not suspected until now that in such matters he might be shy; he could not remember that they had ever made love in the open before.

"*Jesus,*" she said. She was moving rapidly now.

Gently, he put his hands on her.

"*God, I hate you,*" she said. "*I hate you, Nils.*"

She had begun the first of her cries when beyond the arc of her shoulder, through the sweet strands of her hair that moved in a soft breeze (as clearly as if his vision were still somehow aided but no longer magnified by the binoculars), a tiny yellow dot began its fall from the near center of the vast north face of the mountain. It fell

spasmodically as, in succession, each of the *pitons* held for a second
or two, then sprang from the cracks into which they had been
driven, the tiny yellow dot swinging finally like the pendulum of a
clock back and forth across the wall until, after what seemed a long
time, it hung motionless by a golden thread about 70 feet below the
ledge upon which, Johnson knew, a boy in a dark-blue parka held
whatever was left of the life of his friend, desperately, in his two
gloved hands.

"*Betts,*" he whispered in fright as she relaxed at last against him.
"*That lead boy fell.*"

*

She had wanted to go at once for the assistance of the man who
had taken their campsite by the stream, but Johnson had argued
against it. Now, scarcely three hours later and already 400 feet up
the standard north face route, he was confident his decision had
been best, that an hour or more could have been lost in attracting
the help of a man neither he nor Elizabeth could be sure was a
mountaineer. He moved up yet another lead toward the two boys.
The boy in blue was still seated on the ledge, facing out, holding
the rope in his hands, across the small of his back; the rope plunged
over the edge of the ledge, taut to the place where, about 70 feet
below, the boy in yellow was suspended from it as motionless as if
he had been hanged. Johnson reflected that, in addition to the incessant, throbbing anxiety he felt for these young boys, he also felt
a guilty pride in his ability — even after the erosion of years — to
manage such a difficult climb. And he felt, too, a relief, surprising in
its intensity, that he and the woman he had married were joined by
the rope now as they so often had been in their early years together,
he leading the way, she climbing second behind him.

The sun was on the wall, but the rock under Johnson's hands
still felt cool; a warm, westerly breeze gentled against the right side
of his face. He made his moves precisely and out of 20 years' experience, studying through his steel-rimmed spectacles that portion of
the route that lay directly above him, finding and testing his holds,
balancing up from one to the next, placing his *pitons* with care and
at somewhat longer intervals than he would have liked, for he had
not expected to do this extensive a climb and had packed in only a
small amount of gear.

She stood easily on her belay stance 100 feet below him now, anchored to the wall, paying the rope to him as he climbed. Unlike him, she had never been afraid of high places, had never had to overcome the kind of terror he had felt in his first year. Since they had begun their ascent to assist the two boys, she had sustained an attitude toward him that was crisp, efficient and yielded nothing of what he hoped might be her willingness to forget, at least for a while, what had been their recent past.

"Twenty feet!" he heard her call.

"All right!" he answered. His heart beat rapidly.

He had given up calling to the boy in blue above him. Either he had been too stunned by the accident or his mouth was too cotton dry to answer. Apparently, he had not tied the rope off to the anchor *piton* behind him as he should have done by now in order to free his hands. Johnson knew how terrible that weight could be and wondered if the belay had been rigged properly: In whatever fashion it had been rigged, at least it had held; but the boy in yellow had showed no sign of consciousness and Johnson was reluctant to think what that might mean. Although he had participated in many rescues, seen numerous deaths, he had never managed to quite make his own attitude one of protective fatalism that most of his colleagues shared, that was also shared by Elizabeth, whose toughness he had often envied.

He found a suitable position on the wall, anchored himself and turned to face out. From here he could see the falling blue-green forested slope of the mountain and the distant glinting meander of the stream; could watch now, and take in the rope, as she climbed toward him.

She was a natural, a born climber, and he knew if she had spent a fraction of the time he had in perfecting skills, she might have been better than he. He could not help feeling proud of her as he watched her make her careful, efficient moves toward him. It was as if now in their absence of affection, she had become a finely crafted instrument that he had been wise enough, lucky enough, to purchase at a time when the demand for her had been superficial and his own credit had been good. Pausing just long enough to retrieve the *pitons* he had driven, whacking them loose from their cracks with her hammer, clipping them and their carabiners smartly to a loop of rope she had draped from her right shoulder to her left hip across the scarlet jersey she wore, she would glance up along the route, choosing her holds, her quick, perceptive eyes never quite meeting his own.

"You're climbing beautifully," he said when she reached him.

"How much longer will it take?"

"I don't know. A couple of hours, maybe. We're making good time."

"Has he moved at all?" she asked, squinting up.

"No."

"What about the other one?"

"I can't get him to answer. He's probably scared to death."

"We haven't got enough ropes to get them down, do we?"

"We'll rig something."

He had hoped, as they switched positions now, moving gingerly on the steep wall, she might return his compliment; but she was silent and he adjusted the rope where it circled his waist, shifted impatiently the sweat-stained straps of the small red rucksack he carried and into which he had put some sandwiches and candy bars, their first-aid kit and extra clothing.

"Want something to eat?"

"I can wait," she said.

"How about some water?"

"No, thank you."

He put his hand on hers where she held the rope in readiness to pay out to him as he went.

"Betts," he started to say. She looked at him. Her eyes were green and they pooled now with tears.

"Don't," she whispered.

"I just wanted to say thanks for doing this with me. I couldn't have done it alone." And he added, painfully aware that he meant it: "There's no one I'd rather be up here with. Do you believe that?"

She shook her head.

"Don't do this, Nils," she said. "Those boys need our help. If you're ready to go, you better go."

He felt angry that he had opened himself to her and a need now to be cruel.

"All right, fine," he said, already beginning to climb. "Try not to cry, will you, because if you do cry, you'll have trouble handling the rope."

"Don't worry about how I handle the rope," she replied, as if he were no longer a central fact of her life, no longer worthy of her anger. "Look," she said. "There he is."

"What?" he grumbled. "There who is?"

"The one I told you about. The one who took our place by the stream."

He glanced over his shoulder and down. Five hundred feet below the place where he stood balanced now on two small outcroppings of rock, a lone figure in an orange parka waved up: a figure that had materialized, it seemed, out of a void. Johnson blinked. A speck under his left eyelid had troubled him since he and Elizabeth had made love.

"Is he a climber?" he asked, moving up again. He had not bothered to return the wave.

"Yes. I think so. He's got a rope."

"Well, that's not going to do us much good, is it?" he said.

"It could," she said.

"What's that supposed to mean?"

She was silent for a moment and Johnson, in an awkward position on the wall, his confidence threatened subtly by the fact that now, as he climbed, he was being observed, swore softly.

"Give me some slack, will you?" he said. "What do you mean, it could?" Then he heard her laugh, as if she were relieved, as if her instincts about the stranger had been correct.

"Nils, he's coming up," she said. "By himself."

*

The afternoon breeze gentled finally along the surfaces of the range and higher winds began to fill the visible sky with cloud. The lead boy's body, which had bumped against the wall while the breeze had been strong, now hung motionless again from the rope, which had been jerked by the fall from his waist to a point just under his arms. On the belaying ledge, some 70 feet higher, the other boy's legs dangled and were also motionless except when, from time to time, he would bang his boots together as if to restore circulation, creating as he did an alien, helpless sound. Johnson heard it as he stood with his wife, together now on a small ledge 200 feet below the body of the fallen boy, watching as the stranger made his lone ascent.

"He's over halfway," she said, peering intently down. "He's fantastic."

Grudgingly, Johnson agreed, aware that at the rate this stranger was moving up, unencumbered as he was by a second, by *piton*craft and belay, he would very likely reach them before they reached the boys. He climbed almost jauntily, his orange parka tied around his waist, a small green lump of a pack bouncing against the back of what looked from Johnson's perspective like a white dress shirt with the sleeves rolled up, its tails tucked into a pair of combat trousers. He carried a coil of rope over his shoulder and had a way of leaning out from the nearly vertical wall, studying the route for a while, then making half a dozen consecutive moves, some of which would carry him as far as 15 or 20 feet at a time. In his own history as a climber, Johnson had seen no more than a handful of men who moved as well as this man moved, and none that he could remember who had moved any better. It was a performance he respected and envied, for in it was written a talent that he himself had never had; and while he was relieved that he would now have this standard of help in carrying out the rescue, he could not quite put aside a sense of threat that seemed for him to emanate from the simple fact of this man with whom he had not as yet exchanged a word and for whom his wife had expressed a frank, even provocative regard.

"Has anyone ever soloed this face before?" she asked.

"No. I don't think so. I haven't heard of anybody."

"You must know who he is; he's not just anybody."

Johnson wiped his spectacles, which, during his hours on the wall, had become covered with a pumiceous dust.

"I don't recognize him. There are plenty like him these days."

"We're lucky to have him," she said.

"And his rope."

"Of course, Nils. His rope, too."

Johnson went up another 100-foot lead, moving with conscious deliberation, as if, in what had become an atmospheric intensity, he might otherwise be impetuous. He brushed his handholds free of grit, settled his fingers onto them, tested his footholds fussily with the rigid soles of his *Kletterschuhe*. He balanced carefully up in clean motions, assuring himself by the care he was taking that he would not be embarrassed by a fall. Then he found a good stance, a deep, cavelike pocket in the rock from which he could belay comfortably, and leaning against the stone behind him, sitting with his legs straight out, he brought in the slack rope and called for her to join him. Halfway through the pitch, she had trouble removing one of his *pitons*. He could hear her banging it stubbornly with her hammer and, when he leaned awkwardly out from his position, he could see her small hand clenched around the carabiner, yanking it fitfully back and forth.

"Leave it, why don't you?" he called. Scarcely 100 feet below her, the lone man was coming up, moving swiftly now, for here the face was somewhat less steep and offered a variety of holds.

"I'm going to get the goddamned thing," he heard her say. "Give me some tension, will you?"

He took up the slight belly of slack that had developed between them until the rope was taut and she could use both of her hands in her attempt to loosen the jammed *piton*. Finally, with an odd sense of relief, as if it had been driven into his own heart, he heard it spring free, heard her snap it to the collection that hung from her shoulder loop.

"All right, climbing," she called.

"Climb ahead," he said.

The north face was in shadow again, the air cool out of the sun; he had a sense that dusk would come rapidly and that rain would fall. A swallow swept by the place where he sat; he heard the subdued, jetlike hiss of its passing. He was hungry and quite tired now and knew before he could begin the next and final lead the lone man would reach this place.

That lead boy is dead, he thought. *I'm sure of it.*

When she reached him, her familiar face rising suddenly in front of the opening of the recess in which he sat, he drew his knees to his chest in order to make room for her; but instead of changing places with him, as he had expected her to, she kept her position on the steep wall, turning, resting an arm along the threshold of the recess and, in doing this, whether deliberately he could not tell, she blocked his egress from the cave.

"I'm ready to climb," he told her.

"Let me rest a minute, Nils," she said tiredly. "I wore out my arm pulling that damn *piton*."

"You should have left it. We've been doing fine; we've got enough to finish."

"It always seems like a defeat to me to leave one. Hi," she said. She was looking down and had, apparently, spoken to the man who was coming up from somewhere below her. Johnson guessed from the little volume she had used that the man must be close now, and there had been a shyness in her tone that he recognized but had not heard her use in a long time. He caught the distant jingling of the *pitons* and carabiners the man carried, but as yet had not used, and heard his reply, friendly, he thought, but muffled to incoherence by the cave. Johnson moved restlessly, sensing what would be his disadvantage if the man suddenly arrived.

"Come on, Betty," he said.

"I don't know," she said, not speaking to him but to the one who was coming up. "Yes," she said. "I know. My husband saw the fall."

Then the man was standing next to her, keeping his easy balance with a careless touch of his hand to the outside edge of one of the walls of the recess, looking in to the denlike place where Johnson sat. He was a young man, mid-20s, Johnson guessed, and though he had been climbing steadily for a long time now, he showed no evident signs of fatigue. His hair was wavy and brown, fashionable in its length but also, Johnson observed, professionally trimmed. His strength was evident in his hands and wrists and forearms where they showed below the rolled-back sleeves of his shirt; and in his blue eyes, his friendly but unyielding expression, across the tanned surfaces and well-shaped planes of his face, Johnson thought he read privilege: private schools, perhaps, trips abroad, easy and useful connections in high places; and these assumptions seemed to gain validity as, when the young man spoke, his tones warm yet at the same time sober and carrying with them the confidence of one who has not only managed to survive his life so far but also managed to prevail in it, Johnson caught the cultivated accents of the East.

"Hi," he said. "My name's Calloway." And before Johnson could reply, the young man added, as if they had all just met on the approach to a tee on a busy golf course: "Do you mind if I go by?"

*

The lead boy, in fact, was dead. It appeared he had died instantly in his fall, his neck broken, his blond head jutting unnaturally above the bright color of his parka, a weal of blood congealed at one corner of his mouth. Calloway was removing the equipment the boy had carried, adding it impatiently to his own as if it might prove useful — the *pitons,* carabiners, web stirrups and slings — as Johnson came up, belayed by Elizabeth some 90 feet below now in the cave. The sky had darkened with cloud, the air was quite still; already, he had heard thunder.

"How's the other one?" he asked, pausing tentatively on his holds, for he had seen Calloway climb up to the ledge.

"Psyched out. He won't say anything. I tied the rope off for him."

"Does he know about this?"

"I told him," Calloway said. "I don't know if it registered."

Gnats were moving near the dead boy's eyes. Johnson looked away. The meander of the stream was lost in distant shadow now. Soon, he knew, a breeze would rise; almost surely, the late-afternoon rain would come. Below, he saw Elizabeth lean out from the cave, look up, her face a pale, expectant wedge above the fabric of her jersey. He shook his head. She would be saddened, he knew, but not surprised: Though she had not said so, he thought she had intuited from the beginning that the boy had not survived his fall.

"We don't have enough daylight left to get the other one down," Johnson said. "Even if we get lucky and the storm misses us."

Calloway agreed. He seemed to be waiting for the older man to make a decision, perhaps out of deference to his age, perhaps because he had been first on the wall. Johnson, keeping one hand on the rock, removed his spectacles, wiped his brow with the sleeve of his shirt. The urgency of reaching this place had given him an adrenal strength that now was rapidly ebbing away as if to follow what had been his last fragile hope for the fallen boy. Tired, hungry, balanced gingerly on his holds, he felt his legs begin to shake; slight cramps had developed in the lower muscles of his calves.

Calloway looked up in the direction of the summit that towered above them, merging now into what had become a granite-colored sky. He seemed disgruntled, impatient to be on his way, to separate himself from this death and the failure of which it spoke. When he brushed back a shock of his brown hair and looked intently at Johnson again, Johnson sensed the younger man had reached the far limits of whatever refinement had prevented him so far from simply taking charge; and even out of his exhaustion and reluctance to state a position the younger man might challenge, Johnson discovered in himself a need to preserve his place.

"We'll have to bivouac," he said.

"Right."

"There's room on that ledge for two — "

"I think we should do the overhang," Calloway cut in — and it was clear he had worked it out, was sure of himself. "According to the book, that's the standard site. There's room enough up there for six."

"We'd be burning our bridges — "

"We can go on up and finish the face in the morning."

"I don't know," Johnson said.

"I've read the route description," Calloway said. "It doesn't sound bad; I'm frankly not worried about it. We can go one rope of four or two ropes of two: whichever you like. Once we're up there, we can walk down the east ridge. No problem.

"Look," he said. "There's no point in spending a rotten night."

"Do you think that other boy will be up to doing the overhang?"

"He'll do what we tell him to do," Calloway said. "What about this one? We'll need the rope. We can tie him off here or cut him loose."

Johnson poked a finger to his eye where, under the lid, a speck still burned. The younger man had spoken without feeling, and it was not so much this fact that troubled Johnson (he understood it as a logical and useful attitude to hold) but the fact that he could not quite do the same, that when he spoke he knew he would hear along the edges of his voice traces of the pulse of loss he felt.

"I guess there's not much point in tying him off," he said finally. "Not if we're going on. One of us should be up there with the other one, though."

"Go ahead," Calloway said. He seemed more relaxed now that they had reached a decision. "I'll take care of it. What about your wife? Will it bother her?"

"She won't like it, but she's been through this kind of thing before. She'll be all right."

"She's lovely," Calloway said. He had fished a clasp knife from his pocket. Johnson watched as the younger man drew the long blade out with the disk of his nail. The compliment had struck him as gratuitous and he did not respond to it.

"Give me a couple of minutes up there," he said. Then, as he turned to climb, he realized he would not have enough rope to reach the ledge. Calloway saw the problem at once.

"I'll give you a belay," he said. Folding the blade back into its handle, he returned the knife to his pocket and began to uncoil his rope. Johnson could not help feeling a little embarrassed, Calloway having so recently climbed unprotected to the same ledge. He called to Elizabeth, told her the plan, and then, the belay established, Calloway paying out rope from an easy, slouching stance, he went up.

The surviving boy sat on the ledge in his blue parka, gazing vacantly out. His hands were placed on his lap in such a way that Johnson could see where the rope, during his efforts to stop the fall, had scorched the leather of the palms. He was a red-haired, freckled boy, and Johnson tried talking to him, tried to comfort him as best he could, but the boy would not speak, only nodded his head or shook it or simply gazed out at the visible horizon of high mountains and dark, lightning-illuminated cloud.

The ledge was rough, even smaller than Johnson had remembered. When he removed his pack and sat next to the boy, he felt their shoulders touch. The rope, anchored to the wall behind them, bent sharply over the edge of the shelf; and although Johnson did not wish to look at it, he forced himself to, watched it unblinkingly until, suddenly freed of its burden, it sprang lightly up. He wondered then how long it would take for the body to fall and whether or not the sound of it striking the earth might be heard at a vertical distance of almost 1000 feet. He felt an oppressive sense of inevitability. Removing his spectacles, closing his eyes for a moment, he was grateful for what had become a remote yet persistent rumble of thunder.

"I'm sorry about your friend," he said quietly, repeating what he had said before.

"He's my stepbrother," the boy said. And during the time it took for the others to come up, and even after that, these were the only words he spoke.

*

In reduced light, from a standing belay position established by Calloway just below the ledge, Elizabeth payed out rope to the younger man as he climbed on a bold diagonal to the overhang and then, with astonishing swiftness, built a near catwalk of stirrups from the wall to its outer lip. He trailed the belay rope behind him as if it were nothing more than an obligation, and when he stood in the last of the stirrups, his left fist balled into a crack at the edge of the overhang, he leaned out and peered up in what had become his familiar reconnaissance of route, and then, without hesitation once he had hauled up a great belly of slack so as not to be impeded by the rope behind him, he reached up with his right hand, kicked his foot free of the last stirrup, swung out over 1000 feet of space, hung there for a fraction of a second, then went cleanly up and over.

Johnson shook his head. He looked at Elizabeth, saw across the pale, tired planes of her face her frank regard for what Calloway had done. It would be easy for the rest of them to follow, protected from above by the young man whose confident cry of "Climb!" they heard already come indistinctly down.

Elizabeth went first, moving surely to the overhang itself, pausing, then going out from stirrup to stirrup until she stood in the last stirrup and Johnson, who sat on the small rough ledge, belaying her from behind, felt a clutch of fear as he saw this woman who had been his companion through all his adult years and who was the mother of his sons poised in a place almost identical to that where the lead boy had stood just prior to his fall; and when Johnson heard her familiar voice call for tension on the upper rope and saw her scrabble finally up and safely out of sight, he felt such relief as to make him weak, and he sighed and wiped his face.

"Go ahead," he said hoarsely to the surviving boy, once the ropes were secured. The boy was brave, possessed of a courage not buttressed by experience or any special skill. He went awkwardly up and out and over, his wash-blue eyes still traumatized with shock, his legs shaking badly all the while he stood in the stirrups under the dusky overhang, his hands stuttering from hold to hold, trailing obediently behind him the rope from which less than one hour ago the body of his stepbrother had been cut away.

Wearily, Johnson stood. His own legs were unsteady, his shoulders sore where the straps of his pack had chafed them. By the time he had knotted the rope around his waist and ascended to the overhang, the sky had grown so dark he had to wait for flashes of lightning in order to see clearly the ghost-white webbing of the stirrups that advanced outward from the cliff, appearing now as if they had been driven into something as insubstantial as the air itself that eddied indecisively against the face, agitated by what he guessed would prove a quick rising of the wind.

He moved cautiously from stirrup to stirrup, taking them and their carabiners with him as he went, hearing the clink and jingle of the metal as it collected around him, sensing through his finger tips the building charge of atmospheric electricity, straining his ears to hear the warning buzz, hearing only the still-distant roll of thunder, calling to Calloway for tension at last, feeling the rope pull swiftly and hard against him, hoping briefly that it would, in fact, hold him as he let it take his weight, leaned back against it out over the dark void, its engulfing dimensions clear only in the flashes of lightning that would illuminate the sky and earth for several seconds now before they flickered out and the artillery of thunder would boom along the distant range; reaching awkwardly in under the overhang to unclip the last of the stirrups, groping tiredly for some purchase on the sharp-edged rock as, from above, Calloway applied his strength to the rope; kicking and thrashing until at last he managed to deliver himself in the absence of all grace to the abundant area above the overhang where Elizabeth sat next to the younger man, combing out her long brown hair as if she were at the dressing table in the bedroom of their Denver home, and the surviving boy gazed vacantly out, and Calloway popped up and

stretched and said, in his cultivated accents: "Good show. Fine.
Now let's eat."

*

For a while, the lightning played along the far peaks, then the
storm collected itself and moved off into the east, leaving behind its
unfulfilled promise of rain and the light of a luminous moon. The
temperature of the air began to drop, and by the time they had
eaten their rations of food and Calloway had brewed tea for them
all on the small Primus stove he had fished from his pack, the surfaces of the rock around them were damp to touch. Elizabeth sat
next to the younger man in the area of what had become their
kitchen. Johnson, separated from her by the surviving boy, watched
as she applied fresh lipstick, a rust red he knew, close in color to
that of the parka she now wore. He could read nothing in this old
and feminine gesture except her habit of paying attention to her
appearance wherever she happened to be; and yet when she pulled
her lips together and recapped the small gold tube, he was surprised
by a desire to have her sit next to him and sensed at the same time
hów awkward it might be to change positions, how she, or even Calloway, might be amused. Briefly, out of some as-yet-indistinct kin-
ship of soul, he put his hand on the knob of the surviving boy's
knee.

"How are you doing?" he said.

"OK," the boy replied, but he was half-hearted.

"We were lucky we missed the rain."

"I know."

"My name is Nils," he said. "What's yours?"

"Perry."

"Where do you live?"

"Durango."

"Have you done much climbing before this?"

"No."

Johnson nodded. Over the hiss of the stove he could hear the
others talking. They talked easily, as if instead of just having met
during this encounter on the wall, they had known and liked each
other awhile. In his relationship with Elizabeth, played as it had
been until now to the beat of his own drum, he had never experienced anything more than the most innocuous sort of jealousy. She
had been so doggedly loyal to him that he had more than once in

the privacy of his thoughts charged against her a lack of imagination. Now, in the context of her recent efforts to assert herself and the presence of this young, able and magnetic man, he felt a rising threat and she, whom he had taken quite for granted these many years, seemed to become more desirable, even precious, as she moved in spirit away from him.

Later, when Calloway suggested to him they begin next morning in two ropes of two, Johnson, his own practical judgment arguing against it, found that he had agreed. A consecutive rope of four with Calloway in the lead would, in spite of its slowness, he thought, be almost perfectly safe. But the younger man had made his suggestion in such a way as to cast no doubt upon Johnson's ability to lead his own rope; and, therefore, to argue against the suggestion once it had been made would have been, it seemed to Johnson, a confession of inadequacy. In spite of his fatigue, he thought he had climbed well in the first 1000 feet and was reasonably confident that he and Elizabeth could manage to complete the wall, if not with Calloway's finesse, at least with competence. It was only after a general agreement to proceed in two ropes of two that the surviving boy, for the first time, ventured a comment of his own.

"Can I go with you?" he asked Johnson, his voice still unsteady but loud enough for the others to hear.

"Fine." Calloway said at once, as if he sensed the boy did not quite trust him. "Elizabeth and I will lead. We'll take the spare rope. If there's any problem, we can all join up."

"Is that all right with you, Nils?" he heard her ask.

"Sure. Fine," he said. But he felt as if in a game of chess he had been tempted by his opponent into making a move the consequences of which he could not quite anticipate; and he wondered if his voice had betrayed his uncertainty.

Three of them lay down then and tried to sleep in their respective places on the ledge. The last thing Johnson remembered seeing was the silhouette of Calloway, who continued to sit cross-legged, gazing out where the moon rose, sipping his tea.

*

It went well in the first 400 feet. Then, perhaps no longer concerned, Calloway and Elizabeth began to move ahead. At 500 feet above the bivouac ledge, they were one full lead beyond Johnson and the boy; at 600 feet above the ledge, they were no longer in sight. An early wind had risen in the northeast and was blowing hard against the face. The surfaces of the rocks were cold to touch.

Johnson blew on his finger tips, squinted through his spectacles at the route above. He had reached a difficult section and was having trouble making his moves. He guessed the angle of the rock to be 80 degrees here, the small holds it provided infrequent and awkwardly distributed, so that twice he had found the only way he could shift his position and advance was to move down several inches and then reascend, placing his left foot where his right had been. He had tried to protect himself as well as he could, but the wall here was smooth and the few cracks it provided were shallow and he had used up all of his smaller *pitons*. Eighty feet below, anchored to the wall and belaying from stirrups, the surviving boy handled the rope indifferently, as if to him it was not conceivable that a man like Johnson could fall.

He closed his eyes, pressed his cheek against the rock. Transmitted through it he could hear the remote sound, no louder than the ticking of his watch, of Calloway banging a *piton* somewhere into the face above. He wanted to call for help. His pride would have allowed for that, but he knew he would not be heard in this wind and at this distance, knew if he did call he would alert the boy below to the fact they were in trouble, and that could only make things worse.

He looked up, hoping to catch a glimpse of the others, but where the wall tilted toward a less acute angle, he saw only a blue sky full of racing cloud, which, in this perspective, gave him the giddy sense that the mountain itself was toppling forward. Elizabeth had left *pitons* in all the most difficult pitches so far and here, 15 feet above the reach of his hand, he could see two web stirrups tossing like bunting in the wind. To reach these stirrups, he would have to negotiate a section of rock that appeared so steep and generally faultless and barren of holds he could not imagine how Calloway had done it, or he himself had done it a decade earlier, as he must have, though he held no specific memory.

He hugged the wall, felt its harshness against him. He lifted his right foot to a nubbin, slowly let it begin to take his weight, moving up an inch at a time, searching with his left hand, finding a shallow striation into which he could place the pads of his finger tips. His heart beat rapidly. When he made his next delicate move up, he felt the rope tug at his waist, and he angrily called for slack and felt the pressure ease slowly and then saw the rope belly out on the wall below his right foot and knew the boy, who had previously given him too little, now was giving him too much, but he was hoarse and more afraid than he had been since his first years as a climber, and so, without trying to communicate any further with the boy, he committed himself to yet another slight move up this sheerness of rock, found at last a thin crack with his right hand, jammed his fingers in to the second joints, felt the skin rip away, the pulse of blood, a terrible relief to have gotten even this much purchase here, moved his left foot then to a nutlike nubbin of rock scarcely large enough to take the extreme edge of his shoe, felt the wind hurling itself against him as if to dislodge him, heard it wail and sigh in the large pockets and crevices above, saw the rope belly out along the wall below, as if the surviving boy had simply payed out all the slack he had and was waiting passively for this pitch to be over.

Johnson swore, felt a sudden brutal anger that she had left him here alone, had climbed on out of sight and sound with Calloway, who must have passed this way without effort. Why had she not waited as had been their plan? Why had she not left a solid *piton*, thought of him, remembered him? He closed his eyes against the wind, guessed in the irrationality of his anger and fear that she would be Calloway's now, and then someone else's, and someone else's after that. He knew how it went, how insubstantial a bond fidelity was once it had been breached a single time and knew for the first time, felt, even, how she must have felt: the humiliation, old, ancient, of the one betrayed.

He opened his eyes, swore. He was in a half-crouched position now, his right arm stretched at full length above him, his right hand jammed in the thin crack, his left hand flat against the wall, his right foot scraping uselessly, his left leg trembling as he let it take his weight and began to rise out of his half crouch, pushing down on his left foot, pulling up with his right hand; and he had drawn himself to almost a full standing position when the nutlike nubbin broke suddenly and cleanly away under his left foot and he fell abruptly, the right side of his face scraping along the wall, his spectacles tugging up from his ears, bobbling, his left hand flashing up too late to stop them as they swept away from him, buffeted and joggled by the wind to fall the 1600 feet to the ground above which he hung suspended now by the fingers of his right hand, his inarticulate cry cut off by the clutching dryness of his throat. Vision blurred, he felt the strength ebb quickly from his arm, and just as quickly, in what was left of the time he would have, he began to pull himself up, testing the wall with the edges of his shoes until he found at last a small lip that would take his weight, and he balanced gingerly up until he stood pressed flat, his face close to the bloody fingers that had saved him. Then, for five long minutes, with the wind slamming against him, its banshee sound in his ears, he did nothing more or less than breathe.

*

The crack was shallow. It took just over two inches of the six-inch *piton* he drove, but that much of it was tightly wedged and when he slipped a loop of rope over it, down the exposed shaft of the *piton* to the placé where the *piton* entered the crack, and clipped a stirrup onto that loop of rope, the stirrup held his weight and enabled him then to step up slowly and reach the stirrups she had left, and from that point forward, the wall was pleasant again and he and the boy finished it without incident.

Elizabeth and Calloway were waiting at the summit, sitting together in the lee of an upthrust slab of rock.

"Hello, Nils," she said offhandedly. But then she noticed the blood on his hand and the fact that he was not wearing his glasses and she seemed concerned, he thought, when she asked him what had happened.

"I was in the middle of a scramble," he told her. "The wind took them."

"Are you all right?"

"Yes. I'm fine."

"They weren't right for you, anyway," she said.

He smiled tiredly. She seemed like an old friend, the impassivity of her expression familiar, welcome; but she had left him, he sensed it, had gone farther away than she had ever gone before.

"He used to wear horn-rims," she explained to Calloway. "They made him look dignified."

Calloway laughed.

"Let's get out of here," he said.

It was then they heard the sobs of the surviving boy, whom they had overlooked as they talked. He was sitting on a rock with his face in his hands as if somehow he were ashamed. The wind was blowing his red hair. Johnson went over, sat next to him, put a hand on his shoulder.

"It's all right," he said quietly. "We know how you feel."

For a while, the boy's shoulders continued to shake, and Johnson felt a tightness in his own throat and a gathering sense of loss. He looked up at the sky, where the clouds sped by under the impetus of the quick wind. It would be near twilight, he guessed, by the time the four of them got down. Then he and Calloway would go and together they would bury the dead.

WILLIAM SAROYAN

Isn't Today the Day?
Or, Saroyan 1964

(FROM HARPER'S MAGAZINE)

ONE OF THE IDEAS I carry around in my head all the time is,
Today's the day.

And it never is, although now and then it almost is.

Today's the day I'll *really* write, the day I won't have to think
how to do it, the day I'll be with it, unable to do anything wrong,
the great day, my day, the day of the innocent in the world — me.

A *question* I carry around all the time is, Who makes up the
jokes?

Nobody seems to know. Jokes don't happen by themselves, but
nobody has ever tracked down a joke to the guy who made it up.

Another thing, of another order, that I carry around all the time
is a certain amount of remembering of other writers, old friends of
mine, and old enemies.

One of them is a writer I've known thirty-three years, who is a
very good reader, a much better reader in fact than he is a writer,
who quit writing thirty years ago, although to this day he doesn't
act as if he quit at all, he thinks he's been in there all the time writing great books. This writer reads a book and jumps into his car
and races ten miles to the house of another writer to say, "I can't
read William Faulkner, the guy just doesn't know how to write, he
refuses to revise, the stuff goes on and on without punctuation,
even, but I just forced myself to read this new book of his and the
thing *can't* be read, it's impossible to read."

"What'd you read it for, then?"

"*Sanctuary!* Like the Hunchback of Notre Dame hollered, but of course that's the name of the book, too, but it wasn't any sanctuary for me."

And then long years later he'll drive four hundred miles to ask about a writer who shot himself through the mouth with a shotgun. "How do they *do* that?"

"I don't know."

"*Why* do they do it?"

"I don't know."

And then the next day or the day after, I'll remember another writer, only this one not only couldn't write, he couldn't read either, but what he could do, he did for eight straight years, and then zing went the strings of his heart, and his wife was a widow, and his two kids were half-orphans. What he did was write movie scenarios — but seriously, which was probably the secret of his success, because people who make movies like to take the whole thing seriously. Damned if *everybody* doesn't like to take everything he does seriously, except maybe me.

Take plays, for instance, opening nights, actors performing, and then taking curtain calls while a whole buildingful of people clap their hands off, I can't take *that* seriously, I feel sorry for the playwright, who by that time thinks he's done it, I feel sorry for the actors enjoying the applause so humbly, they make tears roll out of my eyes, but the whole thing is a joke, only I never knew anybody who could make a joke *to tell* out of it.

Everybody takes everything seriously. Go to a barber for another haircut, and he thinks he's got something going for himself personally, his own superior way of giving a haircut, of being a barber, not like those bums who drink hair tonic and can't keep a job for longer than ten years. He takes barbering seriously, he believes barbering has got to be taken seriously. If an ape is taught to give a haircut in half the time the barber takes, and it's twice as good a haircut, the barber says, "They hypnotized him. Wait till that boy comes out of it, he won't be no world-beater."

When I got up this morning I hollered, "Today's the day."

While I shaved I didn't care about the way I look. So it's like an old hobo in the doorway of an empty store at daybreak, so what? I didn't care, because I knew the truth: I was young, I was hand-

some, I was a writer, and this was my day. I sang with Chubby
Checker on the radio, "Hooka tooka Mama soda cracker."

And then I got under the shower, and who said anything about
anybody being any fifty-five years old? Not me. Just let me have
my black coffee and my unfiltered cigarette, and watch me go.

Write? Man, I was going to write the Holy Bible in one fell
swoop, but of course I can never come to fell swoop without making
it six or seven other things that sound something like fell swoop,
but I'm not going to do it this time, the hell with it. I was going to
write holy writ. One cup of black, two cups of black, three cups of
black, world, morning, life, me, was there ever a better parlay?

After the first black, a brand-new pack of Chesterfields was
opened, a brand-new cigarette was brought out, a paper match
lighted, the flame carried to the end of the cigarette, a big drag in,
deep, "Man, today's the day."

Ideas? All over the place. Characters? The most wonderful characters that ever occurred to any writer. And away down at the bottom, tobacco smoke bumping into sleeping dogs and making them
jump for joy, run and bugle, because there it was, the scent of the
wily red fox, and this was the day we'd get him, writer, dog, fox,
art, and all. Nothing could stop us now, and all of it would be new,
and good for money too. There wouldn't be an editor in the world
who would dare turn it down, saying (as he was always saying, taking himself seriously), "We liked the way the thing began, but it
wavered in the middle, and at the end we all had the feeling that
we'd been left holding the bag." Instead, he'd just say, "Okay, if
you'll be reasonable about how much you want for it. We get sued
for three million dollars twice a week, and it's expensive. And
don't forget it's not really a short story either, and if you want to
know the truth, we all want it but not one of us can decide *why* we
want it, so don't be unreasonable about how much you want for
it."

For forty-four minutes this morning this was the day. Not only
the day I had been waiting for all *my* life, it was the day everybody
else has always been waiting for, and I felt chosen to be the one the
day would come to, at last. I felt so chosen I could barely tolerate
myself, my doubting self, my disbelieving self, my glum hangdog
bored tired self mumbling, "Take it easy."

I wanted to feel courteous, even to himself, my own lazy fat self, magnanimous if possible, indifferent to his insults, unchosen as he is, as he has always been, and I wanted him to know there just couldn't be any snobbery in me about him: "You come along too, why don't you?" Generosity unbounded, goodwill galore, and Christian charity unfiltered.

Morning, man, and the world is here again. There's a sunflower somewhere with a shopworn bee buzzing around the golden fuzz out of which the yellow petals laugh about the light, the bee intoxicated by the offbeat smell and the dazzling color. It's all *now* again, isn't it, old-timer? The whole thing's here again, isn't it, as if by schedule? This has *got* to be the day. What jokes, what stories, what characters, what fun, what art, what laughter, what writing, what *readable* writing, what readers the writing would make, transforming a lot of half-dead dream-drenched fools into alert, raring readers.

Just get me to my old table and my old typewriter, and watch me go, in spite of the fifty-five years, the bad gimp since 1939, but lately forgotten, the chronic catarrh but ignored, the hissing right ear but excellent for Hooka tooka Mama soda cracker, the dim right eye but useful in support of the left, just get me to the stack of good old blank paper and watch me fill six or seven sheets with great wonders.

Plot? Who needs plot? Form, continuity, style? Who needs them? Man, when the world is the world again, the next day has got to be the day, and this *was* the next day, postponed a little, postponed fifty years, on account of rain, influenza, school, work, war, movies, and the news, the big news, the daily news, but now at last no longer postponed, here at last and exactly on schedule, as promised, totally unpostponed, instant, as instant as the coffee in the fourth black cup, instant and everlasting, all on account of me, the original innocent, the unlettered man of letters, the unschooled founder of the only school, the rejecter of the forms, the story, the novel, the essay, the play, the lawyer's brief, the last will, the free brochure about happy retirement on a hundred a month, the price list, the catalogue, the directory, the phone book.

The coffee's supposed to be wrong because the oil in it gives you ulcers, the cigarettes are wrong because they give you cancer, liking the world is wrong because the world is contemptible, being keen about being alive is wrong because being alive is stupid and in any case how long can it last? Believing is wrong because it has all been disproved. Expecting something good to come out of a new day is wrong because there has never been a precedent for it. Forgetting gimp, catarrh, hissing ear, and dim eye is wrong because they are all there, smiling and waiting, willing and able to make a shambles of a man at any moment. Remembering the fun and the laughter and the girls and the children born of them is wrong, because where is it all now, where are they all now? Everything is wrong because everything is always wrong, but not to the writer, he will not learn, he refuses to learn, he's even too stupid to be stupid, and he says again, "Today's the day," taking nothing and nobody seriously, excepting the day itself, as clean as a sheet of blank white paper.

So he sat down, so I sat down, so whoever it was sat down twelve hours ago at six in the morning, San Francisco still dark, Hooka tooka Mama soda cracker, how about the kids who make up songs, how about the way they sing them?

Every day I hit the sack at one in the morning, wake up at three, switch on the transistor radio, and there they are again, held in contempt by Clifton Fadiman, ridiculed by Marya Mannes, there they are again, bugling at the little red fox, indifferent to the crisis at the *Saturday Review* about how total destruction is drawing nearer because nobody understands the inevitability of it: Elvis Presley, Ray Charles, Fats Domino, Chubby Checker, and the girls, the wonderful little girls who sing he's a walking miracle, or you don't own me, or go now.

Nobody who is anybody wants to take pride in the singing boys and girls, but the fact is *they* are telling the story and we aren't. We're making art, we're being superior, we have read Stendhal, haven't we? We *know*, don't we? We have written stories, novels, plays, poems, and fiery editorials, haven't we, having gone to serious school and having taken every bit of it seriously?

I take pride in them, the singers. I even take pride in the little girls who gathered together in organized groups to scream at the Beatles, four funny-looking Liverpool boys who learned to avoid going to barbers, not to be embarrassed about it, and to wink about the fortune it was bringing them. I take pride in Johnny Cash, Ferlin Huskey, Marvin Rainwater, and Pete Seeger — ticky tacky, Pete sings at three in the morning, every one of them is made out of ticky tacky, every one of the nice people who go to barbers, and in a pinch *become* barbers, and take it seriously. And I take pride in the great fat boy, my own friend can't even remember his name, phoned me one time when he thought he ought to and said, "Anything I can do, man?" — singing everything ever made into a song, "and a little bitty tear brought me down." After I'd heard him sing it on the radio one time I sang it with my son and daughter in Chicago, and the black taxi driver turned around and laughed: "Man, that's the song of my life." Burl Ives, and nobody can do a song better, not even Bob Wills and the Texas Playboys singing "New San Antonio Rose," not even the Sons of the Pioneers singing "How Great Thou Art." The singers do it, the singers have it. The joke-tellers do it, the comedians do it, and pretty nearly everybody else doesn't.

It was the day, so I sat down because it was wrong, it was hopeless and useless, and I knew like the Finn at the top of the ski jump at the Ninth Winter Olympics in Innsbruck on television, brooding, head down, making the man on the microphone ask the lady ski champion of long ago, "Is he praying?" I knew, with the Finn, that wrong or impossible or useless or stupid or ridiculous, it was there to take after, and could be reached, like the crazy little red fox laughing, and then I saw him lift his head, and lunge out and go. I remembered having seen him take off and lean far forward. Over the skis, pushing away out there to the best jump ever, I knew, with him, that if it was possible to do, I'd better try to do it, and if I happened to fall flat on my face, that would be all right too, because you can't even do *that* unless you try, unless you're out there in the damned blue trying.

The counting down had been going on since I had jumped out of bed. From approximately a cool million the counting had moved down to a hot eight, to seven, six, five, four, three, two, one, and go.

So what happened?

Nothing. Try again, then. Three, two, one, go. Nothing again. Again, then. One, go. Nothing. Go. Nothing.

Why?

Isn't this the day? What happened to the day?

Somebody growled on a phonograph record, "I saw the best minds of my time go mad," but even when I first heard it — and first was last, it was enough, more than enough — I didn't believe it, it was a noisy argument, but it had something the matter with it. Everybody went mad, committed suicide, went to jail, or died, and it was supposed to be the fault of — whose fault *was* it supposed to be? The fault of the sons of bitches on Madison Avenue, as if *they* had never gone mad, committed suicide, gone to jail, and died. And they *had*. What they hadn't done was claim it had been the fault of the poets who were chanting their poems on phonograph records.

Again, then. Three, two, one, go.

Nothing again, maybe I'd better start at the top again, with a million, which all red-blooded American boys choose as the number of dollars they shall earn a year or two before they become President. Counting down from a million took the better part of an hour, even though I did a lot of skipping, but again nothing, and it looked as if the time had come to find out whose fault it was. This took sixty-six one-hundredths of a second: it was *my* fault. I had chosen the wrong stupid profession not to take seriously. I should have chosen a practical profession. The profession of writing is wrong, like smoking cigarettes, bad for your health, a diminisher of life expectancy.

What happened to the day? What happened to the jokes? What happened to the writers I was always remembering? Gone, like Ferlin Huskey singing it.

Well, gone, then, move along, there's a day out there somewhere. So I left the table, the typewriter, the stack of blank white paper, and I drove to the sea. I drove to the beach, and nobody there, not even a Japanese, fishing. I walked and looked and listened, and picked up rocks and driftwood. Nothing. The gimp came up because of the soft sand, the ear hissed, the dim eye blurred, the sea gulls came circling around, flying low, as if I had something good to throw to them, or as if I was in fact chosen and it had been ordained that they circle around my head, to mark the fact.

I loafed all day, hungry, cigarette-sour in the mouth, almost as badly in need of a haircut as any of the Beatles, full of memories of the dead, all of them alive in the memories, back, away back to 1928, 1932, 1934, back before the war, back before the bomb, back when everybody laughed, back before death, in those days even the dead didn't die, and you went to a funeral feeling, Have a nice time, Joe. And then as the sun began to move down into the sea I

went back to the coffee and the cigarettes, to the table, the typewriter, and the stack of white paper, and the hell with it, today was
the day all right, but it wasn't. I was there all right, and there were
no excuses, it was nobody's fault but my own, but it got away, the
day got away again.

I don't mind, though. I can't sing, and that's what I'd like to
do. My songs aren't much good, and I don't even bother to put
them on paper anymore, I let them go. I can't read, because I'm a
writer, I chose writing as my profession, but I can't write either. I
mean, I can write, but I can't write, man. Anybody can write, and
everybody does, but after all these years I can't write, I don't know
how. I know how, but I don't know how. I just thought I'd tell
you. It's all right, and not because tomorrow's another day, not
that at all, because that isn't really true at all, tomorrow is *not* another day, it's the same day, but after fifty-five years of it, the only
reason it's probably all right is that yesterday is always there, it is
always unknown, never understood, but man wasn't it great yesterday, let's talk again, like we did last summer Hooka tooka Mama
soda cracker.

PHILIP H. SCHNEIDER

The Gray

(FROM THE KANSAS QUARTERLY)

AARON SLIPPED THE BOW MOORING and swung back over the gunwale just in time to get his footing before the boat whipped out from the dock and plowed into the green wash of the bay. He coiled the line and dropped it in the bow, then climbed to the upper cabin where the man named Leroy stood with his feet spread wide and his bare shoulders and chest gleaming black in the sun as he gripped the wheel.

"There ain't much to know, boy. We get seaward a bit, we slap a chunk of fat from the tub on each of them hooks and we drop 'em over and we wait. Won't be long 'fore the fin start comin' 'round."

Aaron watched as the shining black hands and arms spun the wheel a half turn to the starboard. The boat cleared the breakwater and he moved closer to hear in the rising wind.

"All you got to do is stand back there and give the go ahead when one of them lines go tight, so I'll know when to give 'er the screw."

Leroy swung the wheel another twenty degrees to the starboard and started up the coast. Aaron felt the spray from the bow breaking into droplets on his face and his chest as their speed increased.

"After that you ain't got but one chore. Got to get them other lines back into the stern. I ain't about to rip the bottom out of this rig on account of one of them gettin' fouled up."

Aaron nodded.

"You got all that?"

"I guess."

"Suffocates 'em."

"Huh?"

"Haulin' 'em. Can't get no water in their gills."

"Oh."

Leroy stopped talking and they churned up the coast for another ten minutes before he throttled back and motioned Aaron with him as he climbed back down to the stern. He took a chunk of the bloody fat from the tub and jammed it onto the barbs of one of the giant trebles, then he tossed another of the chunks to Aaron and watched as Aaron pushed the chunk gingerly onto the hook.

"That ain't no little doughball for mudcats, boy. You got to put somethin' into it, make sure it stays."

Aaron tried another. Leroy looked it over carefully and nodded and then they both tossed the chunks out from the stern. Leroy went back up to the cabin and got them slowly under way.

It took less than a minute for the first gray triangle to come sweeping up in a wide spiral around the creeping boat. Then another came, and then a third. Aaron eyed the fins as they circled. He watched them slice the mild surface of the swell, and he watched them dip and smoothly rise and dip again around the boat, coming always closer, and he was still watching them when the port stern went suddenly tight.

He pulled his gaze down to the sound of the line going hard, and he stared down at the new and sudden tension, and at the way the woven steel stretched on less and less of an angle into the sea, and it was another five seconds before he remembered the go ahead. He turned as quickly as he could toward the upper cabin and he started to raise his hand, but Leroy did not wait. The boat planed upward, yanking against the tight steel.

He lost his footing to the move. He staggered heavily backward, and teetered for a long moment with his heels and his calves hard against the boards of the stern as his arms made awkward circles out at his sides. It took most of his strength and it seemed like a long long time before he was able to pull himself around to face the cables that whipped frantically back and forth in the heavy wash.

"Get them loose ones in!" Leroy shouted down from the wheel.

Aaron nodded his head to the shout and reached forward to grip the flailing cables, one in each of his hands. He set his feet against the boards of the stern and rocked his weight back toward the cabin, but the water was heavy in its drag on the steel and the bait, and the whipping of the wash made the woven strands slip and jerk in his grip. He rocked backward once more and he tried to hold the steel against his ribs with the insides of his biceps as he grappled for a better hold, but the strands slipped away from him, making long ragged welts along the skin of his sides, tearing his t-shirt into fluttering rags. His hair fell moistly over his face and blinded him. He rocked backward again, gripping more tightly with the insides of his arms. The steel ground against his ribs, but it did not slip. He settled like a machine to the force that opposed his strength, gripping, grappling forward, gripping again.

It took a long time, so long that he was not ready when the hooks leapt finally from the flow and the pressure stopped. He lost his balance and lurched heavily backward, stumbled, spun halfway around, wrapping himself in cable as he went, and then he crashed down to his elbows and his knees on the rough white canvas of the deck. He lay there with his teeth set hard and his eyes squeezed shut, his arms completely numb. Leroy's voice boomed down from the cabin.

"Where the hell'd you go, boy? This ain't no time for takin' a break. Get them gaffs out of the rack and get set to haul when I cut 'er off!"

Aaron pushed himself to his feet, hinging his elbows gingerly and pulling the coils of cable from around his knees before he jerked the gaffs from the rack. He held one of the gaffs in each hand and he braced himself at the stern. Leroy leapt down to join him when the engine stopped and began to haul in on the cable before he could move.

"Get to it, boy, 'fore they tear 'im up!"

He looked down at the gaffs and up at the rack, wondering for a moment if he should try to put them back or not, and then he looked at the cable, dropped the gaffs to the deck and wrapped his hands around the steel behind Leroy. They heaved in unison.

The shark broke water ten yards from the boat, dead weight on the water. It looked alive in its fixed suffocation as they hauled it alongside, but Leroy did not stop to look at it. He picked one of the gaffs from the deck and plunged it into the solid part of the gray body, just in back of the head. Aaron picked the other gaff from the deck and started forward, but he did not know what to do with it and he wound up standing at the gunwale, staring down at the gray bulk. Leroy shoved the grip of the already secure gaff into his hand and took the other and buried it into the flesh just in front of the tail.

"All set?"

Aaron nodded slowly, and they heaved.

His shoulders dipped with the weight. The muscles in his neck bulged against the tension of his skin and his hair fell down over his face again. Salt ran down from his forehead and into his eyes. He slipped, and staggered, and caught himself, the strain taking away the all of his thought, and then, as he reached the very edges of his strength, the gray thing was suddenly in the stern and both of them were sitting gasping for breath, grinning idiotically at one another from on top of it.

Then they did it again, and again, and it was the same each time until the stern hampers were full and they churned slowly back to the harbor and the town.

Leroy gave him fifty dollars that day when they sold the meat to Ortiz. He spent some of it on liniment, some on rum, and some on a hammock so that he could sleep on deck during the warm Panama nights.

And he learned, during the first few months of their first year together, how to bring in the loose cables without half killing himself, and how to set the gaffs, and his shoulders stopped feeling as though they were coming out of their sockets from the weight, and there were always the grins when the gray came up to the surface and over the stern.

It was at the end of that first year, in the late morning after a long weekend in the town, that Leroy came back to the boat with the girl. It was some kind of deal.

Aaron was sitting on the far gunwale in the sun with his legs stretched out on the deck and he eyed the girl as Leroy led her down the dock and helped her aboard. She was very blonde from the sun and she was not really brown, but burned yellow in a Central-American tan.

"Name's Leah," Leroy said quietly. He bent to pull the bait tub away from where it blocked the cabin stairway.

She stood at the gunwale with her mouth making a hard line

across her face and her lips almost hidden as she drew them in. She glared down at Leroy's back for a moment, then her glance flicked up to Aaron. He looked away, and shrugged, and turned to help Leroy with the tub. They slid it up against the starboard gunwale and lashed it into place, then Leroy took Leah down to the cabin. Aaron watched the way she flipped her soft buttocks first to one side and then to the other as she descended.

He went down later and brought his gear back up to the deck and made himself a place under the awning that covered the stern while they were in the harbor. He put the hammock up, hooking it to the wall of the cabin and to one of the awning poles, then he lay down in the rough netting and let the rest of the gear lie in a loose pile near the cabin wall. The afternoon sun could not reach the deck through the awning, but the heat made the smell of fish rise from the hampers on each side of the stern. He did not mind the smell, though, and he did not really mind moving up from the cabin. He spent most of his nights up on the deck anyway, and he had always had to carry the hammock up and down the narrow stairway. Now he could store it in one of the upper cabin lockers and Leroy would not be able to tell him to keep his crap out of there, the way he usually did.

Leroy and the girl came up from the cabin just as the afternoon sun began to go red over the water. Leroy said that they were going into the town for the things that she had there, but Leah did not say anything to Aaron, nor did she look at him. He nodded as they stepped off to the dock.

"If you go drinkin' and you see Ortiz, you tell 'im we go out again, end of the week," Leroy said back to him as they started away. Aaron nodded again.

And at the end of the week, when the gray came over the stern and they sat grinning at each other with their chests heaving in and out and neither was able to speak, Leah came up from the cabin and looked at them. Leroy turned to her, his grin growing even wider. She came close to them and looked at the shark for a moment and then she turned and she said nothing as she started back down the stairway.

Aaron grabbed the hatchet and began hacking at the tail. Leroy did not move for a long time, then he quietly took the ax from the cabin wall and went to work on the head. They did not speak to one another and there was only the sound of the blades chopping through the meat.

And during the second month Leah was on board, they took only four small gray on all of the trips they made. Money got low. Ortiz came down to the boat in the evening near the end of that month and he and Leroy sat on the bow in the red dusk and talked in low tones for three hours. Aaron watched as Leroy periodically shook his head, less and less emphatically each time, and finally nodded to Ortiz's gestures. Then the two of them went up the dock to the bar that Ortiz owned and Leroy said nothing when he came back late to the boat. Aaron went with him the following night to the broken piers of the free port and they watched as a half dozen men loaded a shallow drawing banana scow. He and Leroy sat together on the pilings and listened to Ortiz whisper harsh orders to the men who carried polyethylene wrapped cases of Canadian whiskey and room-sized air-conditioners and transistor radios into the gaping bow section.

"How long you think you'll be?"

"Couple weeks."

The men finished with the cartons and began to pile the three tons of green bunches around and on top of the contraband. It took another hour.

"You need anything — chow, booze, — you see Ortiz."

"Okay."

"And you look to Leah too," Leroy added quietly as he got up.

Aaron nodded and watched Leroy walk across the pier to the scow, and then he turned and climbed back down into the skiff and rowed back across the harbor.

Leah came up from the small cabin two nights after Leroy left. Aaron did not hear her come. He lay in the hammock with his eyes closed and he did not know that she stood at the far gunwale until she spoke.

"There's no getting out of it, is there," she said, he guessed, about the heat. She stood with her back to him and she fanned herself with the long fingers of her left hand as she looked out over the water.

"Guess not," he said.

She was quiet for a little while. She stopped fanning herself and she let her hands play lightly up and down the awning supports, and then she turned and looked at him for a while, and at first he gazed back at her, but he felt his face growing warm under her glance and he turned his eyes out over the water. She came slowly to him when he turned his face away and she pushed back the hair that hung partially over his face. He tried to concentrate on the movement of a single gull that dipped down in long easy curves to the water of the harbor. He could not. He turned his face up to hers and looked at her, and he felt himself slipping, loosening up where he wanted to hold himself tight. He thought suddenly that he should get up, right then, and go to town, to Cash Alley where it was always dark and wet and green with moss, or to the bars that eclipsed the whole of Calle del Perro, where it cost a little more, and that he would be all right when he came back.

"I hate that nigger," she murmured.

"You're nuts."

Her fingers pushed back more of his hair.

"I hate him," she whispered from low in her throat.

He stared up at her, at the way she looked down at him, and at the way her eyes reflected the dim glow of the shore lights. Then she turned and started slowly away down the narrow steps. He watched the lone gull sweep through one more dipping curve, and then he followed her.

During the third night, as he held her close against him in the lower bunk, she pulled his lips down on her neck and quivered violently under him.

"I'm entitled," she murmured harshly, "I'm entitled."

He drew back and looked at her.

"What?"

She blinked and looked surprised and then she smiled.

"Nothing," she murmured. She pulled his lips down on hers.

But three days before the end of the second week, as he sat on the edge of the bunk and bent to kiss her one more time before he got dressed, things changed. He was halfway down to her lips when the heavy steps started across the upper deck. He leapt to his feet and jerked his trousers from the top bunk, staring wildly up at the sound of the steps, and then he jammed his right foot into the leg, and hobbled, and swayed, and staggered backward, and finally he wound up sitting in the middle of the cabin floor, still staring up at the sound. Leah lay nude in the lower bunk, clutching the sheet around herself as her wide eyes watched him try to shove his left leg down through the cuff that was tangled around his right.

He was still trying when Leroy's face appeared in the passageway. He jerked himself to his feet and finally brought the trousers into place, then he stood swaying in the center of the cabin as both Leroy and Leah stared at him. He felt the blood rushing to his face.

"What's up, boy?" Leroy asked quietly as he pushed his thick bulk into the cabin. His glance flashed back and forth from Leah to Aaron as he moved to a spot almost between them.

"I — ," Aaron began.

"He *made* me," Leah said suddenly from the bunk, "He *made* me do it."

Aaron pulled his glance around to her face, his jaw going slack in disbelief.

"That right, boy?" Leroy asked through clenched teeth. His glance traveled back and forth between them again.

Aaron began to shake his head, slowly at first, then faster as Leroy stepped closer to him. He backed away, one step, then two, and then he turned quickly toward the passageway.

Leroy's fist caught him on the temple just before he reached it. He reeled forward into the narrow space and fell to his hands and knees, and then he pulled himself slowly back upright through the pain at the side of his head and turned to meet the attack, but Leroy had stopped in the hatchway. He looked at Aaron for a moment, then he hitched a thumb toward the upper deck.

Aaron didn't wait for more. He pulled himself up the steps and sprawled in the stern, his chest heaving for breath. He heard Leah's voice, rapid and pleading, below the deck, and then there was the sound of Leroy's open palm coming down against her.

They did not speak to one another after that, except out on the water when they had to. And they did not grin anymore when the gray came over the stern. Leah watched always from the stairway on the trips out, smiling into the wake.

When they were in the harbor, she took Leroy into the town and they did not come back for three or four days. Leroy looked tired when they came back. He slept for a long time. Leah brought hats and red shoes back from the shore and wore them when she sat on the bow and cleaned her nails and took the sun.

It was two months later, on a very hot day, that Aaron stood easily in the stern and wiped his face with the front of his shirt as he watched the lines. The water was smooth. The sun glimmered from the surface of the water and the salt ran down from his forehead and into his eyes and it made him want to keep his eyes closed for a long time. Then one of the lines, the starboard stern, went taut and he whipped his hand up in the go ahead.

The boat did not do what it usually did. It moved easily enough up into the plane, but then it shuddered and lurched several times, and then it slowed almost to a crawl.

"God damn," he muttered to himself.

"One of them lines hang up?" Leroy shouted in question from the wheel.

Aaron looked quickly at the other cables. Both hung loosely from the slow moving stern. The engine growled against the third, the taut one, as it moved evenly out to the starboard.

"Can't be!" he shouted up toward the cabin. He heaved on the slack lines to make sure. They came in easily. Then the Lincoln began to whine, pressured by the tension on the steel. Leroy whipped the bow over to port, away from the direction of the pull. The boat still crawled, shuddering even more.

"Come take the wheel!"

Aaron leapt for the ladder.

"Keep 'er full," Leroy said as he left for the stern.

Aaron worked the wheel to keep the pressure even and he watched Leroy arrive at the stern and stare down at the taut line. Leroy stayed in the stern for only a moment more, then he hurried back to the wheel. His eyes gleamed and his teeth flashed in the sun as he spoke.

"Awful damned big for a fin," he shouted over the scream of the Lincoln.

"Maybe a manta," Aaron shouted back.

"Manta that big'd be takin' us with 'im."

"What else?" Aaron screamed.

"Awful damned big for a fin."

Aaron turned his face toward the stern and saw Leah holding tight to the stairway rail, watching the taut line. She smiled and her eyes followed always the tight steel.

Leroy began to sweep. He worked the boat to the starboard, and then to the port, and then to the starboard again, trying to move the thing on the line into a faster pattern. It did not work at first, and the boat continued to strain, but then he caught it suddenly in the direction that it moved and their speed jarred upward. His black knuckles whitened on the wheel and his grin sparkled in the sun as they gained.

Aaron watched the muscles bulge across Leroy's chest and arms as the big man fought the wheel. He watched the trickles of sweat spray out into the wind as Leroy whipped his head from one side to the other, his eyes flashing almost black in the sunlight. He felt a grin spreading slowly across his own face, and then, just for a moment, the two grins met, and Leroy nodded in a vague kind of approval of everything that was going on.

"Well, don't just be standin' there like a damned fool. Get back astern and make sure that line's holdin' up."

Aaron was already halfway down the ladder.

It was a shark. It came up just a half an hour later while the Lincoln still wasn't moving them fast enough to cut off the water into its gills. And it came up slowly, heavily, all of it in one thick rolling turn, and it did not seem bothered by the line as it went smoothly back down. Leah stood in the stairway. Her eyes widened a little when the gray came up, then she smiled as she watched it disappear.

"God damn, man!" Aaron shouted back to where Leroy gripped the wheel, "It's thirty feet long!"

"Closer to eighteen, maybe twenty," Leroy yelled down at him, "We're only thirty-five."

It did not come back up, but it did start to give. Slowly at first, almost too little to notice, and then faster, and faster still.

"He ain't gonna get no water at this speed!" Leroy finally shouted. The boat lurched even more freely into the spray. Aaron stood at the stern, watching the tight steel that cut their wake.

The Lincoln moved them almost full for ten minutes, and it was another five after that before Leroy throttled back. He left the wheel as soon as the boat settled to a drift and came back down to the stern and together they hauled on the line.

It wasn't like the ten footers. Aaron felt his jaw go slack and he almost let go of the line when the gray broke water twenty yards astern. Leroy shot him a quick scowl, aware of the sudden added stress, and he quickly gripped the cable once more.

When it was finally alongside, they both stood braced at the gunwale and stared down at the thick gray bulk.

"You ready?" Leroy asked, glancing over his shoulder as he spoke. Aaron nodded and Leroy let go of the line and reached for the gaffs.

Leah stood in the stairway, frowning.

Aaron sank with the weight of the shark as it came sudden and full to his arms and shoulders. He felt the tightness grow in his chest and his stomach as he watched Leroy plant the gaff just behind the head, and then the pressure diminished and he gave Leroy all of the weight and he went for his own gaff. He plunged the hook into the meat and felt it bite to a firm hold, then he spread his feet and readied himself.

They heaved, and Aaron felt the shock travel down through his shoulders and back and along his ribs and into his legs, but the gray barely moved. They looked at one another and both of them renewed their grips, Leroy not grinning anymore, sweating thickly, and Aaron staring widely back down to the shark.

They tried again, sucked for breath, once more, again. Aaron's gaff pulled straight from the strain. He turned and yanked the spare from the rack.

"It's not gonna work," he gasped heavily as they eased off on the sixth try. Leroy scowled at him and firmed his grip on the gaff.

"It's got to come, the sonsabitch! It's got to!" then he heaved terribly upward, wrenching at his gaff, not even waiting for Aaron to use his own.

And nothing happened.

Leroy seemed to hang suspended for a long moment in a shroud of sweat, and then he slowly slumped down toward the gunwale with his face set and hard and with his chest pumping harshly in and out. Aaron was suddenly aware of the thick gray that covered his temples and spread back into his hair. He saw the deepening cracks around his eyes and at the corners of his mouth. He saw it all as though he had never seen any of it before, and it surprised him, and it made him a little afraid.

"Suppose," he said through his heavy breath, "Suppose we — cut it up?"

Leroy's face came slowly up to his, the features bent down into a squint, and then Leroy turned and glanced quickly down over the gunwale.

"Right," he said simply, "You leave go there and get one of them coils of rope, down the cabin."

Aaron gave the weight once again to Leroy and slid quickly past Leah on his way to the cabin. He yanked the coil from under the fire buckets and lunged back up to the stern.

"Take a hold here," Leroy said when he got back to the gunwale. Aaron gripped the line and braced himself and Leroy took the coil and slid over the side into the water. He worked quickly in the swell. He started with the middle of the coil and looped a turn around the body, just behind the head, and then another, three feet in front of the tail. He tossed the free ends up over the gunwale.

Aaron waited, his eyes first on Leroy, then on the fins that appeared and disappeared, circling closer each time around the boat. He opened his mouth to bring Leroy back on board, but before he could get the words out over his teeth, Leroy was dripping near him on the deck, straining against the line that encircled the tail. He cinched it tight on one of the gunwale cleats, then he moved to the free end of the coil that lay at Aaron's feet.

" 'nother second," he wheezed, and then the shark hung in the two coils of rope, part way out of the water. Aaron jerked the gaff free and stepped back out of the way as Leroy pulled the ax from the cabin wall. The fins were closer in their circle around the boat. Leah frowned in the stairway.

Aaron felt the red drops spray up over his face and his arms as Leroy brought the ax back up after the first bite. He crouched then along the gunwale and watched the steel cut through the thick gray hide and into the white flesh. Leroy grunted heavily with each thud of the blade, rasping in a new gulp of air each time he brought the steel back up over his head. He was more than halfway through when the first fin surged in and sliced away three feet of intestine that dangled from the gaping hole in the side of the gray. Leroy paused to eye the other fins for a moment, then the blade whacked back to work. There were two more rushes before the gray dipped in two pieces from the rope.

"Gaffs!" Leroy shouted.

Aaron scooped them up, handed one quickly to Leroy, then sunk his own into the tail section.

It came by inches. Neither of them took a breath as it crept heavily up the side of the gunwale under their strain. Sound broke simultaneously from their lips as it finally teetered, half in and half out on the edge of the gunwale, rolled slowly inward, picked up speed, then smacked down in a spray of blood and water to the deck.

The head was heavier. Aaron felt the fringe muscles in his arms and back coming slowly apart in little spasms of pain as he heaved almost shoulder to shoulder with Leroy. Streaks of blood ran down the outside of the gunwale and stained the white paint as the meat sucked noisily free of the water. And then he began to feel numb down along his back and his thighs, and then there was only the weight against him and his force against the weight.

And suddenly, before he knew or could understand what had happened, he was sprawled flat on his back next to Leroy as both of them skiddered awkwardly to rest on a cushion of loose intestines and flesh and blood. He pulled for breath and turned his face to Leroy's and he felt it break quietly into a grin that at least matched the one that leered crazily at him. They lay there for a long time, their chests pumping up and down from the deck, grinning hideously and idiotically, first at one another, then straight up into the sun.

The men on the dock stopped work and some of them came forward to stare in silence at the two stained and grinning men who leapt to the planks and watched Ortiz's boys awkwardly wrestle the two sections of shark to the dock scales.

"Rum!" Leroy boomed down on Ortiz's barboy, who had come to see the shark.

The boy darted up the planks and in through the hinged wooden doors, and then he reappeared and flew down the dock with two thick brown bottles held out to Leroy's waiting hands. Leroy took them and turned and smacked one of them against Aaron's chest, barely giving him time to fold his hands around it before it was released. Leroy gripped the other in his big palm and yanked the cork away and raised it to his lips with a quick and easy motion. The rum spattered out on their chins and down onto their chests as they gulped.

Leah stepped carefully from the stern of the boat to the dock. Her lips drew tight as she swung a half full duffel bag to the planks after her, and then she turned and stood with her chin tilted a little upward, facing Leroy.

Leroy took the bottle away from his lips and lowered his glance and looked at her for a long time, and then Aaron felt the big man's arm come easily down around his shoulder, and then the bottle went back up again.

Leah's glance traveled slowly over the two of them, and then she turned and picked up the bag and walked quickly up the dock toward the town.

BARRY TARGAN

Old Vemish

(FROM SALMAGUNDI)

THE S.S. SOLAR SAILED FROM NEW YORK CITY, pier sixty-two, precisely at ten o'clock on the morning of a clear April for twelve Caribbean days (seven, really, counting off getting there and getting back) and eleven nights. By 10:45 the glistening red, white, and blue ship, about 14,000 tons, its 250 passengers and crew of eighty, had sailed smoothly beneath the Verrazano Bridge through the Narrows into the Lower Bay, and then into the calm Atlantic heading south.

It had been a fine leaving, fruitbasket parties and all, a calypso band, streamers and confetti even. But by 12:30, Clifton Booth had his troubles. Not that he hadn't expected them. As a Tour Director for five years with the Lootens Line and as a specialist in geriatric cruises ("The time to ship out is when you have the time"), the solving of troubles was what Clifton Booth more than half existed for.

About the time the ship had cleared the smokey land for certain, the dramatic Battery shrinking in smudged silvery sticks, the whining complaints began to flicker down upon him like a new and larger confetti than that at the recent dock. Arthur Lewis, one of Clifton Booth's three assistants (they stood watches just like any Ablebodied Seaman), brought him, about every fifteen minutes, a wailing sheath of urgently scribbled protests and pleas: someone had lost his teeth, others were suddenly displeased with their cabins, seasickness swept over them like a plague.

But mainly there was just the grumpiness of the old that flared

whenever they were dislocated, shifted out of the comforting famil-
iarity of personal routines and the securing knowledge of where the
bathroom is in the dark and what all the creaking and vibrations in
their own houses meant. It was just the newness, Clifton Booth
knew, that unnerved them for a while. That is why he stayed in his
cabin for the first two hours of actual seatime and did not heed any
of the yellow notes. By the afternoon the teeth would be found, the
cabins unpacked in and made homelike, and the captain would
have announced that the ship's stabilizers were now operating,
thereby making seasickness modernly impossible, and the last queas-
iness would instantly disappear.

All except Clifton Booth's.

Unfortunately, but in a minor way, Clifton Booth needed a few
hours at the beginning of each tour to regain his "sea stomach," although his difficulty wasn't a matter of equilibrium in the inner
ear.

"Nerves," Clifton Booth said to Arthur Lewis. "Nervousness.
Not *about* anything, do you see; just nervousness *in itself*. Do you
know what I mean, Arthur?"

"Yes sir. I think so, sir," Arthur replied placing the newest messages upon the rising pile on the table next to the Director's
bunk-bed.

"How are they going?" Booth asked, not looking out from under
the damp, cool compress over his eyes.

"About the same, sir. In number and content. The only thing
different so far is a complaint about a bridge partner."

"A *what?*" Clifton Booth said, almost rising. "A *bridge partner?* Oh God," he said sinking back laughing. "And I thought I
had heard them all." He sighed happily. He was feeling much
better. He drifted off to visions of blue St. Croix, of a pleasant
afternoon's talk with Martinson in his cool English garden in the
middle of tropical Guadeloupe, of the Barbados rug by a native
weaver from high in the hills which he had decided at last to buy
for his New York apartment.

He awoke in ten minutes to the yellow rustling by his ear.

"Fewer now," Arthur Lewis said to him, "and the complaints
about the tour are beginning. Phase two."

"Ah," Booth sighed again, his strength and stability almost returned now as the pieces to his pattern, smoothed and worn by five

years of experience, slipped easily almost all into their managed place. "It's going to be a good trip, this one. I can feel it." He took off the compress. All his color was back, replacing the yellowish stain around his temples and the corners of his mouth. "After a while, Arthur, you can *tell* about these things." He sat up. "You can just *tell*."

But he was wrong. He hadn't yet encountered Martin Vemish.

Martin Vemish was sixty years old, a short man, gleamingly bald, but not fat although a little stout. He looked open and hard, smooth-faced but uncompromising, well-tailored but like a man high in the echelons of a Labor union who seemed uncomfortable to be there in his fancy office, remembering as he did the raw battles at Gate Four of Henry Ford's Rouge plant, and things like that. But Martin Vemish's stern appearance owed more, probably, to the fat, inelegant cigar he was always puckered upon than to any individual facial feature. He was, however, *as a person,* what he looked like.

Martin Vemish owned a wall paper and paint store in Ogahala Park on Long Island, about twenty miles from the city, a community at once as old as Eastern America, but as new as last week. He had owned the store early in his life, for forty years, getting into business and a large inventory six months before the Crash, long before latex paints and rollers and do-it-yourself housewives, in the years when wall paper was the major wall covering. For many years now, however, as he watched Ogahala Park turn from trees into houses, he had sold much more paint than paper, though he had his preferences. ("There's nothing *to* paint. Nothing to see, to *feel.* The paint covers. The paper *is!*") But he was in business and so he sold paint.

Still, affection and loyalty paid off. With the new affluence that had descended upon his corridor of Long Island, he sold a lot of paint, but paper made a comeback, and his sentimentally large selection and knowledge of papers had quickly established him as the wall paper center of the Ogahala Park area and even beyond. Because of this more than himself alone, he had grown near to "rich," or what his father would have called "rich." To Vemish, today, it was merely called "plenty." He had "plenty." You had to have it, or someone did, for you to leave your business and go

sailing around the Caribbean for twelve days in the S.S. Solar, not
that he wanted to be there.

He and his gray wife, Sara, were there in the light on the third
deck of the starboard side of the throbbing ship because of their
son, or, more exactly, because of their daughter-in-law, Norma,
whom, even after thirteen years, Martin Vemish had never gotten
to like very much. Still, a man's wife is his own concern, even if the
man is of your flesh, so Vemish had been silent, utterly civil, and
generous at every bad turn of Herbert's faltering business life. He,
Vemish, had maintained Herbert and Norma and the two grand-
children in a manner that Herbert's and Norma's earliest young
hopes for Herbert's ventures had taught Herbert and Norma to expect. They had always lived in a nice house and drove a nice car
and wore nice clothing just as if Herbert were a successful shoe
salesman or civil servant working in the Post Office, which he was
not.

What he had been for eleven years was everything and nothing
— a nice guy looking for a big break who never found it. What he
was now and had been for the past two years was his father's partner.

After Herbert's final failure (selling space in a giant frozen food
locker which he had rented too far out on the Island), Martin Vemish decided to pull Herbert into the business. Years back, even
when the boy was still in the Army, he had offered him. What,
after all, was he supposed to do with the business when he was
through with it? What are sons for, anyway? But Herbert had refused through a glass of larger dreams, and Vemish, and Sara, too,
had let him go in peace, even if they did stand around to pick him
up when he got knocked down.

Vemish and his wife were strong, like rocks, not like rivers.
Their strength was more in remaining than in doing; but they were
parents too. So when the frozen food locker business failed and the
home mortgage payment came due (along with the car and the electric and a dozen others) after eleven years Martin Vemish pushed
his son a little, and from the other side, Norma pushed him a lot.
By the end of a nice evening, Vemish had his man.

Now, two years later, he was reaping one of his rewards: a vacation.

In forty years he had never taken a formal vacation because he and Sara didn't feel anything about them. In the '30's of the Depression no one in a little business took a vacation: there was too much of doing nothing in a day as it was. And later, after the war, it wasn't natural to him to start something new. If sometimes he didn't want to work or Sara wanted to visit her sister in Rochester, New York, or it was too hot, he would simply close the store for a day and sometimes two and go away. That was all. Vacations just never occurred to them. Where they were and what they did pleased them enough. But one of the strongest levers Norma had used on Herbert two years before at the partner-making was that, as his father's partner, he could make it possible now for his father and mother to go on a vacation, to "get away."

"Do you know that they've never, *never*, taken a real vacation?" she had said. "Can you imagine, Herb? Can you imagine? *Forty years with no vacation.*" There was horror in her voice.

Herbert Vemish, like his father, figured that what a man did with his own life was his own affair, but this, as Norma was insistently pointing out, was different. A son, after all, did have some obligations.

"And Herb, darling," Norma had put her hand on his arm, "Martin and Sara aren't getting any younger. It's not so easy anymore." Then, urgently, "Herbie, Herbie, have a little consideration for *them.*" That did it.

Herbert Vemish turned and looked at his father and then at his mother and said, "Ok." He put out his hand to his father. "Partner."

Martin Vemish looked at his son looking at him *that way* and wanted to protest, wanted to make it harshly clear to him that at fifty-eight he, Martin Vemish, was healthy and vigorous enough to make it to seventy-eight, at which time he could be looked at *that way*, maybe. Not until. But the whole point was to get Herbert to do what he was doing right now: agreeing. If Norma's argument worked, so let it. Martin Vemish took his son's hand and shook upon the deal. He and Sara had gotten what they wanted, Norma had gotten what she wanted, and Herbie was pleased to be able to do something good for his aging parents, so what the hell.

Except that Herbie started to do good to them right away. He

was familiar enough with the paint and paper business from high
school days when he had worked after school and weekends so that
in less than a month he could pretty much run things. Besides,
there wasn't much that could go wrong, and, anyway, if Herbert
Vemish hadn't been a success in his commercial ventures, at least
he wasn't a fool. Thirty days into his partnership he began to urge
his father to "Take a nap" or "Take the afternoon off" or "Go up
to the mountains for the weekend." As the summer drew on he
began asking his father where they were planning to go.

"Go? Go where?" his father asked.

"On your vacation," the son answered, a gallon of Bone-white
Flat Interior in either hand.

"Vacations, vacations! Will you stop already with your vacations!"

"No!" the son shouted back. "No! You're fifty-nine! A year
from now you'll be sixty! *SIXTY!*" He said it the way they say
"Bad breath" or "Body Odor" on the TV commercials. "You've
got to start taking it *easier.*"

Martin Vemish walked away from his son that day and disregarded the subject whenever he, frequently, brought it up, but after
two years the father calculated that the weekly turmoil of Herbie's
now obsessive concern was costing him more of his inner peace than
any vacation possibly could: he finally agreed. After all, it wasn't
that he *disliked* vacations; he didn't even know anything about
them.

"All right! *ALL RIGHT!*" he shouted at his son across a rising
square of five pound packages of plaster of Paris that the two of
them were stacking up in a corner of the store. It was February and
snowing, and the son had been at him from the first thing in the
morning. "*ALL RIGHT! I'LL GO!* Make the plans! Buy the
tickets! Send me! Just leave me alone already!"

At supper he told Sara, and even as they were finishing their
after-dinner tea the phone rang with Norma to tell them that she
had selected a Caribbean cruise. She told them how long they
would be gone, where they would go, what they could buy at what
low prices, how warm it would be, and about thirty other things.
She didn't tell them until another time that the cruise was re-
stricted to sixty-year-olds and up, and up. When she did tell them,

the way she put it was, "And one of the absolutely best things about *this* cruise is that you'll have so much in common with everyone else."

Right then Martin Vemish almost cancelled out. It would have been a good day for Clifton Booth if he had.

At three o'clock Clifton Booth put on his lightly braided uniform and called an assembly of his charges, at which time he introduced himself and his assistants much in the manner of a Dean on first meeting with the collected Freshmen. There was a continual bantering going on between Clifton Booth and himself, a delicious interior dialogue that his Graciousness permitted them a glance at — light, fluffy as sea foam, witty, assuring, charming; but firm, too. He told them in detail about the numerous activities that he had planned for them on shipboard. He talked about the games, the dances, the bridge tournaments, the shuffleboard and other contests (and the prizes), the movies, the lectures, the concerts. He told them about the food: its staggering variety, its incredible abundance, its unending availability, and the special dietary considerations that some might need (low salt menus and the like). He explained to them their proper procedure while ashore at the daily stops the ship would make: first the guided tour for those who wanted it ("Though I can promise you that the tours are unquestionably *the* way to see the most in the time available") and then the period for shopping. ("Although I guess the husbands would just as soon we didn't leave the ship at all.") Laughter.

He told a delighting story of a clever woman shopper who bought from an out-of-the-way shop on Martinique what turned out to be a real "find": a handcarved (not turned) salad bowl made of Martinique teak, perhaps the rarest wood in this hemisphere, maybe, even, the world. His audience ooo-ed. Similar things were always happening.

And then he told them of the laggardly pair, continually late for everything, who, after a number of close calls, finally missed the boat in St. Kitts and had to stay there three days before another cruise boat came along to save them.

"*Three days* they lost out of their once-in-a-lifetime cruise. *Three days* in Saint Kitts with nothing to do but sit on the beach and stare at the water." He let his lovely voice show compassion for their loss, but pique at their foolishness. He let his voice rise up to drive into his listeners the critical importance of promptness in returning to the boat.

"Wherever you are," he admonished now, strictly, "keep an ear tuned to the boat whistle. When you hear the whistle it will mean you've got an hour to get aboard ship. *Aboard* it." He said it all again and added details.

This was a no-nonsense thing. Fun was fun, but there were still obligations, duties. "Let's remember," he said, his voice soothing down into his peroration, "while we're all on this ship together, we are like a little world. We've got to be considerate of each other in order for any of us to live happily. We've got to think of the next guy. So let's see if we can't do a better job on the world of this ship, the good old S.S. Solar, than we, as mankind, have done on the world of the old ship Earth."

Somehow it all sounded so familiar, as if they had all been here before.

Still they applauded strongly and started to nod in sage agreement. It sure wasn't an easy thing to do, running a cruise and looking out for the happiness and safety of 250 people. They felt that they should feel thankful to have someone as pleasant and sensible as Director Booth to take care of them. Well, they were going to do whatever *they* could to make it easier for him to make it easier for them. With a little pitching in all around there was no reason why the next eleven days and ten nights couldn't be as nice as any they had ever spent — nicer, even. At least now they had a clearer understanding of why they were here.

Clifton Booth praised them, then, for their considerate attention and announced that an Introduction Tea would start at four o'clock in the Main Lounge. He hoped to meet all of them individually there and that they would all get to know each other. Once more they applauded back what was now their affection.

All but Martin and Sara Vemish, who had not attended the meeting.

Back in the office that adjoined Booth's stateroom, Arthur Lewis reported the Vemishes.

"Are you sure they *knew* about the meeting? Are you sure they *understood?*" Clifton Booth was standing before his mirror straightening himself out. He spoke to the reflection of his assistant.

"Yes sir. When I saw them sitting there I asked them if they knew about the meeting. They did. I explained that it was a very important meeting because it outlined the basic procedures for the cruise."

"And?" Booth was impatient. Recalcitrants were such a bother.

"They said they didn't care. They liked it out on deck."

"And?"

"That was all, sir."

"What do you mean, 'That was all'?" Booth turned and put on his lordly white, black-beaked hat and started for the door.

"That's all they said, sir. That's all they would say," Arthur Lewis said, saying all *he* could say, again to the back of Clifton Booth as he moved into action.

When it came to tactics the only ones that Martin Vemish knew about were grim. In 1948 when Macy's, the first of the big department stores to open branches in the suburbs, opened in the new Ogahala Park Shopping Center and started to move for all the business, including the paint business, in the area — for *all* of it — Martin Vemish fought back the only way a man who doesn't fight much fights when he has to: deadly. Restraint, after all, is a condition of experience, a knowledge earned from the *use* of power. Martin Vemish, lacking experience, knew nothing about restraint. He went for Macy's throat. Macy's was threatening him and it was all he knew what to do.

He advertised for the first time: in newspapers, with handbills, with posters on telephone poles as if he were running for political office. He cut prices below even what Macy's was selling at, and *then* he ran special sales. He wrote sputtering letters to the Chamber of Commerce and worse to the Letters-to-the-Editor page of the paper trumpeting his outrage. He cut the letters out of the newspaper and pasted them in the window of his store between the red and blue signs that were giving his business away gallon by gallon. "Communists," he called Macy's in his letter. He compared them to the Russians overpowering the courageous little countries of eastern Europe. "Un-American," "Death of the Free Enterprise System," "Low Prices Today, Macy's Prices Tomorrow" were some of his titles.

During the winter, when business was slow, nobody painting much of anything but chairs, cabinets, and a few interior walls, he almost went broke. There were bitter days in February when he looked over the classified section wondering about what sort of job he might soon have to get.

But in the spring he won. Macy's relented, withdrawing to its enormous share of the market. From then on Vemish's business rose from the ashes.

Had he known more about the world than he did, perhaps Martin Vemish would not have fought with Macy's the way he had, but he did not know, and he never found out, and, anyway, he couldn't stop himself from fighting against a thing he hadn't started.

Clifton Booth knew none of this as he approached the Vemishes, their eyes shut, their faces uplifted to the western sun, at pleasant ease thirty miles abeam of Stone Harbor, New Jersey.

"Hello," Clifton Booth said, coming between Martin Vemish and the sun.

"Hello," Vemish said looking up into the shadow over him. Sara opened her eyes but said nothing.

"I'm Clifton Booth, your Tour Director."

"*Your* Tour Director, not mine," Vemish said.

Clifton Booth had floundered about in real estate before he became, at forty, a Tour Director, and found his destiny. He was as successful at the one job as he had been at the other, as if large parcels of land were too difficult for him to manage compared to the handling of the smaller geographies of old people on tightly scheduled boats. He was very good at it, at adjusting the old people to his organization for them, for he was, as he had discovered, his century's surrogate king, the *technician* of power, the Manager.

From the start he had indicated great skill in Tour Directing and had moved from an assistantship to his own boat in exactly one year, half the usual time. In the Lootens Line it was generally conceded that no one ran a better, a more orderly cruise than he, a "tighter" ship. There was even talk that he would be the successor to the post of Chief Director, whose responsibility it was to oversee the training of the others as well as to sit in upon cruise policy decisions. All in all, Clifton Booth knew where he stood, and why.

Confidently Booth approached the Vemishes another way. He

had ways and ways. On every cruise he met some petulant, persistently cantankerous anger of an old one, who had been abraded in some way by a petty feature or detail of the planned and plotted existence that he had signed on for for twelve days and eleven nights. The outburst would flash until he, Booth, came and put it out. He understood: it was the way of the old. He was a gentle man, and patient. His patience was a weapon, and a great one. But not his only one. He knew a lot of things to do to people to get them straightened out and running true to his form in no time at all.

Only with Martin Vemish it was different. With him it wasn't some little senile bitching or petty gripe; it was a deeper anger and an abiding one, and over and through it all flickered contemptuous fire. Vemish despised the idea of the cruise itself. He saw it as a shoddy trick that the strong young played upon the weakening old, a facade that children insisted their parents put on as the final price to pay for affection, as the last humiliating demand for their death. Vemish hated it and Clifton Booth, the agent, even as he looked at him for the first time. This *attendant,* the ship his home, this "parent" to the childish and cowered old, himself rooted in no fading memories dissolving in time's acid, stretched beyond no context other than himself, bound to shore by no perdurable threads of kindred love — it was easy for him to imagine things to be other than they were and to manage a world as he thought it was and therefore should be. And wasn't that what he was getting paid by the children to do?

Martin Vemish didn't want to be on the S.S. Solar's geriatric tour, not for twelve days or twelve minutes, but if he had to be, then he would be there on his own terms, which is exactly what he told Director Booth.

"Listen," finally he said, not bothering to take the cigar out of his mouth, "you and your people leave *me* alone and I'll stay out of *your* way. No trouble from either end, ok?" He closed his eyes and eased back in the deck chair.

"Mr. Vemish," Booth began, "I don't think you understand. My job on this cruise is to serve you, to make you as comfortable . . ."

"Fine," Vemish interrupted him. "Fine! Exactly! Good! Serve me by leaving me alone!" He closed his eyes again. Booth changed his voice a little.

"Mr. Vemish, running a cruise is a complicated thing. You don't have to participate but there are certain details about life on a cruise ship that you *do* have to be made . . ."

"Screw!" Vemish said chomping down on his cigar, this time without opening his eyes. Clifton Booth turned to Vemish's silent wife.

"Mrs. Vemish," he began, all but unaware of his tone, the patronizing whine in which he spoke to wives about their childish husbands. But Sara Vemish cut him off.

"You heard him," she said.

Director Booth stalked away, surprised at the motion of the ship.

So *that's* the way it was going to be, Booth thought as he moved sightlessly through the ship's familiar corridors to his office-cabin. So the Vemishes didn't want to play the game by the rules. Well, he'd see about that. He'd just see about *that*. Why in hell, he wondered, did they take the cruise? To make misery? To bring gloom and trouble instead of happiness? It comforted him to think that people who took cruises that they didn't want were just those kinds of oddballs who required the most dealing with, but that it equaled out because the hard-heads were always easiest to handle if they didn't come around, if they didn't *shape up*: he could always throw them out. In five years (four years of his own command) he had done it fifteen times, sent couples home. He would give them a letter of refund credit and arrange a flight out from the next island that a plane could land on. A few times he had to get them space on a returning boat because they wouldn't fly, but he had managed even that.

Fifteen times! Which was about fifteen times more than any other Tour Director had done it. At first the Home Office was disturbed and then appalled, but when the letters from the other passengers, some of them, particularly the older ones, started to mount up, letters praising Booth for his decisiveness in removing the "spoilers" (for he would always make it publicly clear to his cruise why he had taken such a drastic step), his actions took on the stature of policy and Booth found his geriatric *métier*. The Lootens Line discovered that it could guarantee your shipboard ease and pleasure (what didn't fit, throw out), and its advertising began to reflect that. So Martin Vemish had just better watch out. On the last call, if it went to that, the Director always would hold all the top cards.

Clifton Booth sat at his desk with the Vemish dossier in his hand.
He read over the bland particulars: Martin Vemish . . . Sara . . .
Ogahala Park . . . business . . . Down at the bottom of the page-
long form, in the Activities and Interests Section, none of the numerous boxes was checked.

"We've got us a problem case," Booth said over to the other side
of the cabin where Joseph Crenshaw, the second of Booth's assistants, sat recording into the Tour Log the events of the mid-watch,
twelve to four, his responsibility.

Joseph Crenshaw had been a Tour Director himself, once, but he
had been caught by a husband performing a duty beyond his call.
The Lootens Line was a humane one, and it demoted Crenshaw instead of firing him, but it demoted him for good. He had worked
for them for sixteen years now, ashore and aboard ship, and he
would never be a Tour Director again. But he liked the life; he
was obliged to no one but himself and his own pleasures, of which
there were many in the April islands of the azure Caribbean.

"Who's that?" Crenshaw asked not looking up, not caring. He
had sailed with Clifton Booth frequently in the past and preferred
it: Booth took so much of the work upon himself and to his heart
that the Assistant Directors had little more to do than relax and
enjoy the cruise, not that there was that much to enjoy with the
"gerries." Joseph Crenshaw knew, then, what was going on in his
superior; he could imagine, then, what the outcome would be. He
didn't permit himself the luxury of judgment or that expense of
energy. What energy he had he used to pursue his own interests.
Let Booth pursue his own.

"This Martin Vemish," Booth said. "Apparently he thinks
we're going to turn this boat around for him. Well, he's got another think coming, I'd say." Joseph Crenshaw nodded his head
and wrote on. Booth flipped the dossier down on his desk and settled back to think the situation through. He didn't want to lose
perspective.

So far nothing disturbing to the others had actually happened
and that was the important thing. As long as Vemish could keep it
that way, then Booth *would,* in fact, he promised to himself, leave
him alone.

There had been others, after all, on every cruise. On every cruise
there had been those whom you couldn't really think of as a part of

things: singles who had been sent on the cruise to recover from some grief, or to meet someone new; newly married old people oddly shy as they had not been the first time forty or fifty years before; and there were those touched by a sudden, morbid depression. Booth left them. Their sympathy-evoking presence didn't help the gay *tone* of the cruise, but they were no threat to it.

But Vemish was. At the end of it all, Booth knew that finally there would be no way that either of them could leave the other alone. And even if there had been, Booth knew that with a Vemish it would have to come to more than that because he looked at his job in creative terms: he imagined that he was a craftsman.

Booth saw each of his cruises as a separate object, as a made thing, like a sculpture or a painting or a good piece of furniture. It wasn't enough for him just to float his tour safely and comfortably from New York to the Caribbean and back again; he wanted the cruise to be, as every artist wants his work to be, memorable. *He* wanted to remember; he wanted *his passengers* to remember. He kept the collective gift that almost all his cruises had given him as an athlete keeps his trophies, the date of the cruise noted on a tag gummed to the bottom of the gift. He Xeroxed the Tour Log. He had innumerable pictures. At the end of a good cruise he was high; at the end of a bad one, low. And there had been bad ones, at least by his lofty estimation. Every time they had been the result of blighters like the Vemishes, who like dark fists of clouds on the clear horizon, could become in less than an hour black and fearful storms.

In the face of their clear threat to his accomplishment and personal happiness, Booth girded. None of his successes were sweeter than those he had had to struggle for, wresting his shining victory with skill, ingenuity, and courage from the maw of blackness. He mounted, gathered up his thunderbolts, and rode forth.

Bradford Bates stood on the half deck overlooking the chlorine-blue swimming pool set into the stern of the S.S. Solar. Around the pool shroud-white bodies lay variously reposed in files and ranks of deck chairs. Most of the flesh that Bradford Bates looked down upon was nearly formless, like the globs of lard he remembered his whole lifetime ago from the cook greasing a baking pan for biscuits. The amorphic streak in the third chair, second row on the east side of the pool, was the woman to whom he had remained married for thirty-five years. Her name was Charlotte. She wore a two piece bathing suit of which each half of the halter was a different tone — a deep green fading into a dull red; like traffic lights flickering out.

In the pool a portly but solid, shiningly bald man swam, cavorted. He splashed and dived, squirted water out of his mouth while floating on his back like a whale, whooped loudly, and now and again raced across the width of the pool in a frothing channel like that made by an erratic torpedo. No one else was in the pool. Nor had anyone else been in it that day before the bald man. Bradford Bates knew because he had been standing in the shadows of the higher deck for nearly two hours hiding, which was what he usually did.

No one had gone into the pool. Very few people walked about. It was nothing at all like the gay pictures Charlotte and he had looked at in the magazine section of the *New York Times*. It was nothing like what his daughter, a younger Charlotte, had told them. Only the one man in the pool and the waiters moving about bringing liquids and fruit. But Bradford Bates didn't mind.

Off to the opposite side of the boat from him he saw the first of Porto Rico. Minutes before it hadn't been there and now it was. He quivered at the solidness of it as all who have ever been at sea do at a landfall. He wanted to shout out as if he had been high up in a crow's-nest. He moved. He stepped forward out of his shadow. He stepped to the railing as the island became each instant more and more detailed, a place of trees and huts and hovering but transparent clouds, diving and wheeling seabirds against the dark green of the humped-up hills.

"Bradford," Charlotte Bates called up at him. "Bradford," she called, light and swift, the practiced refinement of her voice hissing through the air like a tamer's whip, certain and sure. She waved him to come to her. He sank.

In their cabin Charlotte Bates held forth.

"Once, once in my lifetime we go on a cruise and you desert me, run away. Two days and I only see you when we eat, and not always then. Where have you been? Where do you go?" He knew that he wasn't expected to answer. He stood by patiently as his wife stepped out of her bathing suit as if she hadn't been wearing it. She walked into the bathroom as he watched her clear, etched skeleton articulate without reference to the merest sheath of flesh that slid over it. Before the shower drowned her out she called, "And that man in the pool! Puffing and snorting like an animal! What does he think, that he's the only one on the boat? Who is he, that . . . that *vulgarian?*" The water pounded upon her chest.

Bates felt defensive for the man. What had *he* done? For himself he felt nothing; at least, after battering years, he couldn't think of what he felt as being something in the definite way that he felt something for the bald man enjoying his lively swimming in the pool. He couldn't permit himself to think of himself feeling. He might have liked to swim himself except that he knew Charlotte. He could imagine: "You've come a thousand miles from home, more, for a *swim?* You needn't think of yourself as a . . . a *youngster,* that you must make a spectacle of yourself. Think. Who else is in the pool?" And now that the one person in the pool was someone whom Charlotte had decided against once and for all time, her resistance to his own going into the pool would be glacial. He waited for her to finish her shower and to dress. It was the story of his life.

"When does the ship dock?" she asked him over her shoulder as he zipped her completely into her dress. There was so little of her to hold it.

"I don't know," he said. "Soon, I think. Now, maybe."

"Now? NOW?" She was alarmed. She had not come to San Juan, Porto Rico, to stand around in a cabin explaining to him how he should conduct himself. "Let's go," she said. "Let's *go.*" She hurried out of the cabin leaving him to scuttle after her. Everything in her world was always his fault.

The S.S. Solar had almost docked. The enormous brown hawsers like incredibly long snails in a surreal dream were tightened around the giant black cleats on the wharf below by thick-shouldered men sweating in the Caribbean sun. The gangplank deck of the ship was busy with crew members preparing to disembark the "cruisers." (Clifton Booth had initiated the idea of calling the tour passengers "cruisers" and not "tourists.") And the "cruisers" were gathered and crowded. What noise and excitement they were capable of, they made. It wasn't much.

Individually none of the passengers was so old as to be actually infirm. And what black grief any one of them might at any moment have begun to discover in his body was not revealed in a personal meeting. Everyone, alone, walked vitally enough, had his single — if fragile — strength. It was their collective agedness that oppressed them, all of it together bearing down upon them that silenced them, frightened them. Standing as a group upon the shaded deck about the kaleidoscope of San Juan was like standing in a hall of mirrors: there was nowhere you could look without being reflected, unless you closed your eyes, and that would have been most terrible of all.

Clifton Booth addressed them over the gentle loud speaker system. They came to even quieter attention.

"Well, folks. This is it. First port and a beautiful day. Now let me go over some of the things we talked about earlier." He told them about the guided tours, the free hours, the "better" restaurants if they wanted to eat ashore, to watch out for the drinking water, the places to look for bargains, and lots else, like where the police station was and what to do if you thought you were being taken advantage of by a native and what to say if you weren't feeling well (*"Señor, estoy enfermo. Traigame al barco, por favor."*) Many of the "cruisers" were taking notes. He also told them that although the ship would not sail until two o'clock that morning, he hoped that they would all be back on board no later than ten o'clock that evening.

"Now one last thing." His voice became cautious and serious, and they leaned forward toward him. Then he quickly changed. "Don't spend all your money today. Tomorrow is Saint Thomas, *duty free!* Two hundred will get you four hundred every time." They laughed. A few clapped.

The grate and snap of the section of railing swinging out of place before the incline of the gangplank turned them away from Booth and into the slow funnel that they began to drip down and through on to Porto Rico. From the south rim of the funneling deck Charlotte Bates and her husband moved toward the gangplank. And from the north rim came the late-arriving Vemishes. Near to the gangplank entry Martin Vemish said to his wife, "Well, let's see what it's all about. Maybe there are guides or something we can get to show us around." Sara nodded.

Twice now Vemish had not heard about the pains the Lootens Line had gone to to provide an intricate and interesting guided tour for its "cruisers," for him. And if he didn't know that then he probably didn't know what to do if he got sick or when to absolutely get back to the ship. He might even spend all his money before St. Thomas, not to mention Martinique or Barbados or the rest. Resentment stirred through those around Martin Vemish like brief eddies through anemones in a tidal pool when the tide begins to rise. Who was *he!*

Charlotte Bates heard and balanced her anger at Vemish against the satisfaction of confirmation in her first dislike; he was the man in the pool. She had *known* what he would be like. She hurried to reach the gangplank before him as if his arriving first in Porto Rico would defile it for her. They reached the entry almost together, but not quite. Vemish moved in a half-step before her, Sara on his arm. Charlotte Bates had to stop abruptly; she was not used to having people step in front of her. And Bradford Bates was not used to having his wife stop suddenly once she had begun to move where she decided she would go. He banged into her and started her off again, this time into Vemish. She bumped him.

"Easy, lady," he said back through his contrail of cigar smoke hanging in the still afternoon air, hardly looking at her. "There's plenty of island for us all. Plenty." It was Vemish's kind of pleasantry.

"Some people," Charlotte whispered loudly to her husband and to all the rest. Some of those who heard her nodded the way some always nod before the sibilances of the Charlotte Bateses, as if they dared not. She marched down into San Juan, which had now gone all red before her.

Clifton Booth leaned back against the white plates of the bulkhead hearing and seeing. It won't be long now, he thought.

Robert Clark, the third of Clifton Booth's assistants and the one closest to becoming a Tour Director on his own, sat at the little table near the gangplank reading by the sharp, round light of a hi-intensity lamp. An occasional moth would flutter up from the city to dance in the white cone. If it did not go soon, Robert Clark would snap it out of the air with his hand and cast the crumpled thing away. Since he came on to his watch at eight o'clock, he had been sitting at this table reading and marking off in the Leave and

Return Book those returning. It was 9:45. Then Clifton Booth
was at his shoulder asking,

"Have the Vemishes returned yet?"

"No, not yet," Clark told him.

"Let me know when they do," Booth said and walked away, but
not far, not so far that, minutes later, he didn't see the Vemishes
when they reported in. Clark didn't bother to ask who they were.
They were the only couple of the cruise left to be accounted for.

"Pleasant evening," Clark said as they passed him.

"Wonderful," Vemish said. "Wonderful. Look!" He had
stopped and turned. He took from under his arm a box of cigars.
"Havanas," he said. "Corona Corona. The real thing. I haven't
smoked a real Havana for I can't remember how long. The trip's
worth it already." He put the cigars back under his arm, put his
lighted cigar back in his mouth, and turned into Clifton Booth,
who had come up on them.

"I'm glad to see you folks made it back in time," he said.

"Ah, it's Mr. Ruth," Vemish said.

"Booth," Clifton Booth corrected him. "Booth, not Ruth."

"Have a cigar," Vemish opened the box and held it out. Three
cigars were gone.

"Thank you, but I don't smoke," Booth declined.

"A shame, a shame," Vemish nodded his head. "All this tobacco
and you don't smoke." He gestured out at all the islands of the
Carribbean. "A shame."

"You know, you can't bring Cuban products back into the
states," Booth informed them.

"So I'll smoke fast," Vemish said and with his silent wife passed
on.

But in St. Thomas it was different. The S.S. Solar and its cruise
was scheduled to leave St. Thomas for St. Croix at six in the evening. Passengers were to be on board by five in the afternoon at the
latest. At 6:15 the Vemishes were not to be found.

In his cabin-office Booth sat drumming his fingers on his desk
when the intraship phone rang. Joseph Crenshaw answered it.
"It's for you," he said to Booth holding his hand over the mouth-
piece. "The Captain." Booth took the phone quickly.

"Captain Harley here. Where are your sheep, Booth? I've got
tides to consider, and weather, and docking schedules."

"Yes, Captain. I can appreciate the inconvenience. In ten more minutes I will initiate our search procedure by calling the police, the hospitals, and the tour guide office. I suppose all we can do for now is wait."

"Why don't you start looking for them right away? Why didn't you start earlier?"

"Yes, sir," Booth said. "The Lootens Line procedure is to wait an hour and a half before alerting the authorities." Booth felt how white he was, how all of him that lived had coalesced into his stomach, and there it lurched.

"Well, let me know as soon as you hear something," Captain Harley grumphed.

"Yes, Captain. Yes, I will. And Captain," Booth caught him before he hung up. "I can promise you this: it won't happen again. No, Captain. Oh, no. *It won't happen again.*" Saying it, thinking about how it was true, gave him back his blood.

The Vemishes returned by seven o'clock on their own. Booth called the Captain and in fifteen minutes the ship swung away from its berth and into the still light evening. For an hour Booth left the Vemishes alone. And then he called upon them in their cabin.

"Have you eaten?" was what he asked them first. "If you would rather, I'll come back after your supper. It's a matter of some importance." And there was no hurry. He had all the way to St. Croix to tell them and for them to pack.

"Not yet," Vemish told him. "We haven't eaten yet, no. I need time to recover." At which Vemish sank down heavily upon the bed.

"Recover?" Booth asked.

"From the excitement. What a day." Vemish swung his legs onto the bed and lay back. "Let me tell you Mr. Ruth . . . Booth. I'm not such a young man anymore. This kind of thing can take it out of you."

"What happened?" Booth asked.

"Sara," Martin Vemish said, his eyes closed now, "tell him." Booth turned to her.

"No," Sara said. "You tell him."

"No, no," Vemish said, "I'm resting. You tell him."

"No," Sara Vemish said.

"WHAT?" Clifton Booth shouted. "TELL ME!" Martin
Vemish said:

"A little boy fell into a deep hole with water in it and I jumped
in and saved him. From the water in the hole I got wet, so the
boy's mother took us to her house and cleaned up my clothes and
dried them. That's why we're late, so help me God. But it's all
right, it's all right. Don't worry about me." His eyes were still
closed. "They wanted to throw us a big dinner. They wanted to
give me some kind of medal, you know. But I told them. 'Look,'
I said, 'I got a whole ship of people waiting for me. As soon as my
pants are dry, I got to go.' They pleaded, but I was firm. So here I
am. Offf. What a day. What did you want to talk to us about?"

"NEVER MIND," Booth continued to shout. "NEVER
MIND."

Outside, even in the liquid air of Caribbean dusk, Clifton Booth
was dizzy near to fainting.

About ten-thirty, well after supper but not after the food, quiet
and unused tables of it placed here and there in the great forward
Lounge of the enclosed Promenade Deck, Bradford Bates did the
third bravest thing of his life. Giddy, almost giggling with his daring, he stole away from his wife, deep in her gesticulating story to
her circle, walked up to the smoking Vemish and Sara, and introduced himself. It must have been the salt air.

Vemish looked up at the frail Bates for a moment and then asked
him to sit down. He did, and then they told where they lived (as it
turned out, not far from each other), what they did (Bates had a
small accounting business), how they were enjoying the trip.

"Eeeeh," Vemish said. Bates smiled.

"What about this?" Bates asked indicating, with a small circling
of his thin head, the Lounge.

They were sitting in the middle of what looked like a giant bazaar. Everywhere there was the booty of the day, the treasure of the
fabled St. Thomas. Floating about on the sea of old people, many
awake beyond their ordinary hour, bobbing about everywhere between the blue-haired heads of excited grandmothers and their husbands, were the various, colorful trinkets of the tourists' lust. It
was as if, after three or four hundred years, the Caribbean natives
were turning the game around and buying back their land and soul

with the same humiliating, gaudy baubles and eye-bashing colors that the earlier Spanish masters had raped them with.

"Terrible," Vemish said loudly out of a burst of emphatic smoke. "Terrible." His eyes were hot but not angry. "You ask me, it's expensive crap, even for bargains. Still, it's their money. What do I care."

All day he and Sara had wandered slowly through the inescapable market place that was St. Thomas, annoyed and embarrassed by the ugly squeal flickering at them wherever they went, an animal call sent up by their own "cruisers" as well as from the passengers from the six more cruise ships in the port, for they were not alone on the Spanish Main. All day he and Sara had heard the passionate yelps of pleasure from the stalls around them everywhere as if the women were being serviced by an obscene substitution of wooden bowls and French China and roughly-dyed table cloths. Still in Vemish's ears were the growls of satisfaction of the men as they fondled duty-free cameras and tax-less scotch. He remembered the whistle of the ship ordering the orgiastic climax, the frantic push and drive to conclude the business, giver and taker alike hearing Time's 14,000 ton winged chariot pursuing them; the climax and then the peaceful exhaustion. And later, now, the leering recall of conquest.

"Tell me, Bates," Vemish said leaning toward the little man. He removed his cigar and used it as a blunt pointer, aiming it like a gun just fired. "What do you see here that you couldn't buy exactly the same in the city? Eh?" Bates nodded yes.

"Nothing," Bates agreed, delighted in his friend and in himself. Delighted to be asked a question. "Not a thing."

"Right," Vemish said, loudly enough for any near to hear him. He laughed. "What they don't sell here, in the off season they ship up to Gimbel's. Ha! For *LESS!*" People heard. Vemish picked up the ashtray next to him and examined its bottom as though it was something he had bought. "Made in Japan," he shouted. He and Bates roared. The others, more of them, heard. "Why do they do it, Bates?"

"I don't know," Bates said. He felt a little drunk.

"I'll tell you." Those near to him didn't want to hear, but he spoke so that they had to, that or leave, though he didn't care if they did.

"Nothing to do. We get shoved out of our beds away from family, business, friends, and we're told to *enjoy* ourselves. Have a big time. Chance of your life. Yeah, yeah. God forbid we don't come back with our arms loaded to prove it!"

Bates nodded his head rapidly and giggled at last. A couple nearest to Vemish got up and hurried away. Some others rewrapped their packages.

Bates saw Charlotte see him and start toward him. He hung on. From the other side of the Lounge, behind him, he didn't see Clifton Booth. Both of them arrived in time to hear Vemish proclaim loudly something about getting sick of being dragged from one Caribbean shopping center to another Caribbean shopping center.

"Bradford," Charlotte Bates commanded. For an instant Bates' wrinkled throat was jammed with his desire, but he bit down, swallowed hard, and stood up.

"My wife, Charlotte," he said to Vemish. To his wife he said, "Charlotte, this is . . ." but Charlotte Bates wasn't about to be introduced to Martin Vemish *ever,* and certainly not in front of two-thirds of the "cruisers." And would her husband hear about *that.* She stood draped about by four yards of a bolt of native cotton cloth, mainly orange with a purple thread design; she held the rest of the column of the material almost as thick as herself in her arms like an artillery shell.

"Ah, Mr. Booth," Vemish said, muffled a little from his cigar but still plenty clear enough to be heard far into the quieted Lounge. "Do you ever buy anything?"

"Frequently," Booth said like an announcement. "Every trip, in fact. It's one of the best things about the cruises. Friends are always asking me to bring things back for them."

"Tell them to try Gimbel's, right Bates?" Vemish snorted to his friend, reaching out to poke his knee. But now Bradford Bates was afraid as he considered how the knife of his wife's vision of social rectitude would cut him through the night and the days — and the days.

"I'm sorry, Mr. Vemish, but there is no smoking in this lounge. The smoking lounge is aft." He pointed aft. "If you want to smoke you'll have to smoke there or on deck. You can't smoke here." It was clearly an order.

"So why are there ashtrays?" Vemish asked.

"For when the ship is not . . ." but Booth stopped quickly.

"A floating hospital? Is not full of old people with rotten lungs?" Vemish finished for him.

"*Extinguish the cigar,* Mr. Vemish, or else smoke it where you're *permitted* to." All of the other "cruisers" were watching and listening now. Charlotte Bates, like a Victory, stood thin, orange, and smiling. Bradford Bates was white, tight-lipped, eyes closed. Booth was the total Presence in the Lounge, everybody's son. Vemish ground his Corona Corona into the glass ashtray. Then Sara Vemish said to Booth, like quiet thunder,

"Get out. Get out." Then she screamed like lightning, *"GET OUT!"*

Although it was three o'clock in the morning, Clifton Booth had assembled all his assistants. He was nervous, drawn, and queasy even with the long, lulling yaw of the ship. He doubted that he would sleep until he saw this thing through. Still, he wanted them to be apprised of his decision to send the Vemishes home, which, unfortunately, could not be tomorrow because, instead of scheduled Guadeloupe, the ship was going to Barbados. There had been a small ramming in the Guadeloupe harbor and for at least two days the only possible dockage would be either at anchor or at a hardly accessible wharf, both situations too difficult for the old people to manage with comfort and safety. They would make Guadeloupe on the return.

Tomorrow, then, would be a day at sea. And tomorrow he would tell the Vemishes that once they left the ship in Barbados, that was it. He read to his assistants the report that he had written so far which, when completed, he would send to the Lootens Line home office. He wanted them, the assistants, to hear it now in case later any of his procedures should be questioned. There was always the chance of a court case.

Arthur Lewis, eager to learn and to please as a new, young man on a job always is, carefully watched Booth pace bloodlessly back and forth before them. It was as if he were back in college, poised to take precious notes. Joseph Crenshaw and Robert Clark, however, were curious, and pleased.

Both had sailed with Booth before and knew much about him and his methods from others who knew him too. Crenshaw even

had been with Booth when, twice before, he had sent people home:
a psychopathically belligerent eighty year old who had taken to hit-
ting people with his cane, and an old alcoholic who almost went
overboard twice. But Booth was acting altogether differently now
than he had then or before or was legended to. He seemed frightened of the Vemishes, as if it were he who was being stalked. As far
as Crenshaw could see or could compare, Booth's charges and actions were unfounded. The Vemishes might be giving Booth pain,
but they were hardly disruptive in any direct way. Not that he
cared.

Crenshaw looked on and listened to Booth's tension with be-
mused interest, with the ironical amusement of a raffish beach-
comber on this, his floating island. Robert Clark, however, looked
at the spectacle of Booth's pain with ambition's delight. He
couldn't see where Booth had a case against the Vemishes, and he
would be damned if, later, if it was necessary to support Booth, he
would. Neither Clark nor Crenshaw was going to help him very
much.

"When will you tell them, sir?" young Lewis asked.

"I don't know," Booth said. "Have any of you suggestions?"
They were silent. It was the first time Booth had ever asked them
anything. "Never mind," he said and started to pace again. He
rubbed his thumb against his fingers in a noiseless snap. "It will
come. The time will come." He made it sound mystical. "Besides,
they don't matter. I can tell *them* anytime, even when we're docking, for that matter. There's a flight out of the island at twelve
noon. I've booked them on it already." He stopped. "No, no. It's
what they'll do to the others that I've got to think about. They've
done enough damage as it is. I've got a job to do. We *all* have. And
the Vemishes are trying to stop us. *Don't you see that?*" He turned
from their silent faces and over his shoulder asked them to leave.

In the morning Booth, showered but wan, made the announcement that the ship would be going straight on to Barbados because
of the accident in the Guadeloupe harbor. They would be at sea
the entire day and into the evening. To keep them occupied Booth
had organized the S.S. Solar Sweepstakes, a kind of ship-board de-
cathlon of modified deck games designed more to be looked at
than participated in. He could always count on twenty or so passengers healthy enough to have a gentle go at the rocking horse races,

the deck tennis (with a lowered net), the shuffleboard, and the rest. Most of the excitement for the observers would be in the moderate betting that Booth encouraged but strictly limited. At a table off the main dining room Arthur Lewis set up an entry desk and a manual pari-mutuel, where the "cruisers" could place their bets on their favorites either before or after they saw them. It was all to begin at two o'clock.

After the Sweepstakes, at the height of the "cruisers'" friendly and unified gaiety, Clifton Booth would tell the Vemishes that they didn't belong, that they were going home. Indeed, he imagined that that prospect would even please them.

Now, at ten o'clock, his battle plans arranged, he lay down to try to sleep a little. He could never have dreamed that Martin Vemish would have entered the Games.

Martin Vemish entered the Games and played them with destroying vigor, relentlessly, aggressive as in a rage but without malice. If he threw a quoit, he threw it hard (into the face of his slower opponent and cut his nose). In the horse races he rode down a rider who had staggered a little and veered into him (sprawling the man out of the contest). In the dart throwing he heckled the others as if they were the Mets in Shea Stadium, unnervingly loud and jeering ("Get thicker glasses, grandpa"), and when he himself threw, it was like the javelin. In the golf ball driving contest, though not a golfer, his rushing, dangerous presence threw off those who were. He lost points there, but not many.

And now instead of gaiety in the "cruisers" a slow, fine panic started up out of the confusion between what they were expected to do and what they were doing. In place of light, leisurely time-passing laughter upon the emerald sea, there was instead a grim silence sharpened by the huffing of the struggling men, fighting surprisingly once more in their lives, the wheeze and rattle dry in their throats as they fought. They fought with Vemish. He alone laughed. And Sara.

The shuffleboard began like rifle fire and the men had begun to shout back at Vemish and at each other. Here and there in the crowd a tightly strung woman cracked and sobbed. A participant collapsed and was borne off to the infirmary. The Games went on. Vemish cracked his shuffle into his opponent's so hard that the wooden disk flew spinning fifty feet off a deck stanchion for thirty

feet more into the ankle of a woman who screamed and fell, and
like the man was borne away. A low moaning fluttered through the
crowd. Vemish slammed and slammed again. Old women implored
their old husbands to stop. By twos and sixes people fled while others came and pressed in closer.

Clifton Booth spun in his nightmare. "Mr. Booth," Lewis, as
soaked by perspiration as the players, implored, "what'll I do?
Lots of them are coming back to bet. They demand to bet. On Mr.
Vemish. I *told* them the betting was closed. I *told* them it was just
a fun thing anyway. They won't listen. They won't listen, Mr.
Booth. Mr. Booth, they've gone *crazy*."

"Booth," Captain Harley's voice shouted through the telephone,
"you've got two people in sickbay in fifteen minutes. What are you
running down there, a war? What's happening, Booth? What the
hell is happening?"

"I'll sue. I'll sue you and the whole shipping line," Mr. Robert
Phillips shouted at Booth, nearly shaking his clawed fist in the
Tour Director's white, blank face. "It's broken! You broke
Lydia's ankle, you and your asinine games. You'll hear from me.
You'll hear from *me!*"

Topside again Booth staggered toward the crowded game deck,
the moaning growing louder as he neared. He worked his way
through the "cruisers" to the edge of the playing area. The moaning was loud now, but he could not believe that he was in the middle of it, that it was outside of him. He thought that it was in his
own head. Vemish was before him, fifteen feet away, his sunburnt
head peeling already, glistening, his cigar, a new cigar, in his mouth,
bent, in motion, and the accurate crack of the wood on wood.

"Eighteen to eleven, Vemish leads Morrisey," a scorekeeping
voice said.

Booth stood as still as he could. For him the ship was heaving
as in a hurricane. The old woman next to him grasped his arm,
though she did not know it was he — she was staring at Vemish before her — and said,

"Oh! Oh my! Oh look!"

Vemish's opponent, Morrisey, was bleeding from the nose, from
one nostril, slowly but clearly. Nothing had hit him or bumped
him to cause it. He simply bled. Now Booth stepped forward just
as Morrisey bent to shoot.

"Mr. Morrisey," Booth straightened him up.

"What?" Morrisey said, his concentration broken. "What do you want?"

"I think you had better stop, Mr. Morrisey," Booth said.

"What? What for? What are you talking about?" Morrisey looked around, amazed, impatient, his sweat beaded on his eyebrows.

"You're bleeding," Booth said. "Your nose."

"Huh?" Morrisey said. He looked a little like Vemish, only with more hair, smaller, and no cigar. He rubbed under his nose and then looked at his hand.

"It's nothing," he said, "nothing," and turned to play.

"But Mr. Morrisey . . ."

"Come on, come on," Vemish said.

"It's nothing, I said," Morrisey said. "Nothing. Now leave me alone." Morrisey's sparrow wife pushed forward.

"Albert. Oh Albert, please. Stop this."

"Go away," Morrisey snapped. "All of you, go away and leave me alone. Go *AWAY!*" Booth and Mrs. Morrisey backed off.

The game continued. Vemish smashed. Morrisey bled.

"Twenty-one. Vemish."

And now Booth took the last of his strength and moved forward again. He would wait for nothing now. He would tell Vemish. He didn't care who heard. He hoped they would. He would tell him *now.* He knew his duty and his responsibility. If anything, he had let it go too long. But five paces away from Vemish, Vemish took his shuffleboard stick, his lance, and flung it cartwheeling into the Caribbean and walked out of the Games into the crowd which shrank, cringed, back from him. The S.S. Solar Sweepstakes were over.

Booth stopped only for an instant and then started after him through the still open sea of spectators like Pharaoh after Moses. But he would get him now. Now he would have him. He was his arm's length away and reaching. But what did stop him was the sound of Bradford Bates clapping. And then the tiny man cheered. Alone. And the waters closed up over the Director.

"Shut *up,*" Charlotte Bates smashed at her husband through her clenched teeth, making as though no one would hear, though they did. "Shut up!" She had him gripped by the bony curve of his

small shoulder and started to shake him so that his head bobbed.
"Shut up!" she ordered.

But he would not.

Clifton Booth rushed to the railing and vomited.

The ship arrived in Barbados around midnight and quietly
docked. Only a few, those whose cabins were near to where the
men were working at securing the ship, might have been awakened
slowly, partly, in the near tropic night. The rest of the cruise slept,
except Joseph Crenshaw, whose watch it was, and Clifton Booth.
The two men sat in the office part of Booth's cabin.

"Is there anything I can get you?" Crenshaw asked his gray superior.

"Nothing," the suffering man said. "Nothing." They were silent. Then he said. "I can't get rid of them now, can I? The Vemishes? It's too late now, isn't it?"

"I'm afraid so," Crenshaw said, not quite sure of, and not quite
interested in, his Director's demon.

"He's won, hasn't he?"

"Won what?" Crenshaw asked. "The Sweepstakes, well, they
just . . ."

"The cruise! The cruise is a shambles, isn't it?" Booth pointed
out.

"Oh, I don't know," Crenshaw considered. He started to light a
cigarette, but looking at Booth's color made him reconsider.
"There has been a lot of excitement, after all. I don't think the
people are that displeased. And anyway, there are days and days to
go. *Days!*"

Booth shuddered.

But in the morning when, immediately after their breakfast,
Booth appeared on the gangplank deck to give his Barbados talk
and instructions to the "cruisers," less than a third of the usual number were there. During the day, however, it was reported to him that
most of the passengers did leave the boat but mainly by twos or
fours. Hardly any took guides or tours. Also it was reported that
few were returning with anything, with any packages.

At six-thirty Mr. Elliot Newly, a representative of the Barbados
Visitors Trade Commission, came on board the S.S. Solar and asked
for the Tour Director. Directly and simply he complained that this

cruise ship had probably spent less money than any cruise ship that had ever docked in Barbados in recent times. For it to be a Lootens Line ship was rather amazing. For it to be a Clifton Booth directed ship was almost beyond belief.

"What do you want me to do?" Booth snapped. "Order them to buy? What do you want me to do? Threaten them? Beat them?"

"It's not what I want you to *do*," Mr. Elliot Newly said, rising before the spectral, gaunt, and strident Tour Director. "It's a little late for *that*, after all." He backed toward the cabin door away from Booth's glazed eyes. "It's what you've *done*, I was interested in." And then he was quickly gone.

More important trouble came in Martinique. The cruise arrived there at eight in the morning and was scheduled to leave at six that same evening. It was the tightest day of the tour, leaving the "cruisers" between nine and five to "do" the island, just a working day. But by as late as nine o'clock, 118 "cruisers" were still ashore somewhere.

Captain Harley, never a reasonable man, ranted at the stunned Booth from six o'clock until some time after eleven, when the last passenger was aboard and the unhappy ship was moving off to St. Croix. By that time Booth found some peace, some rest, not in sleep but stretched out on his bed in catatonic rigidity, stiffened the way a man is just after he is hit and before he crumbles. Lewis, Crenshaw, and Clark were disturbed enough by their leader's condition to keep from him the increasing reports coming up from the infirmary of indispositions and near-illnesses. And then illness. Every cruise ship had its normal health and well-being problems; a geriatric cruise would naturally have more. But the S.S. Solar, this time out, approaching St. Croix, was something else again.

The ship arrived in St. Croix three hours off its schedule. The day was five degrees cooler than the more constant Caribbean seventy-eight and, though lovely as day can be, felt chilly to most of the "cruisers." Few left the ship at all, and on board they were mostly hidden in books sullenly read or in slow but ceaseless, bleak walking around the Open and Enclosed Promenade Decks, guilt or defiance by turns their companion. Many wore sweaters. The heated, chlorinated pool-side was deserted. Little if any of the food was eaten. The chefs and their helpers looked with puzzlement at the unordered services on the waiting trays, at the un-

touched portions on the returned plates. They shrugged and shov-
eled the food into garbage cans from which it would be dumped in
the night (to discourage the noisy, screaching seagulls) into the fur-
row of the dark ship.

Captain Harley called a council that evening. He and his first
two mates and the ship's doctor, Doctor Goff, met with Booth and
his three assistants. They were all in uniform. It was all very military.

"It's not my business to meddle with the cruises," Captain Harley shouted, though he was only talking. "To me a ship is for
carrying things over water, that's all — people, crates, bags of
coffee, it makes no difference to me. And whatever has happened to
this cruise I'll never know." Booth's stomach lurched. "But as
Captain I've got two responsibilities, safety and, as near as I can
make it, schedule." He paused a long moment. "To get to the
point. I think when we leave St. Croix we should skip Guadeloupe
and head straight in to New York." Booth almost came out of his
chair. He waited for more, but it was the doctor who spoke next.

"You've got a sick cruise this time, Booth," he said.

"Sick?" Booth said. "Sick?"

"Well, as I mentioned in the reports, there are . . ."

"Reports? *What reports?*" He looked around to his assistants.
They looked elsewhere. Finally Arthur Lewis said,

"When you were . . . sleeping, sir. The doctor reported some illness and . . ."

"You didn't tell me." He looked at each of them. His eyes were
yellow. Rapidly he added new, darker dimensions to his suffering.
"You . . . you . . . none of you told me."

"We thought it best at the moment not to," Robert Clark was
pleased to say.

"But *later?*" Booth's voice was drying up, his throat crusting.

"Mr. Booth," the Captain demanded. The doctor went on at
the Captain's direction.

"You've got God knows how many cardiac possibilities in your
troupe, Booth, and right now I've got four suspicious disturbances
under observation."

"Four? *FOUR?*"

"And I've got a woman who went into insulin shock. I've got
twelve cases of acute diarrhea."

"I told them. I *TOLD* them about the water," Booth insisted, pleaded. What more could he do for them?

"I've got one woman on pretty heavy sedation for her nerves," the doctor continued. "And three cases of what I guess you'd just have to call exhaustion. And, of course, Lydia Phillips with the broken ankle. Mr. Booth, there's no more *room* down there."

"Exhaustion?" he asked in a whisper. "Exhaustion?" Tears were in his blood-veined yellow eyes. "But they haven't *done* anything." The corners of his mouth were tight like little knots and white as polished ivory. "Dr. Goff, this is a *pleasure* cruise. It's especially designed for the old. Exhaustion?" At which something broke in Clifton Booth; there was not a cell left in him capable of protest.

"Mr. Booth," Dr. Goff said gently, "for whatever reasons, this is not a happy cruise."

"So let's go home before it gets worse," Captain Harley boomed, not gentle at all. "We've done it before, shortened a cruise, when there's been serious illness or trouble with the ship or the weather. I remember once we thought we had typhoid," he started to reminisce.

Booth nodded yes. Yes.

"I'll send something up for you to take," the doctor said to him.

When he left the cabin of the meeting, he leaned a little on Arthur Lewis, although he didn't know it.

But things did get worse.

Edward Clanton of Lambertville, New Jersey, aged sixty-eight, one of the four heart condition suspects in the infirmary, died that night.

By nine in the morning three more "cruisers" reported in with pains here or there in their bodies. More beds were moved into the infirmary.

If the death made his job harder, it made it, that morning, easier, too, as Director Booth called together all those people whom he had brought out on the sea so far from their homes. They did look tired, unhappy, and very old. White. Transparent.

He announced the death of Edward Clanton of Lambertville, New Jersey. It doused them, the cruise, like a spray from the icy sea.

And he announced that the ship was heading back to New York

now and would by-pass Guadeloupe. No one complained. Subdued, he promised them a full slate of entertainments and activities
for the pleasant days at sea that lay before them. No one seemed to
care particularly, at first, but by noon, adjusting without clearly
knowing it to the sun riding on their starboard side instead of port,
the spirits of the "cruisers" shifted cautiously.

They were going home. There was nothing more they *had* to do,
at least for the next three days. Then, on the fourth, they would
have to face their children. They tried not to think about that.

The days and the nights at sea were not good for any of them.
The weather was less than it was supposed to be and grew colder as
they moved north. Sometimes the day was cloudy for an hour or
two or three. They seemed to be moving into a front. There was
nothing they wanted to do on the ship, nothing but sit in their cabins or in the lounges or on the decks and think, if they did, about
the cinders of their voyage. Nothing had gone smoothly, they could
remember little of anything they had seen or done, they were too
old for new friendships and none came anyway. And what would
they do with what they had bought? How many pictures were there
left to them to take with their new cameras? On what table would
the rioting table cloth go in their lifetime-full and arranged houses?
More and more they felt that they had spent all their days, and
many of them, at sea — the day before, yesterday, today.

In the evenings, after a supper that they might have eaten at
home — tight, limited, precise, unmindful now of the cornucopia
they dined in, most went to their cabins and early to bed if not to
sleep. Or there were nightly movies. There was even some TV,
fluttery and white. There were nightclub acts: singers, dancers, ma-
gicians. There were slide lectures on subjects ranging from Caribbean history to home gardening. There was a five-piece danceband
(circa 1940) in one of the smaller lounges playing slow waltzes and
squared fox-trots to the gleaming, empty oak floor.

The "cruisers" partook of very little of what was available to
them, and even of that little, they touched it heavily, clumsily.
They were quiet, sodden. When they spoke amongst themselves it
was often about the sick down below. A few, like Charlotte Bates,
pushed on after gaiety as advertised. But the determined whine
from her bridge table or the orderly insistence about the exciting

food hung in the dining room or lounge like the snuff of smoke from a taper in the gray, late light of a winter afternoon, her parodic graciousness and culture muffled in the hollowing of the rooms her sound ever beat in. The S.S. Solar, encapsuled in its own environment and time, steamed northward through the roiled sea into a storm.

It was not a great storm as storms go, but for the "cruisers" it was like a spark to a powdery anger that their journey had ground in them: To be here.

As the ship plunged forward into the heightening waves, the stabilizers to aft slapped about helplessly in the water like the flukes of a shoaled whale. The ship swung back and forth across its center in great arcs like an upside-down pendulum. Or else it lurched in an unpredictable zig-zag that could knock a person down or throw him into a table or against a wall.

That they were here. To have come so uselessly far to be here.

All the rankling ironies of the cruise rose in them and drew them from about the ship to the large, non-smoker's Lounge. And there, in the black storm, they found the communion falsely promised them by the sunny, gaudy brochures, the effusive travel clerk, and by their children. They found another kind.

With dignity they complained. They had not slept well since they left their own beds. They had forgotten to leave a tender for their African Violets and Impatiens at home. They had missed the wedding of a favorite niece, the annual affair of a club they had belonged to for thirty years, more than a week (irrecoverable) of a TV afternoon serial, the close letters from far off kin.

That they were here, in the terrible night, with green water booming over the bow of the pitching ship.

"What a laugh," Martin Vemish said to Bradford Bates, enjoying what he could not change. "Come on," he said cuffing his companion on the back, "I'll buy you a drink."

In the empty bar adjoining the Lounge, Vemish bought his friend a drink, scotch and water.

"You know," Bates told him. "It's been years since I've drunk in a bar." He lifted his glass to Vemish.

"With me too," Vemish said, returning the salute. "How do you like it?"

"Not so much," Bates said. "I'd rather drink at home."

"Your wife lets you?"

"Charlotte's not so bad," Bradford Bates said, squinting down into his glass with one eye. Vemish said nothing, willing to leave any man alone with whatever accommodation he has managed. He lit a new cigar and ordered another two drinks.

Then others, many for the first time since the cruise began, came into the bar, swaying with the ship or crawling along the walls, at times impaled upon them by a sudden severe list. They drank and talked, sometimes fiercely and loud. Men left, others came. All were gray or white-haired, neat, in the main frail, but younger now than in their actual years, refreshed by their outrage.

That they were here.

Vemish grabbed Bradford Bates and, swayed in addition now by storm and scotch, wandered a little until they found the wide-lapeled dance band and bribed them back to the Main Lounge. The two of them led the band back into the larger room to the trumpeter's fanfare and the cheers of the crowd. There looked to be present a good part of the "cruisers," nearly 150.

The band began to play and Martin Vemish began a bounding dance with his Sara. Others joined. The band played loud and faster following the whirling Vemish. The party had begun. The dancers shifted about between the card tables and sofas and the writing desks and reading chairs and lamps. The bucking ship shifted the dancers in exotic movements against the music, forcing them into bizarre but expressive gestures. Comic bumps and staggers. Tittering pratfalls. Puffing guffaws as couples collapsed against each other. Bottles were ordered into the Lounge. Ice, glasses. The great Lounge slid and tumbled about — people, music, glasses floated about in enormously slowed motion, arms grabbed out for balance, hips swung against the turning fall-line of the ship, heads, bellies, knees, old bones angled about free, order gone.

That they were here.

Then the laughter, the assailing laughter, rose up and over them, a saving benison.

At eleven Joseph Crenshaw shook Clifton Booth out of his wet, clenched, but tranquilized sleep.

"You had better come at once. The Main Lounge."

"What? *What now?*" Booth screamed, half certain that he was in a nightmare until he felt the tilting ship and his nausea swirl up in him. He tasted his bile and knew that he was awake. "What? *WHAT?*" But his assistant had left him to return to where he was needed.

As Booth, barely dressed, hurried through the inner passageways of the ship to the Main Lounge, bouncing from wall to wall, running, sometimes careening, downhill, sometimes struggling slowly up, he fought against the centrifuge that was pulling his mind apart. Running through the twisting, snaking tunnels of the ship was too much like the terrible dreams he had been having for him to get it straight now. He didn't know, as when he had first been awakened, if he was still inside the terror of a dreamscape or was really awake and running toward (from?) the terror of fact. When he turned, at last, into the broad passageway leading directly to the Main Lounge, he knew it was the latter.

Three crew men, large and muscular, stood at the entrance to the Lounge and every ten seconds or so one of them would reach out to an emerging "cruiser" and easily but certainly shove him back into the howling room. Booth watched for a minute from twenty feet away, unbelieving; then he rushed forward.

"What are you doing?" he demanded, facing the three sailors. A highball glass lofted through the doorway and crashed against the back of Booth's head, the water and ice running quickly down his back.

"Aggh," he uttered and tripped forward, like a man shot, into the hard arms of one of the crew. Behind his dizziness he heard the other two men move at the door.

"Oh no you don't," he heard one of them say. And then he heard the little grunt and the light, quick scuffle.

He stood up out of the line of the open doorway.

"What's happening? Oh for God's sake, what's happening?" It was a question and a prayer.

"Them old geezers flipped out," one of the men said, grinning.

"The Captain said to keep 'em from bustin' up the rest of the ship," another offered.

"Hey, hey," said the third. "Lookit him go! Will you just *look* at that old rooster go!" The other two pushed in to see. Booth ran past them into the Lounge.

Chaos had come again.

Everywhere the old people were dancing madly to a music they may have heard or not. Some danced together, many alone. They sang or hummed; old voices — harsh, granulated, reedy — babbled pieces of Charlestons, Lindies, WPA work songs, songs from various wars, forgotten Hit Parades. Glass, liquids, overturned furniture, clothing, food, people mixed about above and on the deck of the heaving ship. A ribald crone, bones in a dress, lifted one foot high across her knee, put it down, and lifted the other, threw her head from left to right, and clapped out her personal stuttering tempo.

Across the room Booth saw Clark and Lewis shouldering their way through the rolling people toward the entrance of the bar. Between them they supported a rag-doll man, his legs bent under him, his feet dragging, his chin upon his chest. At that doorway he could see three more crew men knocking mad revelers back into the room. At every moment something was breaking.

Near the center of the room the head of Charlotte Bates was shouting. She reached out again and again to grab at the little man moving easily beyond and around her. As she reached for him some motion of the ship would prevent her, while he, as though in demonic league with the sea, anticipated every lurch. She screamed and clawed at him as he rhumba-ed around her in an eyes-shut caricature of grinning passion.

In one corner Booth saw two people passed out (dead?) on a sofa. In another corner he saw a man retch and retch into a rubber plant until the cords in his skinny neck would snap. Booth closed his eyes against it all. A sharp, breaking pain on his forehead woke him again. Someone had thrown a glass.

"There he is. Our Director." Another glass was thrown against his chest. Booth bolted for the small stage, knocking three, four, five "cruisers" down as he went.

"*STOP IT!*" he screamed from the stage. "*STOP IT! ACT YOUR AGE!*" But they rained him with anything they could throw. He ran through them again and out of the room, knocking down more as he went.

He ran out of the Lounge and away. He was wet with whiskey

and water and blood and his own tears. He ran, he felt, forever, turning through passage after passage until he could not. In a dim alcove off of a promenade deck he fell back against a bulkhead and gasped. Only when he could breathe enough to ease the explosions going off in his gashed and battered head did he smell the cigar. Not ten feet away Martin Vemish sat quietly smoking, watching him.

"You!" Booth said, straightening himself off the cold bulkhead with what was left of his strength. *"You!"*

"Me," Vemish said with his cigar in his mouth. What could he say?

"You!" was all Booth could say, appalled.

"Me," Vemish said, tracing the word with almost a giggle.

"Why?" Booth suddenly shouted, but it took too much from him. "Why?" he whispered.

"Why what? What are you talking about?"

"You . . . you know. This. All of this." Booth fluttered with his hand behind him.

"This is all yours," Vemish said. "None of this is mine."

"Why did you do this to me? What have I . . . why did . . ."

"Nothing. I've done nothing. *You?* You don't even exist. None of this does." Vemish waved his hand more largely than had Booth. "It's all a . . . a big . . . a *little* dirty nothing." He waved his hand in the dark, erasing it.

"I . . . I . . ." Booth stiff-legged the ten feet to Vemish, his arms outstretched as in a monster movie, and grabbed the thick Vemish by the throat. But he could do nothing. He held him and moaned. Vemish sat smoking.

"Get away. Get! You crazy nut, you," Sara Vemish said out of the dark.

"Ahhwk," Booth squeaked, surprised by her. His hands flew up from his shock and he fell down at Vemish's feet, into a puddle more than a shape, and sobbed. "I'll . . . I'll get you," he wept.

"You should live so long," Vemish said and got up and stepped over him. Sara rose. Together they walked off. The sea was subsiding.

By the time the S.S. Solar secured its last mooring at pier 62 on the western shore of Manhattan, the storm was over and the day

showed settling promise but still, like April, was capable of anything. Thronged about at the foot of the gangplank were the
children of the "cruisers," quiet and frightened. Near the gangplank five ambulances awaited. And a hearse. Soon the railing
creaked open and official men, some in uniforms — Port Authority
people and Lootens Line people — swiftly ascended, grim-faced.
They were followed by the white-suited ambulance crews. And
these by the dark morticians.

In time the ship gave up its cargo. Bleary, haggard, unshaven old
men came slowly down. Frazzled, wild-haired old women. Some
limped. Some rolled down in wheel-chairs. Their children waited
like stone.

"Daddy. My God, Daddy, what happened?" a woman asked of
an old man who was shaking slightly in the morning chill. She
hugged him and tightened his coat around him and rushed him toward a waiting car.

"Storm," he mumbled.

All about amazed children reclaimed their loved ones.

Charlotte Bates rushed down the gangplank into the arms of her
duplicate daughter. "Your father," she gagged, overwrought,
pointing behind her at the ship. "Your father," she tried to explain as her voice broke.

"What, Mama? What's happened? Has something happened to
Papa? Mother? *Tell me!*" She shook her mother. Her mother
swung her head no, but,

"Your father," was all she could say through her streaming face.
Her daughter helped her away. The younger woman turned to her
husband.

"I'm going to take her home now. You wait for him," she ordered.

When Bradford Bates finally came down the gangplank he came
like Sir Christopher Columbus to the New World.

"What happened, Dad?" his son-in-law asked, awed. "What's
going on?"

Bradford Bates paused and smiled up at the West Side Highway.
He smelled in deeply New York. "Well, Nelson," he said, "I'll
tell you." And taking the younger man by the arm he directed
him toward a taxi and began.

In another, later cab, Herbert Vemish asked his father and mother,

"How was it? How did you like it?"

"Not much," his father said. His mother nodded to agree.

JOHN UPDIKE

Son

(FROM THE NEW YORKER)

HE IS OFTEN UPSTAIRS, when he has to be home. He prefers to be elsewhere. He is almost sixteen, though beardless still, a man's mind indignantly captive in the frame of a child. I love touching him, but don't often dare. The other day, he had the flu, and a fever, and I gave him a back rub, marveling at the symmetrical knit of muscle, the organic tension. He is high-strung. Yet his sleep is so solid he sweats like a stone in the wall of a well. He wishes for perfection. He would like to destroy us, for we are, variously, too fat, too jocular, too sloppy, too affectionate, too grotesque and heedless in our ways. His mother smokes too much. His younger brother chews with his mouth open. His older sister leaves unbuttoned the top button of her blouses. His younger sister tussles with the dogs, getting them overexcited, avoiding doing her homework. Everyone in the house talks nonsense. He would be a better father than his father. But time has tricked him, has made him a son. After a quarrel, if he cannot go outside and kick a ball, he retreats to a corner of the house and reclines on the beanbag chair in an attitude of strange, infantile or leonine, torpor. We exhaust him, without meaning to. He takes an interest in the newspaper now, the front page as well as the sports, in this tiring year of 1973.

He is upstairs, writing a musical comedy. It is a Sunday in 1949. Somehow, he has volunteered to prepare a high-school assembly program; people will sing. Songs of the time go through his head, as he scribbles new words. *Up in de mornin', down at de school, work like a debil for my grades.* Below him, irksome voices grind on, like machines working their way through tunnels. His parents each want something from the other. "Marion, you don't understand that man like I do; he has a heart of gold." This father's charade is very complex: the world, which he fears, is used as a flail on his wife. But from his cringing attitude he would seem to an outsider the one being flailed. With burning red face, the woman accepts the role of aggressor as penance for the fact, the incessant shameful fact, that *he* has to wrestle with the world while she hides here, in solitude, on this farm. This is normal, but does not seem to them to be so. Only by convolution have they arrived at the dominant submissive relationship society has assigned them. For the man is maternally kind and with a smile hugs to himself his jewel, his certainty of being victimized; it is the mother whose tongue is sharp, who sometimes strikes. "Well, he gets you out of the house, and I guess that's gold to you." His answer is "Duty calls," pronounced mincingly. "The social contract is a balance of compromises." This will infuriate her, the son knows; as his heart thickens, the downstairs overflows with her hot voice. "*Don't* wear that smile at me! And *take* your hands off your hips; you look like a sissy!" Their son tries not to listen. When he does, visual details of the downstairs flood his mind: the two antagonists, circling with their coffee cups; the shabby mismatched furniture; the hopeful books; the docile framed photographs of the dead, docile and still as cowed students. This matrix of pain that bore him — he feels he is floating above it, sprawled on the bed as on a cloud, stealing songs as they come into his head (*Across the hallway from the guidance room/Lives a French instructor called Mrs. Blum*), contemplating the brown meadow from the upstairs window (last summer's burdock stalks like the beginnings of an alphabet, an apple tree holding three rotten apples as if pondering why they failed to fall), yearning for Monday, for the ride to school with his father, for the bell that calls him to homeroom, for the excitements of class, for Broadway, for fame, for the cloud that will carry him away, out of this, out.

He returns from his paper-delivery route and finds a few Christmas presents for him on the kitchen table. I must guess at the year. 1913? Without opening them, he knocks them to the floor, puts his head on the table, and falls asleep. He must have been consciously dramatizing his plight: his father was sick, money was scarce, he had to work, to win food for the family when he was still a child. In his dismissal of Christmas, he touched a nerve: his love of anarchy, his distrust of the social contract. He treasured this moment of proclamation; else why remember it, hoard a memory so bitter, and confide it to his son many Christmases later? He had a teaching instinct, though he claimed that life miscast him as a schoolteacher. I suffered in his classes, feeling the confusion as a persecution of him, but now wonder if his rebellious heart did not court confusion, not as Communists do, to intrude their own order, but, more radical still, as an end pleasurable in itself, as truth's very body. Yet his handwriting (an old pink permission slip recently fluttered from a book where it had been marking a page for twenty years) was always considerately legible, and he was sitting up doing arithmetic the morning of the day he died.

And letters survive from that yet prior son, written in brown ink, in a tidy tame hand, home to his mother from the Missouri seminary where he was preparing for his vocation. The dates are 1887, 1888, 1889. Nothing much happened: he missed New Jersey, and was teased at a church social for escorting a widow. He wanted to do the right thing, but the little sheets of faded penscript exhale a dispirited calm, as if his heart already knew he would not make a successful minister, or live to be old. His son, my father, when old, drove hundreds of miles out of his way to visit the Missouri town from which those letters had been sent. Strangely, the town had not changed; it looked just as he had imagined, from his father's descriptions: tall wooden houses, rain-soaked, stacked on a bluff. The town was a sepia postcard mailed homesick home and preserved in an attic. My father cursed: his father's old sorrow bore him down into depression, into hatred of life. My mother claims his decline in health began at that moment.

He is wonderful to watch, playing soccer. Smaller than the others, my son leaps, heads, dribbles, feints, passes. When a big boy knocks him down, he tumbles on the mud, in his green-and-black school uniform, in an ecstasy of falling. I am envious. Never for me the jaunty pride of the school uniform, the solemn ritual of the coach's pep talk, the camaraderie of shook hands and slapped backsides, the shadow-striped hush of late afternoon and last quarter, the solemn vaulted universe of official combat, with its cheering mothers and referees exotic as zebras and the bespectacled timekeeper alert with his claxon. When the boy scores a goal, he runs into the arms of his teammates with upraised arms and his face alight as if blinded by triumph. They lift him from the earth in a union of muddy hugs. What spirit! What valor! What skill! His father, watching from the sidelines, inwardly registers only one complaint: he feels the boy, with his talent, should be more aggressive.

They drove across the state of Pennsylvania to hear their son read in Pittsburgh. But when their presence was announced to the audience, they did not stand; the applause groped for them and died. My mother said afterward she was afraid she might fall into the next row if she tried to stand in the dark. Next morning was sunny, and the three of us searched for the house where once they had lived. They had been happy there; I imagined, indeed, that I had been conceived there, just before the slope of the Depression steepened and fear gripped my family. We found the library where she used to read Turgenev, and the little park where the bums slept close as paving stones in the summer night; but their street kept eluding us, though we circled in the car. On foot, my mother found the tree. She claimed she recognized it, the sooty linden she would gaze into from their apartment windows. The branches, though thicker, had held their pattern. But the house itself, and the entire block, were gone. Stray bricks and rods of iron in the grass suggested that the demolition had been recent. We stood on the empty spot and laughed. They knew it was right, because the railroad tracks were the right distance away. In confirmation, a long freight train pulled itself east around the curve, its great weight gliding as if on a river current; then a silver passenger train came gliding as effortlessly in the other direction. The curve of the tracks tipped the cars slightly toward us. The Golden Triangle, gray and hazed, was off to our left, beyond a forest of bridges. We stood on the grassy rubble that morning, where something once had been, beside the tree still there, and were intensely happy. Why? We knew.

" 'No,' Dad said to me, 'the Christian ministry isn't a job you choose, it's a vocation for which you got to receive a call.' I could tell he wanted me to ask him. We never talked much, but we understood each other, we were both scared devils, not like you and the kid. I asked him, Had he ever received the call? He said No. He said No, he never had. Received the call. That was a terrible thing, for him to admit. And I was the one he told. As far as I knew he never admitted it to anybody, but he admitted it to me. He felt like hell about it, I could tell. That was all we ever said about it. That was enough."

He has made his younger brother cry, and justice must be done. A father enforces justice. I corner the rat in our bedroom; he is holding a cardboard mailing tube like a sword. The challenge flares white-hot; I roll my weight toward him like a rock down a mountain, and knock the weapon from his hand. He smiles. Smiles! Because my facial expression is silly? Because he is glad that he can still be overpowered, and hence is still protected? Why? I do not hit him. We stand a second, father and son, and then as nimbly as on the soccer field he steps around me and out the door. He slams the door. He shouts obscenities in the hall, slams all the doors he can find on the way to his room. Our moment of smilingly shared silence was the moment of compression; now the explosion. The whole house rocks with it. Downstairs, his siblings and mother come to me and offer advice and psychological analysis. I was too aggressive. He is spoiled. What they can never know, my grief alone to treasure, was that lucid many-sided second of his smiling and my relenting, before the world's wrathful pantomime of power resumed.

As we huddle whispering about him, my son takes his revenge. In his room, he plays his guitar. He has greatly improved this winter; his hands getting bigger is the least of it. He has found in the guitar an escape. He plays the Romanza wherein repeated notes, with a sliding like the heart's valves, let themselves fall along the scale:

The notes fall, so gently he bombs us, drops feathery notes down upon us, our visitor, our prisoner.

ARTURO VIVANTE

Honeymoon

(FROM THE NEW YORKER)

LYING ON A HAYSTACK, Girolamo picks a smooth golden straw — one that the rain hasn't blackened — and makes of it a ring around Fiorella's finger. He does the same in the field with a blade of grass, then stretches it vertical between his thumbs and blows on it, raising a silence-sundering sound. And in the woods he uses gorse. Always on Sundays. On weekdays, he works grazing his flock way up on the slopes of the mountain.

"When are you going to put a real ring around my finger?" she asks.

"Soon, soon," he replies, and wonders. Her head is resting on his arm. They are both looking up at the sky. "Soon," he says again, wistfully.

He has to tend the sheep many more months before he will have sold enough wool, enough cheese, for the ring and the house. She, too, is working at it. She sews all day and knits evenings. She cuts. She embroiders on her cloth and her future. Her life is fleece-white; it is rose; it is golden. The pillow-cases have her and Girolamo's initials entwined. She dreams of the house: the brick floor is waxed; the fireplace in the kitchen is lighted, the flames lick the crown and roots of a chestnut and shine on the brass of the firedogs; the water in the lidded black caldron over the flames is getting hotter and hotter. After supper, Girolamo will lift it off the hook and carry it to the sink for her. The sink is of stone — one huge slab, carved hollow and so smooth no grease will stick to it. The sheet she's hemming is one of a stack. They will smell good in the closet from lavender stems twisted back over the blossoms and tied in the shape of a spool.

Girolamo, too, has visions of what the house will be like. He sees heavy salamis hanging from rafters, hams well coated with pepper, festoons of sausages, drums of cheese oiled on the surface and aging. He wonders if he will have a car. To have one, the road must be improved. The big cobblestones are all right for mules and his donkey, but for a car he must get fine gravel. And the last stretch may be too steep, even in first gear.

The house isn't ready. So far, it isn't much more than a barn — a barn and a pen — on the rim of the hamlet, where the road ends and the paths start that he and the sheep have made. First thing to be built is a staircase. The loft of the barn must be floored, two inside walls put up, doors hung, and several windows. They will have a bathroom. The old people don't, but all newly-weds have them. These things he ponders as he grazes his sheep. Sometimes one strays from the fold. Then he picks up a stone and throws it so it will land beyond her and make her turn back. He can throw stones amazingly far. Last year, he had a dog he could trust. But Tosco died, and the new one isn't so smart. Sometimes he has to walk miles for one sheep, and it isn't fun at night, when you can hear the wolves howl. The women here don't call them wolves but refer to them as *bestiacce* — "bad beasts." As with cancer and hail, there is the feeling that naming isn't very far from invoking.

With the first frosts, the grass begins to wither, and the sheep spend more time in their pens or are taken to greener pastures. When he was a child, they took them down to graze in the lowlands by the sea, where the grass is green all year round. He used to follow the flock down the winding road to the valley, and down the valley all the way to the sea. The journey lasted three days. The flock looked like a cloud down the road, and there would be other flocks at short intervals before them and after. Sometimes in the sky rows of clouds would take the same route down the valley. He followed the sound of the sheep's bells, and often, stick in hand, he would have to drive them to one side to make room for a car. In recent years, the traffic has got so forbidding the shepherds truck their sheep down to their winter pastures or keep them here on the mountain and feed them hay and other fodder. That's what Girolamo does. He stays. He works on the house. He saws timber for rafters. He carries bricks up from a kiln in the plain, and because bricks are expensive he adds stones — beautiful square ones that he finds. He mixes cement, and carries pail after pail up the ladder. But the actual building is done by a mason.

The staircase is finished. It is an outside one, on the south side of the house. Before, to get to the second floor, there was just a ladder to a window. Fiorella will have geraniums in pots on the balustrade. She has half a dozen embroidered new sheets. They are thick, rough, made of coarse linen, and they'll wear a long time. She wonders when she and Girolamo will sleep between them. She'll wash them down at the hamlet's fountain, even if they are going to have running water.

There are many days in the winter when the weather is so bad you can't work outside. Still, each week some progress is made on the house.

The days lengthen. In March, the slopes of the mountain are threaded with green — new green, fresh over the seared blades of last year. In the house, the partitions are up and being plastered. There's a good smell of mortar about. New faces appear — an electrician, a plumber. The house is being wired, is being piped. Now for the finishing touches — the bathtub, the faucets, the bowl, in the kitchen the sink and the stove. Soon Lent will be over, and then . . .

The day comes. A wedding is always in season, but best in the spring. He has a ring for her — golden, just right. They bought it down at the village — ten miles from the hamlet — one Saturday morning. "A beautiful hand," the jeweller said, peering through his thick lenses close enough that his lips skimmed the slender fingers.

The bridegroom, in a blue suit and white tie, looks unfamiliar, so different from when in the fields, his clothes faded, the sweater made of the wool of his sheep. But he isn't self-conscious. He smiles; he seems full of energy, zest. The bride moves nimbly. The white dress she has made fits snug round her waist. As they walk away from the altar, she leans on him. They seem to be hurrying toward the future that beckons there beyond the door, which is open. At the wedding reception they are solicitous, full of attentions, and go around from one guest to the other, welcoming, toast-

ing, inviting people to visit their home as soon as they get back
from their honeymoon — an overnight excursion to Rome, where
neither of them has been.

"Oh, we'll give you time to settle down; don't expect us for a
week or two," a married friend says.

"A week or two? No, you be sure and come along before that!
We like company."

"Company?" someone else says. "You don't need company now.
You've got each other for that."

"I shouldn't want any other company, not for years — not if I
had a warm, good little woman like that," an older guest says, with
a glint in his eyes.

"You go slow, Grandpa, with that kind of talk," a relative says,
and they laugh.

Fiorella and Girolamo are spirited, joyful all through the party.

But on the train to Rome they sit self-conscious in the compartment; they hold hands; they stick close together and talk only in
whispers. His face is flushed. His tie seems to constrict him. His
jacket is buttoned up. And she hardly ever looks around her — she
looks down at her hands or at him. In front of them, a paunchy
middle-aged man is reading the paper. His wife sits erect, stern, dis-
approving. Of what? There are two tourists — a young man and a
girl, in khaki shorts and gray sweatshirts, their haversacks on the
racks and a washed-out look on their faces.

In Rome, the hotel — the first one either of them ever has been
to — recommended by a friend is old, small, near the station. She
looks at the sheets — sleazy, so thin they are almost transparent,
and questionably clean. She touches the radiator, which is warm,
though it is April. At the hamlet, even in winter they'll have no
heat in their bedroom. To warm the bed, after supper she'll put
some live cinders from the kitchen hearth into an open pan, cover
them with ashes, and hang it from a wooden sledlike framework
that she'll slide in between the sheets. It is a luxury that even the
poorest of the poor can afford and won't do without.

The hotel room is meagre, but never mind — for dinner they'll
go to a world-famous place: Alfredo's.

They sit side by side. At a table opposite theirs, by the wall, another couple is sitting, about their age. She is a striking brunette in
a green taffeta dress. Her eyebrows, the curve of her cheeks and

mold of her chin seem to have been carved in one felicitous stroke. She is perfectly at ease. And she assumes poses you don't see up on the mountain. As the young man talks to her, she laughs, once or twice holding on to his forearm. He has a bright look about him; his face lights up when he speaks; he is spare, thin-nosed, tawny-haired, and apparently very entertaining. He's fussy about the wine. He knows just what to order.

Girolamo and Fiorella, on the other hand, are hardly conversing. They often gaze or catch each other gazing across the tables at the couple opposite. The recipients of their attention don't seem to mind. One passing look is all that comes from them. They say a few words to each other, and a knowing smile rests briefly on their faces.

At last, dinner is over. Fiorella and Girolamo go back to their hotel. At last, they are in bed. Sleep should follow love, but it doesn't. She is thinking of the girl in the restaurant, and the way Girolamo looked at her. He probably wishes he were married to her. Up in the hamlet and for miles around, she is the prettiest, but down here where does she stand? She's nothing. Her looks are lost on this city.

He can't sleep, either. He still sees his wife looking at the tawny-haired, smart-looking young man. He is certain she wishes *he* were her husband. And why shouldn't she? What is he, anyway? A poor shepherd, ignorant of the ways of the world.

"Tell me the truth," she says in a whisper. "Do you wish I were that girl who was sitting opposite us at Alfredo's?"

"No, why?"

"You kept looking at her."

"Silly, I wasn't looking at her," Girolamo says. "I was looking at him, thinking you liked him better than me. You had your eyes on him, I know."

"But I didn't!" says Fiorella. "*She* was the one I was looking at, thinking you wished you were married to her."

"And I thought — "

"So did I!"

They laugh. They hug each other. Sleep this time follows love.

They wake at six, the time they usually rise. They can hear the hum of the city. On the mountain, even at noon, everything is so

still that if you see a man chopping wood across the valley you can
hear the sharp blows distinctly seconds after they fall. That is, if
the wind doesn't drown them. It can howl for weeks without
pause, till the whole mountain seems to be shrieking, for the hamlet
is near the divide — this side the rivers flow into the Tyrrhenian
Sea, the other side into the Adriatic. Now, why would they want to
live there? From down here the hamlet seems endlessly high — way
up, near the stars, itself a constellation at night, and in the daytime
a few rocks put together out of the numberless rocks of the mountain. Is it really there? He thinks of his sheep; he knows each of
them one from the other, and he reviews them. It's a good way of
knowing that they are true. He couldn't possibly invent them.
And the house is true, and the stones of the mountain. And the
wind is true, and the cries of the wolves.

After breakfast, they visit the Colosseum and St. Peter's. In the
afternoon, they have to decide which of two trains to take home.
"Shall we take the early one?" he asks.

"Yes," she replies.

Soon the mountains appear in the distance, chain after chain.
Somewhere in that misty blue a white speck is their hamlet, and
new and ready is a house waiting for them; in it a table is laden
with gifts, and a bed is made. The pillowcases have their initials
embroidered; the covers are folded. They have only to slip in. No
— there's still a long way to go. But the train rushes on.

ALICE WALKER

The Revenge of Hannah Kemhuff

(FROM MS.)

Two weeks after I became Tante Rosie's apprentice, we were visited by a very old woman who was wrapped and contained, almost smothered, in a half dozen skirts and shawls. Tante Rosie (pronounced Tante Ro'zee) told the woman she could see her name, Hannah Kemhuff, written in the air. She told the woman further that she belonged to the Order of the Eastern Star.

The woman was amazed. (And I was too! Though I learned later that Tante Rosie held extensive files on almost everybody in the county, which she kept in long cardboard boxes under her bed.) Mrs. Kemhuff quickly asked what else Tante Rosie could tell her.

Tante Rosie had a huge tank of water on a table in front of her, like an aquarium for fish, except there were no fish in it. There was nothing but water, and I never was able to see anything in it. Tante Rosie, of course, could. While the woman waited, Tante Rosie peered deep into the tank of water. Soon she said the water spoke to her and told her that although the woman looked old, she was not. Mrs. Kemhuff said that this was true, and wondered if Tante Rosie knew the reason she looked so old. Tante Rosie said she did not and asked if she would mind telling us about it. (At first, Mrs. Kemhuff didn't seem to want me there, but Tante Rosie told her I was trying to learn the rootworking trade, and she nodded that she understood and didn't mind. I scrooched down as small as I could at the corner of Tante Rosie's table, smiling at her so she wouldn't feel embarrassed or afraid.)

"It was during the Depression," she began, shifting in her seat and adjusting the shawls. She wore so many her back appeared to be humped!

"Of course," said Tante Rosie, "and you were young and pretty."

"How do you know that?" exclaimed Mrs. Kemhuff. "That is true. I had been married already five years and had four small children and a husband with a wandering eye. But since I married young — "

"Why, you were little more than a child," said Tante Rosie.

"Yes," said Mrs. Kemhuff. "I were not quite twenty years old. And it was hard times everywhere, all over the country and, I suspect, all over the world. Of course no one had television in those days, so we didn't know. I don't even now know if it was invented. We had a radio before the Depression, which my husband won in a poker game, but we sold it somewhere along the line to buy a meal.

"Anyway, we lived for as long as we could on the money I brought in as a cook in a sawmill. I cooked cabbage and corn pone for twenty men for two dollars a week. But then the mill closed down, and my husband had already been out of work for some time. We were on the point of starvation. We was so hungry, and the children were getting so weak, that after I had cropped off the last leaves from the collard stalks I couldn't wait for new leaves to grow back. I dug up the collards, roots and all. After we ate that, there was nothing else.

"As I said, there was no way of knowing whether hard times was existing around the world because we did not then have a television set. And we had sold the radio. However, as it happened, hard times hit everybody we knew in Cherokee County. And for that reason the government sent food stamps, which you could get if you could prove you were starving. With a few of them stamps, you could go into town to a place they had and get so much and so much of fatback, so much and so much of cornmeal, and so much and so much of (I think it was) red beans. As I say, we was, by then, desperate. And my husband prevailed on me for us to go. I never wanted to do it, on account of I have always been proud. My father, you know, used to be one of the biggest colored peanut growers in Cherokee County, and we never had to ask nobody for nothing.

"Well, what had happened in the meantime was this: my sister, Carrie Mae — "

"A tough girl, if I remember right," said Tante Rosie.

"Yes," said Mrs. Kemhuff, "bright, full of spunk. Well, she were at that time living in the North. In Chicago. And she were working for some good white people that give her they old clothes to send back down here. And I tell you they were good things. And I was glad to get them. So, as it was getting to be real cold, I dressed myself and my husband and the children up in them clothes. For, see, they was made up North to be worn up there where there's snow at, and they were warm as toast."

"Wasn't Carrie Mae later killed by a gangster?" asked Tante Rosie. "Yes, she were," said the woman, anxious to go on with her story. "He were her husband."

"Oh," said Tante Rosie quietly.

"Now, so I dresses us all up in our new finery, and with all our stomachs growling all together, we goes marching off to ask for what the government said was due us as proud as ever we knew how to be. For even my husband, when he had on the right clothes, could show some pride, and me, whenever I remembered how fine my daddy's peanut crops had provided us, why there was nobody with stiffer backbone."

"I see a pale and evil shadow looming ahead of you in this journey," said Tante Rosie, looking into the water as if she'd lost a penny while we weren't looking.

"That shadow was sure pale and evil all right," said Mrs. Kemhuff. "When we got to the place, there was a long line, and we saw all of our friends in this line. On one side of the big pile of food was the white line — and some rich peoples was in that line, too — and on the other side there was the black line. I later heard, by the by, that the white folks in the white line got bacon and grits, as well as meal, but that is neither here nor there. What happened was this. As soon as our friends saw us all dressed up in our nice warm clothes, though used and cast-off they were, they began saying how crazy we was to have worn them. And that's when I began to notice that all the people in the black line had dressed themselves in tatters. Even people what had good things at home, and I knew some of them did. What does this mean? I asked my husband. But he didn't know. He was too busy strutting about to even pay much attention. But I began to be terribly afraid. The baby had begun to cry, and the other little ones, knowing I was nervous, commenced to whine and gag. I had a time with them.

"Now, at this time my husband had been looking around at other women, and I was scared to death I was going to lose him. He already made fun of me and said I was arrogant and proud. I said that was the way to be and that he should try to be that way. The last thing I wanted to happen was for him to see me embarrassed and made small in front of a lot of people, because I knew if that happened he would quit me.

"So I was standing there hoping that the white folks what give out the food wouldn't notice that I was dressed nice and that if they did they would see how hungry the babies was and how pitiful we all was. I could see my husband over talking to the woman he was going with on the sly. She was dressed like a flysweep! Not only was she raggedy, she was dirty! Filthy dirty, and with her filthy slip showing. She looked so awful, she disgusted me. And yet there was my husband hanging over her while I stood in the line holding on to all four of our children. I guess he knew as well as I did what that woman had in the line of clothes at home. She was always much better dressed than me, and much better dressed than many of the white peoples. That was because, they say, she was a whore and took money. Seems like people want that and will pay for it even in a Depression!"

There was a pause while Mrs. Kemhuff drew a deep breath. Then she continued.

"So, soon I was next to get something from the young lady at the counter. All around her I could smell them red beans, and my mouth was watering for a taste of fresh water corn pone. I was proud, but I wasn't fancy. I just wanted something for me and the children. Well, there I was, with the children hanging to my dress-tails, and I drew myself up as best I could and made the oldest boy stand up straight, for I had come to ask for what was mine, not to beg. So I wasn't going to be acting like a beggar. Well, I want you to know that that little slip of a woman, all big blue eyes and yellow hair, that little *girl*, took my stamps and then took one long look at me and the children and across at my husband — all of us dressed to kill I guess she thought, and she took my stamps in her hand and

looked at them like they was dirty, and then she give them to an old
gambler who was next in line behind me! 'You don't need nothing
to eat from the way you all dressed up, Hannah Lou,' she said to
me. 'But Miss Sadler,' I said, 'my children is hungry.' 'They don't
look hungry,' she said to me. 'Move along now, somebody here
may really need our help!' The whole line behind me began to
laugh and snigger, and that little white moppet sort of grinned behind her hands. She give the old gambler double what he would
have got otherwise. And there me and my children about to keel
over from want.

"When my husband and his woman saw and heard what happened they commenced to laugh, too, and he reached down and got
her stuff, piles and piles of it, it seemed to me then, and helped her
put it in somebody's car, and they drove off together. And that was
about the last I seen of him. Or her."

"Weren't they swept off a bridge together in the flood that wiped
out Tunica City?" asked Tante Rosie.

"Yes," said Mrs. Kemhuff. "Somebody like you might have
helped me then, too, though looks like I didn't need it."

"So — "

"So after that, looks like my spirit just wilted. Me and my children got a ride home with somebody, and I tottered around like a
drunk woman and put them to bed. They was sweet children and
not much trouble, although they was about to go out of their minds
with hunger."

Now a deep sadness crept into her face, which, until she reached
this point, had been still and impassive.

"First one, then the other of them took sick and died. The old
gambler came by the house three or four days later and divided
what he had left with us. He had been on his way to gambling it
all away. The Lord called him to have pity on us, and since he
knew us and knew my husband had deserted me, he said he were
right glad to help out. But it was mighty late in the day when he
thought about helping out, and the children were far gone. Nothing could save them except the Lord, and he seemed to have other
things on his mind, like the wedding that spring of the mean little
moppet."

Mrs. Kemhuff now spoke through clenched teeth.

"My spirit never recovered from that insult, just like my heart never recovered from my husband's desertion, just like my body never recovered from being almost starved to death. I started to wither in that winter and each year found me more hacked and worn down than the year before. Somewhere along them years my pride just up and left altogether, and I worked for a time in a whorehouse just to make some money, just like my husband's woman. Then I took to drinking to forget what I was doing, and soon I just broke down and got old all at once, just like you see me now. And I started about five years ago to going to church. I was converted again, 'cause I felt the first time had done got worn off. But I am not restful. I dream and have nightmares still about the little moppet, and always I feel the moment when my spirit was trampled down within me, while they all stood and laughed, and she stood there grinning behind her hands."

"Well," said Tante Rosie. "There are ways that the spirit can be mended, just as there are ways that the spirit can be broken. But one such as I cannot do both. If I am to take away the burden of shame which is upon you, I must in some way inflict it on someone else."

"I do not care to be cured," said Mrs. Kemhuff. "It is enough that I have endured my shame all these years and that my children and my husband were taken from me by one who knew nothing about us. I can survive as long as I need with the bitterness that has laid every day in my soul. But I could die easier if I knew something, after all these years, had been done to the little moppet. God cannot be let to make her happy all these years and me miserable. What kind of justice would that be? It would be monstrous!"

"Don't worry about it, my sister," said Tante Rosie with gentleness. "By the grace of the Man-God I have use of many powers. Powers given me by the Great One Herself. If you can no longer bear the eyes of the enemy that you see in your dreams, the Man-God, who speaks to me from the Great Mother of Us All, will see that those eyes are eaten away. If the hands of your enemy have struck you, they can be made useless." Tante Rosie held up a small piece of what was once lustrous pewter. Now it was pock-marked and blackened and deteriorating.

"Do you see this metal?" she asked.

"Yes, I see it," said Mrs. Kemhuff with interest. She took it in her hands and rubbed it.

"The part of the moppet you want destroyed will rot away in the same fashion."

Mrs. Kemhuff relinquished the piece of metal to Tante Rosie.

"You are a true sister," she said.

"Is it enough?" Tante Rosie asked.

"I would give anything to stop her grinning behind her hands," said the woman, drawing out a tattered billfold.

"Her hands or the grinning mouth?" said Tante Rosie.

"The mouth grinned and the hands hid it," said Mrs. Kemhuff.

"Ten dollars for one area, twenty for two," said Tante Rosie.

"Make it the mouth," said Mrs. Kemhuff. "That is what I see most vividly in my dreams." She laid a ten-dollar bill in the lap of Tante Rosie.

"Let me explain what we will do," said Tante Rosie, coming near the woman and speaking softly to her, as a doctor would speak to a patient. "First we will make a potion that has a long history of use in our profession. It is a mixture of hair and nail parings of the person in question, a bit of their water and feces, a piece of their clothing heavy with their own scents, and I think in this case we might as well add a pinch of goober dust, that is, dust from the graveyard. This woman will not outlive you by more than six months."

I had thought the two women had forgotten about me, but now Tante Rosie turned to me and said, "You will have to go out to Mrs. Kemhuff's house. She will have to be instructed in the recitation of the curse-prayer. You will show her how to dress the black candles and how to pay Death for his interception in her behalf."

Then she moved over to the shelf that held her numerous supplies: oils of Bad and Good Luck Essence, dried herbs, creams, powders, and candles. She took two large black candles and placed them in Mrs. Kemhuff's hands. She also gave her a small bag of powder and told her to burn it on her table (as an altar) while she was praying the curse-prayer. I was to show Mrs. Kemhuff how to "dress" the candles in vinegar so they would be purified for her purpose.

She told Mrs. Kemhuff that every morning and evening for nine days she was to light the candles, burn the powder, recite the curse-prayer from her knees, and concentrate all her powers on getting her message through to Death and the Man-God. As far as the Su-

preme Mother of Us All was concerned, She could only be moved
by the pleas of the Man-God. Tante Rosie herself would recite the
curse-prayer at the same time that Mrs. Kemhuff did, and together
she thought the two prayers, prayed with respect, could not help
but move the Man-God, who, in turn, would unchain Death who
would already be eager to come down on the little moppet. But her
death would be slow in coming because first the Man-God had to
hear all the prayers.

"We will take those parts of herself that we collect, the feces, the
water, nail parings, et cetera, and plant them where they will bring
for you the best results. Within a year's time the earth will be rid
of the woman herself, even as almost immediately you will be rid of
her grin. Do you want something else for only two dollars that will
make you feel happy even today?" asked Rosie.

But Mrs. Kemhuff shook her head. "I'm carefree enough already, knowing that her end will be before another year. As for
happiness, it is something that deserts you once you know it can be
bought and sold. I will not live to see the end result of your work,
Tante Rosie, but my grave will fit nicer, having someone proud
again who has righted a wrong and, by so doing, lies straight and
proud throughout eternity."

And Mrs. Kemhuff turned and left, bearing herself grandly out of
the room. It was as if she had regained her youth; her shawls were
like a stately toga, her white hair seemed to sparkle.

*To the Man-God: O Great One, I have been sorely tried by my
enemies and have been blasphemed and lied against. My good
thoughts and my honest actions have been turned to bad actions
and dishonest ideas. My home has been disrespected, my children
have been cursed and ill-treated. My dear ones have been backbit-
ten and their virtue questioned. O Man-God, I beg that this that I
ask for my enemies will come to pass:*

*That the South wind shall scorch their bodies and make them
wither and shall not be tempered to them. That the North wind
shall freeze their blood and numb their muscles and that it shall
not be tempered to them. That the West wind shall blow away
their life's breath and will not leave their hair grow, and that their
fingernails shall fall off and their bones shall crumble. That the*

East wind shall make their minds grow dark, their sight shall fail, and their seed dry up so that they shall not multiply.

I ask that their fathers and mothers from their furthest generation will not intercede for them before the great throne, and the wombs of their women shall not bear fruit except for strangers, and that they shall become extinct. I pray that the children who may come shall be weak of mind and paralyzed of limb and that they themselves shall curse them in their turn for ever turning the breath of life into their bodies. I pray that disease and death shall be forever with them and that their worldly goods shall not prosper, and that their crops shall not multiply, and that their cows, their sheep, and their hogs, and all their living beasts shall die of starvation and thirst. I pray that their houses shall be unroofed and that the rain, the thunder and lightning shall find the innermost recesses of their home, and that the foundation shall crumble and the floods tear it asunder. I pray that the sun shall not shed its rays on them in benevolence, but instead it shall beat down on them and burn them and destroy them. I pray that the moon shall not give them peace, but instead shall deride them and decry them and cause their minds to shrivel. I pray that their friends shall betray them and cause them loss of power, of gold and of silver, and that their enemies shall smite them until they beg for mercy which shall not be given them. I pray that their tongues shall forget how to speak in sweet words, and that it shall be paralyzed, and that all about them will be desolation, pestilence, and death. O Man-God, I ask you for all these things because they have dragged me in the dust and destroyed my good name; broken my heart and caused me to curse the day that I was born. So be it.

This curse-prayer was regularly used and taught by rootworkers, but since I did not know it by heart, as Tante Rosie did, I recited it straight from Zora Neale Hurston's book, *Mules and Men,* and Mrs. Kemhuff and I learned it on our knees together. We were soon dressing the candles in vinegar, lighting them, kneeling and praying — intoning the words rhythmically — as if we had been doing it this way for years. I was moved by the fervor with which Mrs. Kemhuff prayed. Often, she would clench her fists before her closed eyes and bite the insides of her wrists as the women do in Greece.

According to courthouse records Sarah Marie Sadler, "the little moppet," was born in 1910. She was in her early twenties during the Depression. In 1932 she married Ben Jonathan Holley, who later inherited a small chain of grocery stores and owned a plantation and an impressive stand of timber. In the spring of 1963, Mrs. Holley was 53 years old. She was the mother of three children, a boy and two girls: the boy a floundering clothes salesman; the girls married and oblivious, mothers themselves.

The elder Holleys lived six miles out in the country, their house was large; and Mrs. Holley's hobbies were shopping for antiques, gossiping with colored women, discussing her husband's health and her children's babies, and making spoon bread. I was able to glean this much from the drunken ramblings of the Holleys' cook, a malevolent nanny with gout, who had raised, in her prime, at least one tan Holley, a preacher whom the Holleys had sent to Morehouse.

"I bet I could get the nanny to give us all the information and nail parings we could ever use," I said to Tante Rosie. For the grumpy woman drank muscatel like a sow and clearly hated Mrs. Holley. However, it was hard to get her tipsy enough for truly revealing talk and we were quickly running out of funds.

"That's not the way," Tante Rosie said one evening as she sat in her car and watched me lead the nanny out of the dreary but secret-evoking recesses of the Six Forks Bar. We had already spent six dollars on muscatel.

"You can't trust gossip or drunks," said Tante Rosie. "You let the woman we are working on give you everything you need, and from her own lips."

"But that is the craziest thing I have ever heard," I said. "How can I talk to her about putting a fix on her without making her mad, or maybe even scaring her to death."

Tante Rosie merely grunted.

"Rule number one: *Observation of subject*. Write that down among your crumpled notes."

"In other words — ?"

"Be direct, but not blunt."

On my way to the Holley plantation, I came up with the idea of pretending to be searching for a fictitious person. Then I had an even better idea. I parked Tante Rosie's Bonneville at the edge of the spacious yard, which was dotted with mimosas and camellias.

Tante Rosie had insisted I wear a brilliant orange robe, and as I walked, it swished and blew about my legs. Mrs. Holley was on the back patio steps, engaged in conversation with a young and beautiful black girl. They stared in amazement at the length and brilliance of my attire.

"Mrs. Holley, I think it's time for me to go," said the girl.

"Don't be silly," said the matronly Mrs. Holley. "She is probably just a light-skinned African who is on her way somewhere and got lost." She nudged the black girl in the ribs, and they both broke into giggles.

"How do you do?" I asked.

"Just fine, how are you?" said Mrs. Holley, while the black girl looked on askance. They had been talking with their heads close together and stood up together when I spoke.

"I am looking for a Josiah Henson" (a runaway slave and the original Uncle Tom in Harriet Beecher Stowe's novel, I might have added). "Could you tell me if he lives on your place?"

"That name sounds awful familiar," said the black girl.

"Are you *the* Mrs. Holley?" I asked gratuitously, while Mrs. Holley was distracted. She was sure she had never heard the name.

"Of course," she said, and smiled, pleating the side of her dress. She was a grayish blonde with an ashen untanned face, and her hands were five blunt and pampered fingers each. "And this is my . . . ah . . . my friend, Caroline Williams."

Caroline nodded curtly.

"Somebody told me ole Josiah might be out this way — "

"Well, we haven't seen him," said Mrs. Holley. "We were just here shelling some peas, enjoying this nice sunshine."

"Are you a light African?" asked Caroline.

"No," I said. "I work with Tante Rosie, the rootworker. I'm learning the profession."

"Whatever *for?*" asked Mrs. Holley. "I would have thought a nice-looking girl like yourself could find a better way to spend her time. I been hearing about Tante Rosie since I was a little bitty child, but everybody always said that rootworking was just a whole lot of n—, I mean, colored, foolishness. Of course we don't believe in that kind of thing, do we Caroline?"

"Naw."

The younger woman put a hand on the older woman's arm, possessively, as if to say, "You get away from here bending my white-folk ear with your crazy mess!" From the kitchen window a dark, remorseful face worked itself into various messages of "Go away!" It was the drunken nanny.

"I wonder if you would care to prove that you do not believe in rootworking?"

"Prove?" said the white woman indignantly.

"Prove?" asked the black woman with scorn.

"That is the word," I said.

"Why, not that I'm afraid of any of this nigger magic — !" said Mrs. Holley staunchly, placing a reassuring hand on Caroline's shoulder. *I* was the nigger, not she.

"In that case won't you show us how much you don't have fear of it?" With the word "us," I placed Caroline in the same nigger category with me. Let her smolder! Now Mrs. Holley stood alone, the great white innovator and scientific scourge, forced to man the Christian fort against heathen nigger paganism.

"Of course, if you like," she said immediately, drawing herself up in the best English manner. Stiff upper lip, what?, and all that. She had been grinning throughout. Now she covered her teeth with her scant two lips and her face became flat and resolute. Like that of so many white women in sections of the country where the race was still "pure," her mouth could have been formed by the minute slash of a thin sword.

"Do you know a Mrs. Hannah Lou Kemhuff?" I asked.

"No, I do not."

"She is not white, Mrs. Holley, she is black."

"Hannah Lou, Hannah Lou. Do we know a Hannah Lou?" she asked, turning to Caroline.

"No, ma'am, we don't!" said Caroline.

"Well, she knows you. Says she met you on the breadlines during the Depression and that because she was dressed up you wouldn't give her any cornmeal. Or red beans. Or something like that."

"Breadlines, Depression, dressed up, cornmeal — ? I don't know what you're talking about!" No shaft of remembrance probed the depths of what she had done to colored people more than thirty years ago.

"It doesn't really matter, since you don't believe — but she says you did her wrong, and being a good Christian, she believes all wrongs are eventually righted in the Lord's good time. She came to us for help only when she began to feel the Lord's good time might be too far away. Because we do not deal in the work of unmerited destruction, Tante Rosie and I did not see how we could take the case — " I said this humbly, with as much pious intonation as I could muster.

"Well, I'm glad," said Mrs. Holley, who had been running through the back years on her fingers.

"But," I said, "we told her what she could do to bring about restitution of peaceful spirit, which she claimed you robbed her of in a moment during which, as is now evident, you were not concerned. You were getting married the following spring."

"That was 'thirty-two," said Mrs. Holley. "Hannah *Lou?*"

"The same."

"How black *was* she? Sometimes I can recall colored faces that way."

"That is not relevant," I said, "since you do not believe — "

"Well, of *course* I don't believe!" said Mrs. Holley.

"I am nothing in this feud between you," I said. "Neither is Tante Rosie. Neither of us had any idea until after Mrs. Kemhuff left that you were the woman she spoke of. We are familiar with the deep and sincere interest you take in the poor colored children at Christmastime each year. We know you have gone out of your way to hire needy people to work on your farm. We know you have been an example of Christian charity and a beacon force of brotherly love. And right before my eyes I can see it is true you have Negro friends."

"Just what is it you want?" asked Mrs. Holley.

"What *Mrs. Kemhuff* wants are some nail parings, not many, just a few; some hair (that from a comb will do); some water and some feces — and if you don't feel like doing either number one or number two, I will wait; and a bit of clothing, something that you have worn in the last year. Something with some of your odor on it."

"What!" Mrs. Holley screeched.

"They say this combination, with the right prayers, can eat away part of a person just like the disease that ruins so much fine antique pewter."

Mrs. Holley blanched. With a motherly fluttering of hands, Caroline helped her into a patio chair.

"Go get my medicine," said Mrs. Holley, and Caroline started from the spot like a gazelle.

"Git away from her! Git away!"

I spun around just in time to save my head from a whack with a gigantic dust mop. It was the drunken nanny, drunk no more, flying to the defense of her mistress.

"She just a tramp and a phony!" she reassured Mrs. Holley, who was caught up in an authentic faint.

Not long after I saw Mrs. Holley, Hannah Kemhuff was buried. Tante Rosie and I followed the casket to the cemetery. Tante Rosie was most elegant in black. Then we made our way through briers and grass to the highway. Mrs. Kemhuff rested in a tangly grove, off to herself, though reasonably near her husband and babies. Few people came to the funeral, which made the faces of Mrs. Holley's nanny and husband stand out all the more plainly. They had come to verify the fact that this dead person was indeed *the* Hannah Lou Kemhuff whom Mr. Holley had initiated a search for, having the entire county militia at his disposal.

Several months later, we read in the paper that Sarah Marie Sadler Holley had also passed away. The paper spoke of her former beauty and vivacity as a young woman, of her concern for those less fortunate than herself, as a married woman and pillar of the community and her church. It spoke briefly of her harsh and lengthy illness. It said all who knew her were sure her soul would find peace in heaven, just as her shrunken body had endured so much pain and heartache here on earth.

Caroline had kept us up to date on the decline of Mrs. Holley. Since my visit, relations between them became strained, and Mrs. Holley eventually became too frightened of Caroline's darkness to allow her close to her. A week after I'd talked to them, Mrs. Holley began having her meals in her bedroom upstairs. Then she started doing everything else there as well. She collected stray hairs from her head and comb with the greatest attention and consistency, not to say desperation. She ate her fingernails. But the most bizarre of all was her response to Mrs. Kemhuff's petition for a speci-

men of feces and water. Not trusting any longer the earthen
secrecy of the water mains, she no longer flushed. Together with
the nanny, Mrs. Holley preferred to store those relics of what she
ate (which became almost nothing and then nothing, the nanny
had told Caroline), and they kept it all in barrels and plastic bags
in the upstairs closets. In a few weeks it became impossible for anyone to endure the smell of the house — even Mrs. Holley's husband, who loved her but during the weeks before her death slept in
a spare room of the nanny's house.

The mouth that had grinned behind the hands grinned no more.
The constant anxiety lest a stray strand of hair be lost and the foul
odor of the house soon brought to the hands a constant seeking motion, to the eyes a glazed and vacant stare, and to the mouth a
tightly puckered frown, one which only death might smooth.

BIOGRAPHICAL NOTES

Biographical Notes

AGNES BOYER is a graduate of Michigan State University. Born and raised in Michigan's Upper Peninsula, she now makes her home in Canada. She lives with her husband, son, and daughter in Oakville, Ontario.

JERRY BUMPUS was born in Mount Vernon, Illinois, in 1937, and is an M.F.A. from the Writers' Workshop in Iowa. His work has appeared in *Esquire* and he has published over sixty stories in literary magazines. His novel *Anaconda* is available from *December* magazine. Mr. Bumpus teaches creative writing at San Diego State University and is married to a genealogist who, in the summer, usually succeeds in luring him and their two daughters onto treks deep into the heartland and into the past.

ELEANOR CLARK was born in Los Angeles and educated both abroad and at Vassar College. Her stories have appeared in numerous magazines including *The Southern Review, Yale Review,* and *The New Yorker.* She has published two novels, *Baldur's Gate* and *The Bitter Box,* and a nonfiction work of hers, *The Oysters of Locmariaquer,* won the National Book Award for 1965. She has also received two Guggenheim Awards and is a member of the National Institute of Arts and Letters.

PAT M. ESSLINGER-CARR was born in Grass Creek, Wyoming, in 1932. A graduate of Rice University, she has a Ph.D. from Tulane University, and has lived in South America. Her stories have appeared in numerous magazines, and a collection of Latin American stories, *From Beneath the Hill of the Three Crosses,* was published in 1970. She has written two novels with Colombian settings, and the opening chapter of a third novel appeared in the Winter 1974 issue of *The Southern Review.* She is presently an Associate Professor of English at the University of Texas in El Paso where she lives with her writer husband and four children.

LEWIS B. HORNE was born and raised in Mesa, Arizona, and studied at Arizona State University and the University of Michigan. His stories have appeared in numerous journals including *Ohio Review, Kansas Quarterly,* and *Descant.* He is presently teaching at the University of Saskatchewan and lives in Saskatoon with his wife and four daughters.

ROSE GRAUBART IGNATOW is an Associate Editor of *Chelsea.* She is a full-time writer and summer painter and attended the Cooper Union Evening Art School and The Art Students League. Her stories have appeared in a number of magazines including *The Carleton Miscellany, Confrontation,* and *Jewish Dialog of Canada.* She teaches Puppetry Workshop and Magic Painting to children during the summers in her community.

MAXINE KUMIN was born in Germantown, Pennsylvania, in 1925, and received her A.B. and A.M. degrees from Radcliffe College. She is the author of four books of poetry, the most recent of which, *Up Country,* won the Pulitzer Prize in 1973. She has also published four novels. The short story in this collection grew into *The Designated Heir,* published by Viking Press in 1974.

MARY LAVIN has recently been awarded an honorary degree of Doctor of Letters by University College, Dublin. She has twice received a Guggenheim Fellowship, and has been honored with many prizes such as the Eire Society Gold Medal in 1974. Her stories have frequently appeared in *The New Yorker.* She was President of the Irish Academy of Letters for 1972–1973.

JOHN L'HEUREUX is an Assistant Professor of English at Stanford University and a Contributing Editor of *The Atlantic.* He is the author of four books of poetry, an autobiography, and two novels. His short stories have appeared in *The Atlantic, Transatlantic Review, Esquire,* and many other periodicals. "A Family Affair" will appear in his collection of stories, *Family Affairs,* which Doubleday will publish later this year.

PHILLIP LOPATE, poet and teacher, was born in New York City in 1943. He works with children in poetry, film, and videotape, and is project director of Teachers and Writers Collaborative at P.S. 75 in Manhattan. He is now writing a book, *The Change Agent,* about his experiences in the schools, which will be published by Doubleday in 1975. His book of poems, *The Eyes Don't Always Want to Stay Open,* was published by Sun Press in 1974.

STEPHEN MINOT was born in Boston in 1927, graduated from Harvard College in 1953, and received an M.A. from the Writing Seminars Program, Johns Hopkins University, in 1955. He is the author of *Chill of Dusk,* a novel, and of twenty-four stories and articles which have appeared in such magazines as *The Atlantic, Harpers,* the *Virginia Quarterly Review,* and *Playboy.* He is the author of *Three Genres,* a textbook on writing, and is co-editor of *Three Stances,* a critical anthology of contemporary fiction published by Winthrop. His latest publication is *Crossings and Other Stories,* which will be brought out by the University of Illinois Press in 1975. Mr. Minot is married and has three sons. He has taught at Trinity College, Hartford, Connecticut, since 1959 and during 1974–75 is serving as Visiting Writer in Residence at Johns Hopkins University.

BEVERLEY MITCHELL was born in 1930 and grew up in the Fraser Valley. She is a member of the Congregation of the Sisters of Saint Ann, a Canadian order whose chief works are teaching and nursing. For eighteen years she taught in the schools of her order in British Columbia. A graduate of Seattle University, she received her master's from the University of Calgary and is presently completing her Ph.D. in Canadian literature at the University of New Brunswick. Her short stories have appeared in *Fragments, The Journal of Canadian Fiction,* and *The Fiddlehead.* "Letter from Sakaye" will be broadcast on CBC radio's "Anthology" and is to be included in the Macmillan (Canada) anthology, *Stories from Pacific & Arctic Canada.*

MICHAEL ROTHSCHILD was born in Maine in 1947. His stories have appeared in *The Paris Review, Works in Progress,* and *Antaeus. Rhapsody of a Hermit and Three Tales* was published by the Viking Press in 1973. He lives in Strong, Maine.

PETER L. SANDBERG was born in Winchester, Massachusetts, in 1934. While doing graduate work at the University of Colorado in 1958, he took up the climbing of mountains and writing of stories. Since that time his work has appeared in *Saturday Review, Playboy, The Literary Review, The South Dakota Review,* and numerous anthologies. A Lecturer in English at Northeastern University in Boston, his first novel will be published by Playboy Press in the spring of 1975. He lives with his wife, Nancy, in a cottage on the shore of a New Hampshire lake.

WILLIAM SAROYAN, now 66, divides his time between his home in Paris and his home in Fresno, with frequent visits to San Francisco, and none ever under any circumstances to Los Angeles. He also frequently visits London, Lisbon, Clovis, Chicago, and Chowchilla, favorite places, and now and then, if all is in order and the weather is right, Venice, Florence, Genoa, Naples, Palermo, Messina, Catania, Beirut, Haifa, Athens, Istanbul, and Odessa. One year he even got to Bitlis where the Saroyans lived for centuries until 1905 when his father, Armenak of Bitlis, went to New York and about a year later was joined by his wife, Takoohi of Bitlis, and the first three of their four children. Being the fourth, he was not born in Bitlis but in Fresno. He says, "When you finally see a fabled city like Bitlis you are supposed to become disenchanted. Not so. Bitlis is in the highlands. At the very top was where the Saroyans had their houses. In 1964 I sprawled upon grass and wildflowers there, where our own house of stone had stood for so long. Nothing lost. Everything gained. Bitlis is mine, and always will be."

PHILIP H. SCHNEIDER was born in upstate New York in 1941. His stories have appeared in *Quartet, Nimrod, Kansas Quarterly,* and

The Mediterranean Review. Mr. Schneider lives with his wife in Wichita, Kansas, where he teaches in the Creative Writing and Composition Programs at Wichita State University. He is currently working on a second novel.

BARRY TARGAN was born in Atlantic City, New Jersey, in 1932. He was educated at Rutgers University, University of Chicago, and Brandeis University, from which he received a Ph.D. in English Literature. He has published short stories, poetry, and essays in such magazines and journals as *Esquire, The Southern Review, American Review, Salmagundi,* and *Quarterly Review of Literature.* He lives with his wife and two sons in Schuylerville in upstate New York.

JOHN UPDIKE was born in Shillington, Pennsylvania, in 1932, and attended Harvard College, graduating *summa cum laude.* He is the author of six novels, five collections of short stories, three of poetry, and a miscellany, *Assorted Prose.* His latest book is *Buchanan Dying,* a play. He lives in Ipswich, Massachusetts, with his wife and four children.

ARTURO VIVANTE was born in Rome in 1923. He is the author of *Poesie,* a book of poems; *The French Girls of Killini,* a collection of short stories; and of two novels — *A Goodly Babe* and *Doctor Giovanni.* Since 1957 he has been a regular contributor of short stories to *The New Yorker.* He has been writer in residence at the University of North Carolina, Boston University, and Purdue University. He lives with his wife and three children on Cape Cod.

ALICE WALKER was born in Eatonton, Georgia, in 1944. She attended Spelman College and received her B.A. in 1965 from Sarah Lawrence College. She has taught at Jackson State College and Tougaloo College in Mississippi, at Wellesley College and the University of Massachusetts. Ms. Walker is the author of *Once,* a collection of poems; *The Third Life of Grange Copeland,* a novel; *Revolutionary Petunias and Other Poems; Langston Hughes,* a biography for children; and *In Love & Trouble: Stories of Black Women,* published by Harcourt Brace Jovanovich in 1973 for which she

received the Richard and Hinda Rosenthal Award presented by
the National Institute of Arts and Letters. She was awarded a
grant from the National Endowment of the Arts in 1969 and a
Fellowship to the Radcliffe Institute, 1971–1973.

THE
YEARBOOK
OF THE
AMERICAN SHORT STORY

January 1 to December 31, 1973

Roll of Honor, 1973

I. *American Authors*

BAKER, D. W.
My Father's House. Western Humanities Review, Summer.

BAMBARA, TONI CADE
The Lesson. Redbook, January.

BARTHELME, DONALD
Cannon! Georgia Review, Winter.
One Hundred Ten West Sixty-First Street. The New Yorker, September 24.

BECKER, STEPHEN
The Endless Night. The Atlantic, September.

BENNETT, HAL
The Ghost of Martin Luther King. Playboy, August.

BENSON, R. MICHAEL
Tittie Whistle. Massachusetts Review, Summer.

BETTS, DORIS
Benson Watts Is Dead and in Virginia. Massachusetts Review, Spring.

BLACK, DAVID
Laud. The Atlantic, January.

BOYER, AGNES
The Deserter. Prism International, Spring.

BROMELL, HENRY
Early Sunday Morning. The New Yorker, March 3.
Heart of Light. The New Yorker, July 30.

BUMPUS, JERRY
Beginnings. TriQuarterly, Winter.
Travelin Blues. December, Vol. 15, Nos. 1 & 2.

BURN, HELEN JEAN
To the Manor Born. McCall's, January.

BUSCH, FREDERICK
Tax. Carleton Miscellany, Spring-Summer.

CARVER, RAYMOND
The Summer Steelhead. Seneca Review, May.

CHEEVER, JOHN
The Triad. Playboy, January.

CLARK, ELEANOR
A Summer in Puerto Rico. Southern Review, Spring.
Dr. Heart. Southern Review, Autumn.

CLEARMAN, MARY
The Granddaughters. Georgia Review, Spring.
COLWIN, LAURIE
Dangerous French Mistress. Antaeus, Summer.
Mr. Parker. The New Yorker, April 14.
COOVER, ROBERT
The Public Burning of Julius and Ethel Rosenberg. TriQuarterly, Winter.
COPE, JACK
The Violin Maker. The New Yorker, April 21.
CULLINAN, ELIZABETH
The Perfect Crime. The New Yorker, August 27.

DAVIS, BURKE, III
Points of Intersection. Virginia Quarterly Review, Summer.
DAVIS, JOANNA
Life Signs. McCall's, April.
DEEMER, CHARLES
The Idaho Jacket. Prism International, Spring.
DELISSA, RICHARD
The Legend of Hank Boone. Event (Canadian), Spring & Summer.
DOWELL, COLEMAN
The Birthmark. New Directions, Fall.
DOWNEY, HARRIS
A Religious Happening. Michigan Quarterly Review, Summer.

ELKIN, STANLEY
The Making of Ashenden. TriQuarterly, Winter.
ESSLINGER-CARR, PAT M.
The Party. Southern Review, Summer.

FETLER, JAMES
The Indians Don't Need Me Anymore. Literary Review, Summer.

FISHER, M. F. K.
A Question Answered. The New Yorker, July 9.
FRANCIS, H. E.
William Saroyan, Come Home. Georgia Review, Summer.
FREDERICK, K. C.
California Dreams. Shenandoah, Spring.
FREDERIKSEN, ALAN
Captain Han E. Soo. Sewanee Review, Spring.

GARBER, EUGENE K.
The Father. Ohio Review, Winter.
GOLDBERG, LESTER
The Reckoning. National Jewish Monthly, June.

HARTSHORNE, NATHANIEL
The Last Swan. Family Circle, April.
HELPRIN, MARK HENRY
Elisha Hospital. The New Yorker, October 8.
HENDERSON, ROBERT
Marta and Leni. The New Yorker, July 23.
HERMANN, JOHN
Brothers. Virginia Quarterly Review, Spring.
HORNE, LEWIS B.
The People Who Were Not There. Kansas Quarterly, Summer.
Mansion, Magic and Miracle. Colorado Quarterly, Autumn.
HOWER, EDWARD
Miramur and the King. Atlantic, August.
HUGHES, MARY CRAY
The Rock Garden. Southwest Review, Spring.

ICE, RUTH
You Have to Pay. Kansas Quarterly, Winter.
IGNATOW, ROSE GRAUBART
Down the American River. Shenandoah, Summer.

IRVING, JOHN
Almost in Iowa. Esquire, November.

JONG, ERICA
From the Country of Regrets. Paris
Review, Spring.
Mad. Ms., October.

JORDAN, EILEEN
Promises. Woman's Day, December.

JUST, WARD
A Guide to the Architecture of
Washington, D.C. The Atlantic,
February.
Nora. The Atlantic, May.
Journal of the Plague Year. The
Atlantic, August.

KALECHOFSKY, ROBERTA
An Apostrophe to the Long Dark
Street. Western Humanities Re-
view, Autumn.

KUMIN, MAXINE
Buying the Child. American Review
16, February.
Opening the Door on Sixty-Second
Street. Southern Review, Autumn.

LAVIN, MARY
Tom. The New Yorker, January 20.

LEAMON, WARREN
Hester. South Carolina Review, November.

LEVIANT, CURT
The Yemenite Girl. Literary Review,
Fall.

L'HEUREUX, JOHN
A Family Affair. The Atlantic, June.

LOPATE, PHILLIP
The Chamber Music Evening. Paris
Review, Spring.

LOURIE, RICHARD
Next Train to Warsaw? Playboy,
August.

McGUANE, THOMAS
Ninety-Two in the Shade. TriQuarterly, Winter.

MACLEOD, ALISTAIR
In the Fall. Tamarack, October.

MALAMUD, BERNARD
In Retirement. The Atlantic,
March.

MANFRED, FREDERICK
The Voice of the Turtle. South
Dakota Review, Autumn.

MARTIN, RICHARD
Substitutes. Virginia Quarterly Review, Summer.

MATTHEWS, JACK
Amos Bond, The Gunsmith. Mich-
igan Quarterly Review, Summer.
Invaders of the Fields. Yale Review,
Autumn.

MEREDITH, WILLIAM
Rescues. Shenandoah, Summer.
The Dolly Varden. Virginia Quar-
terly, Autumn.

MERWIN, W. S.
Port of Call. The New Yorker, October 1.

MINOT, STEPHEN
The Tide and Isaac Bates. Quar-
terly Review of Literature, Vol.
XVIII, Nos. 3–4.

MITCHELL, BEVERLEY, S.S.A.
Letter from Sakaye. Fiddlehead,
Fall.

MORGAN, BERRY
The Hill. The New Yorker, March
24.

MORRIS, WRIGHT
Trick or Treat. Quarterly Review of
Literature, Vol. XVIII, Nos. 3–4.

MORTON, FREDERIC
The Golden Christmas Ducat. Playboy, December.

NEUGEBOREN, JAY
My Life and Death in the Negro
American Baseball League. Massa-
chusetts Review, Summer.

OATES, JOYCE CAROL
Democracy in America. Shenandoah,
Spring.

PACKER, NANCY HUDDLESTON
Second Wind. Southwest Review, Summer.

PETESCH, N. M.
A Brief Biography of Ellie Brume. Kansas Quarterly, Winter.

POWERS, J. F.
Farewell. The New Yorker, August 6.

ROSKOLENKO, HARRY
The House-Painter, Two Sisters, One Slave. Literary Review, Winter.

ROTH, RUSSELL
For Those Who Have No More to Give. South Dakota Review, Winter.

ROTHSCHILD, MICHAEL
Dog in the Manger. Antaeus, Summer.

SANDBERG, PETER L.
Calloway's Climb. Playboy, September.

SAROYAN, WILLIAM
Isn't Today the Day? Harper's Magazine, March.

SCHELL, JESSIE
Alvira, Lettie and Pip. Greensboro Review, Spring-Summer.

SCHNEIDER, PHILIP H.
The Gray. Kansas Quarterly, Summer.

SILMAN, ROBERTA
A Bad Baby. The New Yorker, July 16.

SIMPSON, EILEEN
The Revenant. Southern Review, Autumn.

SINGER, ISAAC BASHEVIS
The Bishop's Robe. The New Yorker, June 2.

SPEER, LAUREL
Two Stories. Georgia Review, Fall.

STOUT, ROBERT JOE
McLamb. Twigs, Spring.

SUKENIK, RONALD
On the Wing. North American Review, Spring.

SYLVESTER, WILLIAM
Waging Love. Iowa Review, Summer.

TARGAN, BARRY
Old Vemish. Salmagundi, Fall.

TOLSON, MELVIN B.
All Aboard! New Letters, Summer.

TRIVELPIECE, LAUREL
A Few Little Things. Western Humanities Review, Spring.

TYLER, ANNE
The Base-Metal Egg. Southern Review, Summer.
Spending. Shenandoah, Winter.

UPDIKE, JOHN
Son. The New Yorker, April 21.

VIVANTE, ARTURO
The Jump. The New Yorker, January 6.
The Bell. The New Yorker, February 10.
Honeymoon. The New Yorker, November 26.

WALKER, ALICE
The Revenge of Hannah Kemhuff. Ms., July.

WASSERMAN, J. F.
Soaring. Event (Canadian), Spring.

WEAVER, GORDON
Some Killers. The Southern Review, Spring.

WEST, CRISTY
The Hunt. The New Yorker, September 24.

WILDMAN, JOHN HAZARD
Folly Fighting Death. Southern Review, Summer.

WILLARD, NANCY
The Childhood of the Magician. Quarterly Review of Literature, Vol. XVIII, Nos. 3–4.

II. *Foreign Authors*

DELBO, CHARLOTTE
Phantoms, My Faithful Ones. Trans. by Rosette Lamont. Massachusetts Review, Spring.

FORSTER, E. M.
Ansell. Intellectual Digest, August.

HERNANDEZ, JUAN JOSÉ
The Godchild. Trans. by H. E. Francis. Southern Review, Spring.

JHABVALA, R. PRAWER
Bombay. The New Yorker, October 15.
Prostitutes. The New Yorker, December 10.

KIELY, BENEDICT
The Night We Rode with Sarsfield. The New Yorker, August 20.

LITVINOV, IVY
Old Woman. The New Yorker, June 16.

NORRIS, LESLIE
A House Divided. The Atlantic, May.

O'BRIEN, EDNA
The Creature. The New Yorker, July 30.

PRITCHETT, V. S.
The Rescue. The New Yorker, April 14.
The Spree. Playboy, December.

SAMARAKIS, ANTONIO
50 Kilos of Mothballs. Trans. by Catherine Raizis. Literary Review, Spring.

STANEV, EMILIYAN
Death of a Bird. Trans. by Francis Salter. Literary Review, Winter.

TONKS, ROSEMARY
The Hospital. Southern Review, Summer.

VASSILIKOS, VASSILIS
The Departure. Trans. by M. Byron Raisis. Literary Review, Spring.

WALKER, TED
The Morning Shouter. Quarterly Review of Literature, Vol. XVIII, Nos. 3–4.

WOOLF, VIRGINIA
The Introduction. Ms., July.

YEHOSHUA, A. B.
Early in the Summer of 1970. Trans. by Miriam Arad. Commentary, March.

Distinctive Short Stories, 1973

I. *American Authors*

AARON, CHESTER
Hold Your Breath! North American Review, Winter.

ADAMS, ALICE
Alternatives. The Atlantic, April.
Sex and the Subdebs. Redbook, April.

ADLER, RENATA
Brownstone. The New Yorker, January 27.

AMFT, M. J.
What's Going to Happen to Letitia? Redbook, January.

APRIMOZ, ALEXANDRE
The Rattle Snake. Canadian Fiction Magazine, Spring.

AUCHINCLOSS, LOUIS
The Cup of Coffee. Ladies' Home Journal, July.

BARKER, MILDRED
Payday. Ms., June.

BAROLINI, HELEN
The Finer Things in Life. Arizona Quarterly, Spring.

BEATTIE, ANN
Victor Blue. The Atlantic, December.

BERGES, RUTH
La Romantica. Literary Review, Winter.

BERNSTEIN, LEONARD S.
The Unusual Courtship of Gendlemen's Daughter. Michigan Quarterly Review, Fall.

BLAKE, FORRESTER
The Lake. South Dakota Review, Autumn.

BORENSTEIN, A. FARRELL
The Visions. Kansas Quarterly, Summer.

BOVEY, JOHN
Concert. Quarterly Review, Winter.

BRODKEY, HAROLD
A Story in an Almost Classical Mode. The New Yorker, September 17.

BROMELL, HENRY
Mime. The New Yorker, July 9.

BROOKHOUSE, CHRISTOPHER
The Afternoon Gordon Dies. Sumus #1.

BYALL, PAUL
Whispers of Lost Options. North American Review, Spring.

CARDWELL, GUY
An Island World. Virginia Quarterly Review, Spring.

CARRIER, JEAN-GUY
So Many Children. Canadian Forum, February.
Whatsis Name. Canadian Forum, February.

CHERNOFF, SANFORD
A Matter of Time. Partisan Review, Winter.

CLARK, ELEANOR
The Man for Her. McCall's, June.

COHEN, KEITH
Natural Settings. Paris Review, Spring.

CORPORA, JAMES
The Castellan. Massachusetts Review, Winter.

CUEVAS, ERNESTO
The Important Thing. Canadian Fiction, Winter.

CURLEY, DANIEL
What Rough Beast? Massachusetts Review, Spring.
The Eclipse. Hudson Review, Summer.

DIXON, STEPHEN
Darling. North American Review, Summer.

DOKEY, RICHARD
Blue Period. Michigan Quarterly Review, Winter.

DRAKE, ALBERT
I Remember the Day James Dean Died Like It Was Yesterday. Epoch, Spring.

DRUM, CHARLES S.
One and Won. Southwest Review, Spring.

EATON, CHARLES EDWARD
Skunk in the Skimmer. Southwest Review, Winter.
Rooster on the Roof. Ohio Review, Spring.

EDWARDS, MARGARET
The Color Wheel. The Greensboro Review, Winter.

ELLISON, RALPH
Cadillac Flambé. American Review, 16.

FAESSLER, SHIRLEY
Lucy and Minnie. The Atlantic, March.

FISHER, M. F. K.
The Wind-Chill Factor. The New Yorker, January 6.

FRANCIS, H. E.
Passageways. University of Windsor Review, Spring.
The Fire in My Face. Southwest Review, Fall.

FREMLIN, CELIA
If It's Got Your Number. Ellery Queen's Mystery Magazine, November.

FRIEDMAN, BRUCE JAY
Lady. Esquire, January.

FROEB, JEANNE
Pretty Things. Southwest Review, Spring.

GALLANT, MAVIS
His Mother. The New Yorker, August 13.
An Alien Flower. The New Yorker, October 7.

GARDNER, EDWIN
The Ark. Sewanee Review, Autumn.

GARRETT, GEORGE
Here Comes the Bride. Gone Soft, Spring.

GERALD, JOHN BART
Luke's Song. The Atlantic, October.

GHISELIN, OLIVE
The Spacious World of Aunt Louise. Western Humanities Review, Spring.
The Testimony of Mr. Bones. Michigan Quarterly Review, Fall.

GOLD, HERBERT
  The Writer and the Distinguished American Cop. Ohio Review, Winter.
  Time-Sharing Man. Fantasy and Science Fiction, December.
GORCHOV, ROBERT D.
  Mrs. Blasingame Poteet. The New Yorker, May 12.
GOYEN, WILLIAM
  Come the Restorer. Southwest Review, Autumn.
GRATION, GWEN
  Pilgrim Father. South Dakota Review, Winter.
GREEN, CLIFFORD G.
  Benny: The Epilogue. The Literary Review, Fall.
GREENBERG, ALVIN
  Footnotes to a Theory of Place. Antioch Review, Vol. XXXII, No. 3.
GRIFFIN, TOM
  Flies, Snakes, Fat Benny. Playboy, August.

HARDIN, DAVID
  Now. Kansas Quarterly, Summer.
HARTER, EVELYN
  A Drift of Incense. Kansas Quarterly, Winter.
HAWKINS, TOM
  Putting a Child to Bed. Greensboro Review, Spring-Summer.
HÉBERT, ERNEST
  The Island. Fiddlehead, Spring.
HEMENWAY, ROBERT
  Troy Street. The New Yorker, June 9.
HENKIN, BILL
  Drive Interrupt. University of Windsor Review, Spring.
HERBST, JOSEPHINE
  I Hear You, Mr. and Mrs. Broun. Aphra, Winter.

HERRMANN, JOHN
  Macula. North American Review, Spring.
ICE, RUTH
  The Chicago Seven. Literary Review, Winter.
IGNATOW, ROSE GRAUBART
  My Mother's House. New Letters, Spring.

JACOBS, HARVEY
  The Tooth Fairy. Woman's Day, November.
JOHNSON, CURT
  Before the War. Western Humanities Review, Spring.

KALESCHOFSKY, ROBERTA
  The Wind. Western Humanities Review, Autumn.
KASS, JERRY
  Across the Line. Literary Review, Summer.
KENNEBECK, PAUL
  Baldessari's Dead Sea Flights. Harper's Magazine, August.
KIRMSER, JEUNE
  Night Flight. Kansas Quarterly, Winter.
KRANES, DAVID
  Dealer. Esquire, August.

LARSEN, ERIC
  Notes on Three Unwritten Stories. Miscellany, Winter.
LARSON, CHARLES R.
  Portrait of Henry James as a Young Lady. Literary Review, Fall.
LEE, LANCE
  Frederic's Door. Literary Review, Summer.
LELOWITZ, ALAN
  Marvin Gardens' Revenge. Ploughshares, Vol. I, No. 4.
LILLIAN, GUY
  Dead Niggers. Greensboro Review, Spring-Summer.

PHELAN, R. C.
Helping Can. Yale Review, Winter.
PHELPS, DEAN
Happy Jack. Wind, Number Nine.
POLK, JAMES
The Phrenology of Love. The Atlantic, October.

QUERTERMOUS, MAX
The Artists of the Living Room. Virginia Quarterly Review, Summer.

RANDALL, FLORENCE ENGEL
The Sounds of Summer. Woman's Day, October.
RASCOE, JUDITH
In the Place Where Everything Is Perfectly Clear. Ms., October.
RATH, ROGER
The Trim. Carleton Miscellany, Spring-Summer.
ROBINSON, BARBARA
Last Train to Elm Grove. McCall's, May.
ROGIN, GILBERT
The Sans Souci Launderama. The New Yorker, April 28.
ROSE, LOUISE BLECHER
The Beautiful View. Redbook, August.
ROTH, HENRY H.
Separate Courses. New Letters, Spring.

SADOFF, IRA
The Books That Will Change Your Life. North American Review, Spring.
The Nightmare, Charlie's Wife and the Desert Island. Carleton Miscellany, Spring-Summer.
SAROYAN, WILLIAM
Picnic Time. Ladies' Home Journal, July.
SCHOENEWOLF, GERALD
Wedlock. North American Review, Spring.

SELZER, RICHARD
The Harbinger. Harper's Magazine, July.
SILBERT, LAYLE
The Skywriter. South Dakota Review, Summer.
SINCLAIR, THOMAS
La Ronde. Twigs, Spring.
SINGER, ISAAC BASHEVIS
The Briefcase. The New Yorker, February 3.
The Son from America. The New Yorker, February 17.
Her Son. The New Yorker, May 12.
SMYTH, DONNA E.
Chrome & Yellow. Canadian Fiction, Winter.
SONNETT, SHERRY
Dreamy. Ms., August.
SPIELBERG, PETER
Jury Boxes. Ohio Review, Winter.
STEPHENS, M. G.
The Last Poetry Reading. TriQuarterly, Winter.
STERN, DAVID
Agnon, A Story. Response, Spring.
STOCKDALE, J. C.
Better to Burn. Fiddlehead, Fall.
STOUT, ROBERT JOE
The Wooden Elf. Southern Humanities Review, Fall.
STUART, JESSE
The Betrayal. Kansas Quarterly, Summer.
SUKENIK, RONALD
Out. Massachusetts Review, Spring.
SUTHERLAND, BARRY
Adam. Canadian Fiction Magazine, Spring.
SWEENEY, KEVIN
The Sounds of Sadness. Unspeakable Visions of the Individual, Nos. 1 & 2.

TEVIS, WALTER
The King Is Dead. Playboy, September.

THOMPSON, KENT
   A Broken Bottle: A Suicide for Barbara Ann Shea. University of Windsor Review, Spring.
   I Live in Canada. Fiddlehead, Spring.
   What Costume Shall the New Man Wear. Fiddlehead, Spring.

VIVANTE, ARTURO
   Of Love and Friendship. The New Yorker, May 26.
   The Letter. The New Yorker, September 3.

WALKER, ALICE
   Everyday Use. Harper's Magazine, April.

WEALES, GERALD
   The Country of Silence. Ellery Queen's Mystery Magazine, May.

WEAVER, GORDON
   The Two Sides of Things. North American Review, Summer.

WEIGEL, HENRIETTA
   Bambi. New Letters, Summer.

WHELAN, GLORIA
   The Best of Two Worlds. Literary Review, Summer.

WHITE, FRED D.
   Three Stories. Michigan Quarterly Review, Winter.

WHITE, JAMES P.
   Wives. Kansas Quarterly, Winter.

WIEBE, RUDY
   Along the Red Deer and the South Saskatchewan. Prism International, Spring.

WILLIAMS, TENNESSEE
   Miss Coynte of Greene. Playboy, December.

WYATT, LAURENCE
   Persimmon Summa. Twigs, Spring.

YAMAMOTO, JUDITH
   A Long Time to Be Gone. Redbook, September.

YU-HWA, LEE
   The Sandalwood Nostalgia. Arizona Quarterly, Winter.

II. *Foreign Authors*

ARGUEDAS, JOSE MARIA
   Puppy Love. Trans. by Hardie St. Martin. Antaeus, Spring.

BRENNAN, MAEVE
   Family Walls. The New Yorker, March 10.

CALVINO, ITALO
   The Road to San Giovanni. Shenandoah, Summer.

DAGERMAN, STIG
   To Kill a Child. Trans. by Peter Stenberg. Prism International, Spring.

ELLISTON, VALERIE
   The New Woman. Redbook, September.

GILLIAT, PENELOPE
   Iron Larks. The New Yorker, January 13.

GORDIMER, NADINE
   The Conservationist. Playboy, March.

HAWKES, JOHN
   The Universal Fears. American Review, 16.

IBBOTSON, EVA
   A Heart That Was Tender. Ladies' Home Journal, May.

IOANNOU, GEORGE
The Bed. Trans. by M. Byron Raisis. Literary Review, Spring.

KNOWLES, JOHN
Neville. Cosmopolitan, April.

MÁRQUES, GABRIEL GARCÍA
Death Constant Beyond Love. The Atlantic, July.

NORRIS, LESLIE
Percy Colclough and the Religious Girls. The New Yorker, April 28.
Cocksfoot, Crested Dogs-Tail, Sweet Vernal Grass. The New Yorker, July 2.

PETROV, IVAYLO
The Student from the Attic Apartment. Trans. by Francis Salter. Literary Review, Winter.

PRITCHETT, V. S.
The Rescue. The New Yorker, April 14.
The Marvelous Girl. The New Yorker, December 24.

RACHLUS, NAOMI
Wedding Bath. Shenandoah, Summer.

ROBBE-GRILLET, ALAIN
The Still Abode of David Hamilton. TriQuarterly, Winter.

Initiations: A Cycle. Harper's Magazine, September.

SANGUINETI, EDOARDO
The Game of Goose. Trans. by Marcia Nou. Prism International, Spring.

SEVERNYAK, SERAFIM
A Sentimental Incident. Trans. by James Karambelas. Literary Review, Winter.

SOWDEN, LEWIS
You've Got to Be Civilized. Literary Review, Winter.

TAYLOR, ELIZABETH
Madame Olga. McCall's, August.

VEZHINOV, PAVEL
Lunch Hour. Trans. by Francis Salter. Literary Review, Winter.

WARNER, SYLVIA-TOWNSEND
Four Figures in a Room. A Distant Figure. The New Yorker, February 24.
Scenes of Childhood. The New Yorker, June 2.

ZIPPER, JACOB
The True Image. Trans. by Sacvan Bercovitch. Prism International, Spring.

Addresses of American and Canadian Magazines Publishing Short Stories

American Review (formerly New American Review) 666 Fifth Avenue, New York, New York 10019

Americas, Organization of American States, Washington, D.C. 20006

Antaeus, 1 West 30th Street, New York, New York 10001

Antioch Review, 212 Xenia Avenue, Yellow Springs, Ohio 45387

Aphra, R.F.D. Box 355, Springtown, Pennsylvania 18081

Ararat, 109 East 40th Street, New York, New York 10016

Argosy, 205 East 42nd Street, New York, New York 10017

Arizona Quarterly, University of Arizona, Tucson, Arizona 85721

Arlington Quarterly, Box 366, University Station, Arlington, Texas 76010

Atlantic, 8 Arlington Street, Boston, Massachusetts 02116

Brushfire, Box 9012, University Station, Reno, Nevada

Canadian Fiction, 4248 Weisbrod Street, Prince George, British Columbia, Canada

Canadian Forum, 30 Front Street West, Toronto, Ontario, Canada

Carleton Miscellany, Carleton College, Northfield, Minnesota 55057

Carolina Quarterly, P.O. Box 1117, Chapel Hill, North Carolina 27514

Chicago Review, University of Chicago, Chicago, Illinois 60637

Cimmaron Review, 203B Morrill Hall, Oklahoma State University, Stillwater, Oklahoma 74074

Colorado Quarterly, University of Colorado, Boulder, Colorado 80303

Commentary, 165 East 56th Street, New York, New York 10022

Cosmopolitan, 1775 Broadway, New York, New York 10019

December, Box 274, Western Springs, Illinois 60558

Ellery Queen's Mystery Magazine, 229 Park Avenue South, New York, New York 10003

Epoch, 252 Goldwin Smith Hall, Cornell University, Ithaca, New York 14850

Esquire, 488 Madison Avenue, New York, New York 10022

Event (Canada), Doughlas College, P.O. Box 2503, New Westminster, British Columbia, Canada

Event (U.S.A.), 422 South Fifth Street, Minneapolis, Minnesota 55415

Falcon, Mansfield State College, Mansfield, Pennsylvania

Fantasy and Science Fiction, Box 271, Rockville Centre, New York 11571

Fiction, 193 Beacon Street, Boston, Massachusetts 02116

Fiddlehead, Department of English, University of New Brunswick, New Brunswick, Canada

Florida Quarterly, University of Florida, 330 Reitz Union, Gainseville, Florida 32601

Forum, Ball State University, Muncie, Indiana 47302

Four Quarters, La Salle College, Philadelphia, Pennsylvania 19143

Georgia Review, University of Georgia, Athens, Georgia 30601

Gone Soft, Salem State College, Salem, Massachusetts 01970

Good Housekeeping, 959 Eighth Avenue, New York, New York 10019

Green River Review, Box 594, Owensboro, Kentucky 42301

Greensboro Review, University of North Carolina, Box 96, McIver Building, Chapel Hill, North Carolina 27401

Harper's Bazaar, 572 Madison Avenue, New York, New York 10022

Harper's Magazine, 2 Park Avenue, New York, New York 10016

Husk, Cornell College, Mount Vernon, Iowa 52314

Iowa Review, University of Iowa, Iowa City, Iowa 52240

Kansas Quarterly, Kansas State University, Manhattan, Kansas 66502

Ladies' Home Journal, 641 Lexington Avenue, New York, New York 10022

Laurel Review, West Virginia Wesleyan College, Buckbannon, West Virginia 26201

Literary Review, Fairleigh Dickinson University, Teaneck, New Jersey 07666

Lotus, Department of English, Ohio University, Athens, Ohio 45701

Mademoiselle, 420 Lexington Avenue, New York, New York 10022

Malahat Review, University of Victoria, Victoria, British Columbia, Canada

Massachusetts Review, University of Massachusetts, Amherst, Massachusetts 01003

McCall's, 230 Park Avenue, New York, New York 10017

Michigan Quarterly Review, University of Michigan, Ann Arbor, Michigan 48104

Mississippi Review, Box 37, Southern Station, University of Southern Mississippi, Hattiesburg, Mississippi 39401

Ms., 370 Lexington Avenue, New York, New York 10017

National Jewish Monthly, 1640 Rhode Island Avenue, N.W., Washington, D.C. 20036

New Directions, 333 Sixth Avenue, New York, New York 10014

New Letters, University of Missouri, Kansas City, Missouri 64110

New Orleans Review, Loyola University, New Orleans, Louisiana 70118

New Renaissance, 9 Heath Road, Arlington, Massachusetts 02174

New Yorker, 25 West 43rd Street, New York, New York 10036

North American Review, University of Northern Iowa, Cedar Falls, Iowa 50613

Northern Minnesota Review, Bemidji State College, Bemidji, Minnesota 56601

Northwest Review, Erb Memorial Union, University of Oregon, Eugene, Oregon 97403

Occident, Eshleman Hall, University of California, Berkeley, California 94720

Old Hickory Review, P.O. Box 1178, Jackson, Tennessee 38301

Panache, 221 Nassau Street, Princeton, New Jersey 08540

Paris Review, 45-39 171 Place, Flushing, New York 11358

Partisan Review, Rutgers University, 1 Richardson Street, New Brunswick, New Jersey 08903

Pathway Magazine, P.O. Box 1483, Charleston, West Virginia 25325

Penthouse, 1560 Broadway, New York, New York 10036

Perspective, Washington University Post Office, St. Louis, Missouri 63130

Phylon, Atlanta University, Atlanta, Georgia 30314

Playboy, 232 East Ohio Street, Chicago, Illinois 60611

Ploughshares, P.O. Box 529, Cambridge, Massachusetts 02139

Prairie Schooner, Andrews Hall, University of Nebraska, Lincoln, Nebraska 68508

Prism International, University of British Columbia, Vancouver, British Columbia, Canada

Quarry, College V, University of California, Santa Cruz, California 95060

Quarterly Review of Literature, 26 Haslet Avenue, Princeton, New Jersey 08540

Quartet, 1701 Puryear Drive (Apt. 232), College Station, Texas 77840

Queens Quarterly, Queens University, Kingston, Ontario, Canada

Redbook, 230 Park Avenue, New York, New York 10017

Remington Review, 505 Westfield Avenue, Elizabeth, New Jersey 07208

Roanoke Review, Box 268, Roanoke College, Salem, Virginia 24513

Salmagundi Magazine, Skidmore College, Saratoga Springs, New York 12866

San Francisco Review, P.O. Box 671, San Francisco, California 94100

Saturday Evening Post, 1100 Waterway Boulevard, Indianapolis, Indiana 46202

Seneca Review, Box 115, Hobart and William Smith College, Geneva, New York 14456

Seventeen, 320 Park Avenue, New York, New York 10022

Sewanee Review, University of the South, Sewanee, Tennessee 37375

Shenandoah, Box 122, Lexington, Virginia 24450

South Carolina Review, Box 28661, Furman University, Greenville, South Carolina 29613

South Dakota Review, Box 111, University Exchange, University of South Dakota, Vermillion, South Dakota 57069

Southern Humanities Review, Auburn University, Auburn, Alabama 36830

Southern Review, Louisiana State University, Baton Rouge 70803

Southwest Review, Southern Methodist University, Dallas, Texas 75222

St. Andrews Review, St. Andrews Presbyterian College, Laurinsburg, North Carolina 28352

Sumus, The Loom Press, 500 West Rosemary Street, Chapel Hill, North Carolina 27541

Sunday Clothes, 51 Sherman Street, Deadwood, South Dakota 57732

Tamarack Review, Box 157, Postal Station K, Toronto, Canada

Texas Quarterly, Box 7527, University Station, Austin, Texas 78712

Transatlantic Review, P.O. Box 3348, Grand Central Station, New York, New York 10017

Transpacific, P.O. Box 486, Laporte, Colorado 80535

TriQuarterly, Northwestern University, Evanston, Illinois 60201
Twigs, Hilltop Editions, Pikeville College Press, Pikeville, New York 41501
Virginia Quarterly Review, 1 West Range, Charlottesville, Virginia 22903
Wascana Review, Wascana Parkway, Regina, Saskatchewan, Canada
Western Humanities Review, Building 41, University of Utah, Salt Lake City,
　Utah 84112
Western Review, Western New Mexico University, Silver City, New Mexico
Windsor Review, University of Windsor, Windsor, Ontario, Canada
Yale Review, P.O. Box 1729, New Haven, Connecticut 06520